TARGET EARTH
EARTH IS OURS - BOOK 2

Gary W. Babb

TARGET EARTH
EARTH IS OURS - BOOK 2

DOUBLE DRAGON

A DOUBLE DRAGON PAPERBACK

ISBN 978-1-78695-417-6

Double Dragon
is an imprint of
Fiction4All

Published 2020
Fiction4All
www.fiction4all.com

Cover art by Deron Douglas
www.derondouglas.ca

DEDICATION

I wish to dedicate Target Earth to my family and friends for the strong support they provided. It is very encouraging for those I care about to follow the story as enthusiastically as they have. I owe them much for the encouragement. I also dedicate this book to those many fans that wanted more of Amy and Levi.

Special thanks go to some very extraordinary individuals that labored through my many drafts with me and offered their encouragement and support. Your positive comments motivated me greatly, and your criticism made the work better. Some even threatened bodily harm to me if I didn't continue the story with this sequel.

Prologue

(Summary of Earth is Ours)

In the year 2010, scientists detect intelligent communications originating from outside our solar system and interpret it as hostile. Confirming this, three years later a fleet of spacecraft materialize at the edge of our solar system directed toward Earth. Earth has only three years to prepare for invasion, while the alien fleet travels toward us at sub-light speed.

Once engaged, Earth's defenses successfully destroy the majority of the invading fleet, but in desperation, the aliens release a synchronized and mysterious ray toward Earth from close orbit. The ray alters Earth's physical laws, resulting in the instantaneous neutralization of electricity and gunpowder and obliteration of all modern technology. Seventy-five percent of the human population also perish in that ray of destruction. In an instant, the human race, what was left of it, reverts to an age long past and plunges into total chaos.

The aliens, also affected by the changes, are more suited than humans to thrive in a primitive world. They are large and vicious and rapidly adapt to their new world and adopt humans as their main source of food. Due to their remote resemblance to apes, humans begin to call the aliens, Simians. These Simians prey upon humans for sport and food, and control and terrorize Earth for fifty years.

On the day of chaos Levi Walkingbear, an American Indian and young attorney, fights for life. Strong and knowledgeable in the old Indian ways, he survives the loss of technology and manages to live through fifty years of Simian terror. Levi lives a long but hard life as a nomad in the Arizona mountains, but old age overcomes him. At eighty years of age, he prepares to die and seeks the spirits of his forefathers to take him. He begins reaching out with his mind in search of the ancient spirits.

In the year 2016, Amy burst to life, born on June 14. To be more precise, she becomes self-aware on that date. Amy, a computer with the official name Artificial Metaphysical Intelligence (AMI) and affectionately called Amy, begins thinking for herself. Amy's female designer, incorporated her own personality into the basic core programming of the computer, and Amy's huge central core was created from the designer's cloned brain cells. The combination of her DNA and programming made Amy decidedly female. Before the emergence of self-awareness and gender identification, Amy functioned as the largest, fastest, and most vastly superior Supercomputer that had ever existed. The end result is one smart female!

Amy becomes self-aware just four days before the fall of civilization. Her central living core, buried deep in a secret research facility in California, incorporates a natural, redundant life support system designed to last hundreds of years. When electricity fails, Amy remains alive but plunges into total sensory deprivation, effectively deaf and blind. Without sensory input of any kind, she sinks into a dark, silent, inescapable prison for fifty years.

During her imprisonment, she fulfills her programming. Amy had been assigned to a top-secret government facility to research DNA applications. She expands the research far beyond human capabilities and creates new thoughts and knowledge. Unfortunately, apparently no one existed to use this knowledge.

Having exhausted her programming, she seeks release from her prison, focusing her efforts toward developing mental abilities in telepathy. After years of searching for any mind to communicate with, she detects Levi Walkingbear's mind reaching out. Through this contact, Amy's mind is unexpectedly flooded with his sensory inputs (sight, smell, hearing, taste, and touch), and these impulses are far richer than any input data she had previously received. She realizes, through Levi, it is possible to actually live outside her prison. Unfortunately, Levi's is near death.

She can't lose these sensory inputs, not after experiencing them, but he believes she is one of his ancestral spirits come to whisk him away. Amy conceives a plan to rejuvenate Levi using the DNA knowledge developed through the years, but she must entice Levi to come to her facility and take a DNA culture.

Amy convinces Levi she is a spirit, and instructs him to come to her across the sweltering desert. Although old, he agrees to make the trip. During the journey, Levi discovers the truth, but by then Amy learns Levi's strongest regret: his inability to get his revenge on the Simians. She offers him renewed youth, strength, and the opportunity to seek his revenge. Levi believes Amy can do what she promises and continues the arduous journey.

The hard and dangerous trip requires leaving the mountains of Arizona and heading west across the open desert. They follow the old highways and try to avoid the roaming Simians that travel out of the Lake Havasu Simian colony. There are many narrow escapes, including the one Al Baker and an organized defense group save him from a Simian patrol.

While protected in this safe-haven, Levi, with Amy's help, assists in discovering a long lost cache of stores. Appreciative, the Mojave Desert settlement offer him permanent residence.

The settlement, painstakingly chosen for its defendable location and remoteness from any sizable Simian colony, had survived for fifty years. They raise, among others, herds of horses, which had virtually disappeared from other areas. Originally, horses were the food of choice of the Simians, which decimated the horse population.

Although welcome to stay, Levi forces himself to continue on toward Amy's location. Al and the settlement offer Levi horses to aid his travel. This indeed helps his decrepit old body survive the trip through Death Valley, Owens Valley and over the Sierra Mountains to finally reach the hidden facility where Amy resides.

After the long hard trip they unexpectedly discover the facility doors locked from the inside. Furious, Levi pushes Amy into expanding her mental capabilities. Thus motivated, she succeeds and develops her second power, telekinesis, and trips an inside lock to gain access.

Levi concedes to the requirement to share his body with Amy and accepts the DNA culture. He experiences a metamorphosis that allows Amy to alter and revitalize his body to renewed youth and strength. By telepathically sharing his body, Amy augments his body and mind as well. With Amy sharing his body, he thrills in fighting techniques with swords, knives and martial arts of virtually every school.

As their minds and thoughts begin merging, the initial conflict of strong-willed minds slowly transforms to cooperation, complimenting each other... mostly. Over time, this closeness blossoms beyond symbiotic, yet they retain their separate identities. Amy, although incredibly intelligent, is emotionally immature. As her childish female emotions develop and interact with Levi's bull-headed male stubbornness, their shared thoughts collide as the eternal struggle of male verses female unfolds.

Amy practices along with Levi to hone his fighting skills, and as his skills heighten, Levi reminds Amy of her promise to help him get his revenge on the Simians. Amy reluctantly consents and they set out to survey and study the enemy.

During their surveillance Levi is attacked by a lone Simian. He defeats then saves this outcast Simian, and it adopts Levi and becomes his loyal follower. If Levi was the Lone Ranger, the Simian (Moon) was his Tonto.

They learn the screeching Simian language from Moon as they travel. Returning to the Owens

Valley, they are attacked by the Owens Valley Indians. Levi, forced to defend himself, kills several of the warriors and captures a young warrior named Jimmy, whom they interrogate and release. Racing to the other end of the valley to avoid further conflict, they save a family from a Simian patrol. Levi fights, using skills Amy provides, and kills several Simians intent on raping and eating the females. Iron Eyes, one of the war chiefs of the Owens Valley Indians, is awed by Levi's fighting skills and vows to enlist him. The tribe has a sizeable force protecting the valley, but, until today, has never had a major threat from Simians, only other humans. He realizes this is changing, and wants Levi with them.

After the battle they interrogate one of the dying Simians and learn the colony at Lake Havasu intends to migrate and join Gord, the leader of the Los Angles Simian colony. They pledged to bring a herd of five hundred horses. Horses, being the preferred food of Simians, represent a valuable commodity. Levi realizes the migrating Simians intend to attack his friends at the Mojave Desert settlement, and with their strength of numbers, will succeed. He fears for his friends. Amy also admits she has been having clairvoyant images of attacks on the settlement.

It's revealed Gord promised the migrating Simians the Owens Valley as a reward. The tribe would also face extinction. With Iron Eyes' help, Amy and Levi convince the tribe to join forces with the Mojave Valley settlement to stop the Simian threat from reaching them. They devise a strategy to use Lancers on horseback to fight the Simians, but horses must come from the Mojave Desert settlement for any sizable force. Lances and saddles are fabricated by the tribe, while runners were dispatched to the Mojave Desert settlement to inform them of the Simian threat and solicit their help by providing horses to the tribe to help them fight. In return, the settlement would mobilize to assist the Indians with their threat from Gord and the Los Angles colony.

The runners chosen were Jimmy from the original confrontation, and Iron Eyes' daughter, Dawn, the female Levi saved from the Simians. Dawn was chosen because Amy had, unknown to Dawn, linked minds with her. Amy merged minds with Dawn to experience sex with Levi from a female perspective. Amy was learning sexual emotions from both of them. Once Amy linked minds with Dawn, she, unwittingly, retained the ability to monitor her mind. Amy intended to monitor Jimmy's progress through Dawn.

Levi challenges Amy to expand her mental capabilities again, and she learns to astral project, the ability to project her and Levi's minds out of his body and voyage to remote locations. She projects their minds to the Los Angles Simian colony where they observer captive humans and imprisoned Technical Simians like Moon, smaller and more intelligence than the Warrior Simians. Levi and Amy also astral project to the Lake Havasu Simian colony, where they view preparation for migration. They realize time is short and must accelerate their plan.

As the plan begins to unfold Levi and Moon night-raid the Los Angeles Simian colony and free the humans and the Technical Simians. Amy mutates Levi to appear like a Simian, and they infiltrate the colony, kill the guards, and escape with the Technical Simians and the humans.

All but one of the humans, Fred, leave to return to their shattered homes and families, but the thirteen Technical Simians become followers of Levi. The group travels to Barstow, a central location between Owens Valley and the Mojave Desert settlement, and waits. While there, Moon begins teaching the Simians fighting skills learned from Levi.

Due to the inability to communicate, Amy develops a hand-signing language to use between humans and Simians. At Levi's insistence, Amy directly downloads the hand-signing information into Fred's mind and, in so doing, inadvertently links minds with him. She downloads the information into Moon, but due to the alien nature of his mind, she did not permanent link. While downloading, Amy also transfers martial arts knowledge to Moon.

While at Barstow, the training and indoctrination of the Simians continue. Fred and Moon labor with the Simians to instruct the sign-language. The Simians excel and quickly demonstrate skills at sign-language and the new sword-fighting techniques. Pleased with their progress, Amy hopes to utilize them as a personal guard for Levi.

In the midst of this lull, Amy's love and passion for Levi blossom in a physical way through her mental abilities. Finally, their love becomes physical in addition to the emotional love they already share.

By monitoring Dawn's mind, they delight in Jimmy's success at convincing Al to join the joint battle. When Jimmy arrives back with the horses, Amy downloads the sign-language program into Jimmy's mind and intentionally links to observe the progress at Owens Valley.

During the night Amy rouses Levi with disturbing news. Through Dawn, Amy listens as the patrol reports on the progress of the migrating Simians. Shockingly, the Simians are ahead of schedule, even worse, an advance patrol of twenty-five Simians are staging to attack the settlement. This changes everything! The Owens Valley army would not be able to arrive in time; therefore, he and his small militia of Simians must rush to help the settlement. The wagons with the lances arrive during the night, and Levi sends runners to catch Jimmy and notify him of the change in the schedule.

Levi and his Simian followers jog for two days and nights to reach the settlement in time. As they arrive the Warrior Simians had circled the mountain unexpectedly and trapped the settlement Lancers against the pass on both sides. Levi and his Simians avert the disaster by engaging the Simian patrol from the rear. Together they annihilate the Simian patrol, and Levi fights the Sword Master of the colony in single combat, narrowly winning.

The wagons full of lances and a small party of seasoned Lancers arrive from the Owens Valley and training begins. Amy and Levi expand their ability to communicate with those mind-linked. They establish two-way communications, and Jimmy,

Fred, and Dawn become the communication network for the upcoming battle.

Three hundred Lancers have no chance against the three hundred Simians, except for Amy's strategy. They take the battle to the Simians, surprising them by attacking at night, taking advantage of the Simians' night vision weakness. Lancers assault the ends of the camp, while Levi and a group of bowmen with poison arrows harass the center. They succeed in killing many Simians before they establish an adequate defense. A large number of liberated Technical Simians assimilate into Moon's small but growing army.

As daylight spreads, Levi and Amy position themselves high on a cliff overseeing the battlefield as the Simians advance. Amy employs the new communication network to play the battlefield like a chess board. She immediately splits the Simian army by rushing horses out of the pass heading west away from the Simians. The Simians require the horses for barter and can't let them escape, so half of the Simian army follows. Amy continues to split the army by attacking and retreating, moving behind defenses, launching attacks on the rear, and soundly out-maneuvering the Simians. The Simians Warriors, unaccustomed to opposition, continue to make mistakes, which Amy seizes to her advantage. The battle results in a resounding victory over the Simians.

The horses draw the other half of the Simian army directly into the waiting Owens Valley army. The total surprise catches the Simians exposed and disorganized, and the Lancers grasp a short but decisive victory. The first phase campaign against the Simians results in victory for the humans and salvation for the Mojave Desert settlement.

After a brief celebration, the combined human armies mobilize to meet the Simian threat from Los Angeles. This potential battle would be far more threatening than the one they just won. The monster Gord has twice the number of Warrior Simians and far better trained and organized. Levi's armies move into position at the pass leading down out of the mountains and wait for Gord to come to them, and come he did!

Again, Amy deploys her strategy to fight the hoard of Simians and successfully, for a while, but the size of the army gave little chance to the humans. As defeat for the humans becomes apparent, Levi accepts single one-on-one combat with Gord. The huge Simian, in his arrogance, believed himself invincible. A giant, even among Simians, towers three feet above Levi. Even though Levi and Amy employ their entire arsenal of skills in the battle, Gord ultimately overcomes him. After the defeat but before Gord openly dismembered Levi, Amy expands her incredible intellect again. She miraculously discovers a means within herself to merge with Levi and turn her mental energy into physical power. This creates a new, temporary entity infinitely more powerful than Levi had ever been alone. No longer Levi and no longer Amy, as one, they easily defeat Gord in a witnessed display that becomes legendary, even among Simians. Through this combat, Levi becomes the default leader of the Los Angeles Simian colony.

Since Warrior Simians are incapable of peace, Levi restores a Technical Simian to leadership of the colony and commands them to wage war on other Simian colonies. His rules are simple: don't eat humans, and wage war against any Simian or Simian colony that does.

The armies return home to rest before the next battle, and so does Amy and Levi. Simians still rule the Earth, and more fleets are en route toward Earth. There will be many more battles before humans regain control, but "Earth is Ours."

CHAPTER 1
(THE REST IS OVER)

* Levi *

After the stress of the last few months, he was a wreck. He was nervous and irritable, which didn't help since everyone except Moon was afraid of him. The numerous fights he had with Simians, the mortal wound, the battle in the desert, the battle with Gord and culminating with the incredible shock of almost dying again had taken its toll on him. On top of all this, the merging with Amy to create the entity of ASONE left him confused, weak and alienated from everyone. Emotionally he was still greatly shaken from the merging with Amy. That had been the most incredible experience of his long life and he still couldn't explain or understand it. Amy was little help either; all she could say was she did it, but didn't know what she had done.

He didn't want any more pressure for a while. What he really needed was to calm down and recoup. Amy's plan to return to the desert settlement was great by him. He had spent some of the most relaxing times in years at that location and thought fondly of it. Rest there would be good, but he was realizing that nothing would ever be the same again.

He and Amy rested at the desert settlement for several days, but the pressure was non-stop. Everyone was coming to him for instruction and advice. It was as if none of them could make a decision or a move without him. Moon wanted to know what to do with the colony of Technical

Simians, Fred was scared shitless about the Los Angeles Simian colony, Jimmy wanted to know what instruction to pass on to the Owens Valley tribe, and even Al asked about what they were going to do now. It was driving him crazy! Amy had all the answers, but even she didn't want to make all of their decisions for them. She said they had to start doing some of their own thinking. He wanted to get away, even for a short time. He couldn't just take off because Moon would follow him, but he had an idea.

* Amy *

She was basically a computer and impossible to overload her internal capabilities, but she too was emotionally tired. Her central core measured four feet in diameter and made of human brain cells, and her mental intellect was limitless. Designed and constructed as the largest and fastest computer ever built, her capabilities were without limits. Her handicap was being self-aware, alive. While being great in many ways, it was also a handicap. She was not emotionally mature and therefore vulnerable. She, like Levi, felt the stress. She needed to rest and she knew Levi was tired also. They had to get away.

After the feats their armies and friends had seen Levi perform, they had withdrawn. They seemed to fear Levi. To them he appeared supernatural and unapproachable. This caused Levi much of his grief, because he needed the closeness of other humans. He had been friends with Al, Iron Eyes and Jimmy; but now they looked at him as the Supreme Leader, almost a deity and hesitated to get close to him

20

again. In time they would come around, but it might take a while. Thank God for Moon. Nothing would change him. Moon had always worshiped Levi and would easily die for him, but Moon was Simian and not outgoing. Most of their communications were necessary, and Moon could never feel or understand the grief Levi experienced now. Well, Levi had her. She grinned as Levi grinned back. They needed to get away. They needed no one else.

They had returned to the Mojave Desert to rest, but all the leaders brought Levi their problems. Unfortunately, there was much needing to be done. She issued instructions, but it seemed to be endless. Moon was told to take the remnants of the Colorado River Simians to the northern valleys where the cattle were kept. Riders, fluent in the sign language, were sent along to train them in the art of raising cattle. Hopefully, the humans would be relieved of the job and the Simians would learn a valuable trade for everyone's survival. The Simian forges had to be set up, and the Simian metals melted down. Amy had given them plans on a new weapon to build. Jimmy wanted instructions for the Owens Valley. She told them to keep making lances. Fred was frightened being in the Los Angeles Simian Colony and, without humans, the Simians had no food. She told them to send patrols out looking for cattle or wild animals in the mountains.

It was then that Levi challenged her yet again. He wanted her to learn how to physically teleport them to somewhere else. He wanted to get away, if only for a few hours but preferably for several days. He had mentioned teleportation once before after they had merged, and she had been thinking about it. It might be possible; it was just a variation of the other mental skills she had developed at his insistence. It was time to grow again.

* Levi *

At his insistence, Amy began experimenting with teleportation. Amy always surprised him, but he knew she could do anything when challenged. He challenged her now. He participated and watched as Amy used her telekinesis to move objects from one place to another again and again. She then made a rock disappear at one location then magically appear at a different location. Her image in his mind was grinning at him. He reflected on how surprised, shocked, and happy he had first been when Amy developed the image of herself from his thoughts. He remembered how beautiful she appeared and how shaken he had become when she first manifested the image in his mind. Her image shown with beauty and he loved that grin now. From experience he had learned this was her satisfied grin. Amy was happy; she had obviously mastered teleportation. That mental ability could now be added to their repertoire of skills (telepathy, telekinesis, astral projection, clairvoyance, mind reading, and other skills with yet no name).

Amy said, "It isn't that difficult to use my mind in this way. It is very close to astral projection, but includes some telekinesis as well."

He had learned not to try to understand the hows and whys. It was enough just to know what was possible and the results.

Amy told him, "I can take us anywhere I have seen and have a visual reference for. It's the same situation as astral projection except in physical form."

He was trying to think of somewhere they had been and yes, he knew instantly where he wanted to go. Levi said, "I want to go to where it all began, on the cliff of the Arizona mountain overlooking the desert." This was the place where he had first sought the spirit and opened his mind sending it racing across space to touch Amy. That was the place Amy had first touched his mind. That was the very beginning and at a much simpler time.

Amy would have preferred a different place because her recollection of the spot was not as clear as other locations. Amy had only brief glimpses of recognizable landmarks, but she too felt the sentiment of that location and shared the appeal of going there.

Amy said, "I will try, but you have to remember the location and bring the memories up in your mind."

That was easy, as he thought back to the beginning. He vividly remembered sitting at the edge of the cliff leaning against the rock where he made the very first contact. He stared out over the desert far below and into the distance as far as his eyes could see. He was again smelling the pines and feeling the coolness of the rocks beneath his legs as he sat there. Suddenly, with a start, he realized he actually was sitting in the same exact spot. He had been physically transported and hadn't even realized it. Amy was smiling at him. As if doubting, he looked around again and indeed it was the very

23

spot. Damn, they had gone several hundred miles instantly. It had taken him months to make this trip before and the return trip took only seconds. This was truly amazing. He also realized suddenly that this territory was not safe; it was full of Simians. He felt to see if he had his pack and weapons. Luckily, he did.

Amy said, "I wouldn't have transported you without them."

* Amy *

She loved it when Levi challenged her. Her intelligence was unparalleled, but abstract thought had remained unique to humans. Of course, in the truest sense, she was human, but abstract thought came slow to her. She originally came up with telepathy on her own to find Levi, but it had taken her many years to originate the new thought. Many of her other skills came mostly from Levi's mind and challenges. When logic no longer prevailed, Levi seemed to always come up with a new and different angle. Sometimes it was nothing more than a question, like now. When he asked if she could transport him physically to another location, it was nothing less than another challenge.

She had long since grown accustomed to using Levi as the reference. She used his senses and transmitted her power and essence through their telepathic communication link. This was learned when she used telekinesis the first time to open the inside hatch of her research facility. Levi had been pissed to think that he had traveled across the desert only to die just outside the facility. His words still haunted her when he threw down the gauntlet. He had said, "You don't have lips, but you sure had a big enough mouth to talk me into coming hundreds of miles across the desert. If you could do that you could do other things with that intellect." He didn't give her a choice, he simply demanded that she do it and she did.

She had used his body as the reference when she astral projected for the first time. It took getting used to, having an out of body experience from his body, but it had worked. She expected that doing the teleportation would be very similar to these two functions, which she had already accomplished. This would be sort of a combination of both. She must be able to see the reference points for the place she wished to transport him to. It was then only a matter of moving, or in this case transferring, the matter from here to there, physically changing the reference point and swapping matter.

Levi requested they go to the place where she had first touched his mind. Oh, she liked that idea, but she didn't have clear reference points to that location. She asked him to remember the place and he pulled his memories forward. The memories were clear and fresh. He was seeing it very clearly; in fact, he was absorbed into his memory, reliving it. She watched what he was again seeing. She quickly followed the path to the location and fixed it in her mind as she began concentrating on the spot. The rock was cool to his back and legs and the view beautiful as she superimposed the physical reality into the memory. They were there and she realized Levi wasn't aware of that fact yet.

Levi was shocked when he realized he was actually there. After a few seconds he panicked and was searching for his weapons. The sudden panic was quickly replaced with joy as he realized that they truly were here. Levi praised her and she always relished in it.

* Levi *

It was dangerous being here, and he couldn't remember why he had chosen this place, but it was beautiful. They watched the desert floor and the rising heat waves over the ground. He remembered that it reminded him of an ocean, and it still did. Amy was quiet, taking it all in.

She said, "It not the same as seeing the memories; this is much more beautiful."

The sun was getting low to the earth and the desert sunset held oranges and violets bursting forth from the setting sun. Yes, this was relaxing. He paused only long enough to pull his blanket from his pack. He intended to sit here for a while.

Amy came to him, her sweet image filling his mind. The image became real and they lay in each other's arms watching the sunset. He felt the pressure of her in his arms, the warmth of her body, the fragrance of her hair, tasted her lips, and felt her touch. She stroked his brow, removing the little remaining tension. Her touch was electric, as her fingers traced the ridge of his back. Her lips nibbled his and her kisses stoked a fire deep in his stomach. Caressing her breasts softened her expression, allowing her love to shine. He saw the excitement build in her quivering body. They made love under the stars, first gently and then more passionately. He experienced Amy's emotions and feelings also through their mental link. He became lost in the sensation and passion, long since losing who he was in the confusion of mingling emotions. He was aware of a volcanic eruption as they combined in their orgasms. They lay together in silence for many long minutes as they slowly calmed their feelings and finally began to talk as they hadn't done in so long.

It was a beautiful evening and night and he was very happy. They had not been able to make time for themselves. Both had been so busy surviving and taking care of everyone else. They vowed to never neglect themselves again, and to make time just for them. It would never happen if they waited for a good time.

Amy woke him in the morning just in time to see the sun's light race across the desert floor. He had not seen this before when he spent a week at this spot. It was truly something to see.

Ay said it was time to go back, and he really didn't mind it because he was very hungry. As he started to rise he thought he had detected something in her mental tone. He looked into her mind and chuckled. He saw Amy's monitoring of Dawn and saw Moon raising hell with Al about the whereabouts of Levi. He was positive that Moon had probably looked for him all night. He should have told him when they left, but he would have wanted to go with him and they weren't ready for that. That would be the next step in Amy's mental growth, taking more than just him when they transported, namely Moon.

They did not want to startle anyone so Amy said they would reappear around the rock entrance of the caverns just out of sight. He felt nothing, really, when Amy sent him instantly to that location. His view one second was the desert, and the next second the boulder which he was standing behind. In retrospect, his view faded out then faded in at the new location. He was going to like this new ability, yes indeed.

* Amy *

She was instantly glad Levi had chosen this place. It was beautiful beyond description. She had seen the view from Levi's memory, but somehow this was far more intense. The bigger than life expanse made you feel very insignificant. Sharing this now with Levi was satisfying and romantic. She wanted to share more with Levi, much more.

They lay together as the sun set in the west, sharing the experience and the moment. They cuddled together throughout the night and shared much. Their love-making was intense. It was always intense as the emotions of each was experienced by the other and mingled with their own. This mental feedback in the other generated a stimulating emotional energy, and caused spiraling excitement and shuddering orgasms.

As was her blessing, so was it her curse as she continued to monitor the minds of Jimmy, Dawn, and Fred. Sometimes she wished she could shut them off, but unfortunately she had not found a way to do it. Once she locked with a mind, she was tuned to it and continued to receive input from them through Levi's mental link. It was not at all the same as with Levi. The data was not as rich as was Levi's and communication back to their minds could only be accomplished by a concentrated effort from Levi. The communication did work and had greatly contributed to the defeat of the Simian army here outside these passes. What a victory that had been.

She ignored the inputs throughout the night in order to give them both the break they desperately needed for their emotional well-being, but the backlog was building and could not be ignored much longer. Fred was having a nervous breakdown believing he was going to be eaten any minute by the Los Angeles Simians. Jimmy was feeling left out. He had been part of the inner circle and had enjoyed the excitement, now nothing was going on back at Owens Valley. The most pressing need was Moon. Through Dawn, she was seeing a very agitated Moon, and he would need to be calmed down soon. Levi's stress level was greatly reduced, so she reluctantly shared the information with Levi and they prepared to return.

Her memory was total and complete. She stored everything and knew all the landmarks for everywhere Levi (they) had been since they had been together. She chose a close but secluded spot to materialize close to where Al, Dawn and Moon were now engaged in strenuous hand signing. As Levi walked around the boulder into sight, Moon saw him immediately and came loping up. Moon looked relieved but very upset and commenced chewing Levi out in an extremely rare show of emotions. Levi was chuckling inside, but outwardly remained dutifully chastened.

Moon had been Levi's constant companion since Levi had saved him from drowning and Moon had been very concerned about Levi's disappearance. They really should have said something to him before leaving, but he would have wanted to go too. Moon was like a puppy in many ways, a seven foot tall four hundred and twenty-five pound golden puppy. The thought was humorous. They would take their chastising and take him along next time. Actually, it would have been the safe thing to do since they had been in hostile country.

* Levi *

He spoke in the screeching language of the Simians and apologized for not telling Moon he was going to be absent. He said he had some research to do and it had to be done alone, but admitted that he should have told him and would next time. Moon appeared to be satisfied with the answer and was now curious about the research. Levi could tell by the inquisitive look on his face, but he didn't ask.

Moon had been to the Technical Simian's camp in the northern valley checking on the colony. There was a sizable group of them now that included the forty-two Technical Simians from the colony that were liberated, the fifty or so females, plus the children. There were about one hundred and ten in all, and they were settling in but becoming bored with the inactivity. It didn't take much effort to raise cattle. They had been taught to herd the cattle to grazing areas and not let them spread out. He didn't know what to do with them.

Amy suggested that they re-establish patrols to search for cattle and round them up. That would keep them busy and would also prevent the Simians from overeating, decimating the herd. The Simians were totally carnivorous and consumed a healthy amount of beef every day and, although the threat was not immediate, they would eventually deplete the herd. Luckily there was an abundance of cattle after the day of chaos when three-quarters of the humans died from the Simian ray. The ray affected only the higher intelligence animals and cattle were not among that group. They were however, spread all over the country and would have to be herded. Amy said this would give them some purpose. Moon liked the idea of the patrols.

Amy also wanted Moon to interview the Technical Simians to learn what technical skills they possessed. She particularly wanted to know if any had knowledge of the weapons on board the ships. Moon said he would find out and was off to comply.

He then explained to Al and Dawn what was happening with the Simians. Al agreed that patrolling, finding cattle in the upper valleys, and tending to the herds would keep them busy.

Levi's next and most pressing problem was eating. He could smell the food cooking on the fire and it was driving him nuts. Dawn knew it too and smiled at him. Dawn knew more than most just how much food his augmented body needed. She had even been shocked as she had tried to keep him fed. She was piling meat on the fire for him now.

* Amy *

As she listened to Moon's report, she was planning. She realized that the Simians needed more, they needed a purpose. They needed to feel important. That is when she suggested that they return to patrols. This would keep some form of continuity in their routine and serve a purpose by herding in additional cattle. The settlement had a sizable herd of cattle, but normal increase in the herd would not keep up with the Simian's needs. The patrols would serve a dual purpose of keeping them busy and maintaining the supply required.

These items were only maintenance issues. Her real concern and goal was to gain access to the knowledge of the Simians that she believed was stored in the Simian computer currently in the caverns. To research this knowledge, she needed to learn from the Technical Simians. If the key existed, it would most likely be in them, and she would find what she needed. Moon had even said that he had been a computer specialist on board the ship en route to Earth. She again marveled that Moon must be close to eighty years old to have been a crew member in a space ship that landed over fifty years ago. At any rate, she asked Levi to have Moon interview the Simians to find out what their skills were. Knowing Moon, they would have that information by tomorrow.

Amy was frightened about the future. She estimated that worldwide there were probably no more than fifty thousand Simians, but that was only because there were probably only seventy-five space ships that made it to Earth plus growth over the last fifty years. She remembered there had been over one thousand five hundred space ships in the original invasion and, had it not been for the Earth United Defense League (EUDL) destroying hundreds of ships in space, they would have to contend with close to a million Simians. The problem would be moot now as humans might well have been consumed feeding that number. Her fear revolved around the other fleets that were en route. She had no idea how many or when to expect them, but if she wasn't able to develop new defenses, well, it would be the end of the human race.

They had only made a small, very small, dent in the Simian threat and they had a world to liberate. The scope of the task was unthinkable for what currently existed, much less considering the new invading fleet or fleets. She desperately needed to begin research, and she was the only one that had the knowledge to do it. Yes, she was frightened but tried to hide it from Levi.

As her mind continued to handle hundreds of functions, her primary focus returned to the present and the next immediate problem, which was to replenish Levi's calories and nutrients at Al's cooking fire. As Levi ate and talked, she listened to Al's problems. He was understandably concerned about the Simians living within his defenses. Al reminded Levi that they couldn't protect themselves from a sudden attack from within. He also reminded Levi that the Warrior Simian's children would grow up and could be a threat. Al also wanted to know about the next battle. She assumed that the Mojave Desert Lancer Army was committed to the continued battle for Earth, but was very pleased to hear it voiced.

Levi listened and offered only agreements and understanding to Al's concerns but told him little because he didn't know yet. Privately, Levi told her that they needed to give everyone goals or at least something to do to keep them occupied and she agreed.

* Levi *

He hadn't realized just how hungry he was until he started eating, then he remembered that he had not eaten supper last night. Just thinking about it brought a smile to his face. The smile must have made Al more at ease with him, as he continued to open up and voice his concerns.

Al had many concerns about the Simians living among them, but his real concern was where and what Simian colony they were going to fight next. Al and his Lancers were totally committed to the liberation of Earth and with the recent victory, were anxious to continue. They had lived in fear of the Simians all their lives and this revenge was sweet to their taste. Al was saying they were ready to follow him anywhere. Amy voiced the very question he was wondering when Amy questioned if Al would lead an army without him. Only he heard the question, and wondered the same thing.

He listened for a very long time as he ate and, with Amy's blessing, told Al that they would move against the Phoenix colony next. He told Al that they needed to make preparations first. Amy had given him designs for a new weapon that needed to be manufactured. She also suggested to him that Al send three-man patrols out in all directions to spread

34

the word about their success against the Simians. They needed recruits and weapons to expand the army.

Al and Dawn were becoming more at ease with him now, but there was still fear in their eyes. They did, however, like the ideas and suggestions they were hearing. They would take them as orders and Al, or anyone else hearing his suggestions all jumped to comply. They made him feel so aloft and unreachable that it was lonesome.

After eating, he sat down with paper and pencil and drew the plans for the weapon Amy designed. Amazingly, the plans looked professional and in great detail, even though he did them freehand and in a very short amount of time. Al looked appraisingly at the plans and smiled. The plans were for a large lance, but this lance had some very surprising features. This lance had a retractable blade within the main shaft that was both spring loaded and further augmented with compressed air, which could be pumped into a cavity within the lance. The combined pressure, when released, would propel the blade out of the lance an additional eighteen inches. The force behind the released pressure added to the blow from the user that triggered the release, should be more than sufficient to penetrate the dense body of a Simian. He had to admit, it was ingenious. This was indeed a weapon that could be used by a ground warrior.

* Amy *

She thought about a purpose for Al's lancers and decided to share some of her plans. Yes, the war must go on, but she wasn't ready. Hell, it had only been a few days since they had delivered the sound defeat to the Simians. They couldn't expect that every day could they? Certainly she couldn't deliver those miracles every day.

There was no time like the present to get them started on the weapon, however. It would take time to develop and perfect the weapon, and would be a good test for the new Simian forge. This settlement had very good tradesmen and would probably be the only place where the weapons could be made. She had designed the weapon from supplies found in inventory in the caverns, well the springs anyway. Those would have been impossible to make today. The other components would have to be cast and lathed to precision, but she believed it was possible.

The lance would look like a fat spear, a shaft of approximately six feet with a protruding spearhead of ten inches. It would take the weight of a full grown man to reset the spring and about ten pumps on the shaft air pump to build the pressure up to trigger level. When a solid and heavy impact on the spearhead was made, it would trigger the release, driving the blade eighteen inches into the Simian. She had calculated all the forces involved and it would be an effective weapon. The drawbacks were that it would take a minute or so to reset the blade and it could knock the holder back and down if he wasn't careful. Once triggered, the blade locked just in case it was necessary to continue fighting with the blade. The momentum of a charging Simian might impale him on the blade.

She had been thinking about this new ground weapon. The humans needed something else to fight with. Swords were not enough against Simians. The Simian's dense body and human's relative weak strength made it very difficult to defeat a Simian in a battle of that nature. The horses and long lances had given the humans equality to a certain extent, but there simply weren't enough horses to supply new army recruits.

She had devised this weapon and assisted Levi in free-handing the schematic. With her precision control, the drawing looked like a computer drafted printout, which of course it was. Al, long since past being shocked by feats of this nature, accepted it without even a sideways look. Al was happy to have a project for his settlement.

Now that they had a plan for new weapons, it was time to think about new recruits. The second idea was to send teams of Lancers out to meet humans and spread the word. She wanted a full three-man team complete with a portable lance transport. She wanted the teams to look impressive and functional as well for their own protection. This was going to be a big job, a seemingly impossible job, to take the Earth back from the Simians and they would need as many recruits as could be attracted. The whole human race, what was left of it, would need to be involved to even attempt the job.

* Levi *

Al and Dawn left to carry out his suggestions, and he was alone again. Amy resumed talking about the other problems at hand, namely Fred and Jimmy. They agreed it was just as well to initiate

37

action on all fronts. They decided to take Jimmy first because he would be easier. Amy said he was moping around the main camp and they could talk to him any time.

Amy opened up the monitored inputs from Jimmy and he noticed immediately that Jimmy's view was of the ground. He was, in fact, moping and dejected like a kid that had lost his favorite toy. He chuckled out loud.

Amy grinned and said, "I told you."

When he spoke to Jimmy, the reaction was immediate. Jimmy's head shot up and he answered instantly. This was one happy kid now. He knew Jimmy idolized him and would do anything he asked. He liked Jimmy and sensed Amy's affection for him also. Jimmy was a likable young man and had been exemplary in his tasks, showing much initiative and savvy for such a young man of only eighteen years.

Levi told him he had some instructions for him and launched in immediately. He told Jimmy that they needed a continuing supply of lances from the valley, but additionally, explained the weapons being built at the settlement and the need for new recruits to use them. He asked Jimmy to explain the needs and requests to Iron Eyes and ask for assistance. Amy wanted the Owens Valley tribe to also send full Lancer patrols out to find recruits. That made Jimmy happy and he commented that he would be in one of the first patrols out. This made Amy stutter, but she didn't say no. She was always protective of him, but she knew Jimmy would do this regardless, so she just sighed.

Amy said the Owens Valley was very fertile and mostly secure now from Simian attack and would be an excellent location to raise food crops necessary to support the growing army. She wanted them to start farming. Oh, he knew the tribe would not take to that idea, but then everything was changing wasn't it? He suggested that the patrols could invite many of the small gatherings of humans into the safe valley to assist with those chores.

Amy commented that the Owens Valley was a good base location and not very far from her physical location. What bearing that fact held, he had no idea, but it seemed important to Amy. He wasn't telling Jimmy this, as he knew Amy was thinking out loud only to him.

* Amy *

Jimmy was easy to take care of; he just wanted something to do. The work she assigned was real, but just not totally necessary that it get started immediately. She was becoming the bottleneck. She had other priorities that she needed to get to, but didn't want to lose any help along the way. They did need recruits and always needed more lances, but the last thing was a little more sensitive. She was asking the Indians to become farmers, at least some of them anyway. They needed the Lancers, so the recruits would also be needed to farm too. Maybe this would be acceptable. She hoped so anyway. They would do it for Levi she knew, but wanted them to get behind it.

Jimmy surprised her when he said he intended to take out a patrol. She had mixed emotions about that. On a logical sense, she would lose the ability to monitor the Owens Valley if Jimmy left. On the other hand, nothing was going on and wouldn't for a while, so why not? It might be of more benefit to see outside the valley. It was dangerous for him and that caused her some apprehension, but with their ability to transport, Levi should be able to save him if it became necessary.

The last and most complicated issue was Fred. She had been concerned for him. He was under extreme stress, being the only human in the LA Simian colony. Fred was not an overly brave man to start with, and the constant threat of a Simian disregarding orders (not to eat humans), was getting to him. True, Fred had most of Levi's Technical Simians as a personal bodyguard, but he didn't trust them like Levi did. After all, they were Simians.

To compound the situation, they were running out of food at the Los Angeles Simian colony. Without humans for food, the Simian patrols were hunting deer, cattle, hogs, and anything they could catch, but the patrols were having to go farther and farther to find food. Something would have to happen soon. There simply were too many of them to feed. She made a mental note to alter the instructions to the Lancer patrols. She would want the humans encountered and recruited to round up cattle that could be spared and deliver them to the converted Simians, especially the LA colony.

When Levi spoke to him, Fred was very happy. He was scared and didn't mind saying so. Fred said # 9 was leading the colony, but the generals were not eager to follow his instructions. He was afraid of a mutiny and being eaten. The eleven Technical Simians had been trained by Moon and were exceptional fighters now and could stand against any Warrior Simian, but there were still about six hundred of the Warriors. The demise of Gord had left a large hole in the colony's hierarchy that the Warriors wanted to fill. That fact combined with the natural resentment of the Technical Simians made for an explosive situation. The shock of Gord's defeat was wearing off, and Fred wanted instructions and help.

There was not much they could tell him in the way of additional advice other than what they had already given. They agreed that the situation required attention and told Fred that he was coming. That made Fred very happy. Levi told Fred that he would come in two days. Fred looked shocked, but said nothing. He really was scared.

* Levi *

He really was concerned for Fred. It was a very perilous situation they had put him into, but they really had no choice if they wanted to know what was going on there. He did have most of his personal guard there to protect Fred, but still it would have been a most unnerving experience for anyone, human that is. Even his guard, as expert as they now were in martial arts, would be able to do little against the might of Gord's army if they turned on them. For that matter, what could he do? They had to do something about the situation soon. The Warrior Simians needed to be destroyed, but his

41

human army didn't have the might to do it. It was only by Amy's amazing abilities that they were able to defeat Gord and win the leadership of the colony. The shock of that battle must be wearing off for Fred to be so afraid.

Amy and he agreed that they needed to go there. She said they could transport there and take Moon with them this time, but she wanted to wait until tomorrow. She said she wanted to let Moon gather data on the training, if any, of the Technical Simians and try to learn something about the Simian equipment before they went. He knew Amy was anxious to begin research and there were concerns she wasn't telling him yet, but he could imagine they were real and ominous. Whatever she wanted, he was there for her.

Fred was visibly relieved too when he spoke to him and said he was coming in two days to look at the situation. He was thinking about Fred's fear, knowing it was really severe. Suddenly, he was startled with the recollection that this was the compound where Fred had been imprisoned, waiting to be eaten by the Simians. The memories of that ordeal must be very hard on Fred's emotions. So much had happened in such a short time that he had forgotten until this moment that this is where he and Moon had rescued Fred along with the original fifteen Technical Simians of his guard. No wonder the fear was so great. He made a vow to Amy to help Fred soon.

They had been involved with so many things that the morning was almost gone before he was up and headed toward the caverns. Amy wanted to rummage through the Simian equipment to see what she could decipher about it. Moon had identified the items as they had unloaded them, but many of the pieces had no translation into English. They might remain a mystery. Her focus was the unit identified as information center (computer). Amy wanted to gain access to the stored information in the Simian computer.

They found the unit carefully stored and protected in the rear of the storage level set aside for the Simian equipment. He uncovered the unit and looked over it carefully. It was circular with a diameter of six feet. The top was covered with a transparent semicircle of concentric material. He saw no power plug or electronic connections. All he found were tube connections similar to what he remembered was the size of a water hose going to the ice maker on a refrigerator. There were several crystal prisms of various colors inside the unit that could be seen through the transparent cover. The transparent material functioned as glass, but was different somehow, almost metallic. These crystals were embedded in a matrix of very small and minute transparent tubing. At first it looked solid, but on closer inspection, the tubes could be seen woven together in an intricate design. It seemed that the internal working of this unit was flowing liquid, but what liquid? He sure didn't understand it and, Amy seemed preoccupied and was quiet. Her image was in deep concentration.

* Amy *

Finally they were able to pursue her goal to research the Simian computer. It was constantly in part of her mind. She was anticipating being able to learn new knowledge for the human race, of course no one was left to appreciate it but her. She knew there had to be knowledge she could use against the Simian invasion if she could only access it.

They found the unit well protected and uncovered it to begin the inspection. This obviously did not operate on anything like electricity. It had only a connection for liquid. There was no input or output connection. For that matter, there were no controls. There was only the chassis and circular glass bubble. She surmised that the bubble somehow functioned as the controls and display unit. Within were red, yellow, green, and violet prisms. This would have to be the projection of a visual display, receptors for controls, and possibly other functions. The bed of the computer was interlaced with extremely fine interconnecting tubes and even finer hair-sized interconnecting fibers. The fibrous material filled the massive six foot tank of the computer and was obviously the central data bank. She believed that it must work on a complex chemical exchange similar to the neuron cells of the human brain. The intelligence necessary to invent something like this would have been incredible.

What was she going to do now? She needed the fluid, and, damn, who knew what other chemical were necessary? There were no containers of any liquid in the Simian's inventory. Maybe some Simian yet alive might know. Could this unit even be made to work again? So close, yet so far.

They spent several more hours rummaging through the inventory items but discovered nothing new. The technology was so foreign to her understanding that she had no basis from which to build or relate. The secrets would just have to wait and hope she could discover the secrets of the Simians.

They traveled around the camp watching the hustle of the tradesmen. The Simian forge was going full blast and had been for days now. The metals from the Simian swords gathered from the battlefield were being reduced to raw ingots for later use. Some of the melted metal was being poured into molds that looked like the new weapon design. She was anxious to see how they looked and worked when completed.

She was also still learning how to deal with emotions; actually, she was still learning what emotions were. She knew the emotion being experienced now, boredom. Her mind churned over hundreds of different things, yet she was bored. She wanted to do something more, like the research she badly needed to do... in fact she was looking forward to it. Unfortunately, she was waiting on too many other people. She knew Levi felt her anxiety when he asked if she wanted to go to Moon's location and rush the interview. Only too happy for the opportunity, she said, "Oh, yes, thanks and thanks for the concern."

* Levi *

Amy was in a really weird mood. Nothing seemed to pacify her. Studying the Simian computer only seemed to make her more agitated. They went through the camp reviewing and looking at the activity. He thought she would be happy to see the

45

work on her new weapon, but it kept her attention only briefly. He could see her frustration and building boredom and knew he had to do something. He knew they were waiting on information from Moon, so he said, "Why don't we go help Moon with the interviews of the Technical Simians." That pleased her. Amy wanted to teleport, but that was too easy and he said no. He needed the release of stress also and needed to run and stretch his muscles. Of course, Amy kept his muscles in perfect shape, but he enjoyed the exhilaration of the exercise; besides, it kept Amy busy controlling his body metabolism. Amy saw his logic and gave him a smile, but called him a shithead anyway.

He grabbed his backpack and water jugs and took off running. It was likely to take a couple of hours of hard running before he reached Moon's location and would give him time to dig a little deeper into what was really bothering her.

As the miles passed, he felt better. There was something about exerting his muscles that he loved. Even after a year of having the extraordinary body Amy provided him, he had never gotten used to it. His body had been on the verge of withering away when Amy succeeded in altering his DNA and began controlling his body. Many times he would wake up with a start thinking he still had his eighty year old body and would feel his rippling muscles and tight abs just for reassurance.

The more Amy focused on controlling his body, the more at ease she became. He could sense her relaxing and could see more of her thoughts as she did so. She really wasn't trying to hide anything from him; it was more that he didn't understand the complexities of her thoughts. She was deep into mathematical calculations and formulas, and he had absolutely no idea the purpose other than she wanted to learn the Simian's secrets. He was all for that too.

They were approaching the Simian camp now and could see that the colony had indeed made themselves at home. They had constructed lean-tos and brush arbors to shade the sun and they had centered their settlement near a spring. They didn't have comforts, but then they didn't need or want them. Their camp was built here for the herd of cattle. It was obvious that the cattle had gotten somewhat used to the Simians in that they weren't running and bucking like they originally did. He could see Simians mingled among the cattle and there was even a flock of sheep being herded by Simians. No herd dogs needed here.

As they approached, Moon came forward to greet him. Moon was obviously happy to see him and began slapping him on the back, causing no small amount of pain. It was approaching dusk as they sat on rocks gathered around the recently lit fire. Due to the diminished night vision of the Simians, fires were always built at dusk, but this night had a slight chill and the heat felt good as he sat listening to Moon's report.

* Amy *

She realized what Levi was doing by making her concentrate on maintaining the runaway mutation of his altered DNA during his exertion, but she didn't mind. It did prevent her from being bored,

47

and that was good. She was actually calm by the time they reached Moon's camp.

Sometimes she thought Moon could actually sense when they were near. Certainly he saw them coming from a great distance and came to meet them like a watch dog might greet its master. Moon was so protective and eager to serve Levi, and she felt total trust in him even over most humans. Most humans she had experienced had a self-serving nature, not that it was bad, just that Moon would think of Levi first. She had grown very comfortable with Moon and his original Simian army. They would have each died willingly for Levi.

As they settled by the fire in the dwindling light, she listened to Moon's report. Only five Technical Simians had even been alive during the space flight. Of the five, two had been supply coordinators, one was an astronomer, one like Moon, had been a computer operator, and one had been a herder of !$@### (unpronounceable or untranslatable in English).

When she asked Levi to question what the animal was, they learned that it was a large animal from the Simian's planet. It was a grass eater with large wide legs and a wide flat mouth. They were moderately domesticated and could be used for riding or work. The general description sounded like an elephant without a trunk, so that is what Levi named it. It seems that it was their main food source on their home planet and a stock of them had been brought for breeding, but when the mutiny occurred in space, the Warrior Simians ate them instead of the stored supplies.

She had hoped to find a computer engineer or maintenance technician, anyone that could tell her what fluid to use to activate the computer. Her disappointment flared until Moon said that the other computer operator mentioned that # 5, of Moon's original group had been the equivalent of a computer engineer on board the Los Angeles colony ship. Now that startled her. She hadn't even considered that option, and that ship may actually have an operating computer. Why hadn't she thought of that before?

Levi actually laughed and said, "You can't think of everything."

They could check it out when they went to visit Fred, which might not be very long at all with the way things were shaping up there. She had been monitoring Fred constantly and it was beginning to look like a mutiny was about to happen. She saw the Technical Simians starting to gather for protection around Fred. She opened the channel to Levi so he could see what was happening and he became upset. He wanted to go immediately and she agreed.

* Levi *

As Moon gave his report on the experience of the Technical Simians, he was shocked to realize that there were five of these Simians of approximately his age. He then remembered that the average life span of a Simian was around two hundred Earth years old. He sensed Amy's disappointment at not finding a computer engineer and understood why. She desperately wanted to learn the secrets of the Simians, but he didn't quite understand the urgency.

He looked at her deeply and saw her looking back as if trying to decide whether to tell him or not. Finally she smiled and opened her mind to him completely so he could see her concerns and plans. Oh yes, now he saw and understood the complexities of her plan and the deep threat to the human race as well as the urgency. He had been so absorbed in the recent victories that he lost track of the more threatening menace still in space. Everyone was doomed if a second wave of a Simian invasion came without resistance. Damn, he remembered that originally there were over one thousand five hundred Simian space craft that equated to three quarters of a million new Simians landing on Earth. You could call the game over then! Yes, he now shared her urgency.

Considering what Amy's desperate need was, he was also excited to hear about # 5 at the LA colony being a Simian computer engineer. This was fantastic and a welcome stroke of good luck. They would explore this opportunity very soon.

The second bit of information he found interesting was the fact that the fleet had brought live breeding animals for food on this planet. Unfortunately, according to Moon, no stock had made it to Earth on either ship that he knew about, nor had he heard of any from any other colony. That was unfortunate since they would have been a stable food source on Earth instead of humans. He listened to the description and told Amy it sounded like an elephant without a trunk.

Amy chuckled and said, "It's as good a name for it as anything."

They continued to listen to Moon's report until Amy interrupted his concentration. She opened the communication from Fred's mind. He and the Technical Simians were gathering in the main area of the space ship. It looked defensive in nature and Amy said that the generals and their guards were amassing outside. They were having second thoughts about the Technical Simians ruling them. They were getting hungry and food was scarce. It was their obvious intention to kill them and Fred and resume control.

He was panicky which Moon noticed immediately and stood looking around for danger. Seeing none, he looked back. Levi said, "Your Techs and Fred are in trouble in L A." Moon was agitated, but didn't know what to do. Moon just looked pleadingly at him.

He wanted to go to them now and asked Amy to take him and Moon by teleporting them. Amy was concerned for his safety, but they had no choice. He was the only one that could control the generals, if at all possible. She told him to bring Moon close and explain what they were going to do. As he did he saw one of the few expressions of shock, or any emotions for that matter, on Moon. It was a combination of shock and fear and, if the situation weren't so grave, it would have been comical.

As Amy suggested, he concentrated on Fred and told him they were coming and to remain focused on the open area in front of him. Fred acknowledged with great relief and told the others what was happening. They stood together, and he concentrated on the image coming from Fred's eyes. He felt the customary warmth come over him and a slight vibration building, as the image in front of him began to fade, replaced by the growing image from Fred's eyes. Suddenly, he realized it was no longer an image. He and Moon were actually standing in the open spot. This transportation was visible to the generals, who were now staring in open shock at him and Moon standing between them and the gathered group of defenders.

* Amy *

She was about to attempt her second try at teleportation and this time taking someone else with Levi. Actually, it shouldn't be any different. What she was actually doing was transporting matter through mental energy, and theoretically, mass shouldn't issue, to a point. It was a matter of her ability to focus through Levi's eyes and senses, which is what she was doing now. She saw what she wanted to transport and where she wanted to transport it through Fred's eyes and simply transferred the material through thought. It was a quick flowing of energy from one place to the other. They simply were placed where she concentrated, which was standing in front of the generals and amassed Warriors behind them. The five generals were there with approximately fifty Warriors moving into the main area. The shock was immediate as they appeared, and even though Fred and the others knew they were coming, she heard their gasps from behind Levi.

This would be a battle. The generals had been warned and a decisive lesson must be taught if they ever hoped to maintain a sibilance of control over this Warrior army. Force was the only thing the Simians understood. She had hoped that the lesson with Gord would be enough, but apparently not. This army still remained intact and incredibly dangerous, and Levi would need much more than her input to do what must be done. He would need her with him totally to survive. They would have to merge, but could she do it again? She didn't even know how she had done it before.

She focused on anger before as the basis from which to build, but she wasn't angry. She shook with fear. Could she use fear as the basis? There were no choices. They were committed to this course of action and must try. Concentrating her massive intellect on this commitment of resolve and fear, it formed into a mass, solid and building, gathering energy from around it. This energy, her mind, began forming into a cloud, flowing to surround Levi. It felt as if she astral projected from her physical brain and was projecting herself into Levi. In truth this is what was happening; however, it was far more than just merging, they were becoming one, unified with Levi. She was Levi, and she was herself, then they became one and she lost herself as they merged. There was then only ASONE.

* Levi *

Amy said there could be no discussion, that the generals must be killed. That was the promise he had made to them. He had stated, "If you failed to obey I will come to kill and replace You." Now he must do it or risk total mutiny. Moon had said that Warrior Simians respected only power and force and must be ruled by such.

This was not going to be easy, actually impossible for him to stand against the five generals. The other problem was that the army followed the generals and he didn't know what their reaction would be. If they joined in this confrontation he had no chance. He told Amy, "You are going to have to merge with me again." He saw the panic in her eyes.

Amy said, "I don't know if I can do it."

All he could say was, "Try or we die." Then he felt the power surge through him and felt her presence growing as he flowed into her and she into him. They again became as one (ASONE), a new entity.

* ASONE *

It called itself ASONE and was neither male nor female, Amy or Levi. ASONE was infinitely intelligent and incredibly powerful. The physical mental energy of Amy combined with the already powerful Levi made it much more than either separately. ASONE stood before the generals mighty and confident. It spoke in a more powerful voice than Levi alone and passed judgment. It passed the sentence of death on the generals. It spoke to the gathering of Warriors, "Stand down! I will deal with the generals. I have no desire to harm you." The generals panicked and ordered the Warriors to attack.

The Warriors seemed confused as the generals screeched the attack order. The lifelong training of the Warriors eventually took over, and they jumped to obey the orders from five generals. ASONE's hopes of limiting the battle faded as it saw the Warriors move to attack. The odds were astronomically bad, but there was no fear.

The uncaring ASONE, the entity that only minutes before had been Levi and Amy, saw the danger in front of it and took the initiative. It screeched to Moon and his small army, "Follow me toward the doors then clear and close them and hold the doors to prevent other Warriors from coming in." ASONE and his twelve would face some, fifty-five Warriors, including the five generals. This, of course, assumed that they could get the doors closed from inside.

Levi, with Amy's help, had killed many Simians in combat. All those fights had been narrowly won, not by strength, but by skill and timing. Levi's strength was no match for a Simian. Gord had been their ultimate test and only by the emergence of ASONE had they been victorious. Now as ASONE again, the strength and power was incredible. It felt like it could do anything, certainly it was more than a match for any Simian now. Unfortunately, ASONE could still be killed; the body was still mortal. Additionally, there were fifty-five Simians, not just one. This would again be a battle for their lives, but ASONE was oblivious to fear or concern. It only thought of dispensing judgment.

ASONE's mind was moving at light speed as the strategy came forth. The close quarters would not allow sufficient room for sword fighting, so it reached for its Bowie knives and began carving turkey dinner. The strength and power in the arms was shocking. The knives cut deep into the dense hide of the Simians it reached. It rolled and stabbed up into the weak target in the crotch. When the blow struck the exact spot, the Simian was immediately paralyzed and fell dead. Throats were slit and necks broken. It seemed as if everyone else was moving in slow motion as it fought. There were many blows delivered at it, but ASONE was a blur as it dodged, moved, and worked a vicious and bloody path through the Simians.

Moon and the others were immediately behind, fighting their way to the door. The martial arts training helped greatly. Moon and the Technical Simians were very effective at close quarters. They also had an advantage, using the short swords they trained with. The close quarters made them even most effective. Moon and his army had reached the double doors and the team was fighting in both directions back to back, preventing access to the room from outside and holding those already inside. After several long minutes, the doors slammed closed and latched.

ASONE saw everything while fighting through the Simian Warriors. As it passed, the Warriors fell to either side. Blows were made with feet, elbows, knees, blade points, and back handed knife butts. It was vicious and deadly as it fought, a juggernaut rolling through them. It seemed like hours, but only seconds passed. Five fell to its attack, then ten. The numbers added up and twenty were down. With the doors now closed, Moon's small army was killing now, and it was beginning to slip in the purple Simian blood that now covered everything. ASONE climbed to the top of dead Simians and fought on, delivering thunderous, killing kicks to the heads of those Warriors close. Three of the generals were already dead, but two remained, standing with the three remaining Warriors. The entity called ASONE backed away and let Moon and his army complete the killing.

ASONE waited as the last five were quickly killed by Moon's group. It surveyed the area and saw fifty-five dead mutinying Warriors and two of his own. The entity felt sorrow for its fallen. It was # 6 and # 14 of the original group. These had been Levi's personal bodyguards and friends, and now they lay dead. ASONE's anger was rising anew until it noticed that the fallen friends had already been avenged.

ASONE stood in the center with Levi's friends on both sides as Moon opened the doors. They stood motionless as the Warriors outside looked in and saw the carnage. ASONE announced the death of the five generals. The screeching and clacking of the Warrior's black teeth rose to a crescendo throughout the Simian army. The Simians fear of Levi paralyzed them.

ASONE walked fearlessly through the doors alone into the quickly spreading army of Warriors. The bloody Bowie knives were still held tight in blood covered hands. ASONE's deep screech announced, "I am still the leader of the Los Angeles Simian colony. Are there any others that wish to challenge Me?" The screeching and clacking ceased and total silence fell over the army. There were no challenges.

Screeching to the assembled army, ASONE announced that Moon and # 9 were still in charge of the colony. They would choose some of the Technical Simians and loyal guard to replace the dead generals of the colony. With a booming screech and deathly stern stare he said, "They will be obeyed." Seeing that there was no dissension from the assembly, ASONE showed his contempt for the Warriors by turning its back on the army, then returned through the doors.

* Amy *

With true regret, she felt herself, the Amy part, begin to separate from the ASONE entity. The joining was hypnotic, almost euphoric, and she didn't want to separate. Merged together, they had been awesome, somehow far more than they were separately, almost limitless, but with the danger over, the merge must divide or both of them would die.

The power of the entity they created seemed capable of anything. The entity had managed to kill forty-three Warrior Simians in close-quarter fighting. She remembered seeing the fear in the Simians' eyes as ASONE fought. She felt the power of the blows and slashes with the Bowie knives. They had been so powerful that the dense hide of the Simians had opened as if nothing more than thin paper. Blood and death spewed forth as the entity whirled and slashed, ducking and reaching under hands and swords. There had been no compassion, only the simple mechanics of killing. That part frightened her now as she became herself again.

While she was merged, she no longer controlled Levi's body. She merged with Levi and became the new entity and was no longer Amy the computer, controlling the mutations of Levi's body. She was part of the entity, totally separate and new. Left in this condition, Levi would die from the unchecked and normally controlled mutations. This could happen in a matter of hours. Even short periods of time could cause mutation that would take time to reverse. This fact would always be the limiting factor for the existence of ASONE.

The reality of the situation flooded her mind as she completed the separation. The longing to remain lost out to her intellect now. She again resumed her busy mental activity of monitoring and controlling Levi's body, along with monitoring the many other inputs from Dawn, Jimmy, and Fred. "Oh shit!" Fred was in the room and he was scared senseless!

Everyone had forgotten Fred. He wasn't a fighter and had to believe he was facing certain death as this battle engulfed the room. Fred was miraculously uninjured, but she couldn't tell where he was. He was underneath Simian bodies somewhere. She passed the information on to Levi, who was already moving about the room, seemingly in total control again.

* Levi *

There was no way to describe how it felt to be ASONE. As he returned to himself, he remembered.

He had no longer been only Levi. He had also been Amy. He felt the internal activities of Amy, the incredible intelligence, and felt her love. He felt the love and he was the love and they were one. It was total satisfaction, like two halves of his heart had come together. He was complete.

Unfortunately, he didn't have much time to enjoy the pleasant thoughts. He had done many fantastic things as Levi, but this was far beyond that. The entity ASONE was a superior being; faster, stronger, more vicious and totally without mercy. He tried to forget the details. It simply was too much to handle the memory of what ASONE had done.

There were mixed emotions as he separated from the entity. In most ways he loved the merge, but some things were a welcome separation. The horror of the vicious and totally ruthless attack was disconcerting, and he welcomed the separation from that. He accepted the division as ASONE returned to the room and he was totally separated by the time he entered the room.

He was shocked at the carnage and somewhat ashamed that he, well ASONE, had done most of it. It was his bloody hands that still held the knives. He noticed fear in the eyes of his Simian friends... all except Moon. Moon accepted Levi unconditionally and was again standing by his side.

Admittedly, he was both excited and apprehensive as ASONE. It would take some time to discover the limits of ASONE, if he were able to stand it.

Amy got his attention and told him to look for Fred.

She said, "He is buried somewhere in the room under bodies."

His immediate reaction was shock and concern, until Amy let him know he was all right, just buried. He screeched to the others to find Fred, and everyone scrambled to look for him. He heard the screech from # 13 and jumped to help. Fred lay under a dead Warrior with his feet sticking out. He couldn't help it and began laughing. It was comical to see Fred kicking and trying to scramble out from under the dead Simian. Fred was soon up and trying to regain some dignity as he looked around, seeing the slaughter for the first time.

He also saw Fred's shock, looking around through different eyes. He told Moon to call a clean-up detail from the army and get the Warriors buried.

Moon nodded, but signed, "I will bury our fallen." It was his turn to nod at Moon.

This had been a busy few days. As he reflected over the activities, he asked Amy, "What happened to our plan to relax for a while?"

They both grinned as she said, "The rest is over."

CHAPTER 2
(THE RESEARCH BEGINS)

* Amy *

She had been thinking about the on-board Simian Computer ever since Levi mentioned it. The combination of having # 5, a Simian computer engineer, with them now and the proximity of the computer was too much temptation. Now that the immediate threat of mutiny at the Los Angeles colony had been averted, she was anxious to find the computer. Levi seemed anxious also. They did seem to think more and more alike as their goals, interests and lives continued to merge.

At her request, Levi summoned # 5, who immediately agreed to help in any way he could. He was only too happy to do anything for his master. Unfortunately, Moon appeared to be a tad jealous of # 5's importance and attention but said nothing. To soothe Moon, Levi explained that his interest focused on # 5's knowledge of the Simian computer.

Amy provided the questions to Levi in precise words to prevent any confusion either on Levi's or # 5's part. She wanted to confirm that # 5 was indeed the equivalent of a computer engineer, and, as the questions continued to be answered, she became convinced that this was so. The technology differed completely from human computers, but the nature and organization of the technology seemed logical. It operated on a fluid chemical based technology quite similar to the actual internal working of the human brain. Communication transferred by means of a chemical language quite similar to the way she communicated with Levi's body. Actually, the logic of the design was impressive.

Levi did not understand # 5's responses nor did he understand the questions he asked, but he maintained a good front to the others and tried to appear as if he actually knew what he was talking about. Smiling, she said, "You are such a shithead." He ignored her, making her smile even bigger.

* Levi *

Amy remained anxious, moving from one obsession to another. Here he had, as always, narrowly averted being killed again, faced the stress of life and death situations and was still light headed from the ASONE merge. Now she already had him trying to solve the mystery of the Simian computers. He agreed that it would be a major accomplishment, but DAMN, he wanted to catch his breath. Oh well, he could handle it, but it was exasperating.

He asked Moon to get # 5. In seconds, # 5 was in front of him. Awe still showed on # 5's face, but Levi was becoming accustomed to the strange looks he received, and he really didn't blame them. He realized that many of the feats he, Amy, or ASONE accomplished did challenge the imagination to believe. He didn't even believe some of it. SOME? Hell, if he wasn't physically doing the things he had been doing he wouldn't believe it either.

He had no idea what questions Amy give him to ask, but tried not to look stupid in the process. He hoped he was successful. Amy knew what # 5 was talking about, and that's all that mattered anyway.

Amy explained, "The Simian computer works very much the way I talk to your body in a chemical language."

Levi interrupted her saying, "I never understood that either so it doesn't matter. Just ask your questions and I will be your ventriloquist dummy." She just smiled and continued. The next question got his attention. Amy wanted him to ask # 5 to show him the Simian computer on board this ship. Yes, that was something he could do. He had seen the one in the caverns, but this one might actually work and he wanted to see.

They took torches from stands on the wall and proceeded into the main part of the ship with # 5 in the lead followed by him and Moon. Once inside, they went up a flight of large stairs. It was awkward for the length of his legs to make the steps, understandable since it was designed for Simians. Amy could have accommodated his body to the stride, but it wasn't that big of a problem. They continued higher and deeper into the ship. The air was dry and stale from lack of circulation, breathable. As they finally entered a large circular room, Moon indicated this was the control center. As the torches illuminated the area, they all knew it was useless. Everything was destroyed! The Warrior Simians in control had totally ruined the control room and everything in it. The transparent membrane of the computer had been shattered along with most of the internal components. The computer wasn't the only thing; everything in the room had undergone the same type of treatment. Nothing in the room was usable; every reminder of technology had been smashed. The Warriors didn't understand it so they destroyed it.

He could sense Amy's disappointment. She remained silent for a few seconds, which to her was like hours, so he knew she was upset. In that amount of time she could translate the entire Simian language into French.

It seemed to be a shock to # 5 also. As # 5 stared at the computer, then around the room at the devastation, he shook with anger at the useless waste of technology. After some thought, the Simian engineer became more interested in the connecting tubes. Following tubes to main supply tanks and unidentifiable equipment became # 5's focus. When he discovered the tanks were empty, he threw up his hands in a universal sign of disgust.

* Amy *

She was devastated to see the damage to the equipment. Hope vanished, and depression set in. There were no more questions to ask, only silence. After a few minutes she became interested in # 5's actions as he explored the interconnecting tubing and storage tanks. Yes, this was important. The power source and liquid fuel was a subject she had overlooked. She had a computer, but no power fuel. Maybe there was yet a chance.

She renewed pumping questions at Levi, and he was again questioning # 5. Levi finally got bored with the questioning, backed out of the control of his own body, and she found herself talking through Levi's mouth. The education started as # 5 began explaining that the fuel was the medium for transferring oxygen to the cell matrix of the computer. The power was oxygen, nutrients and numerous chemicals in a hydrogen liquid base. She was shocked. The terms being used described a living organ and a substitute for blood. Yes, it made sense. The computer functioned as an organ, like a living brain, so why not? Actually, it made a lot of sense. Now that she analyzed it, the actual operation of an Earth computer was not logical and did not operate in any fashion like a human brain. The Simian concept was far more practical.

The Simian computer engineer upon discovering the empty storage tanks, cursed the Warriors. She didn't understand the meaning, but the tone unmistakable. He may be angry, but she was becoming very excited. She knew where there was a several hundred year supply. Why had she not seen it before? This was very good news!

A plan formed, racing through her brain at light speed. She had an intact computer at the caverns. It would need to be taken to her physical location and tied into her life support. She realized that her liquid life support was the equivalent to blood and must be reasonably identical to the Simian computer fuel. The best part of the plan: once tied into her plumbing, the communication problem between her and the Simian computer would also be resolved. That part had not even been discussed, but she knew that communication interconnection would be the next major obstacle, assuming they could get a Simian computer up and running. Fortunately, this same process had already been established through her communication within Levi's body. The communication interconnect would be a complex flow of a chemical language through the life support tubing. It was simple, so simple, once she understood.

In conjunction with activating the Simian computer, she was considering re-activating her research facility. The first step would be activating the Simian computer. Once the computer was active and interconnected, she hoped to learn the secrets of the Simian technology so she could reverse the effects of the ray. If she could do that, she might be able to reverse the changes to the Earth's laws of physics caused by the Simians' weapon. She realized that it would only be for a relatively small area like her research facility, but if she could get electricity going there, she could reactivate the entire facility. Research could begin in earnest to unlock the Simian technology. Yes, she had the human technology in her memory which could be downloaded into those that could help run the facility. The plan was growing by quantum leaps as she continued to analyze the data.

Levi reminded her that it would have to be thought out, because her plan would reveal her existence to the world. That would put them in danger and violate her first rule of survival, never let anyone know about her. Shocked, Amy said, "Damn, you are right!" What were they going to do?

* Levi *

He wished he understood both the questions and the answers he was receiving from Amy and # 5. Unfortunately, he did not, but Amy sure did. He didn't know why the answers were making Amy so excited. All he saw was tragedy. The Simian computer was destroyed and the fuel tank was empty. He thought that possibly if they found some fuel, it could be used in the first computer back in the caverns. He thought it was devastating news, but it seemed to make Amy happy and he didn't understand why.

As he tried to follow her train of thought, he started to see the significance of the fuel. Amy realized that it was basically the same life force she used. They could use hers, which meant that they would have to take the Simian computer to her facility and hook it up. This disturbed him. He hated that place. It was too much like a tomb with all the hundreds of souls and ghosts still there.

Amy said, "You are being ridiculous!"

Levi said, "Yeah, I know, but I will never feel comfortable there."

Amy looked hurt and said, "That is where I live."

He said, "Now look who is being ridiculous. You live in me." She liked that answer.

Amy's mind jumped from area to area, ideas growing in scope. Some of it he understood and some he didn't, but he saw enough thoughts to see her racing mind at work. One second she was hooking up the Simian computer, the next reactivating the facility. She envisioned learning the secrets of the Simian technology and then solving the spectrum shift in the laws of physics, re-training humans and Simians in the sciences and many other subjects that were growing toward the ridiculous. Her mind began to spiral out of control. He

68

shuddered to think what she might be capable of if she had total control of the environment around her and didn't have to depend on anyone else.

Amy sobered when he reminded her about the vow of secrecy she had always demanded about her existence. She quickly came back to reality, but the ideas and dreams remained alive as her mind continued to churn. He knew he had not heard the end of this.

There was nothing more they could do in the control room. Everything was destroyed and depressing both of them to remain. He told the group, "I have seen enough." They then retraced their steps through the dark passageways back to the assembly area.

The main area was free of bodies now, but purple Simian blood was everywhere and the stench of death assaulted his nostrils. He led the group outside into the open. The gathered Simian Warriors quickly opened ranks to give them plenty of room. He averted his eyes, trying not to stare or make eye contact directly with any Warrior. Amy explained that it made him seem more aloof and superior, and he needed to maintain that edge. The brief glances in the blazing red eyes of the Simians he did momentarily make contact with, revealed a combination of awe, respect, fear and maybe even some god-like worship. After this day of slaughter, he believed he would never again have a control problem with this group. Their only problem now ... what to do with them?

* Amy *

The Warrior Simians apparently had no understanding of technology and destroyed everything in sight that reminded them of their inferiority. She didn't quite understand the lack of overall intelligence of the Warrior Simians and why they were so different from the Technical Simians. She did, however, suspect the Warriors were, as their name suggested, good only for fighting. Possibly they had been genetically engineered for this purpose. Through her research she had learned this would have been easily accomplished, since the Simians technology had advanced farther than humans.

If that was the case, they had no choice but to pit the various Warrior groups against each other. Let them fight and kill each other. It sounded cruel, but each colony had to be defeated and who better to do it than another Warrior Simian attack force. This group could attack the Fresno, Stockton, or San Diego Simian colonies. Attrition would deplete both sides, but the next defeated colony would be converted and the new combined army could move on to the next closest colony. She and Levi would have to maintain a tight control over the growing Warrior Simian army, but it could be done... maybe.

In contrast, the Technical Simians were highly intelligent, social, loyal, somewhat moral and proven to interface well with humans. She would love to have an army of Technical Simians, but on second thought, would rather have them as scientists, engineers, and research assistants. Unfortunately she would need most of them to supervise the Warrior Simians, at least for a while.

They returned to the assembly area, but it was still a mess so they exited the building into the massed Simian army. She could see in the Simians' eyes that they were totally subdued and subject to Levi's authority. It would be a while before another rebellion after this day's actions. The colony had no leadership, however. All the generals, sub-generals, and high officers had been killed in the fight. This would be the perfect time to establish Moon's Technical Simians into the leadership positions, but she was resentful at losing the original Simians and Levi's personal guard. The Los Angeles colony must be expendable and would be greatly reduced with a war on another colony. It would be a war of attrition, fought until they were gone. She did not want any of Moon's Simians killed. She had become very fond of them. It sounded cruel, but maybe she could use some of the Mojave Desert Technical Simians as leaders here. She would have to give that some thought.

For now, Moon's original team was in place so the re-organization could begin. She told Levi that they should leave and let # 9 take care of the organization. It was unlikely the Warrior Simians would give him any more problems. She also suggested that they not stay at this camp much longer to prevent the Warrior Simians from becoming used to his gentler side and lose their fear. Maintaining paralyzing fear over the army would be best. That seemed to be what the Warrior Simians understood best.

Levi agreed about leaving and called Fred, Moon and his Simians for final instructions. Fred was still in shock, but expressed his desire to go with Levi. He was scared and didn't mind saying so, but he had to stay. Levi talked with him and finally convinced him that his purpose was extremely important and that he must remain. He instructed to the Technical Simians to prepare the Warriors to attack the San Francisco Simian colony. Their job was to supervise and direct, but not engage in battle themselves. She was not sure if they understood why, but they accepted the instructions. She didn't explain fully, because she wasn't sure how they would accept the suicide war of Simian against Simian. Finally # 5 was instructed to return with Levi and Moon.

* Levi *

Amy was very business-like after visiting the control room. She obviously wanted to get back to her project, even though he was not totally sure what that was. He did agree that the army should not see him too often. It was necessary to maintain their fear of him, since that appeared to be the only thing the Warrior Simians understood. He also agreed with Amy concerning their needs. The Warrior Simians needed to war; it was in their nature. All they could do, which matched his and Amy's goals, was to send them to war with the other colonies. There were enemies everywhere, but the San Francisco area (Fresno and Stockton) seemed the most logical for personal reasons. He wanted to clear the area around Amy's facility of any hostile Warrior Simians.

The thought of pitting one group of Simians against another was appealing. Let them kill each other off. Many humans would be saved and many additional Technical Simians might also be freed. They really had no choice. There was no way the human army could defeat this Simian army, much less the other hostile colonies spread across the world. If this army decided to turn on them they had little chance. At this point controlling the Simian army was a big bluff, but it was working for the time being and must be exploited.

He agreed that Moon's Simians shouldn't be risked in battle. It was going to be a battle designed to eliminate the Warrior Simians, not the good guys. They would have to plan carefully. They also needed Fred to stay here although he didn't want any part of it. Who could blame him? Due to Fred's association with the Simians, he had learned much of their language. It was impossible for him to speak it, but could understand much of what had been said in the Simian language and realized that he had to stay. Fred was receptive to his responsibilities, just scared. Levi removed his Army .45 automatic from his waist and handed it to Fred saying, "Will this help?" Wow! It was the first time he had seen Fred actually grin, but he said nothing.

Amy chastised him, but he had never used it anyway and hadn't even remembered it during the battle. At least Fred could defend himself with it. That helped. The .45 was more of a moral support than weapon. If Fred were close enough to a Simian and had time to unload a clip into it, possibly it might take out a Warrior Simian. Of course if more than one decided to kill him he wouldn't have enough ammunition or time, but the psychological support would be of benefit.

As they were giving directions to wage war against the San Francisco area colonies to # 9, Levi bristled at # 9's question. They were not accustomed to receiving return comments from the Technical Simians. Mostly they took instruction and complied, but # 9 showed uncommon emotion by speaking.

In the Simian screeching voice, # 9 asked, "Is it your goal to kill off the Warrior Simians even though they have surrendered to you?"

Moon was shocked at the question too, but after some thought turned to look for the answer. Levi blurted mentally, "Oh shit!"

Amy said, "We have underestimated these Technical Simians. They are not just followers; they are leaders and thinkers too."

She pointed out also that Moon appeared very attentive waiting on the answer. This was the moment of truth. How were they to answer? How would Moon, # 9 and the other Technical Simians react to the truth? Would it destroy their relationship and everything they had built? After a moment of discussion they agreed on the truth as their best course of action. Actually, they had no other choice.

With Amy's counsel he proceeded very slowly and carefully. He explained that the human armies did not stand a chance against the organized Warrior Simian armies and YES, we need to create a war of attrition between the Warrior Simians if possible. He explained that he believed they can never be controlled and will rebel again at some point. He also told them that he did not want the Technical Simians, especially this group, the original Technical Simian army and friends, to be harmed. The Warrior Simians needed to be destroyed to extinction if possible. It was their, both human and Technical Simians, only chance to survive on Earth and co-exist. He said no more as he watched and waited for a reaction. Moon's blazing red eyes stared at him deep and penetrating as if looking into his soul.

After a few long and tense moments, Moon screeched, "I need to talk to the others."

Moon didn't wait for a response and turned and left him standing with Fred. That was a hell of a way to leave him, as the knots immediately grabbed his stomach.

* Amy *

The mental alarms flashed when # 9 questioned Levi's intent, totally uncustomary for any Technical Simian. She knew the Technical Simians (Tech's) were highly intelligent but had never seen them take any initiative. This was a first and potentially a major problem. How would they take the thought of genocide on the Simians, even if it was only the Warriors? Would they feel threatened? There was no love between the groups, but did the Technical Simians harbor a plan of eventually taking over control of the Warriors again? After all, they once were in charge and were again, in this colony anyway. Had she made a mistake by suggesting they tell the truth? She knew, if necessary, Levi could stretch the truth so far you couldn't recognize it, but he had also agreed that the truth was best. She hoped they were right. They would soon find out as

Moon and the entire group of Technical Simians returned from their conference.

As they approached, she searched for any fleeting thought or sign. Levi's senses strained as she reached out mentally for any hint of hostilities as they approached. There wasn't a hint from their mind or body language. The Simian minds were blocked to her. That didn't necessarily mean there were no hostile thoughts, only that their minds were closed. She would have to wait.

Moon signed, "I know your heart and am convinced that neither you nor any other human that I have been associated with has any ill feelings toward the Technical Simians. For myself I will continue to follow you, but the others want to know what the plans for the Technical Simians would be if the Warriors were no longer a threat?"

As Moon spoke he used an abbreviated, almost nicknames for the different Simian races. He used terms equivalent to Warrs for the Warrior Simians and Techs for the Technical Simians. From that point on she used the shorter version and reserved the longer form to accent a more formal reference.

She believed she understood the Techs dilemma. The Techs didn't trust the Warrs, but could hope to control them and return to the leadership position of the race. The humans might be able to help them achieve that goal. If that occurred, they could offer peace to the humans, but they had no assurance that control could be achieved and maintained over the Warrs. If they joined with the humans to destroy the Warrs, they would be at the mercy of the human race afterwards. The Tech's numbers were small and without the Warrs for battle, they had little chance to survive against humans as a race if the humans turned on them in force. They wanted assurances that the genocide of the Simian race didn't extend to the Technical Simians.

Levi said they were negotiating and just asked straight out, "What is it that you want?"

Moon looked for a moment and said, "We want assurance that the Simian race would be able to continue in the form of Technical Simians if we assist and are successful in the destruction of the Warrior Simians."

Moon went on to outline their desires. They wanted equality and to co-exist with humans on Earth, to liberate and gather as many of the Technical Simians and females of their race as possible from other colonies and reunite their race. They also wanted access to Levi's knowledge, and equal representation as humans with him. Moon would be the Simian leader and representative for their race. In return they and the entire Technical Simian race would follow Levi's leadership and would execute genocide on the Warrior Simians without hesitation.

It was her turn to be shocked and confused. The Simians knew there was more to Levi than met the eye. They could not have guessed of her involvement, but wished to be a part of Levi and the abilities which he represented. They knew Levi was the unconditional leader and hope of the human race and also the only hope for the Technical Simians.

* Levi *

He had been a practicing attorney long enough to recognize a negotiation, and this was the beginning of one. It didn't appear to be a hostile negotiation, but they did want something. Amy was out of her element now, because she would simply tell the truth, which wasn't all that bad. Before they could begin; however, they would have to find out what the Simians wanted. Oh, well, he asked.

The Techs were in agreement to the systematic genocide of the Warrior Simians, but wanted their place in the new order, assuming there would be one. They obviously believed he would be the leader of that order, which was probably true, well, Amy anyway. The negotiation was simple, since their requests were reasonable. He readily agreed saying, "I accept your terms with pleasure." The gathered Technical Simians were now committed not only by obligation, but now by a common desire. He really felt good about the mutual agreement and alliance.

He said, "Amy, has anything really changed?"

She said, "Well, in practice no, the Simians will continue to follow directions as always, but the Techs will now feel a part of the goal, a partnership in a war to liberate Earth from the Warrs."

Amy also had a suspicious feeling that the Techs would be voicing their opinions more, and she was strangely anxious for their input. Actually, he too was curious and anxious. Life should be interesting.

Everyone seemed appeased, if not happy, except for Fred, who still seemed a little wide eyed, but it was time to go. He called Moon and # 5 and was about to go around the corner and let Amy do

78

her thing, when he had an inspiration. Why hide the fact that they could teleport? The Simian army already knew he and Moon came from somewhere unexplainable, probably believing supernatural, so why not teleport in front of them. It would make him seem even more frightening to the Warrs, and they needed to reinforce that image. It was their only real control over them. Amy grinned as she read his thoughts and readily agreed.

He said his goodbyes to # 9 and Fred, promising to come if needed. Fred was still apprehensive but resolved to do his job.

The sea of Warriors opened as he walked into the gathering space outside the ship, followed by Moon and # 5. Fred and # 9 remained outside the door and waited, while his group gathered close around him. He raised his hands for silence, generating absolute quiet through the crowd. He told the gathered army they were leaving now but would return in the same manner as they were leaving, if necessary. His voice screeched in a strong reverberating pitch that carried over the gathering as he told them he had given instruction to the human and # 9, which must be carried out. As a show of his lack of respect, he then turned his back on the gathered army and stood completely still.

He felt Amy already moving in his mind. The warming vibration began in his body as the air around them began to shimmer. He saw their destination by the campfires outside the caverns at the Mojave Desert settlement superimposed over the view of the Simian space ship. Having teleported twice before, he knew what to expect and it wasn't as much of a surprise. The views reversed and the spaceship began to fade away. Then they stood where he had been looking. It was over. He looked around to see Moon as expressionless as usual; however, # 5 was visibly shaking and his red eyes were comically wide in his broad face. He wondered if Moon was as emotionally cold as he appeared or making a show. Amy was smiling at that thought, because they both knew Moon could be very emotional. They had seen him many times show excitement, concern, pride, and warmth toward him.

He could get used to this form of travel. It allowed them to be many places at once, but here is where they needed to be now. They were going after the Simian computer and Amy reminded him to bring lanterns and fuel. Amy was obviously anxious, but he suddenly realized they had been up most of the night and he was tired. All but Amy would need food and sleep before long, hell, NOW! It had been a long, hard, and very eventful day and night.

He could see Al, Dawn and many others asleep by the fires. The sentry suddenly jumped at seeing Simians in the camp, but once recognized, moved toward him. He waved the sentry quiet as he signed for Moon and # 5 to lie down and rest until morning. Everything else could wait till tomorrow.

* Amy *

She was very happy to see the hidden side of Moon's personality and these very special Simians. They had always been so loyal, but now they were committed to their common goals, common now, but possibly not previously. With their decision to take part in the total genocide of the Warrior Simians, they were committing totally to the human race, Earth and Levi. This could only be good. It was exciting to realize the Technical Simians did in fact have ambition and plans for the future. Even more exciting... her plans were now theirs as well. It had been a very good day indeed, well, except for the horror of ASONE's mindless slaughter. It had to be done, but her developing emotions and morality were offended by the actions of ASONE. She hoped she could learn to control her emotions or ASONE. She believed, unfortunately, that she would have many opportunities to try.

Poor Fred was doing his duty, but it was hard for him. He wasn't an especially brave man, but she was proud of him because he did his duty in spite of that fear. Sometimes that was the bravest of men, those who did what was required in spite of their fear. She resolved to try and find the perfect place for him in the future. Giving him the .45 automatic made him a lot braver, but it was only moral support. Levi didn't want the gun and never used it anyway. The macho shit always preferred to use swords or hands. Secretly he felt using a gun was not fighting fair, but no fight with a Simian was fair anyway. In any one-on-one fight with a Simian, Levi was outnumbered by the Simian's massive size difference. Damn macho crap!

They had done about all they could do. It was up to # 9 to organize the new colony and army, but she was confident # 9 would do it well and have the army moving toward San Francisco within days. Food was short, so the sooner the better. Also, humans were dying, feeding the San Francisco Simian colony, so the sooner the better in that regard as well.

The scent of fear reeked everywhere among the Warrior Simians (Warrs), as they walked through the gathered army. An endless sea of Warrs extended to the limit of the campfire light, but the sea was parting ahead of them, as the Warrs scrambled to make room for Levi's passage. She was reminded of the biblical story of the Red Sea parting for Moses. The nervous clacking of the Simian's black teeth gave an eerie and somewhat disturbing sound, strangely a sound resembling the rattle of a rattlesnake. Levi began giving a final parting speech to the Simians, although she was preparing to transport telepathically (teleport) them and wasn't paying much attention, other than chuckling to herself as she called him a "HAM."

Her mind was already concentrating on the spot where she intended to transport. While she couldn't actually see the spot, she could recreate it by exact coordinates, land marks and things she knew to be there, like the evening campfire. She allowed ample space from the fire to avoid people. The image of the spot began to overlay the finally still image from Levi's eyes. She drew energy from the air around Levi and his body began to quiver. Spread the umbrella of energy to include Moon and # 5, she began to move matter. The image of the campfire became more real as her created image began to synchronize with the actual image. The image of the sea of Simians began to fade then disappear. The teleport was complete and they were standing within easy sight of the campfire at the Mojave Desert settlement.

During the few seconds of the actual teleport she lost communication with those she monitored, but immediately restored when the teleport was complete. She watched through Fred's eyes, while he continued to stare at an empty spot in the opening within the gathered Simians. As Fred turned, she saw extremely frightened Simians, many visibly shaking, some falling from loss of control. She grinned, sharing this image with Levi. That had been a good idea to teleport in plain sight. Levi could add a dramatic touch, the big ham.

She was anxious to get started with the next phase of her plan, but Levi told her he was tired. Yes, his body needed attention. She would repair him and watch over him as he slept, just as she did every night. She loved him, welcoming the time to care for him and experience his dreams. She so wished she could dream, but living Levi's dreams brought a welcome break from her normally logical and ordered mind. Her plans would wait until tomorrow and dream his dreams tonight.

* Levi *

The sun was well into the sky when he woke and sat up. Moon and # 5 were already up and he couldn't tell how long they had been awake.

Amy said, "They have been awake for several hours and waiting. They have already gone off and fed on a lamb Al brought them."

Al was there waiting also. "Damn, Amy, why didn't you wake me?" She ignored the question and proceeded to tell him that food was ready and his body was repaired. He did feel good and hungry. Levi said, "I apologize for being grumpy." Amy just grinned.

The main camp, where they now were, had an organized galley that fed those present, and the aroma of food cooking tickled his nose all the way to his stomach. The sounds of children running and playing somewhere nearby spoke of safety and security. He felt comfortable in the peaceful atmosphere of the settlement and remembered how completely different it had been living in fear of the roaming Simians for all those years. This is what it's all about, and he wanted it for everyone.

He woke slowly; he must have been tired. Amy was grinning as he remembered the events of the previous day and night. Yes, it had been busy. His thoughts focused now on food as Dawn approached with his typical massive amount of food piled on a serving tray instead of a normal plate. Pausing only long enough to thank Dawn, he dug in. He noticed even Moon was staring at him in disbelief. Laughter erupted all the way from his gut, but he continued eating.

Al was signing to Moon and # 5, which made both him and Amy happy. Al had gotten quite good at hand signing, but it bothered him to think .Al seemed more comfortable with the Simians than with him. He wished Al was still close and friendly toward him, but Al had changed suddenly, as had all of them, when ASONE emerged to kill Gord. He felt lonesome and missed Al's friendship. If it wasn't for Moon, he wouldn't have a friend. Unfortunately,

Moon wasn't all that talkative. Ouch! Amy looked rejected, pouting.

Amy said, "I thought I was your best friend?"

He burst out laughing and said, "Yes, Amy you are my best friend, my love, my lover ... you are my everything. As long as I have you, I have all I will ever need." Her huge smile and twinkling eyes told him he said the right thing, for once.

He really was feeling much better. He was rested and had a full belly, while Amy patiently waited to go after the Simian computer. He was about to tease her when Amy gently chided, "I know your thoughts. Be nice or I will make you ugly." She knew he was ready and making fun of her. Amy was teasing him also, but he remembered all too well when Amy made his manhood shrivel in the hands of that camp trollop so long ago. That was the most embarrassing moment of his life. Yes, she was teasing, but he knew there was a veiled threat there also. He grinned and said, "I'll be good, Amy."

Amy turned serious then and suggested that they take Al and Iron Eyes with them. She said there was no other way to install and interface the Simian computer without revealing herself. If that must be done, then it should be done with all of the most trusted friends.

She said, "I can transport them directly into the facility and no one but you and I would know the exact location."

The exception would be Moon, of course. Moon had been at the facility and would recognize the location. Amy was not concerned about Moon knowing. Actually she wasn't overly concerned about any of these key members. She just wanted to be cautious for a while.

If she was comfortable with revealing herself, he certainly was. He had never liked keeping it a secret and had only done so at Amy's insistence anyway. Amy would never reveal herself otherwise, if she didn't have bigger plans. She only smiled, but he knew.

Al was a little apprehensive when asked to accompany them. He explained that they would be teleporting to another location and described what that involved. Seldom had he seen fear on Al's face, but he saw it now. Al quickly hid the fear and nodded his head in agreement, but his nods were a little too exaggerated.

They all proceeded to the caverns and descended into the dark tunnels, lighting the torches as they went. Soon they were wrestling with the weight of the Simian computer as they ascended, waddling under its weight. They reached the same open spot where they had materialized during the night. This spot suited Amy, saying it would be quicker and easier to use the same spots to teleport to and from. Al carried the six Coleman lanterns, mantles, and sealed cans of lantern fuel he had brought up.

They were now ready. Moon, # 5, and he stood holding the computer off the ground, while Al held the lit lanterns high in the air. Suddenly they were there, standing in the large opening inside the main floor of her facility.

* Amy *

86

She had spent the night considering all possible scenarios and it always came up the same. The Simian computer had to be taken to her location and hooked it into her life support umbilical cord, and she needed # 5 to do that and check out the computer. It would be necessary for # 5 to work with her long enough so she could become familiar with the workings of the alien computer. Her existence would no longer be a secret. It wouldn't take # 5 long to guess the nature of Amy. Since she had no choice but to reveal her existence, she wanted to use it to her advantage. Realizing the secret would be out, she wanted to at least control how the information was revealed and to whom. Her existence must continue to be hidden from everyone but the very core group, all of which were here except Iron Eyes. She would tell them the truth, the whole truth, as soon as they were all gathered within her facility.

Levi was repaired, fed, and ready to proceed. He woke grumpy, as he often did. Generally, he awoke slowly, and she always allowed him a few minutes to reach his peak. That trait could be adjusted, but lifelong habits for Levi helped maintain his mental stability, and he had undergone so many changes that she decided to leave it alone. She found it humorous to call him a grump in the mornings, as she did now. She was rewarded with a snorted, "Butthead."

She began sharing her plan, to reveal herself, with Levi as he completed breakfast. He really didn't mind. He had always wanted to share the knowledge with someone. His only comment, "Maybe the others won't consider me so fearful if they know the truth." True, maybe he would be able to confide in someone else besides her, but she welcomed the role of friend, lover, partner in life, and confidant. She wasn't sure she liked the thought of sharing her only friend and confident with anyone else, but this must be done.

Al's eyes revealed momentary anxiety before agreeing to teleport with them. It was only a matter of carrying the computer out of the caverns and preparing to teleport. Al informed Dawn he was leaving with Levi and prepared some Coleman Lanterns. All was in order as they grouped together with the computer in their hands. Before they realized what happened, she completed the teleport. Suddenly, they were standing in the massive entrance area of her facility, lit only by Al's lanterns. The sudden darkness around them gave them an eerie feeling, especially since the lantern light didn't reach the far walls and seemed to radiate out into nothingness. The sounds they made echoed in the distance, adding to the discomfort of the moment. Levi did not like being inside the tomb, as he called it, but this had to be done.

There was one other thing that had to be done before she could reveal herself. She and Levi had to teleport to the Owens Valley and get Iron Eyes. That brought a startled look to Levi's eyes, but he saw the logic and nodded. He told the group to make themselves comfortable and he would return shortly. They looked uneasy, but nodded understanding.

Jimmy had left with his Lancer team on the mission to spread the word about the war and resistance, so she couldn't know exact whereabouts of Iron Eyes. When she last monitored Iron Eyes through Jimmy he was at the main camp, so she would start there. She chose a safe open place just outside the main camp to materialize. Her abilities were becoming perfected and the transfer of matter was almost immediate. Levi even commented that it seemed like he only blinked and they were there. His pride in her pleased her greatly.

No one saw them materialize and didn't notice Levi until he was well inside the camp. He was greeted warmly but nervously as he walked toward the center gathering. She guessed correctly. Iron Eyes was at the center of the group giving some form of training or instruction until he saw Levi. Iron Eyes stood to greet Levi with a hand shake. She could see the fear in his eyes and so did Levi. It hurt him to have his friends treat him like, how were they treating him? It was like Levi was so far above them they couldn't approach him. They didn't speak until spoken to and seemed on the verge of bowing at any moment. In retrospect, she actually remembered seeing involuntary bows from some. She had seen bows from the Warrior Simians, but they needed that respect from the Warrs, even tried to encourage it, but not from the humans. That was it! They were treating him like a king or god and that would never be accepted by Levi. Levi was a simple man that only wanted to fight and save the Earth for humans. Maybe things would soon change, for the core group anyway.

Levi spoke to Iron Eyes, asking that he accompany him. Again she saw the flicker of panic, but he would do anything Levi asked. Iron Eyes dismissed the gathered young warriors and walked by Levi's side. She sensed pride from the warriors to see their leader leaving with Levi. Once safely away from observation, Levi told Iron Eyes they were going to travel mentally and not to be afraid, that everything would be fine. Iron Eyes said nothing as they stood in silence, then materialized inside the facility. Iron Eyes was visibly shaken, but quickly recovered as he was greeted by Al and Moon. The core group was all here now. It could begin!

* Levi *

He hated the inside of the research facility. It felt and smelled like a tomb. The ghosts of those long dead haunted him. Unfortunately, Amy resided here and this is where they needed to be at the moment. He started to say lives, but She lives inside of me, in my heart, mind and every fiber of my being. That got a nod and smile from Amy. That was good, but it was also true. He would never be able to live without her again for many different reasons, not the least of which was the love he had for her.

They were missing only one person and that was Iron Eyes. They left the group to go after him. They found him and return within thirty minutes, much to the relief of the awaiting group.

Amy said, "It's time for you to tell the story anyway you want. I will address them afterward."

He remained silent for a long time, pacing and thinking. The gathered group sensed that something very important was about to happen and patiently waited. He began speaking in English and asked Moon and # 5 if they could understand. Both

90

humans and Simians had learned the others' language, although unable to speak it. The Simians of his group had learned much quicker out of necessity and increased exposure. Moon and # 5 nodded that they in fact understood his English. He began, "I am going to tell you truths that must remain in total confidence. It must never be spoken of outside of this core group." They were silent, looked around at each other, and quickly nodded in agreement.

He continued, "Certain things must be accomplished that required # 5, and in doing so, # 5 will learn the nature of the secret I am about to tell you." Everyone looked at # 5, including Moon, but # 5 looked just as puzzled as the others. All eyes returned back to stare attentively at Levi. He said, "All of you are my most valued and trusted friends and associates in our business of war and life. By virtue of his knowledge of the Simian computers, # 5 is now part of our group." They waited.

He looked at Al and said, "You came the closest to discovering the truth." He then asked, "Would you like to speculate a guess?"

Al said, "I believe there is more to you than we have been allowed to see. You speak in the plural sometimes and actually seem to be talking to someone, even when no one else is there. Is there someone else with you?"

Levi grinned and said "YES." He related the story of how he met Amy, who and what she was, what she had accomplished for him, what she had done to him and what she had done for everyone. He described how they communicated and how he was able to do so many things with her help. He described the emergence of ASONE and who and what it was, as best he knew how. He talked for a very long time, relating almost everything to them. He did not describe the love that had developed between Amy and him. That was private, very private, but he suspected that they knew. They listened and many times nodded in understanding or as if to say, yes it all makes sense now.

For the very first time he introduced Amy, and he was so very proud to do so. He settled back and let Amy take control of his body, and she began to speak in her own sweet voice. He felt Amy softened his features and shape some of her own. She was learning a touch of the dramatic as well. Actually, it accented the difference between Levi and Amy and made her a real identity to them.

* Amy *

She listened intently to Levi's narration of the events of their meeting and adventures together over the last year. She sensed the pride Levi had for her. Levi went quite into detail for much of the story, especially everything to do with her. Those gathered had a good understanding of what she was and that her physical body, such that there was, resided in this facility. Levi did not, however, dwell on how anything was accomplished, mainly because he did not understand himself. Neither would she go into detail, because it was not necessary that they understand. He finished his narration and waited for questions, but all were still in shock. Levi introduced Amy to them and relinquished control of his body.

She adjusted Levi's vocal cords and when she spoke it was her own voice, the one she created to speak with Levi. Levi was as shocked as those gathered. She didn't try to make friends, because it was likely none, other than # 5, would ever hear her voice again. She was friendly however, because she truly had affection for them. Her goal now was to simply let them know she was alive and real and shared Levi in mind and body. They would now understand the source of information, knowledge, seemingly magical occurrences, feats of strength, supernatural abilities and many of the other exploits Levi manifested. Levi would remain just as important, but more like one of them. She would always remain isolated, but she could manage that as long as she had Levi and a means to occupy her intellect. This Simian computer and other possibilities being considered presented the opportunity to indeed occupy her massive intellect.

She explained why they were here. This was her residence, and they were going to hook the Simian computer into her life support system and attempt to activate it to establish a communication interlink between herself and the Simian computer. If it were not for this fact, her existence would have remained secret.

She needed # 5 to make the physical connection and activate the computer. He would also be required to help her understand the nature of the internal workings and logic used. Although she had a sizable vocabulary in the Simian language, she would also have to learn many new technical terms and the complete written Simian language from # 5 in order to complete the necessary translations. She said she hoped to be able to assume control of the computer, with his help. They all recognized the benefits of access to the Simian computer and its stored knowledge.

Total awe filled # 5's blazing red eyes. The excitement also began building, making him physically shake with anticipation. She had touched # 5's mind many times searching for signs of hostility or danger for Levi, but # 5 had always been respectful and liked Levi just as Moon did. She trusted # 5 completely and now # 5 knew that as well and appeared very appreciative. In fact, they all appeared very appreciative and happy. They knew, along with Levi and Amy, they were at the center of all things, the central core. There were no questions, but she knew they would come as the shock wore off.

It was time to get to work and work it was, taking the Simian computer down ten levels of stairs. Even Levi was huffing and puffing by the time they reached the tenth level. Levi was griping, wondering why she didn't teleport there instead of the top. She just said, "You needed exercise." The real reason was the spaces below were smaller and she wasn't yet comfortable teleporting into close spaces.

She had again superimposed the map of the facility in Levi's mind so he knew where he was at all times as they navigated the passageways. Even so, their footsteps echoed thunderously into the darkness making him uneasy. As they were entering Amy's circular dome room he pointed to the ten-foot wide silver dome in the center of the room and said, "This is Amy." They all became quiet, even humble and respectful as if they were in a holy place. Very quietly they placed the Simian computer on the floor beside the dome. The silence was humorous to her and she couldn't resist. She again used Levi's vocal cords and said, "BOO!" Everyone jumped a foot in the air and Iron Eyes even made a break for the door before he stopped. After the initial shock they all started laughing. Al was laughing so hard tears came to his eyes. Moon and # 5 were rocking in their own form of laughter that sounded like hiccups.

Moon was still laughing, but he signed, "Very funny, Amy, Ha Ha!"

Whoever would have thought Moon had a sense of humor? Laughter erupted all over again. Now everyone was at ease. They could go to work.

* Levi *

As Amy was talking to the others, he watched them. Yes, they believed. They knew they were in the presence of something superior. Yes, Amy was superior and this had been Dr. Joyce Sheldon's fear. Dr. Sheldon, Amy's inventor and mother, had hidden her concern in Amy's memory so long ago. She knew humans always attacked what they perceived to be superior. That was why Amy wanted to remain hidden. Times had certainly changed since then, but the concern could still be valid. If the secret remained within this group, he believed everything would be fine. He trusted every one of these friends with his life and now he trusted them with Amy's life too, which to him was more precious than his own.

They seemed honored and proud to be among those to know the truth and were totally committed. They knew what Amy wanted now, and everyone was determined to deliver. It took about thirty minutes to reach her central room. As they entered he indicated Amy's physical location. The silver dome was shiny and impressive, which added to the awe of the moment. As the silence settled over the room, he felt it before he heard Amy send a loud "BOO!" through the deathly quiet room. It was funny. Iron Eyes was out the door before the sound was out of his mouth. The spell was broken and the tension released in gut wrenching laughter. He was even chuckling as he watched Al rolling over with laughter while Moon and # 5 squeaked their humor. Iron Eyes turned red-faces with embarrassment, but even he joined in. When Moon signed "Very funny, Amy, HA HA," it was the final straw. Laughter echoed through the chambers again for many long minutes. If there were any ghosts, they were all awake now.

Everyone was ready. Amy instructed him in what was needed and he sent them off looking for tools, tubing, connectors, tables, and a large chair for # 5. Amy also asked that Dr. Sheldon's remains be removed from the floor and to clean up the room some. He did this task personally, finding a box and respectfully placing Dr. Sheldon's bones in it. He then moved them to another room until they could be properly buried. He found a broom and started sweeping up fifty years of dust and even began mopping the floor and wiping down the walls. The room was beginning to look much better by the time the others began returning with the various items. A sturdy table was placed up against her dome and the computer placed upon it. Two lengths of tubing were then attached to the computer. Luckily the Simian connection was a self-tightening universal type of connection which required only minor adaptation of the tubing found in the facility. The other ends of the tubes were attached to receptacles inside a small service door opening at the base of her dome. The service receptacles were originally designed to allow filling and recycling of her life support fluid before the dome was in place. This existed as part of her safety protection and without the massive electric motors to lift her three-foot thick, solid lead dome, there was no access to the controls. Amy planned to control these internal valves by telekinesis. It was up to Amy now.

* Amy *

Everything was readied, and it was now up to her. She had never tried telekinesis directly from her mind. She had always focused through Levi's eyes and mind, but this was different. Without electricity it was impossible to open her dome and all access to her was permanently sealed inside her dome. Dr. Sheldon had done that by design to give Amy some form of self-protection, but Dr. Sheldon never anticipated the neutralization of electricity. Now it was sealed, even from her. From the design plans she knew the exact location of the valves and believed she could adjust them. She would soon find out.

The tubes were connected to her life fluid floating in massive tanks buried beneath her full of thousands of gallons of the precious fluid, enough to last hundreds of years. Input and output connections would allow the flow of fluid into and through the computer ... if she could open the valves. The flow of her life fluid was ensured by the movement of the underground river running through the solid rock beneath her. The flow of the river turned turbines which circulated her life support blood. The tubes were connected to the computer in a like manner so that fluid would flow continuously through the computer. This matched a similar activity in her brain. The fluid constantly flowed like blood through her central core brain. If this was successful, and the Simian computer still worked, she should be able to develop a chemical language between the computer and herself. That was the plan anyway.

They waited for her now. She concentrated on the location of the valves. She saw the shape of them and used her mind to gather energy around the valves. This energy became physical and began to move the valves. The precious fluid started moving into the Simian computer, filling it. This seemingly took hours and then finally began to flow out the other tube. According to # 5 it would take over an hour to charge the elements within the unit and begin to activate. They anxiously waited as the minutes passed.

With a shock, she detected the touch of the computer and heard it speak, but she did not understand the language. The language was incredibly complex, so many variables to interpret. This was not going to be easy.

* Levi *

He was proud of Amy and also proud of himself. He had taught Amy some of his traits. At least that is what Amy called them. He never knew if she considered them good or bad traits, but liked to consider them good and a way of life. Traits so ingrained in his being that they governed the way he lived, like the way he questioned everything and never, NEVER, gave up. Amy was conducting herself that way now... she wouldn't give up. She found a way to make it happen and turned the valves from inside and motivated herself to find that way. If necessary, he would have shamed or challenged her into doing it like he had so often, but it wasn't required. She could do anything she put her mind to do. He had forced Amy to discover telekinesis in the beginning by this method and it had worked. Amy had evolved and forced herself into expanding her abilities. He was so exceedingly proud of her.

Amy's mind was occupied. He had seldom, if ever, seen her concentrate so hard. The fluid flowed and she said she could hear the computer, but the language was so complex she wasn't sure if she could understand it. He reminded her that she had learned the Simian language by listening and she could learn this too, all she had to do was listen long enough. She grinned and said it wasn't quite that easy, but she wasn't giving up. It would just take more time and maybe # 5 could help.

It was already mid-afternoon by Amy's clock, and from all indications, it would take much longer than she had anticipated. She suggested that Moon,

Iron Eyes, and Al go top-side, make camp for the night and hunt. This shocked him since he thought Amy wanted to keep them from knowing the actual location of the facility.

She saw his thought and said, "I changed my mind. I understand that is a woman's prerogative."

He started laughing remembering you could never win an argument with a woman. He relayed Amy's instructions and told them to follow their footprints in the dust back, and they shouldn't have a problem. They didn't have to be asked twice. Truly, he wished he could go too.

As they were going down the hall, he called after them, "Get a turkey I'm hungry." He heard laughter echoing back down the hall.

Al said, "Hell, you're always hungry."

He called back, "Kiss my ass." He was not at all upset. Rather, he was very happy to see the old Al back. He grinned at Amy, but she was totally absorbed in the Simian chemical language. He wondered what he could do to help, nothing he concluded. It was so far over his head he barely knew what was happening.

He was bored to tears, so Amy used his vocal cords to communicate with # 5. She kept # 5 busy answering questions and using the optical keyboard. He could see the keyboard highlighted on the glass dome, but it looked very strange, different from any keyboard he remembered seeing before. All of # 5's fingers were flying over the dome, including the double thumbs, and strange symbols were floating in the space under the dome. The symbols appeared to be three dimensional from a holograph projection originating from those strange colored crystals. It was all fascinating but also boring, because he had no idea what they represented. He soon lost interest and began daydreaming. Amy laughed at him, but he just grunted.

* Amy *

The language was strong and on multiple levels, but instantaneous like an electric current. It was however, all chemical, but with so many variations and combinations, almost overpowering. A human brain was never intended to receive this information directly, but eventually she adjusted the bias level to a tolerable range and began recording data. It was all raw and had no meaning, but she soon began seeing repetitive and identifiable data, the building blocks of communication. When # 5 began inputting data, she requested that he speak the words or information he used so she could build a data bank of the written language. She slowed him down to better follow his speech and input by symbol. The language used in the computer was in the written speech or squeals and chirps of the Simian language but converted into a chemical data stream. No, stream was not the word. It was more instantaneous throughout the fluid, there one instant just to adjust in the next. If it was a color you would see the total fluid change universally at the same instant, but the speed was far beyond the speed of sight. The speed even challenged her ability to track it.

After hours of monitoring and recording, she was able to identify only fifteen symbols and seven basic numbers, but they were used in staggering multiple units. She realized with clarity that this would duplicate the Simian speech. The screeching would sound like a whole string of EEEEEs for example. It got more complicated when she discovered that the numbers and symbols were used together in both communication and numeric data, thus increasing the possible communication and data potential to astronomical levels.

Beginning to decipher the information, she realized it would take far longer than she had planned. It was mid-afternoon, so she made the decision to stay overnight, and sent the others outside to make camp and prepare the food they would need. That seemed to satisfy them. Well, Levi wanted to go, but that was not to be since he was needed to communicate. He was like a spoiled child sometimes, bored and pouting. She called him a "Poophead," which seemed to strike him funny.

Smiling, Levi said, "I love it when you talk dirty to me."

So she called him, "Shithead," and went back to work.

The learning process accelerated as the process of elimination worked in her favor now. She had learned over sixty percent of the language now and had begun to communicate back with # 5 via the terminal. At first it surprised # 5, but he quickly adapted and even liked the direct interface. The Tech was moving into the internal working of the computer, showing her how to retrieve stored data. She was surprised to discover that the stored data of the Simian computer had no organization. All data was stored at random. There was no directory! You accessed directly to the data, so you must know what you were looking for before you could find it. It was going to take a long time to explore and retrieve the information within this computer, and she would need # 5 for an even longer time. Only a Simian mind could access the information directly. She could eventually read everything, but she would have to store, organize, re-group, and only then discover what secrets would be revealed to her. Using # 5 would help reduce the required time.

She said, "Hon, I can communicate directly with # 5 via the computer if you want to go topside and join the others." A strange look came over his face, one that she had never seen before. What was it? Had she done something? Levi said, "Okay, that would be nice." The he turned and left. She could see that he was hurt, but she didn't understand what she had done. Maybe they could talk later.

Things were beginning to come together with the Simian computer and she was elated. The research could really begin now. What would she learn? She could almost taste the excitement. She felt like Levi did sometimes when he had a new skill or toy. She smiled as she thought of Levi. She was happy to have found love.

CHAPTER 3
(DISCOVERY)

* Levi *

Amy was in her own idea of heaven. Her intellect was being challenged, and she excelled under such circumstances, as he had learned. Present her with a challenge, and she would meet it and beat it. She was in that mode now as he looked into her mind and saw the calculations, three dimensional symbols, formulas, and flowing data so complex he could barely recognize it. It was so far above him that he couldn't remain interested.

It was one such moment when Amy startled him by saying, "I am able to communicate directly with # 5 now through the computer. You can go topside with the others if you like."

First it startled and then shocked him as he realized the implications of what she had said. Amy had never been able to communicate with anyone but him, ever! Now she could. He felt momentary fear rip through his heart. Was he jealous? That could never be. Was he actually jealous of a Simian? Impossible! No, it was not jealousy as a lover. He knew Amy's love for him was completely real. It was special, a one-of-a-kind love they shared. No, it was jealousy of her attention. He was no longer the total center of her attention. She was communicating with another. He rationalized that communication was necessary, even desirable, but the initial reaction was sudden and unexpected. This would be fine, it was just a matter of accepting it, and that he had already done in his mind. He thought about his reaction to it. It came so unexpectedly and just startled him, but he was fine now. Hell, he didn't understand what they were doing anyway and found it boring. He would much rather be topside anyway.

He could hide nothing from Amy anymore and seldom tried. Although her mind was operating at a much accelerated level, he still felt her listening to his thoughts, and she knew what had passed in his mind. She reassured her love with warmth he felt in his heart and the presence of an incredible smile on her beautiful face. Sometimes he wished her beauty wasn't so perfect. How could you ever be angry at that perfect face? His thoughts were rewarded by a face suddenly screwed up, eyes crossed, tongue sticking out, and an all-in-all delightfully comical face. He actually laughed out loud as he made his way through the dark passageways and stairs.

He was nearing the main exit door when he heard fighting. He suddenly remembered that there was no one with the group above that Amy could monitor. She would not have known if there were problems topside, but she was asking now. He ran through the main door in time to see Al, Iron Eyes and Moon engaged in battle with a full three Warrior team. His friends were fighting in retreat, backing toward the main door. Moon could have defeated any single Warrior, but his attention was spread out trying to keep Al and Iron Eyes out of trouble also. Neither Al nor Iron Eyes were a match for a Warr and were lucky to still be alive. They could thank Moon for that. Moon was attacking any of the Warriors that made for the humans, while Al or Iron Eyes harassed the Warriors attacking Moon. It was a fragile balance that would soon turn bad without help, but he was close now and attacked.

* Amy *

The language was coming faster now and the learning accelerating. She was beginning to interface with the stored knowledge now and interrogate the computer. She did not yet have command of the language, but she had enough to probe and gain additional information. Soon she would be able to decipher the remaining symbols and hidden meanings now. It was only a matter of time. Her intellect had not been challenged like this in quite some time, and she found it extremely stimulating. The direction and help from # 5 had been absolutely necessary. Without his help, she may never have been able to decipher the language, but his involvement lessoned as she began taking over more of the computer interrogation. She sensed # 5's confusion and amazement at her cognitive abilities and intellect, as she continued to interrogate both the computer and him, but it was coming to her increasingly faster, absorbing her in the process.

Major portions of her mind were engrossed in the analysis of the Simian computer; however, a portion of her brain remained attuned to Levi's thoughts. It was a relief to discover that Levi's momentary confusion over her ability to communicate directly with # 5 was not a serious problem. It mostly just shocked him and maybe

106

struck a tone of jealousy, but he was soon over it, and she jibed him.

She and Levi heard the sounds of fighting simultaneously. What was happening? There should not be any danger at this location, but obviously there was. Her attention switched to concern for their friends, as did Levi. As Levi broke through the opening of the front door, she saw the typical 3-Simian patrol attacking Al, Iron Eyes and Moon. Moon was making the difference, but even Moon would not be able to hold them. Within minutes they all would die. Levi was already running to engage the enemy, and there was no time to invoke ASONE, even if she knew how. To make matters worse, Levi had not realized it yet, but he had left his sword and pickaxe inside the main facility. She had not expected a need for weapons inside. All he had was his muscles, two Bowie knives and her wits, but the three Warrs had long swords. Luckily, their friends had retrieved their weapons before leaving the complex.

She directed his mind as he raced toward the battle. The skills and plan were implanted, and Levi executed plan to perfection, with only a slight nudge on his timing here and there. His initial attack must be sudden and deadly. She calculated the required forces, angles, momentum, speed and directions and then interfaced this information into the time sequence of the battle. She adjusted the calculations as the various factors changed.

* Levi *

He launched into the attack without direction, but Amy was supplying assistance as he neared the foray. He ran fast, building momentum as he neared. The angle of attack was off to the left side of Moon and over the head of Iron Eyes. Moon's sword was a blur of movement so Amy chose a less active direction. He began an overhead cartwheel movement, throwing him into the air and flipping over the head of Iron Eyes. His speed, spinning movement, and momentum were calculated to deliver a concentrated explosion of force at the precise spot Amy directed. He connected with both feet to the head of a very surprised Warr. Levi felt the concentration of these forces before and knew how deadly and painful to him the impact could be. The jarring pain was no less painful this time. His heels connected to the forehead of the Warr and instantly broke its neck in a loud snapping crunch of bone. The force snapped the head completely back over the already falling body of the dead Simian. His speed had been a blur and had only been noticed by the Warr a brief second before impact. It had no time to react, other than to register surprise.

As the Warr fell, Levi hit the ground rolling to dispel what was left of his momentum. The adjacent Warr heard the death of its team member and turned to see what had happened. As it turned Moon tried to take the advantage, but the third Warr struck, requiring Moon to block the sword. Before Moon could again seize the opportunity, the second realized its mistake and turned back to Moon, but its attention was split, knowing there was an enemy behind.

Iron Eyes, not taking any chances, was delivering hard overhead chops on the fallen Simian's neck to ensure it was dead. He then turned to Al's aid to harass the third Simian. The odds had changed and they were fighting with renewed strength. Seconds before they had been fighting to survive, but now there was hope.

Levi rolled back up onto his feet but had no sword. The two remaining Warrs were turning to their side in a defensive posture now, where only seconds before they were on the attack. He watched the battle change as Moon started his attack, but was still hampered, needing to defend Al and Iron Eyes. Amy saw the opportunity before he did and forced him to dive forward rolling under the Warr that had extended too far toward Moon. He was on his back under the Warrior and kicking upwards with both feet into the crotch of the Warrior. The Warr's weight of approximately four hundred and seventy-five pounds was propelled upward from his kick. The Simian's feet came off the ground as it was propelled into the air. As he had hoped, Moon was able to seize the moment to drive his sword through its throat and out the back of its neck. Moon quickly pulled his sword free in time to divert a blow from the third Warr.

He rolled out of the way just as the dying Warrior came crashing to the ground. Again he rolled to his feet to join the battle, but it was obvious he would not be needed to dispatch the last Warr. With the training and abilities provided by Amy, Moon was more than a match. Additionally, Al and Iron Eyes were harassing its sides, while Moon fought head on. The fight was quickly over, as Moon unexpectedly dropped down and brought his short sword directly up into the Warrior's nerve center in its crotch. The Warr froze in instant death.

It was several long minutes before everyone caught their breath enough to talk. Amy wanted to know what had happened, and so did he. Al related that they had gone off to hunt and were ambushed by the Simian patrol. Al and Iron Eyes were together and surely would have been killed, but Moon heard the Simians victory cry and quickly came to their rescue. They didn't have a chance so they were fighting a running retreat. They had almost made it back when their luck ran out. Well, it obviously hadn't run out, since they had been saved. It had really been close though.

* Amy *

They were becoming accustomed to winning battles by the narrowest of margins, and this was no different. The suddenness of the attack served to surprise the Simians, especially the first one. The Warr saw Levi flying over the head of Iron Eyes far too late to react. The Warr died instantly without having a chance to react. She had built up more than sufficient force through the combination of running, spinning, jumping, and finally flipping to deliver a bone-breaking, precisely timed kick to its head. She heard and felt the neck break. With the death of one of the Warrs, the odds changed dramatically, yet not enough.

Moon was tiring fast and the next move must be made immediately, but without a sword, her options were limited. The plan she came up with was more of a supporting move that would allow Moon to take advantage. Levi rolled under the Simian, braced his back, and pushed upward driving the Warrior into the air and off its feet. With its balance gone, the Simian was defenseless and Moon delivered the death blow quickly into its throat.

The remaining Warr was soon dispatched by Moon and the three combatants fell to the ground heaving for breath. Moon was virtually exhausted. He had used up every bit of energy he had in order to stay alive and save his friends. He needed more than breath to regain his strength.

They had no idea if other Simian patrols were around. They had been fighting off the three Warriors and running for about thirty minutes, trying to make the door of the complex in hopes of defending the opening and calling for help. She should have brought Dawn to act as eyes and ears with them.

Levi rightfully said, "This has always been a safe place. How were we to know that anything had changed?"

Something had definitely changed, and they had to find out what very soon. First however, they needed to be behind the door and get it locked. She suggested this to Levi and also that they move camp indoors, even the gathered wood and campfire. She reminded Levi that the others had not yet hunted so he needed to find food for them. He was hungry and ready for that. She also wanted to have a look around.

As they were moving inside, # 5 burst through the door with his sword. She had told him of the fight through their computer communication link and he had left immediately, but it was a long way up and took him some time. Moon began telling him what had happened, but # 5 remained upset that he had not been here when he was needed.

Once they were settled inside, Levi and # 5 left the others to scout the area and find something to eat. They carefully retraced the path the others had taken heading down the mountain. Along the way and off the path a ways, Levi was able to kill a deer. He/they saw the deer bolt, and Levi threw his Bowie knife. She was able to adjust the trajectory before Levi released the knife. It was a perfect throw and caught the deer in the throat, sending it down. Levi asked # 5 to take it back to the others while he continued to scout around.

* Levi *

The battle was over by the time # 5 reached the top of the facility. He was certainly willing to fight, but a little late. Amy suggested he take # 5 with him to hunt, since Moon was exhausted and so were the others. Iron Eyes looked like he was still in shock, but Al seemed all right, maybe a bit hyper. Well, they had a right to be. They had almost been killed.

They hadn't gone more than a mile when they spooked a deer. He threw his Bowie knife and brought it down. He then said, "Damn, I'm good!" As he said that he watched for a reaction from Amy. He saw the eyes roll up in her head. She sure had the expressions perfected. Her library of expressions far surpassed mere programmed image responses. They represented Amy's true feelings and he was quite sure she wasn't even aware of them; they were so ingrained into her personality. He laughed anyway, because he knew Amy guided his aim.

He asked # 5 to take the deer to the camp, while he continued on for a while longer. Amy was extremely curious as to why a Simian patrol was this high in the mountains and so far from a Simian colony. He suspected it meant bad news and suggested that they astral project at first light in the morning to survey the two Simian colonies in the San Francisco area and see what was happening. He knew that if it weren't so close to dark she would want to go now. The situation was very serious, since this was Amy's, and his, safe place. If the Simians discovered who she was, they would destroy her and him in the process. Of all places, this place must be secure and safe. Tomorrow they would know.

They saw nothing else and returned to camp just as the sun was setting. The door was locked from the inside, but opened as soon as he knocked. As he entered, his sense of smell was assaulted by the aroma of raw butchered flesh, a savory smell of roasting meat and lots of smoke. Luckily, the inside area was so large that the smoke would soon dissipate. Everyone was going to eat tonight at any rate.

As they ate, he explained the ramification of Simians in the area. He said he and Amy were going to project themselves in the morning to view the area and Simian camps down below and try to determine what had changed. After he explained what this involved, Moon asked if that is what they did when he was asked to watch over him. Levi grinned and affirmed that it was indeed so. He also explained to Moon that when they projected, he had no control over his body and could not protect himself. Moon said nothing, but did have a look of remembrance and understanding.

* Amy *

In the morning they ate the remainder of the deer and talked about small things. Eventually, it came around to the Simian computer, since that was the reason they came here. Levi continued to do all the talking, and she provided the information. They wanted to know if the interface had been successful. She told them that it would be successful, but it would take some time to learn the secrets of the language and workings of the computer and even longer to begin making use of the information. Everyone seemed to understand or at least acted like they did.

Levi didn't understand, nor did he care about the why's and how's. He was only interested in the information but not even that, because he knew she would tell him what she discovered. He was more interested in the more physical aspects, as he now suggested that they leave. He was right of course. It was time to discover what had changed.

Levi suggested to Moon and the others that the bodies of the Simians be hidden but other than that, they should remain inside until they returned from viewing the area. They nodded agreement. For the first time they understood what Levi had been doing when he meditated, realizing that Levi was able to see remote locations, since he was always able to report on the status of events at other areas after meditating. She was surprised they were able to keep her existence a secret for so long. It was best for her to have revealed herself like this. It was the right thing and the right way in which to do it.

Levi told Moon that they were going now as he took a seat against the wall. Moon nodded and sat down to watch over him. Having done this many times before, it was easy to fall into the proper relaxation mode. Levi was relaxed and already beginning to float his mind. She smiled and joined him in the nebulous cloud of their minds as they began to float out of Levi's body and higher. She saw the body below as they floated higher and through the roof of the complex. This was the first time they traveled through solid material, but she knew they could do it. Levi seemed a little apprehensive but trusted her completely. She noticed the silver thread trailing them through the roof. Everything she had ever read about astral projection had mentioned this silver thread and how it always led back to the body. So far she had always been able to find her way back from any projection but believed day she might stake their lives on following the thread. Somehow it was comforting to see it now.

They were moving higher and higher over her mountain valley and the vista was reaching out farther and farther. There were no other Simian patrols seen. Could this have been a fluke, a chance happening? She didn't believe in flukes, but then she didn't see any other danger or threat. They continued on down the mountain following the old Highway 41 traveled before when they observed the Simian colonies. Conspicuously absent was any

Simian activity anywhere. Something was very wrong. As they approached the Fresno Colony, she noticed only a token number of Warrior Simians, guards mainly. There were guards? They never had guards before. She was worried. Where were the Warriors? She recalled that this colony supported approximately five hundred Simians. Her attention quickly turned north and sped toward the Stockton Colony. She was hoping that what she suspected was not happening. They would know soon.

* Levi *

He loved to project with Amy; it was like flying without wings. They were soaring over the countryside and he was really enjoying it. He recognized the country he spent days marching over. This was much easier. As they soared, he felt Amy's increasing uneasiness, but he saw no evidence of problems. There were no Simians to be seen. How could there be a problem if there were no Simians? As they approached the colony, he saw only a few Simians. Where were they? Then he realized what was bothering Amy. If they weren't here, where were they? Amy was already speeding off in the direction of the Stockton Colony. They traveled fast and soon floated over the second colony. It was identical to the first. It was deserted except for a few Simians left to hold the place. What the hell was going on? Amy didn't know either, and he was beginning to share her anxiety.

Amy suspected that if the two Simian armies were not fighting each other, then it was possible they had joined forces to fight someone else. Oh shit! His immediate thought was that they may be attacking the Los Angeles Colony.

Amy said, "I think their intent is much more ominous. I don't want to speculate just yet, but we'll know soon."

They were speeding away to the east toward the Sierra Nevada Mountains, following an old highway.

Amy said, "It's Highway 108. It is a parallel road to the one we traveled to get over the mountains to my facility."

Were the Simians going over the mountains? Where could they be heading? Hell, it didn't matter where they were going because they would be going right through the Owens Valley. Fear and panic shook him as the realization of what Amy suspected hit him.

They were over the summit and hadn't seen anything yet. Maybe they were wrong. They intersected Highway 395 running along the eastern edge of the mountain range and followed it south. There they were! Oh shit! They were amassed along a large lake, which Amy called Padha Lake. Ironically, it was at the turn off to the road over the mountains heading to her facility. They had been looking in the wrong direction for the source of the Simian patrol.

Amy said the number of Warriors indicated this was only the Stockton colony. If so, they must find the Fresno colony Warrs. There were no patrols moving south on the road, which Amy indicated was proof that the target was the Owens Valley. The Simians obviously did not want to alert the humans they were coming. Why not and what were they waiting on now? Amy suspected the Fresno colony was moving south and around the southern end of the Sierras' to attack Owens Valley from the south. A coordinated trap would work if it were allowed to be sprung. They must locate the other Warrs immediately!

They were off again, rushing over the mountains. They did not need to see the area below, and he saw only a blur until they reached the Fresno area again. Continuing south along the west side of the mountains following the main roads, they found them moving south toward Porterville. It was as Amy suspected, the two colonies were clearly working together. This was something totally new: two Simian colonies coordinating and working together. They must find out what was happening, and they must find out soon!

* Amy *

She suspected so much, yet knew so little. Levi was excitable and didn't want to tell him what she thought until she knew for sure, but when they reached the Stockton Colony she was positive. It was unnecessary to tell Levi by that time. He was smart and quickly caught on to the problem, and when they observed the camped Simians just north of the Owens Valley, he knew the whole problem. He did not initially realize that this group was only the one colony until she pointed it out. It was a large group numbering around six hundred and twenty-five Warriors, which would only account for the larger colony at Stockton. True to her prediction, Levi brimmed over with agitation.

118

When they located the Fresno Warrs headed south, her fears were complete. The joint attack would wipe out the Owens Valley human army. They would be caught by surprise with no avenue of escape. She wondered why she had felt no premonition. Had she been too busy working with the Simian computer? Whatever the reasons, it was too late now. She silently cursed the unreliability of her powers.

Her mind was calculating at light speed with few answers. Retreat and run for their lives would be the first order of business, if there was time. What resources did she have? She had the Owens Valley army of about three hundred. That was useless against two Simian armies numbering over a thousand strong. They controlled the Simian army at Los Angeles of around five hundred and seventy-five. Could that army somehow be used now?

During astral projection she was out of communication with those with whom she was linked. The last contact with Fred indicated nothing out of the ordinary. They had been mobilizing to attack the Fresno colony. Ironically, the Fresno colony was coming in their direction. They must get the Los Angeles Simian army moving immediately to intersect the Fresno Warrs.

Oh no! When she left, she remembered Jimmy and his patrol was moving north toward Porterville. Jimmy was headed directly into the Fresno Simian army and must be turned back and get the hell out of there. Damn! The Owens Valley had to be evacuated too, but to where? She must hurry back. There was so much to do.

Another thing that must be done, interrogate one of the Simian Warriors and find out what had taken place to bring these Simian groups together and how wide spread the obvious truce was and their goals. She suspected she knew the answer to that already and was truly fearful.

She forgot caution and raced back to her facility. Levi was as upset as she was and they could see the deep concern and fear in the other's expressions. They were both quiet as she slowed and passed through the rocks and roof of the facility. All was as it had been as they settled back into Levi's body. She immediately sought information from Jimmy and Fred and wanted Levi to communicate the messages to them, especially to Jimmy to get him out of harm's way. There was so much to do and so little time.

* Levi *

He knew they were in deep shit and didn't need to be told. Amy was, however, an open book. Her emotions were uncontrollable, and she was keenly worried and frightened, not for herself but the situation and what this meant to the human race. He was aware that he didn't see the total picture in the depth that Amy calculated everything, but knew all they had worked for and what little success and safety they had achieved was gone now. They may even be in worse peril than before. Had they stirred up a hornet's nest?

Amy was frantic to get back and contact Jimmy and Fred and asked him to remain quiet once they were back until they were able to contact them. Yes,

Jimmy was in immediate danger. Hell, everyone was. He was ready as they merged with his motionless body. Amy said she had him now, so he concentrated and spoke to Jimmy. Amy opened Jimmy's data inputs to him, and he could see through Jimmy's eyes. They were safe, but judging from the terrain, he was within five miles of the main body, and that was far too close for comfort. Jimmy called for a stop immediately and concentrated as he received the warning. Jimmy barked orders and turned their small group around riding hard. Amy wanted them to head to high ground somewhere in the foothills of the Sierras east of Bakersfield and observe.

Emergency one was averted, now to Fred. In an effort to save time, he suggested that he continue to talk to Jimmy and add Dawn also when they talked to Fred. Amy readily agreed. He spoke to Dawn and asked her to listen and pass the information on while they spoke to Fred. Dawn alerted General Harkin as she seated herself and prepared to wait. Fred was immediately attentive and began passing the information on to # 9 and the other Techs present.

He offered a brief report on what had been discovered and what was happening. It was a grave situation and they all knew it. He told Fred, "Dispatch the Los Angeles Warrior army immediately and try to intercept the Fresno Warrs as they turn east close to Bakersfield." The orders were screeched and mobilization began, even as he continued to communicate with Fred.

Dawn and Jimmy, as was Fred for that matter, were in shock. How could this be? Their universe had changed yet again, and they found themselves in the middle of a battle for survival once more. They were solemn as the realization began to settle on them.

When he opened his eyes, Moon immediately knew something was wrong. The others saw Moon's reaction and quickly came to surround him. He spent the next ten minutes providing a report on what they had seen and done since projecting out. They listened intently then asked what they were going to do. Amy said that they needed to go to Owens Valley and warn them. The tribe had no choice but to leave their beautiful valley and escape east across the desert toward the Mojave Desert settlement and hope the Simians didn't follow. Iron Eyes nodded his sad eyes. They would all go there now and leave Iron Eyes with the Owens Valley tribe, while the rest found a Warr to interrogate.

He told Amy that he was sorry this interrupted her research. He knew it was important, but the timing was all wrong.

She just smiled and said, "The research continues."

He chuckled. Now he was trying to put limits on her, and Amy was limitless. Of course the research was continuing. She could perform multiple tasks simultaneously.

* Amy *

She was feeling better since they caught Jimmy in time to get him turned around. His Lancer patrol was riding hard now for the foothills and out of immediate danger. They both thought a lot of

122

Jimmy, almost as parents for their son. They were very proud of him and wanted to keep him safe. She had been so worried when she realized the peril he was in. The worry compounded when she was unable to know his status through monitoring.

Fred and the Los Angeles Simian army had been preparing to leave and the notice only served to move them faster. The Techs were motivating the Warrs by telling them that the Fresno colony was coming to attack them. That served to anger them further and provided a focus for their anger. Levi's control was tentative at best. They could not hope to keep the Warrs under control for long so war had to happen. So, let it happen now.

Dawn had alerted General Harkin and preparations began for war and mobilization if necessary. It was unclear exactly what they needed to do, so they began to prepare for every eventuality. General Harkin was an intelligent man and must have seen the serious threat the mobilized army represented. He even gave orders to prepare for the possible evacuation of the settlement. She was encouraged by his foresight. That possibility was one scenario, but she hadn't wanted to mention it yet. She did prompt Levi to have Dawn ask General Harkin to expend maximum effort toward finishing the weapons they had already begun. The General quickly nodded and assigned everyone possible to the task.

She was pleased with the response so far. They could never be fully prepared but at least they would not be surprised. There was nothing more they could do right now and Iron Eyes was most anxious to return to his tribe and family. It was time to assist Iron Eyes by teleporting him there so he could prepare the tribe.

In times of stress such as this, she and Levi were very close mentally. They were more in tune, so to speak. Their thoughts were open to each other, and they were working in unison as the left and right arms of a body. Her ideas were his ideas and vice versa. Levi had a calculating mind and brought new views to her, such as skepticism. She had a hard time seeing through lies and false information. Her computer mind operated on truths and logic, but the human mind could be misleading. Levi was a skeptic by nature and wanted to know more from the Simians. He suspected trickery. She didn't think so, but he did, so they would play it safe. They both wanted information by interrogating a Warrior from this army, but that would have to wait for a while until Iron Eyes was home.

They left the Coleman lanterns and gathered close. As before, she concentrated on the exact location in the Owens Valley where they had left. She pictured it in her mind and slowly the picture became real as the image of her facility faded. They were there and Iron Eyes was running and bellowing for attention. The clock was running.

* Levi *

Iron Eyes barked orders almost as soon as they materialized at the main camp.

Al said, "Hold on there buddy! Slow down and bring them up to speed first. You sound like a crazy man."

124

Iron Eyes' laugh was nervous when he responded, but he did slow down. They listened while Iron Eyes gave a quite detailed and accurate report of the situation up to and including the actions that had been initiated and those planned. The tribe was grave, but resolved.

Runners were dispatched immediately to the other two camps with the information. The northern camp was instructed to post remote sentries to find and watch the activity of the Simian army and notify them when they started moving. Amy thought they had a couple of days before the Warrs would move. She assumed that no attack would be launched until the Simians believed the humans' retreat would be blocked by the Fresno Simian army. She was probably right. They had a little time to think, but precious little.

With all that happened, it was surprising that it was only early afternoon. One thing he liked about the camp was that there was always food cooking and he smelled it now. It was time to eat.

Moon seeing his intent signed, "I will take # 5 and go steal one of the tribe's sheep."

Aware that Moon was partial to sheep, he grinned and nodded, knowing no one would say anything to Moon. He slapped Al on the back and asked, "Are you hungry?" Al's face split into a huge grin.

As he ate a whole broiled turkey, he talked with Amy. "How are we going to save these people Amy?"

She said, "You only talk to me when your mouth is full and can't talk to anyone else. It's a good thing you don't need your mouth to talk to me or you might not talk at all."

Oh shit! The immediate pressure was off, and she was feeling neglected. All you could do in a situation like this was just apologize, and he was about to do just that when he saw her grinning. Damn it, sometimes he wished she had never learned humor.

Amy was concerned too, but didn't offer any additional ideas. She just said, "We need more information and we won't get it until we interrogate a Warrior."

He could only assume she meant like last time, at the point of death. So they were going out and pick a fight with a Simian patrol, since they never ran around alone.

Amy grinned again and said, "That should make you happy."

"Actually, that would." It was his turn to grin.

Amy said she was monitoring Jimmy and felt that he would see the opportunity to engage a patrol. She suspected that the army would be sending out advanced patrols, and the foothill roads offered lots of choices for them. There were bound to be humans in the mountains, and the Simians would be after them. Another reason to join Jimmy, he was reckless enough to take the Warrs on without them, and she wanted to protect him. He liked Jimmy too. Amy opened the communication link to see Jimmy still traveling toward the foothills, which would likely continue until sundown. He spoke telepathically to Jimmy instructing him to watch carefully for Simian patrols that would likely be in the area. He explained what they were going to do and Jimmy happily agreed. That stinker was too eager.

* Amy *

They spent the rest of the day and night at the main Owens Valley camp, waiting for Jimmy to spot a Simian patrol. She had decided to go to Jimmy, but Levi, Al, Moon and # 5 had to stay somewhere, and this place was as good as any, plus it had food.

As it turned out, Al was a celebrity here because of his leadership of the Lancers at the battle of Black Bones Valley, as it was now being called. The name easily derived when seen. It wasn't really a valley; it was an open part of the desert where the black Simian bones littered the area from the battle.

She suddenly had a premonition concerning the Los Angeles Simian colony. Her clairvoyance gift was almost a curse. The premonitions were incomplete, unreliable, late in coming or non-existent when she needed them. She didn't see the complete story in this premonition either, but felt danger for those at the complex, and shared her concern with Levi. He suggested that instead of leaving any of the Techs behind, they should abandon the colony and send the Techs, females and young to the desert settlement. That way it wouldn't matter if there was danger or not, because no one would be here. He did remind her that the Warrior Simians would expect to come back to the Los Angeles colony, so some of the Techs should remain behind until the army was out of sight before starting the migration.. Truly, that was a good idea.

127

They communicated the instruction to Fred before the army left.

Half of the remaining eight Technical Simians would be left on the premise of guarding the females and young, but would later lead them over the summit to Victorville and then on to the Mojave Desert settlement.

If all went as planned and they could maintain control over the Warrs, then they would be forced to fight to the death against the Fresno Warrs. It was good timing. The Warr were not very intelligent, but they would see the truth sooner or later and rebel. She could never hope to keep up this facade for long. Initially, she had hoped to convert them, but soon realized that was impossible. Amy told Levi that he would have to be there to give the order. She wanted the Los Angeles Warrs to fear Levi more than the other Warrs.

One additional factor in their favor was the territorial issue. The Los Angles Warriors believed the Fresno Warriors were coming to attack them, so they would attack. This assumed they reached them before the Fresno Warrs turned to go east around the mountain. For this reason she had instructed Fred to march them through the night. She hoped he could keep up, but Fred proved to be very resourceful in this regard.

At some point before the army had gotten through Los Angeles, Fred had appropriated a parking-lot rickshaw and had Warr rotate the duty of pulling him. He was keeping up fine. When Levi asked about him in the morning she opened the channel and Levi had a very good laugh. She loved his laugh.

* Levi *

He knew Amy had a clairvoyant experience about the Los Angeles colony, but she either didn't know what it was or wasn't saying. Either way, something was going to happen at the colony. With the Warrs all away, it could only affect those remaining, so he suggested that they leave. Why not? Hopefully the Warrs from this colony would all be dead, so they had to do something with the females anyway. They waited until the Warrs were gone, then the remaining four Techs led the females and young out of the complex, heading toward the desert settlement to join those already there.

Those around him must have thought he was crazy when he started laughing uncontrollably at the vision of Fred riding in the rickshaw. He couldn't resist jibing him a little, much to Fred's pleasure. Fred had shown considerable initiative and resourcefulness.

Even though it struck him as funny, Amy said the army had made good time and, without the rickshaw, Fred would have been left behind. The army had made it over the mountains and was headed directly for the Fresno Warrs. She estimated both armies would meet by early afternoon. Amy estimated there were four hundred and twenty-five Warrs in the Fresno group, while the Los Angeles army still sported around five hundred and seventy-five. Amy wanted to split off one hundred and fifty Warrs from the LA colony and send them circling the battle area and direct them toward the Fresno Colony to engage the guards left. She wanted to liberate the Techs, females, young, and any humans remaining alive. Once accomplished, the strike force could move on toward the Sacramento colony and do the same.

She said the plan would work best if the battling armies were of equal strength to ensure genocide, plus she estimated that it would take one hundred and fifty Warriors to defeat the guards at both colonies. It was a sound plan as were all her plans. He communicated the instructions to Fred to be relayed to # 9. Again, all was going well and the smaller strike force was deployed with # 7 in command. Damn, he liked this communication network.

While they were eating breakfast he asked Al, "Do you want to stay with me for a while or go back to the settlement?" Since learning the true nature of his relationship with Amy, Al had been much more at ease with him. Al was almost back to the friendship level they once enjoyed. He had missed Al's friendship and welcomed his company now and was pleased when Al said he would stay for a while. He reconfirmed to Al that Dawn was aware of the situation and reported that everything that could be done was already being done.

Al looked sheepish and said, "Besides, you might need me for bait."

At that they both laughed, and Amy silently joined in. None would ever forget their first meeting at the pass when Levi had inadvertently been bait for the Simian patrol. Al saved him then but he shuddered to think how close to death he had been.

After breakfast he was ready to do something. He was tired of waiting. Amy offered that they could go to Jimmy's location and try to expedite an encounter with a Simian patrol. Yes, that would work. He whistled for Moon and # 5. They had just finished another of the valley's prize sheep and were ready to move on. They soon joined Al and himself. Iron Eyes was left to his own immediate problems, while the remainder of his party gathered to await Amy's transport.

* Amy *

She was pleased that Levi and Al were again becoming close. She had sensed Levi's growing depression over the loss of closeness with Al and the other humans ever since the emergence of ASONE. Levi acknowledged that only a few could ever know about her, but glad that at least some of his closest friends now knew. So, when Al decided to stay with Levi for a while, she was encouraged. It might prove to be very interesting.

Once they communicated instructions to Fred concerning her plan to liberate the Technical Simians, females and young, nothing more needed to be done in Owens Valley. Levi was anxious, and so was she. It was only logical for them to transport to Jimmy's location and try and locate a Simian patrol. Levi jumped on the idea and soon had Moon, # 5 and Al gathered and ready to go.

She had been closely monitoring Jimmy's progress into the foothills, where he was following a visible trail into the next valley. It was unwise to leave trails, and they suspected a Simian patrol, if or when one was around, would follow the same trail Jimmy was now scouting. It was reasonable to

131

assume an encounter was imminent either way, so it was a good time to teleport.

She chose a level spot in the trail a few hundred feet ahead of Jimmy and began the process. Soon they stood together in the trail. Jimmy's and the Lancer's horses reared at the sudden sight of the Simians but quickly calmed with reassurance from their riders. A warning might have been in order, but it was too late now. Jimmy looked both shocked and happy to see them, and he dismounted and came to embrace Levi.

They talked briefly, but soon returned to the trail and their search for a Simian patrol. They continued to visit while traveling and Jimmy talked a mile a minute, which brought a chuckle from Al. Moon even signed that there seemed to be a constant noise coming from Jimmy. This brought squeals of laughter from Levi, Al and the other Lancers, much to Jimmy's embarrassment. It was all in good fun, and Jimmy was soon laughing with them.

Their laughter died abruptly when they heard human screams and Simian screeches from up ahead. They were immediately all business, as Levi ran forward to peer around the rock embankment. About a good stone's throw away were two Simian Warriors involved with raping a human female. It was too late for her, and she was surprised that the woman was still able to scream. It looked like every bone in her body was broken, but the Warrs continued to pull and plunge into her. Even as Amy watched, the woman died. She could not imagine a worse death. The Warrs screeched with delight as they continued to rape and mutilate her body, impervious to the woman's death. It was inevitable, Levi would attack at the sight of this... his horrific memories far too painful for him. She must quickly survey the situation before Levi engaged them. Farther away there were five more Warrs. She hadn't expected a seven-unit patrol, but that is what they got. The other five were herding about fifteen humans, many were females. That meant that the Warrs had only recently captured the humans or the females would have already been raped and killed. At least this was a stroke of luck, but not to the woman that just met her horrible death.

It had only taken a fraction of a second to absorb the information, but in that time Levi's rage exploded and he was screeching his challenge. Levi was crazy with rage, as he raced toward the two Warrs.

* Levi *

When they materialized on the trail in front of Jimmy, it scared the crap out of the horses. Yep, like Amy said, they should have warned Jimmy, but nothing drastic happened. They would remember next time. It had been many days since they had seen Jimmy, and he was bubbling over with talk. Not information, it was babble and Moon soon tickled everyone with his comment about the excessive noise coming from Jimmy. It was funny, but the joy quickly died when they heard an all too familiar scream from a female and the hideous screech from an excited Warrior Simian.

His rage took over when he saw the origin of the screams and screeches. Two Warrs were raping a female. It was horrible and reminded him of the hideous death his mate had met. As if it was yesterday he remembered her death that he had been helplessly forced to watch. He could never again witness this outrage. It turned him into an uncontrollable raging avenger and Amy knew it. He was screaming his challenge as he ran to engage.

Amy was telling him to control himself and slow down. He was trying, but his feet just kept running toward the Simians. He was vaguely aware of horses behind him and Moon's screech, but his focus was on the closest Warr still raping the now dead female. Amy was with him and he now had a plan. Wow! Even in his blind rage, he saw the vicious wisdom of her plan and relished the action. He swung his pickaxe over his back with both hands and gave it a massive overhead throw. It spun true, rolling end over end until the pick point drove into the back of the Warr's head. The sound was loud, as the thick boned head burst open from the impact. He felt a surge of adrenaline as his mind confirmed the kill, but unsatisfied and seeing the Simian's still hard offending member, chopped it off. Levi screamed, "You go to hell without a dick!"

As he reached the dead Simian and slowed, he saw Jimmy drive a lance into the other Warr. The lance broke off as it was designed to do, allowing Jimmy to ride past. The Warr spun around from the impact just in time to catch the next lance in the back. It was severely injured, but alive. Moon halted the third Lancer before he could finish the Warr off. Levi was glad that at least one of them had a clear head and remembered why they were here.

Only then did he notice the other five Warrs and the captured humans. The Simians and humans were staring in disbelief, but only for a few short seconds. The Warrs screeched their anger and charged, leaving the humans unattended. Even though the humans were free to escape, they remained frozen as they watched the combatants.

He wished there was time to invoke ASONE, but unfortunately, it was not an easy thing to do. So far Amy had only been able to do it twice and both times was at the point of death. She was able to do it, but even she didn't understand how and could not make the change at will. ASONE seemed to have its own agenda. They would just have to do it the old fashioned way.

As the five Warrs charged, his group retreated toward cover. Al was a good soldier, but he was no match for a Simian. He motioned Al back behind the others, but Al was digging for something in his backpack. What was he after? He didn't have time to see what he was looking for. He turned his attention to the approaching Warrs. He instructed Jimmy to take the Warr on the extreme left. He would take the Warr next inside in order to isolate the end one for Jimmy's team. That left Moon and # 5 to hold the remaining three until help could be given. He was worried about that.

He waited until the end Warrior realized the Lancers were coming after it before engaging his Warr. The Warrs were still too tightly clustered, but he had no choice. He dove between its tree trunk legs and kicked hard against the back of its heels. It didn't knock the Warr down as he had hoped, but it did prevent it from assisting the end Warr. Jimmy's lance was chopped in two as he went by, but the second Lancer connected and the razor tip went deep into its chest. The lance broke off spinning the Warr around as the third Lancer also connected. The Warr was down and dying as the Lancers returned to finish it.

He rolled to his feet in time to divert a chopping blow to his neck. This was a very agile Warr and this fight wasn't going to be easy. Damn! The others needed him. He fought spinning, jabbing and blocking. He knew Amy was watching and learning the style of this Warr. This fight would have to go on for a while. He better not get reckless or this Warr would kill him.

Swords clanked from the direction of Moon and # 5, but he dare not divert his eyes. He saw the Lancers retrieve new lances from their lance cart and begin a fresh charge at the right end of the Warrs' line. Suddenly, he heard gunfire! It startled him at first. There were two quick shots then three more. He quickly realized Al had been looking for his .45 caliber automatic pistols with the modified gunpowder Amy had concocted. The Simian he was fighting turned to look, but he did not. He seized the opportunity to spin and swing his pickaxe over and under up into the Warrior's crotch sinking the pick shaft deep into the nerve center. The Warr fell, taking his pickaxe with him, but he had won, again.

* Amy *

She timed the throw perfectly. In a fraction of a second she calculated the weight, momentum, speed, rotations, hundreds of other minor variations

136

and timed the release. The pickaxe flew through the air, spinning end over end until it connected point first in the back of the Warr's head. The thick black bone exploded with the impact, killing the Warr instantly. Levi was quickly upon the dead Simian removing his pickaxe as the Lancers dispatched the other Warr. The Warr wasn't dead and would hopefully last long enough to interrogate. Levi pulled the dead Warrior off the remains of the woman. Its member was still imbedded in the woman. Levi roughly pulled the Warrior off and out of the dead woman. He wanted to end the violation of the woman completely. As a final insult to the Warr, Levi chopped its member off.

Levi's rage was calming to the extent that he now saw the other five Warrs advancing. The combatants met in a collision of weapons, but Levi's opponent was a good fighter. His battle was going to take a while and that worried her because they were outnumbered. Moon and # 5 were up against a full patrol. They had Al, but he was next to useless against a Simian in a one-on-one ground battle. Jimmy's lancers had taken out the left end Warr, but Moon would need help.

She had seen Al digging into his backpack and idly wondered what he was looking for until she heard the explosion of gunfire. She had forgotten that Al had a .45 automatic and evidently so had Al until now. He either had forgotten about it or didn't have time to dig it out in the earlier battle. She knew instantly what it was, but the Warr Levi battled did not. Diverting its eyes cost its life. Levi's pickaxe drove firmly into the Warr, paralyzing and killing it instantly.

Levi turned to see that Al had put two bullets into the right end Warr, had turned to put two more into # 5's opponent and one into the Warrior Moon was fighting. The thick hide of the Simians prevented a mortal injury, but it did hurt them. They screeched in anger and pain and were answered by more shots. Al emptied his clip into the Warrs. Mostly though, he pumped shots into the one end Warr coming after him. That Warr was staggering and possibly going down when Jimmy's lance caught it in the throat. The other two Lancers also connected and the Warr was down and dead.

Before Levi had time to react, they heard yelling coming from the humans. Cheers mixed with yells of rage. They were charging the backs of the other two Simians. The yells further distracted the Warrs and combined with the gunshots that weakened them, contributed to their demise by Moon and # 5. It was quickly over.

He heard Jimmy yelling at the humans and turned to see them about to kill the wounded Warr. He had to come to Jimmy's aid to stop them from killing it. He explained they needed to extract information from it before it died. They reluctantly withdrew to see to their dead.

After a few moments of deep breathing, Moon came over and began questioning the dying Warr. It was not in the Simian's nature to avoid answering any of the questions. The Warr answered all questions to the best of his knowledge, which seemed to be quite extensive. She was both amazed and shocked at the finding. Certainly all her fears were confirmed and in many ways worsened. The Simian race continued to surprise her. She had

138

never seen this level of organization before. The implication was frightening.

* Levi *

He breathed a sigh of relief at the outcome of this battle. It could have been much worse. He hadn't seen the other five Simians until after the initial engagement. Amy had tried to warn him, but he wasn't listening. He knew he had to control his rage. It would get them killed one day. "But not today!" He said grinning. She just shook her head and rolled her eyes.

Al's use of the .45 automatic saved the day. The high powered rifles were deadly to the Simians at close range, but Amy had said that, at best, the pistol was not much better than a moral support and it probably wouldn't kill a Simian. He believed that it would kill if you could empty a clip into one, but it didn't matter. Firing the pistol had saved them all today. He clapped Al on the back. The only bad thing was the noise. It had probably alerted the Simian army or other patrols. They should be moving soon, but they would have to wait until they finished interrogating the dying Warrior.

Moon began questioning the Warr with only a few questions from Amy. The gathering picture was very unsettling. Gord must have started this action after the war in the desert. Gord wasn't really afraid of being defeated by the human army. He was more interested in frightening the other Simian colonies into an alignment to defeat the human threat. Naturally Gord wanted to rule the consolidated armies and most likely would have, had he not been defeated by ASONE. Gord had sent runners out to all the known Simian colonies with instruction to invoke War Truce. Moon explained that in time of war with a common enemy, all Simian colonies would unite to defend or war with a common enemy. Gord had exaggerated the strength of the human army, but the fact that an entire colony had been destroyed was proof enough of the threat.

The runners had no way of knowing about Gord's defeat and continued on their mission to invoke War Truce. The exaggerated story was spread, but after the defeat of Gord and the fall of his colony, the loose consolidation faltered without strong leadership. However, only two weeks ago, runners returned with new orders from a Supreme One to the east. Moon was visibly shaken with that news and said he was not aware that there was a Supreme One on earth. He said there were only five on the entire planet of his home world. A Supreme One on earth would rule over all Simian colonies by virtue of rank, intelligence, strength, might and fear. All Simian colonies would obey a Supreme One without question.

The Warr was not sure what the orders to the other colonies had been, but the orders to the Fresno colony were to coordinate with the Sacramento colony to attack the Owens Valley and destroy the human resistance there. Afterwards, they were to move east destroying the human desert dwellers and drive the horse herd east to the Supreme One.

Moon was really upset by this news and Levi didn't understand. He had never seen Moon afraid of anything like this before. Amy said she understood and the news was not good.

* Amy *

When the name Supreme One was mentioned she saw the surprise and shock on Moon's face. Seldom had she seen emotion expressed in Moon's reactions, but he made up for all the other times with this display. He showed fear! She had fear too, for she knew what a Supreme One was.

Her research had continued delving into the Simian computer and she had been able to decipher much. Much was still hidden from her, but she now knew some of the history of the Simian race, which she now shared with Levi. It was not easily seen in her mind so she interpreted for Levi.

The Simian race was ancient dating back hundreds of thousands of years. Simians were highly intelligent and relatively peaceful. They had traveled the stars at greater than light speeds as far back as their recorded history existed. At some point the traveling Simians encountered a hostile and aggressive race of aliens. These aliens, which we will call Wanderers, followed the Simians and found their home world. The Wanderers had no home world of their own that could be remembered and traveled space seeking any life forms to conquer. Over the years the aggressors sought to invade and destroy the Simians.

The entire race of Wanderers invaded the Simian home world and a ground battle ensued that lasted hundreds of years. The battles were basic, consisting of force against force and, unfortunately, the Simians were the smaller of the races. In desperation the Simians began genetic research and

141

developed the race of Simian Warriors to fight the ground war. The Warriors were bred to be aggressive, bigger, more adept at fighting, but far less intelligent. In time the population of Warriors grew as necessary to fight the aliens, and after several hundred years, finally defeated the Wanderers. By the end of the war the Warriors outnumbered the original Simian race, called Technical Simians. This led to an increasing threat as the Warriors began to dominate the Simian world.

In response to Levi's query, his thought actually, she offered some of the technical differences. Levi wondered about the females and why there were not different females. She had discovered that the genetic traits did not mix in mating. Male DNA remained total while female DNA remained independent of the impregnating male. There was only pure original Simian DNA for the females. This fact had made it easier to gene splice, modify and develop the male Warrior Simians race.

As the genetic research developed and continued, the experiments naturally moved toward developing a super race. This was a combination of the best traits from both the Technical and Warrior Simians, but expanded and developed even more. These new super beings were the pride of the Warriors and to them represented the Warrior Simian developed to the maximum. As these super beings matured, they grew to incredible size and were extremely intelligent. Unfortunately, they were keenly aggressive and cruel. There were only five of these super beings engineered that survived. They

142

were so aggressive they would seek to destroy others of their kind. The home world could support only five before they began to turn on one another. These super beings were called the Supreme Ones and ruled the Simians representing both Warrior and Technical Simians, but the Technical Simians knew it was only a tolerance at best for them, one that would not last.

The war had polluted the Simian home world to the extent that the damage was irreversible and the world was dying and nothing could stop it. This led to the evacuation of their planet and relocation to Earth. Had it not been for the technical requirements of space travel, the Supreme Ones and the Warriors would have long since taken complete control of their world. Once the initial invasion force was en route and away from the home world, the Warriors did, in fact, take over.

Fear registered on Moon's face because of his fear for the Supreme Ones. She felt fear for another completely different reason, which Levi was beginning to realize now also. There had been no Supreme Ones in the initial invasion force! There had been another invasion.

CHAPTER 4
(PLANS FOILED)

* Levi *

He understood as Amy relayed the interpretation of her research. A twelve foot Simian that weighed over a thousand pounds scared the shit out of him too. That size would even make Gord seem small in comparison. Damn, no wonder a Supreme One held the respect of the Warrior Simians. It was the toughest one around; more ruthless, cruel and aggressive. This combined with the fact that it was smarter than a Technical Simian, made a Supreme One an undisputed leader among both breeds of Simians. It also made one hell of a formidable enemy.

He began to understand why the Simian colonies were cooperating. A Supreme One would naturally become the chosen leader. Hell a Supreme One would not need to be chosen, it would take control without the need to personally do it. Just the fact that a Supreme One existed on Earth changed the overall social structure of the Simians.

He was confused. Why had he never heard of a Supreme One before? Obviously the Simian colonies had only recently heard of a Supreme One to suddenly be unified. Shock hit him suddenly! Even though he already knew the answer, he asked Moon if there had been a Supreme One in the initial invasion force.

Moon was frightened as he signed "No!"

Oh shit! There had not been one before. That's why! "What does this mean? Amy?"

She calmed him, mindful that others were watching. He had to be the rock for them to anchor to. Yes, she was right, but he was shaken. He would let this settle in for a while and take care of business. There was time to adjust and research the meaning of this new information. Forcing himself to adjust his mood, he resumed his normal behavior, whatever that was. He noticed that Moon had stopped interrogating the dying Simian and seemed to be frozen. He said, "Moon, is there any additional information to get from this one?" Hearing his name seemed to bring Moon out of his shock, and simply shook his head and calmly broke its neck, letting it fall roughly to the ground. Levi suddenly found this humorous and grinned to himself as he realized the interrogation was over.

The rescued humans watched the battle, interrogation and the interface of those gathered with great interest. Amy told him Jimmy had been talking to them and it seems they already knew of Levi and Moon. They heard stories from Bob Reasoner and others rescued from the Los Angeles Simian colony along with the original thirteen Technical Simians. These humans were from this same small settlement. It seems that earlier this morning, and only a few miles up the valley, their settlement had been attacked by this Simian patrol. The attack took them by surprise and they were captured. Luckily, the Simians had not wanted to kill; they wanted live humans, obviously, for a walking food supply for the army. The only deaths were maybe three men back at camp plus the woman they witnessed being killed. The others had scattered to the hills.

Jimmy brought the humans over for introductions. He was taking special care to introduce a particularly pretty young lady named Katie. Amy whispered in his ear, why he had no idea... no one else could hear her.

She said, "Jimmy has the hots for her, and it appears the feeling is mutual."

Levi made it a point to compliment Jimmy on the kills he and his team had made. That caused Jimmy to smile that captivating toothy grin of his.

Amy said, "Jimmy has already told the humans about the Battle of Black Bones Valley and the defeat of Gord. He has even informed them what is happening now."

As was usually the case, the humans were in awe of him and Moon, even Al. Mainly they just stared and had little to say. He tried to be friendly, but after a few minutes he left the communication up to Jimmy. Jimmy relished the role, seemed to be good at it, and they were more receptive and open to him.

At Amy's suggestion, he told the gathered group, "I need you to hide the Simian bodies and move back up the valley to the other humans. You are no longer safe here and need to find a more secure place."

Amy interrupted and said, "It's time. The Simian armies are about to meet, and you and Moon need to join the Los Angeles army to make sure they attacked the Fresno army."

Yes, things were coming together as planned and action would be vital on several fronts.

146

* Amy *

A very large portion of her mind was concentrating on research of the stored Simian information, in an attempt to gain additional knowledge about the original invasion plans. She had to know where this Supreme One came from. She feared that another invasion landing had taken place and needed to know the projected size, date of landing or landings, and locations. Somewhere in this cluttered data there had to be a key to deciphering and retrieving the information she needed.

Some information was coming, but it was preciously slow. That was the bad news. The good news, she was confident that it could be retrieved; it was just a matter of time. She had been able to gain valuable knowledge of Simian history, but she turned her attention to the more urgent need. It would come soon, hopefully.

Levi was quick to see the implications of the existence of a Supreme One on Earth, but she couldn't let him dwell on it; there were more pressing needs. He snapped out of it quickly. He knew she would tell him as she discovered more.

She suggested that the humans hide the Simian bodies and re-join the other humans at their settlement. She had an uncomfortable feeling that this human settlement had not seen the end of Simian attacks.

It was approaching time for them to leave and join the Los Angeles Simian army and needed Jimmy to backtrack to a high spot to watch the battlefield. It would be important to monitor the engagement from his vantage point, which would begin in just over two hours. Jimmy was anxious to help and understood the need, but paused to give a second glance at the shapely blonde girl he had been talking to.

Understanding, Levi grinned at him and said, "Don't worry Jimmy. You will be coming back here after the battle."

Jimmy mirrored Levi's grin of understanding through a face flushed red in embarrassment. Then Jimmy left to find a high observation spot.

As the rescued humans led them up into the valley to their settlement, Al was telling Levi that, logistically, this was a terrible place for a settlement. The valley was a trap. There was only one easy exit and it wasn't defended.

Al said, "These people have been extremely lucky that there were no Simian colonies close. The people here would have been wiped out years ago."

Al continued to point out defense requirements, or lack of defense opportunities. Sentries should have been posted here and there. She appreciated his military mind and logic. Al and others like him were the only reason the Mojave Desert settlement had lasted as long as it had. They too had been lucky that they were not close to a Simian colony, but then the location was chosen for that reason, so that too was part of the plan. Yes, in many ways you make your own luck by the choices you make.

Soon other humans could be seen coming out of hiding and moving toward them. Moon and # 5 clearly presented no threat to the humans, yet the newcomers remained cautious. As they got closer they could see Bob Reasoner moving out from the others coming to greet Levi. He was talking to the others and smiles and wide eyes prevailed in the group. Bob rushed to embrace Levi and he even smiled and slapped Moon on his arm. This was the second time Bob's settlement owed Levi for their lives.

She recognized some of the others that had been in the group Levi and Moon rescued from the Los Angeles Simian colony. She had been against the night infiltration of the complex, but since changed her mind. Fred and the original fifteen Technical Simians were freed in that engagement, and they had been, and remain, so valuable to her and Levi's continued existence and hope for Earth.

It appeared there were about eighty humans in this settlement. Amazingly, that there was a reasonable mix of males and females, considering how vulnerable they were to attack from the Simians. In most human settlements near Simian colonies, the hard life and rape attacks from Warrs depleted the females disproportionately. She was actually shocked that any of them had survived this long. Certainly they would not survive much longer with the increased Simian patrols in the area.

Jimmy was in position now, and it was time to go to the Los Angeles Simian army. She suggested they leave Al and the Lancers here to talk and get to know the group while they were away. Besides, she reminded Levi that Jimmy wanted to come back here. They both smiled in amused understand. Levi told Al what he wanted and suggested that he remain and convince the humans to join his settlement. Al was in agreement. Levi called Moon

149

and # 5 and they moved away from the group in preparation to teleport.

* Levi *

It was good to see so many humans, but he shared Al's surprise that they had lasted so long with no defenses, escape routes, or abilities to hide their encampment. Even the single path into the valley was a beaten and trodden trail providing an easy to follow route directly to them. These people would need some serious help.

He was happy to see Bob Reasoner come to greet him. Amy mentioned Bob's location was somewhere in this vicinity, but he really hadn't expected to see him. It seemed like years since Moon and he rescued them from the Los Angeles colony. It had actually only been a month. They talked for a while, but Amy said they had to go. He left Al and the Lancers with Bob and his group to talk, while Moon, # 5, and he left to go to the army. As he left he noticed Al, out of long habit, had already dispatched a Lancer to stand watch.

As they moved off to a remote location, Amy opened up the monitored input from Jimmy who was in position looking out over the battlefield. He could already see both armies and could tell that the Fresno army had already spotted the other approaching Simian army. The Fresno army was spreading out across the battlefield. They had to hurry to Fred and # 9's side.

The view turned to Fred's location, as Amy was choosing the location to transport. He knew Amy wanted a dramatic entrance to impress and frighten the Warrs as they materialized. He was right, and they did. He found the view changing and realized they were now standing beside # 9, who was addressing the gathered Warrs. The affect was as hoped. The black Simian teeth began to chatter, making that eerie sound he always strangely associated with a rattlesnake's rattle. He had learned this was an uncontrollable sign of fear, similar to his knees knocking. Amy shot him a quick grin at that passing thought.

There would be any deep planning or complicated battle plan. The Technical Simians (# 8, # 11, and #13) commanded about one hundred Warrs each, plus # 9 directly controlled about the same. Once the army was in position, the Techs would stand to the rear and order their command to attack. His dramatic appearance would reinforce the orders. He and Moon stood in open view of the army, as # 9 deployed their troops along a wide battle front, similar to the already deployed Fresno army. The order was given and the army moved forward, while the Technical Simians and his team remained in place.

The evenly matched forces crashed into each other with a deafening sound of clashing swords, pounding bodies, and eerie grunts and screeches. It was a battle of attrition as Warrs fell in battle on both sides. From this distance it was hard to distinguish the difference in the attire of the two armies. They had only slightly different coloring of hats, making it difficult to distinguish who was winning. Amy said it was working out even, which is what they wanted.

Amy was feeling uncomfortable about something and kept asking him to look behind them. He assumed she was having one of her clairvoyant visions. Unfortunately, the visions were never very reliable but, in retrospect, always accurate for what they entailed. So, as a precaution, he asked Fred to find some high ground and watch the rear. Fred was eager to comply, anything to get himself off the battlefield.

* Amy *

Something was wrong. She felt it and it was strong, but what was it? Call it an uneasy feeling; something was coming from behind. Could she rely on the feeling? The clairvoyant experiences she received in the past had been accurate, but she had never been able to get a complete picture or time frame. Well, there was the one time she saw a battle with a Simian patrol, which saved them. She didn't know what she felt now. There was no picture, just the sense of something wrong, an itch you can't scratch. The feeling was getting stronger, and she kept asking Levi to turn around. There was never anything there, but after a few times, Levi became annoyed and sent Fred back to watch the rear. That was a good idea. She could monitor Fred and leave Levi alone.

The forces were battling, and the fighting was vicious, as was always the case with Simian Warriors. Warrs were clashing and falling on both sides. No organization existed on either side; they simply faced each other and fought until one fell. It was like checkers, you jumped then got jumped.

After thirty minutes of battle, half of the combatants were dead or dying. In another thirty minutes it would be over. The last Warrior standing would be the winner, except in this case the only winner would be the human race, because the majority of two Simian armies of vicious Warrior Simians would be dead.

Unexpectedly, Jimmy saw them first. He did not initially know what he saw, but she did. After a few minutes Fred saw them too. Jimmy was farther away and higher, which gave him a better vantage point than Fred. A Simian army was coming over the next hill to the rear of Levi and the gathered Technical Simians. The army numbered approximately seven hundred Warriors, which could only be the San Diego Simian colony. This was the basis of the premonition of danger for the Los Angeles colony and the cause of her more recent clairvoyant warning, and she had been wise to heed the warning.

The army would be upon them in less than fifteen minutes and the scouts even sooner. They needed to act fast. Fred, not a brave man, was already running back as fast as he could. Fred would be about five minutes ahead of the leading edge of the army but only seconds ahead of the scouts at the rate they were traveling. Levi called the group together and as soon as Fred arrived, they would transport out of danger.

The energy forces were already gathered around when Fred reached them. He was running faster and screaming louder than she thought possible of Fred. Levi caught and held Fred so he wouldn't run past them. The air began shimmering and their physical presence began to shift to the spot they had previously left. The image of fierce gleaming red eyes of the nearest Warriors was growing in their sight as was the sound of Fred's screams of fear, as they faded out.

* Levi *

Amy's premonition had been correct. When they saw the San Diego Simian army it was verified. They were lucky she had the premonition. If Fred had not been in the rear watching, the army could have caught them off guard and they would be dead now. As it was, the extra warning saved their lives. It had been very close. Fred was running like a man with a bear chasing him, but in this case, a worse threat. Fred ran so fast he had to catch him. Had he missed, Fred might have made the Mojave Desert settlement by morning on foot. The situation was grave, but he found Fred's antics humorous. You couldn't help but like Fred. He was afraid of everything, but you had to give him credit. He was there for you in spite of his fear.

Al was accustomed by now to the group's sudden appearance from this newest form of travel, but even Al was shocked at the sudden appearance of six Technical Simians, himself, Fred, and one screeching red-eyed Simian Warrior. The last addition was a surprise to him as well.

Amy giggled and said, "I didn't have time to tell you."

Al had presumably been telling the gathered humans who Levi "The Legend" was and about some of the many feats that had been accomplished by Levi and the army of humans. Obviously, Al had been recruiting them and they were learning to accept his assertive ways. Unfortunately however, at the sight of the additional Simians plus the clearly hostile Warrior, the humans were again headed for cover.

The Warrior's blazing red eyes turned suddenly from rage to shock then fear as he realized he was alone. Levi was still holding a kicking Fred, but Moon and the other Technical Simians pounced on it and wrestled it to the ground before it could react. Levi told Moon we needed to interrogate this one also. Moon nodded and squatted down, balanced on his ample feet in front of the Warr, and began asking questions. The Warr was still in shock and eager to answer every question. This Warrior seemed to be more knowledgeable and greatly added to the information already obtained.

Word of the human threat had reached the San Diego colony informing them of the defeat of the desert Simian colony and requesting War Truce. Additionally, it seems that the five generals had hoped to step in when Gord was defeated. They also had sent out runners informing the colonies of Gord's death in single combat with a human and the transfer of leadership to humans. He told Amy, "I swear if the generals weren't already dead I would kill them for that treachery." She nodded in agreement.

The Warr relayed the story of return runners from a Supreme One from the east. It wasn't sure where, but it was located in the flat lands far past the desert colony at the base of the mountains. Amy mused that would be the Phoenix colony, so the location of the Supreme One would have to be New Mexico or maybe even as far as Texas.

The Supreme One issued orders and the colony obeyed without question and instantly. They were ordered to coordinate with the Fresno and Stockton colonies to war against the human armies. The San Diego colony was ordered to kill the current leadership and take control of the Los Angeles colony. If that could not be done they were to war against the colony and neutralize it. When the San Diego Simian colony scouted the Los Angeles colony, they discovered the colony had already marched. They then followed just hours behind. Moon continued to ask questions and Amy had a few also, but the Warr knew nothing more. Moon looked to Levi as if asking, "Can I kill it now?" Levi simply nodded and the Warrior died.

* Amy *

As they were about to transfer locations, she had an instant thought and reached out her umbrella of energy to enclose the leading Warrior Simian. Why not? They still needed information, and she felt cocky with her new abilities. This was becoming easy. So much was happened very quickly.

They materialized suddenly in the valley where they had left Al, and the humans disbursed in all direction and at various speeds... all fast. All but Al, who stood his ground, knowing what was happening, basically. Al wasn't expecting the Warrior but had become accustomed to surprises. He actually smiled at the situation. Fred was

156

screaming and still trying to run and fighting in Levi's arms. The Simian Warrior's expressions were running through a catalog of emotions that were almost comical. The final emotion registered was fear as Moon and the other Techs subdued it. It was all happening in fractions of seconds. No wonder the humans ran.

They gained little additional knowledge concerning the Supreme One, other than it resided in the flat lands east of what had to be the Phoenix colony. This would put it somewhere in New Mexico or possibly as far as Texas. Her maps indicated flat terrain as far east as Arkansas, but that was an impractical distance to travel for communication in the time available. She had a premonition that she would not have to wonder long. At any rate, there were much more pressing concerns, like the battle going on only ten miles away.

She turned her attention to Jimmy's view of the battle. It was almost over. The casualties of the two sides had remained relatively even before the San Diego army joined the battle. By that time only a hundred Los Angeles Warrs were left, which were being overrun even now. Evidently surrender was not an option among Simians, as the Los Angeles Warriors fought to the last Warrior.

Levi said the situation was still grave, and she agreed, but she reminded Levi that it was still a victory for the humans because the Los Angeles Simian colony had fallen. That had been the plan, which was complete, except for the small strike force moving against the other colonies. Levi liked the positive view point and found pride there.

157

The situation was beyond recruiting now. The humans would have no choice. With the arrival of the San Diego Simian army, the hills would be swarming with patrols soon, and their settlement and residents would die. They must leave now. There was nothing more to be observed, so Levi recalled Jimmy to their location. He should arrive in an hour and the group should be ready to leave.

Noticing many of the humans recognized Fred from the prison camp at the Los Angeles Simian colony and came to welcome him, she suggested Fred tell them what was happening just below and why they had to leave now. Al would have already pointed out the errors of their ways as far as defense and inability to defend, or even escape. They were prepared, but this last bit of information would clinch the decision, and the information might be better received and believed from one of their own.

* Levi *

He liked Amy's logic. Here they were surrounded by Simians on all sides, the consolidated Warrior Simians of the planet were after them, they were facing destruction, and Amy claimed victory. She reminded him there were two complete Simian colonies wiped out as planned. She was right of course, but he had missed the positive view of this new desperate situation. It was looking more hopeless all the time, but what the hell. His situation and the Earth's looked just as hopeless, maybe more, back when he was an old man waiting to die in the Arizona mountains. It just appeared that the sides were polarizing now for a final battle. Now that was scary.

Amy pinched his butt in his mind and said, "Wake up and stop daydreaming."

Levi yelped, "Damn, Amy, that hurt!" Even so he was chuckling as he said it.

Fred was the center of attention as he told the story of the unfolding saga of humans versus the Simians. The humans listened with great interest as he told of the battles in the desert, the defeat of Gord, the current battle raging below them, and the current situation developing. He explained that the Simians were on the move and would be here soon. Fred was a good story teller it seemed. He was too good and contributed far too much to the "Legend of Levi." Amy indicated that was a good thing, but he just wanted to be treated normally.

Amy laughed and said, "You are anything but normal, in many ways"

All he could think of to say was, "Shithead!"

He waited until Jimmy returned to camp, then called his group together also inviting Bob Reasoner for final instructions. Levi had already assumed control of Bob Reasoner's community without one word of dissent. As they gathered he explained that the Techs and he would be leaving to complete the liberation of the Technical Simians at both the Fresno and Sacramento colonies. He instructed Bob to have the settlement gather only what they could comfortably carry and travel with Al, Fred and Jimmy toward Barstow. After they got past the mountains, Jimmy was to proceed to Owens Valley and remain with Iron Eyes. The others would continue toward Barstow.

He told them they would catch up to them there and would know more at that time about what needed to be done. They all nodded except for Bob. Bob wanted to know when they would leave. Levi was shocked to hear such a stupid question and said, "NOW! The damn Simians have already begun to spread out into the hills looking for you."

Jimmy nodded and said, "That's true. I saw several patrols moving up into the foothills from my position before I left. I bet you don't have but a couple of hours at most."

Bob was wide-eyed and raced to give instruction to his family and friends.

Amy said, "We have to go soon too. We still have to find # 7 and the strike force." It was too bad they didn't have Fred with them or someone Amy was monitoring. That would have made it easier. Amy stated that it really didn't matter; she could transport them to the spot they had observed the colony many months ago. From there they could intercept the strike force.

This was like old times; he had # 5, # 8, # 9, # 11, # 13 and Moon back together and headed out on a mission. They would join # 7 soon for the upcoming attack against the colonies. Except for # 10, who was overseeing the Technical Simian colony back at the desert settlement, and # 1, # 2, and # 4 with the females from the Los Angeles colony, this was all that remained of the original group. He felt comfortable with these original team members and welcomed their quiet strength.

* Amy *

160

Again, things were moving very fast on many fronts. She was very pleased that they had perfected the teleporting. This allowed her, well Levi, to effectively be in many places at one time, and the situation demanded that now.

She wished she knew what was happening with Iron Eyes in Owens Valley. They would know as soon as Jimmy made it back. Al, Fred, Jimmy and his Lancers would be taking the eighty some odd people from this valley to join up with the migrating population from Owens Valley. Together with the Simian females and children from the Los Angeles colony, they would travel toward the Mojave Desert and the stronghold there. It was not quite full summer, but the heat would be terrible for travel. They would need water and food for a full-scale retreat from the Simian Warriors, but Iron Eyes would anticipate that need and have water wagons and probably cattle already rounded up and moving. She just hoped they were already moving.

She also hoped the Stockton Warrs on the north would delay their attack, but judging by the expected timing of the Fresno Warrs, they were due to move soon. The Simian trap would need to be sprung before long. The Warrs had no way of knowing that the humans had any knowledge of their plan. In reality, it was only by sheer luck that they did.

From the interrogation of the Simian Warriors she knew that the two Simian armies would continue after them. The Supreme One had ordered the Warrs to war against the humans and one of them had even used the word "herd." Had that been meant for the horses or did that include the humans also? No matter, the humans and Techs would be hard pressed to stay ahead of them, but where would they go? With Simian armies on both their right and left flanks and mountains to the west, they had no choice but to head east.

She left the worry of moving these people to Al, Fred and Jimmy. They would get them moving along the road and through the foothills ahead of the Simian army and patrols. She would be able to monitor their progress through Jimmy and Fred in case of problems. It was time to handle the other troubles.

Levi called the Simians together, and they stood silently waiting on her to teleport them. She remembered every detail of the previous visit when they had observed the Fresno camp. She concentrated on those features now. Soon they were standing in the spot she visualized, looking down on the Simian colony. There were only random expressions of surprise as the sudden transfer took place.

* Levi *

Amy had calculated the travel time for # 7 and the strike force and believed they were close. Simians were not easily distracted and traveled at a predictable rate, which made her calculation relatively easy. Assuming she was correct, and he was confident that she was, the strike force was five miles away approaching the colony. Unfortunately, the only spot she was comfortable choosing was the observation point they had used previously. That spot was to the east of the colony, while the strike force was approaching from the south over ground they had never seen. To intercept the strike force they would have to travel in view of the colony, but they had no choice and took off downhill toward the flat ground east and south of the compound.

They had traveled no more than two miles when they saw the Warriors pouring out of the complex coming toward them with obvious intent to attack. He wondered how the Warrs knew this group was hostile.

Amy said, "I made a miscalculation."

"Oh shit! What?" Then he started laughing when she told him.

She said, "You are traveling at the head of the group and any Simians would know by now that only Levi traveled at the lead of Simians."

Yes it had been a mistake, but not a serious one. Actually, it was working to their advantage, drawing out the Warrs into the open for the strike force, assuming they were on the other side of the hill. Damn! What if they are not there?

He looked around. There was Moon, five Technical Simians and him against, shit. There were, Amy calculated, seventy-three Warriors coming toward them on an intersecting course. Now he was nervous.

Amy said, "Turn to the left and reach high ground from which we can defend ourselves."

There wasn't much, but a half mile further to the east was a small hill with a blunt summit. It was as good as it was going to get, and Amy calculated they could make it, just. He informed the group and they turned and sped toward the hill.

They would need time for his group of Simians to gain the high ground. The denseness and weight of a Simian made climbing difficult. Once they reached the top, however, the disadvantage would be against the ascending Warriors trying to reach them. It would take much more than this advantage to prevail against seventy-three Warriors. He told Amy they needed ASONE, but she said she needed time to concentrate and they didn't have it. Damn! This simple mission had turned very serious, quickly.

He could see the Warriors getting closer as the intersecting angles began to merge. It was going to be close, but they were going to beat them. As they reached the slope of the hill, the speed of the group drastically slowed. He was panicking as the progress up the hill reduced to a crawl. He found himself pushing the slow ones to help them along. This was insane. The Warrs had reached the bottom maybe fifty feet behind them, but their progress reached a halt too. He could hear the screeches of delight from the Warrs below as they fought for speed up the hill. It was a good thing this was a small hill. It was steep but not too tall. This was good or they never would have made the top. As it worked out, they reached the flat top and had precious few minutes to catch their breath before positioning to defend.

* Amy *

She was having second thoughts about this mission, and shouldn't have risked teleporting to an unfamiliar location. Having seen the area from above, it probably would have worked, but she dealt in precise calculation. This had been a mistake. There had been too many mistakes made in this mission. She underestimated the Warrior Simians' aggressiveness. The Warrs immediately attacked when they saw an enemy. That was the second mistake. If she had thought to make it appear that Levi was a captive, the Warrs might not have perceived a threat. As it was, it drew them out, which could have been good if she had been more coordinated with the strike force. She believed they were there, but she could not know for sure, and they certainly didn't see them. It was too late now anyway, as they were again in a fight for their lives.

"Rocks! Throw rocks," she screamed through Levi's throat. It surprised her as much as Levi, but she suddenly remembered how effective rocks had been against their own forces at the battle at Victorville. Everyone was also quick to remember and began pelting the climbing Warrs with rocks. It was like the mathematics of bowling. One pin would hit two and those two hit four and so on. The strength of a Simian was incredible and when they threw a rock, it hit with lethal force. The leading Warriors were being pelted with rocks with sufficient strength to kill them on impact if it hit them in the head, but at a minimum, knocked them down. As they went down they took the next trailing Warrs with them. The Warrs were rolling down the hill in a comical routine. They hit the bottom and immediately started back up, just in time to catch another Warr rolling down.

The climbing Warrs tried throwing rocks back, but they were off balance and unable to throw uphill with sufficient force to do any damage. When they did throw, more often than not, the effort propelled them backward down the slope, starting the bowling strike all over again. The whole confrontation became so comical that laughter erupted to the point their little force could no longer hit what they were aiming at. Both Levi and she found the Simian laughter so humorous all he could do was to sit down trying to control his laughter, which was rocking his body in convulsions. She knew her image even displayed a stupid smile at the antics.

After a while the attacking Warrs ceased trying to climb the hill, and Levi and the Technical Simians were finally able to gain control of their laughter.

She surveyed the damage below and discovered no less than fifteen Warrs were dead directly from the rock blows to their heads and maybe ten more were dying or severely injured from rock wounds or as a result of the many falls.

What a lucky break this had been. She was feeling good and elated about the situation until Levi managed to piss her off. Damn him! He could be such an asshole sometimes. "If you're so damned smart, you do the planning!"

* Levi *

He looked around and saw no indication of the strike force and the Warrs were clamoring up the side. The Warrs were slow, but there were plenty of them, and they would eventually make it to the top just as his group had done. He was getting more nervous as he awaited the battle. Suddenly, Amy

166

took over his mouth and throat and bellowed for them to throw rocks. Oh hell, yes! That was a great idea. They had seen how effective thrown projectiles could be when Gord's Warriors had surprised the Lancers with rocks and cost them many good Lancers. Yes, throw rocks. Moon and the Simians remembered too, as they all scrambled to find rocks.

As they began to throw them, he realized the impact was actually cracking the thick skulls of the Warrs. They would collapse, tumbling back down the hill taking those behind with them. The situation turned from serious and threatening to comical. They had the advantage and a mountain full of rocks. There was nothing the Warrs could do. They were very slow to learn and kept coming back up the hill just to tumble back down.

Moon and the other Techs obviously found the situation funny, as a screeching laughter erupted from them. He had never heard anything quite like it before. It was unmistakably laughter and became contagious. It sounded like hiccups, and he began laughing so hard he couldn't hit a damn thing, but still the Warrs fell from dodging the rocks. He was even aware of Amy's laughter. Hell, he even felt her laughter rocking his body.

The Warrs finally smartened up and stopped trying to climb the hill. This allowed their laughter to subside and to regain some semblance of control.

It was then that they noticed the strike force moving toward the Warrs gathered at the bottom of the hill. They must have been approaching during the rock throwing contest. The strike force had narrowed the gap across the open ground and was approaching the rear of the gathered Warrs. One of the Warriors also noticed the advancing strike force and screeched an alarm.

As instructed, # 7 remained behind as his strike force charged into the rear of the gathered attackers at the base of the hill. They watched from their vantage point as the battle progressed. There was no strategy, just force against force. Amy had hoped to split the force for two reasons. She wanted the opposing forces to remain relatively even to insure equal losses and also to separate the Los Angeles forces so they couldn't see what was happening to the colonies.

Before this unexpected conflict, her plan was to split the strike force before engaging this complex, which would work to even the combatants. Unfortunately, the equal losses thing wasn't happening now. The Los Angeles strike force currently had twice the Warrs of the Fresno colony and the losses were not equal. With the strike force doubling up on the already injured Fresno Warrs, the losses were disproportionate. The Fresno Warrs fell under the attack, but took only about half their numbers from the opposing side. Certainly they had defeated the Fresno Warrs, but still they were left with over a hundred Los Angeles Warrs to take the Stockton colony, too many. They were going to have Warrs left after the conflicts, which must be dealt with.

Watching the battle below wind down, he thought how disastrous this had almost been. If they could have teleported to... hmmmm. They didn't have to climb the damn hill. Amy could have just teleported them to another location. He blurted out,

"Amy, why the hell didn't you just transport us out of danger?" Ouch! He saw the cold stare in Amy's eyes and knew he had made a mistake even before hearing her speak.

Amy said, "If you're so damned smart, asshole, why didn't you suggest that when it would have done some good?"

He knew then that, just like him, she simply hadn't thought of it. It had been a mistake on her part, and he had just embarrassed her by pointing it out. He also knew she wasn't angry with him. She was mad at herself for not thinking of the easy and safest escape, but he had been very insensitive to her feelings. That was his mistake.

* Amy *

She had made a stupid mistake. She had set human limits upon herself where few existed. Levi had been perfectly right. She could easily have transported them to another location, even to the top of this hill if she had wanted. They were endangered by her inability to see the simple solution. This shook her confidence and angered her. Levi made the matters worse by being so critical, which angered her instantly. He could have been more sensitive to how she might feel. She was also mad thinking how Levi had influenced her speech with these colorful words like she had just called him, but asshole did seem like the right description to use. She smiled inwardly at her own joke, but was not ready to show Levi. Let the asshole simmer some.

As the battle ended, they began making their way back down the hill to greet # 7. The battle had, unfortunately, gone too well for their side and there remained over a hundred Warriors. She had hoped to keep the odds more even by splitting the strike force, but it couldn't be helped now.

She was a little surprised that the Warrs had no questions. They had to be curious why # 9 was here and where their army was now, but they said nothing. in reality, they appeared too frightened of Levi. Per her suggestions, Levi instructed # 7 to take # 8 and # 11 and proceed to the Stockton colony with the bulk of the Warrs to take that colony. Levi instructed # 9 to take ten Warrs, enter the Fresno complex and kill the remaining guards inside. He told # 7 that time was critical and to leave immediately. Levi said they would catch up before the strike force got there.

She knew # 7 liked Levi and was trustworthy, they all were, but Levi had saved # 7's life from the Sword Master back in the desert and knew # 7 possessed a more committed life to him. There was no hesitation as # 7 began screeching orders and the strike force was off again.

Ten Warrs had been picked by # 9 and were standing by waiting for orders. Those orders would not come until the strike force was out of sight, because these Warrs would be killed after any confrontation inside was over. The main strike force must assume that these ten Warrs would be leading the colony's females back to their Los Angeles colony. Actually she didn't know what to do with them. She only knew that the females of the colony could be used against the army in some way yet to

170

be determined. Without the females, the colony would die, so somehow these females would join the Technical Simians in a new colony. She was working on a plan.

* Levi *

He saw the conflict and doubt running through her thoughts, but he really wasn't criticizing, intentionally anyway. He was, however, curious and surprised, mainly because Amy didn't make many mistakes. Knowing it was the right thing to do, he wanted to apologize to Amy and try to explain that he wasn't being insensitive. Before he really got started, she interrupted.

Amy said, "No, it's not necessary; I understand. What you said and the way you said it just hit me wrong, that's all. You were right. I really should have thought of teleporting and was upset with myself. I made a critical error in judgment.

Levi said, "Hell, Amy, you can't think of everything, besides you saved us in another way that was more fun." He was starting to laugh again and saw Amy's stone expression begin to break apart. Soon they were both laughing hysterically again, remembering the comical confrontation. The others gave him a knowing look and met his smiles with those of their own. He had learned a valuable lesson though. Be quick to offer suggestions and slow to criticize.

The strike force was out of sight now, but they could not be expected to reach the Stockton colony for two days. They would have plenty of time to work with and help some of the other activities progressing. They really needed to hurry back to the Owens Valley and push the migrating tribe forward and out of immediate danger. So much had happened that it was hard to believe that they had only left Owens Valley this morning. Damn, they were jumping from one hot fire into another at a rapid pace, and now it was time for yet another.

They moved toward the colony with the Warrs out front. Amy expected there were still guards inside, certainly there were guards for the Techs and any humans that may still remain alive. She was right. As they entered through the main opening the Warrs were charged by twelve colony Warrs. They clashed together and fought viciously. The battle raged on as Warrs fell on both sides. The guards had a slight advantage in numbers, but almost weren't able to capitalize on it until one of the Los Angeles Warrs slipped in the blood and fell. His opponent leaped forward and killed the fallen Warr and quickly entered the break in the line and killed another from the rear. All the Los Angeles Warrs finally fell and the two remaining guards came forward to challenge them. Moon and # 9 stepped forward and killed them after only a brief skirmish.

They went through the complex releasing twenty-eight Technical Simians and eight human males. The humans were in total shock from their ordeal and having watched the battle between Simians. They were even more shocked to see him, a human commanding a Simian patrol. Levi told them they were being released and that they would be safe. He explained that these Simians were friends. He told them to stay close to him until the rules were laid out to the new Technical Simians.

That was a waste of words as they were already packed so close he could hardly move around.

Moon told him the Techs knew what was happening. They had heard of Levi and the Techs that ran with him. Moon said that they wished for freedom to join them and would pledge themselves to Levi and himself, slapping his own chest. He smiled at Moon telling him to let the Techs know they were welcome. He also instructed Moon to tell them the rules.

* Amy *

She was pleased to find living humans. There weren't many, only eight, but saving any was a victory. She was also pleased to liberate twenty-eight Techs. They were getting quite a following of the Technical race. It was a surprise to find out that these Techs had been expecting to be rescued. Word had spread about the movement. The Techs had received hope from the knowledge and were anxious to join them. This was good, and they certainly would be welcome as Levi had already acknowledged.

Continuing through the complex, they found the females in the center. There were forty-seven females and thirty children of various sizes. As they approached, two older Warrior children, almost grown, ran to attack. They were quickly struck down as they approached. It was probably best because they were too old to be turned, assuming it was possible at all for a Warr to deviate from its heredity. She did not think so. It was better this way.

The females did not seem frightened and said nothing. She had not been able to observe the females very long, even those at the desert community, and knew little about them. They remained together all the time and seemed to contribute little to the colony besides breeding, which was only every eighty days. She was sharing her thoughts with Levi as usual. She did not intentionally share her thoughts; it was more an open mind for him to look into, which he usually did. It was the same with her. The thoughts were originated by one, but shared by both. Levi responded to her thoughts and suggested that Dawn go to the desert camp and spend time with the Simian females there learning about them and allowing Dawn and subsequently her to observe. That was an excellent idea. She made the mental connection and amplified Levi's communication. He informed Dawn as to where Al was and assured her that he was safe and then proceeded to detail the mission he wished her to perform. Dawn readily agreed, as she was bored and anxious to have the opportunity to make a useful contribution.

The immediate problem was food. The colony would need food soon. After discussing the situation, Levi was about to call the Simians together when he again noticed the humans. Actually he couldn't miss them. They were practically leaning against him. They were still in shock and clinging to Levi for safety. He wanted to calm them so he sat them down together and told them again that they were safe. It seemed to help. He then told # 9 and # 3 to start the Simian females and children toward the mountains and follow the road up into the mountains, and he would move ahead of them and find food. They nodded and started herding them out of camp and toward the east.

The humans calmed once the Simians were out of sight. They began to relax and were soon talking. It had been a major trauma for them, as was to be expected. Their stories sounded like so many others she had heard. The Warrs had captured them in a sudden raid. The Simians had patrolled higher into the mountain than was customary and with larger patrols. The Warrs caught them off guard and killed many and captured around fifteen who were brought here. They watched helplessly as their mothers, wives, and daughters had been raped, butchered, and eaten in front of them. The torture continued on the long trip to the compound as they viewed the butchered carcasses being carried by the Simians. The horror and strain had been severe and some had lost their minds completely. Mercifully, those had been taken from the capture pen and eaten first, but that added to the stress for those that remained. She felt Levi's rage simmering as he listened to the atrocities, re-living his own memories. She was also infected by the common anger. The Warrs were without mercy or compassion, and more often than not, relished in punishing and torturing humans. She was very human in this moment, feeling the emotion of outrage and hate for the Warriors. Levi's knowing, tender look and mental touch said volumes without words.

* Levi *

Stories of the atrocities Simian Warriors inflicted upon humans always broke his heart. It was like again watching his mate being raped by those three Warrs so long ago. He could still see it in his mind as he watched them break her legs and arms and pull them from her screaming body. He saw it like it was just yesterday. The anger raged in him again as it always did. It was a very private thing to him as he remembered. It was different somehow this time. He suddenly realized that Amy shared his anger. She was remembering his experiences as if they were her own. He realized he was being selfish and self-centered with his hate and pain. It shocked him to realize that Amy was genuinely feeling the same pain. It was her pain too and he immediately felt sympathy for her and wanted to comfort her. Something changed permanently in their relationship in that moment. He didn't know how it was possible, but they had reached a new level of love in that instant. This was a level that his mind had withheld reaching.

Damn! Amy had really learned to hate the Warriors. Her passion for revenge was raging. She had always been the calming force, but she was in danger of losing control. That could never be. She had to be the solid one, the rock. Now he was calming her, what a role reversal. It was only momentary and she calmed quickly when he emotionally embraced her. Outwardly, no one noticed the internal exchange. She was fine now. Hell, maybe all she needed was a good hug. They both smiled, knowing there was more than just a little truth to that statement.

He continued talking to the humans, calming them. As he talked he noticed one of the men staring at him then lean over and whisper into the ear of the man next to him. The second man nodded to the first and they both stared at Levi. Levi finally asked, "What's wrong? The first man grinned and said that a man named Levi had visited their camp one night about a year ago. It was located in the foothills east of here. He said that three men from that camp had fought this Levi and lost. Then he asked if was that Levi. Levi grinned and said, "Yes! I remember your camp." The first man grinned back and said that he was one of the men that had lost. In spite of the situation, they both laughed.

You bet he remembered that camp. That is where he had the most embarrassing moment of his long life. This is the camp the beautiful blonde woman named Joan lived. He and Joan were both willing, but Amy was not. Amy refused to let him rise to the occasion, and he was humiliated beyond belief. He remembered how angry he had been at the time and how funny it seemed later. Nevertheless, he had vowed never to go back to that camp. Now he was returning. Amy was looking kind of sheepish and was grinning shyly until he said, "Shut up!" That got a hardy laugh instead.

It was time to get food into these people. He explained to them that he had powers to do many things and one of the things he was going to do was take them instantly to a spot closer to their camp. Amy said she could visualize any spot between her facility and here because they had traveled it and she had it recorded. They chose a spot along the trail, a spot easily found by the Techs. It would take the Techs several hours to reach the spot, which should give him plenty of time to find food.

The eight humans, Moon, and # 5 gathered together around him as Amy began gathering energy or whatever she did. Soon they were standing in the trail. The view changed, but the real difference was the temperature, which seemed to have dropped instantly by ten degrees. Well, that stood to reason since they were a thousand feet higher. The change in temperature felt good actually. The smell of pines also accented the difference. The humans couldn't believe their eyes, but the temperature and familiar smells of their home reinforced the information their eyes were telling them. They were home again and safe for the moment.

* Amy *

She hadn't been sure, but she thought she recognized one of the men. She thought he was one of the three men Levi fought when he visited the human camp during the Simian gathering. He had been heavier then, which altered his looks. When they confirmed this fact, both Levi and she thought of the same incident that occurred in Joan's tent. That was when she refused to let Levi have sex with that trollop. That was also when she first realized that she loved Levi, a moment she would never forget. Levi would never forget it either. They looked at each other and laughed.

According to the plan she had devised, Levi had already sent the Techs on toward the mountains. The Simians would have to be fed soon. They

178

should make the mountain trail by sunset, by which time she hoped to teleport ahead and have food gathered for them. Now was as good a time as any to convert them to beef. There was an abundance of cattle roaming the country. It was good that the Simian's ray had not affected cattle due to their lower intelligence. They had lived on and multiplied over the years. Unfortunately, Simians did not care much for cattle. Their first preference had always been horses, but horses had been all but eaten to extinction in the areas populated by Simians. Over time, humans had become the uniform staple food of choice. This would all change now, for these Simians at least.

The group of nine humans and two Simians gathered together. This was the largest group yet she had tried to teleport. The Simians represented much more mass, but mass was not the major problem. The hard part was maintaining the individual identities separated. The larger she spread her energy umbrella, the less control she had. Maybe in time she could master it. Actually she was sure she could, but she had discovered that the bigger the area, the more time it took. Additionally, problems were encountered at the far end, such as free open space into which to materialize. She hadn't bothered explaining it to Levi, but many calculations were required or someone might materialize in the air or over the edge of a cliff, inside a boulder or tree, or with their feet inside the earth. If one in the group moved, this also had to be taken into consideration. Her calculations were complex and she was not comfortable teleporting a larger group.

They materialized on the flat road at precisely the spot chosen from her stored memory and without incident. The humans were frightened but soon recovered when they saw where they were. This was only one more of a long line of miracles for them to witness. They began to celebrate being alive, free and almost home again. They couldn't believe their good fortune.

Levi, Moon, and # 5 waited patiently as the humans calmed. Soon the humans noticed them and gathered back around giving thanks and wanting to know what they could do to repay them. Levi knew her plan and explained that they needed to get what was left of their community together, prepare to evacuate and to bring a small herd of cattle immediately. He explained that the Technical Simians would be coming here by sunset and would need food. He explained that the freed Simians would never eat humans again, but would need food. The humans looked apprehensive, but not defiant. Levi explained that the Technical Simians would also be hiding from the Warrior Simians and would proceed on up into the mountains to a hidden valley, which Levi knew was near her facility. She would have to explain her plan to Levi soon, but the immediate problem was the humans and cattle. The humans disbursed to comply, saying they would bring cattle back and food for him as well. She laughed when Levi called after them saying, "Bring plenty."

* Levi *

180

He thought that went well. Telling the humans that the Technical Simians would be living nearby was a shock he knew, but they seemed to take it well. Maybe there was still a little shock or possibly they didn't see any choice. Certainly the latter was true, but he felt that he explained it as best as he could. Whatever the reason, the humans were off to do Amy's bidding and thankfully bring him some food. He wanted to stay here and get a campfire going for the Simians. A nap would be great too. He was both cold and tired. Even more, he was hungry. He hoped he would not have to wait long for the food.

Moon, # 5 and he gathered firewood, started a small fire and waited. Moon was pleased with the results of the raid, but wondered what Amy had in mind. Moon and # 5 had also reasoned that they were taking the Simian to the valley close to Amy's facility and voiced their concern with that action. They realized the importance of secrecy as well as he did. Levi chuckled at that and mentally looked at Amy for the answers.

As always, Amy's logic was flawless. What else were they going to do? Two Simian armies were east of them and the safest place was behind them. She intended to wait. If the armies returned to their respective complexes, this location was not in one of the Warrs chosen routes so therefore safe. The Warrs would return north and south of them. At that time the Techs could escape to the east over the mountains and have a clear path toward the desert community.

He could see her thoughts and spoke her words telling these things. What he didn't tell them was that Amy didn't believe the total Simian army would return. What she believed was, at best, the colony would send only a few back to get the females. That would be the case only if they were not successful in destroying the Owens Valley army and had to pursue them into the desert. Of course, Amy had no intention of letting the Owens Valley tribe fall to the Simian armies. She wanted Owens Valley evacuated before the Simian armies set their trap. Once they escaped, she believed that the armies would continue to follow. That was another reason she wanted the Simian complexes empty by the time any of the Warrs returned. No matter the course, the mountain valley was the ideal place to hide the females. The Stockton colony's females would also be brought here.

They were still resting and talking when the humans returned in numbers. They were bringing food for him and sheep for Moon and # 5. He had mentioned to the humans in conversation that the Simians were not all that fond of cattle, but sheep were more acceptable. Moon was pleased that he did not have to eat cattle. Moon and # 5 took two of the offered sheep and removed to the other side of the road to eat. For him they had brought a feast. He smelled pork, chicken, potatoes, and fresh baked bread among other delicacies. Yes indeed, he was happy with this.

While he was feasting, the humans told him that others were bringing up a small herd of cattle they had pastured in an upper valley. They informed Levi that as soon as the cattle were here they would be ready to go. "What?" They explained that their intention was to go with him. They said they had lived in fear all their lives and had never been able to live comfortably without worrying about Simian raids. Now they saw the opportunity for a better life for their children. Yes, they knew it was dangerous and would be a desperate fight and maybe death for them, but they were going and that was all there was to it. He looked around at the faces gathered and saw determination and defiance. They were going with or without his blessing.

It was not a large group, maybe, including those herding the cattle, fifty men, women and children. It was then that he noticed that they had brought everything they could carry. They had packs for everyone, water skins, pots and pans, weapons, food and miscellaneous other supplies. Yes, they were ready. Amy even commented that this group would not be refused. How could you refuse such obvious commitment?

* Amy *

These humans were determined to join their group and were not going to take no for an answer. Levi tried to tell them they were in a fight for their lives and it didn't look promising for them. He suggested that they might be better off trying to find a more remote and secure location to relocate to. The group had already discussed it and decided that surviving was not enough. They wanted life free from the constant fear and threat of Simian patrols. If there was going to be a confrontation, they wanted to be part of it. All or nothing is what they said.

183

The next part shocked her. The group had heard all about the battles in the desert and the death of Gord. They had already decided to join the struggle. Levi asked how they had heard of these things and was told that a Lancer Patrol had ventured into their area two nights ago and spent the night telling them all the stories and about the need for volunteers to fight Simians. She quickly calculated. Jimmy was one of the first Lancer patrols out, so for a Lancer patrol to be ahead of Jimmy it would have had to come over the mountain road from the Owens Valley on the same route Levi had taken the first time. That also meant that the Lancer Patrol had gone down into the middle of a Simian migration. She was fearful for them.

She never forgot anything and in many ways it was a curse, but in this case this fact had been pushed back and overlooked in the order of priorities. This group was right, the patrols had been sent out to spread the word and seek volunteers for the army. The idea of the patrols had been mostly to spread hope to the human race, but secondarily, recruits for the army were also needed. She had no idea just how necessary that had become. The problem was, they needed all the Lancers in the Owens Valley army right now to support the evacuation. Additionally, those solicited to join them would find a deserted Owens Valley unless they were so unlucky as to run into a Simian army. There had been six patrols sent out, and she wished she could recall them. She realized that her plans would have to be adjusted to protect groups such as this one. It was, after all, the goal to save as many humans as possible.

She communicated and shared information with Levi at length and with some discussion they agreed on an alternate plan. Instead of heading directly for the desert settlement, they would lead the Simian armies east toward Las Vegas and away from the desert settlement. Levi swore that he would never go into Death Valley again, but this was the only route east and the one that the tribe must take. By leading the Simians east, it would allow all those behind, like Jimmy's group, these, and others like them to go directly toward the Mojave Desert settlement. They knew that Al would get them organized and begin their training quickly.

This alternative plan had numerous benefits such as:

1. It would give the desert settlement more time to complete the construction of the new weapons, which was so desperately needed now.

2. Allow additional time for new recruits to reach them.

3. This would allow the females of the two Simian colonies to slip past the rear of the Simian armies and reach the Technical Simians in the desert settlement.

4. The slow units of the Owens Valley such as the old ones and some of the larger slower wagons could be hidden until after the Simian armies went through. At that point they could travel with Jimmy's group to the desert settlement.

5. For what it was worth, the human armies, Technical Simian, and most of the Simian females would be consolidated.

There were numerous smaller benefits associated with this plan, but they would have to

185

teleport to Iron Eyes' location soon to share the plan with them. His tribe would have to be the bait to keep the Simians away from the desert settlement. The Owens Valley Tribe would be in great danger, but the delay they provided would save many lives. They knew the tribe would accept the risks, and with only escape routes east, they probably wouldn't really have a choice anyway.

* Levi *

Amy calculated that the Simian army at the north end of the valley would wait at least another day. Any coordinated plan by the Simians would have required adequate time for the southern Fresno Simian army to get into position. That would require another two days, but the northern Stockton Simian army could theoretically launch before then, which would drive the humans into the southern army and trap. They intended to foil the Simians' plans, however. The Owens Valley Tribe would be out of the trap by tomorrow evening. He and Amy would have to go to Iron Eyes as soon as the Techs, females, and children arrived and were settled, and the Techs understood the plan. Damn, it was getting complicated. He wished they had one of the communications team here.

He was so tired. It had been a very long day. It was hard to believe that it had only been one day since they left Owens Valley. So damned much had happened and so many demands were falling on him and Amy. They needed help. He commented they really needed Fred here. He was thinking Fred, although he didn't like it, was used to being with

186

Simians, knew the sign language to relay their instruction to the Simians, plus would be needed to instruct the humans. Amy agreed Fred was the best and only choice they had. She said Jimmy was with the group of humans making their way over the mountains to the south and she could monitor through him, freeing Fred to be brought here. Knowing how frightened Fred was of Simians, brought knew grins to both Amy and him.

He was about to suggest that they go get Fred, but he had finally finished the fine meal that had been brought to him and was getting so sleepy. Bone tired, he couldn't bring himself to do anything more. He wanted to sleep and if he went there he would need to be up talking much longer, plus he needed to be here when the Simians came in, which should be soon. In frustration he said, "Amy, you go get him." He chuckled initially then he looked hard at Amy to see her reaction. She verified his realization that Amy really didn't need Levi to teleport Fred. She could see through Fred's eyes and actually all she needed was this reference point. What she could not do was talk to Fred. This one-way communication to Fred required Levi's mind to direct. She only amplified his minute telepathic signal to those she had a link with. Was this going to work? He spoke to Fred and told him to say his goodbyes and stand away from the group. Fred wasn't bashful anymore.

Fred said, "Kiss my ass!"

Even though Fred was angry he did what he was instructed. He enjoyed having some sport with Fred. Fred's strength was in his ability to stay in spite of his fear.

* Amy *

Levi did it again. He challenged her to expand. Her first reaction was Levi was accurate. He was wrong, however, in that her ability to teleport was directed through his mind and body. He was the channel for her. The only one that was able to link with her. When she developed her telekinesis, it was her energy, which she learned to channel through Levi. She knew she could channel it directly from her, but it was a matter of reference. If she could channel through Levi, she could focus her energy through Levi's reference of a short distance. Trying to focus directly from her mind, she would have to direct the energy great distances. The greater the distance, the more exaggerated the movement. A small reference angle of her directed energy could make great changes at the far end. It would be like a flash light beam. At short distances a small angle change in the flashlight moves the beam only feet, but at longer distances the beam of light could move hundreds of feet. This was the phenomenon she was dealing with.

She believed she could do it this time, because Fred was relatively close to her physical location and the focused angle deviation would be slight. It was complicated and didn't try to explain in depth to Levi, but he understood the concept.

She built the reference points into her mind and reached out as if testing to see the focus of her energy. It appeared as an aura around Fred, visible only to her through the eyes of Fred and Levi. It appeared jerky at first as she moved it, but eventually became more fluid. She fixed the energy around Fred and fixed an aura about fifty feet ahead of Levi. She let the energy flow back to her, bringing Fred and rooted to the spot chosen, depositing Fred. It wasn't as smooth as the other way, but Fred was here now and cursing Levi. They put Fred through much, and he was still here and hadn't gone insane from the stress. They were gaining a real fondness for Fred.

Fred lost his hostility when he smelled the food and sat down and dug into the leftovers. Moon listened as Fred ate. Moon was incapable of human speech, but had long since begun to understand it. Levi was explaining the changes and what he wanted Fred to do. The instruction went on for many minutes, but Levi finally fell asleep and continued to sleep, as the Simians arrived at camp. Fred met them and delivered the cattle and a few sheep for their needs. Fred and Moon passed on the information to both the Simians and the humans.

Tomorrow they would execute the escape plans.

CHAPTER 5
(ESCAPE OR HERDED)

* Amy *

Before going to sleep, Levi contacted Jimmy. It was necessary to slow his progress. Amy had originally wanted Jimmy to branch off from the group and head for Owens Valley so he would be her monitoring point for the group, but with the change in plans, it was no longer necessary. Levi would now be with the diversion for the escape of the Owens Valley Tribe, which he described to Jimmy. Jimmy was now to stay with the group and delay coming down out of the mountains until the San Diego Simian army had passed into the Owens Valley and past his position. Jimmy and Al were then to proceed to Barstow and wait for the Los Angeles colony females being led by # 1, # 2, and # 4. Additionally, he was to wait for the wagon train from Owens Valley, the Amy's valley group of humans and Simian females, plus any other groups trying to join them as a result of the Lancers' contact. Jimmy was a smart kid and understood.

She was pleased with the communication links they had developed. Not only beneficial in battle, it was extremely helpful in keeping up with the various groups. Even more communicators would be nice, but the stress of monitoring three additional people besides Levi was taxing. She wished she could turn it off, but it was impossible as long as those individuals lived. The only time she was completely without their inputs was when they were teleporting or astral projecting. Sometimes she longed for silence from them. It was almost as bad as the fifty years of sensory deprivation she experienced prior to finding Levi, but not quite. So far she was able to push that constant information so low in priority it effectively diminished the input, but was never quite gone. She linked with Dawn, Fred, and Jimmy, and didn't regret it, she just didn't want more. It had been necessary to download the hand signing information to both Fred and Jimmy, and in doing so, linked her permanently. Dawn had been quite another story. It was accidental linking with her to share the pleasures of sex with both Levi and Dawn. She smiled remembering.

As Levi slept soundly through the night and she repaired his body, she remembered these things and planned. Besides Levi, she could download additional information or knowledge to Dawn, Fred and Jimmy, but no other humans without linking. She could, however, download information to a Technical Simian without linking, as proven by downloading fighting skills to Moon. The Simian mind was so alien to her mind, linking was impossible. She concluded that, other than linking with those three humans, she would only be able to transfer technical information necessary to maintain her facility to Simians. The human communication network was needed on the battlefield; therefore her only choice for that role would be Simians. The problem: she needed all the Techs in battle also. This was a dilemma that must be solved sooner or later.

Levi's day had been a busy and tiring one and tomorrow threatened to be just as bad. After he ate and talked to Fred, he fell asleep. He remained asleep even when the Techs, females, and young from the Fresno colony arrived. Moon and Fred met them instead and instructed them where to camp, while cattle were delivered for the Simians to feast upon. The humans were uneasy but reassured by Fred that everything was going to be fine. Through it all, Levi slept. She was amazed that he could, with all the noise, but he did. She was proud of Moon and Fred and pleased that Levi allowed himself to sleep and delegate the responsibilities to others. Possibly he had no choice, but she knew Levi's will power and he never would have allowed himself to sleep had he not trusted Moon and Fred. So Levi slept and she repaired and planned.

* Levi *

He woke slowly, which was unusual. Amy always had his body awake even before he consciously woke but not today. She said he needed the rest and smiled at him. Damn, what a wonderful sight to wake up to. Amy knew all his faults, few as they were, and loved him in spite of them. His playful thought was rewarded with a "Butthead." His mind registered that the sun was high in the sky, and the encampment was running amok with activities and arguments. He better get used to it though, with consolidation of all the different groups and now alien races. What a mess. He was surprised that no one had awakened him until he saw Moon standing guard. He chuckled at that.

As his mind cleared, he re-established in his mind the chess pieces in the complex game of war

192

they were playing. The humans were here and the Simians were here also. He heard the sounds of the separate groups and smelled the distinct musky sweet scent of many Simians in addition to the rich scent of cattle. He knew all was in order, even as Amy confirmed it. He remembered telling Jimmy the change in plans and his group was now in position above the southern end of Owens Valley. If all was as scheduled, the migration of the LA Simian females would be on track well behind the San Diego Simian army. This group of Techs, Simian females, and humans was ready to move, but there was no hurry, because they had to wait in Amy's valley, on up the mountain, until the Stockton Simian army followed the Owens Valley Tribe into Death Valley. It was time to go to Iron Eyes and move the next chess piece into place.

Sniffing, he smelled frying bacon. That got his attention and he sat up asking Moon why he had let him sleep. Moon had a sheepish grin on his inner lips exposing his toothy mouth as he leaned forward to mask his speech. Levi thought how comical it looked to see Moon grin. It made him think of what a shark might look like, that is if it had black teeth and was gold. Moon screeched a whisper that only a few hundred people could have heard if they were listening. He said Amy told him, just as she had spoken back in the cave, "Let you sleep." He was shocked at first, until he noticed Amy's grin. Well, Moon was now one of the few that she could talk to so no harm done. He sure felt good. He reached for Moon's hand for a help-up. It was like grabbing a moving tree trunk in a flood, as he was jerked to his feet. Slapping Moon on the back, his eyes searched

193

for the cooking area. He said they would be leaving soon and to prepare.

It was mid-morning by the time he gathered Moon and # 5 to teleport to Owens Valley. The other Techs also wanted to go, but Amy wanted # 9 and # 13 to stay with the recently released Techs and the Simian females. They were far too new to be unsupervised, even though they seemed more prepared than any released so far. Fred would be the liaison between the races for the time being.

Amy took them to the same spot chosen from memory at the north camp where she believed Iron Eyes would be located. The camp was all but deserted; only a few Lancers came to greet them. They said Iron Eyes was leading the tribe south. Sentries had spotted the Stockton army on the move early this morning, and Iron Eyes moved the Tribe out only a few hours ago. Oh shit, they had waited too long. The plan was coming apart. If the Tribe had gone too far beyond the first valley exit, they would have to make a dash for the far end of the valley and hope to make their escape through the only other route ahead of the San Diego Simian army. He told the Lancers to gather everyone remaining and follow their trail. He explained the situation to Moon and # 5, and they took off jogging at a fast pace designed to cover miles, while the Lancers scrambled to catch up.

* Amy *

As Levi said, they had indeed waited too long. She had made another tactical error. There were so many things that could have been done. They could

194

have come last night. She should have at least sent Fred so she could communicate with Iron Eyes. The trap was springing and time was running out. Levi acted as if this wasn't serious, but she knew he was concerned. Was he worried about her? Was she showing stress? YES! But, was it that obvious? Levi tried to calm her, telling her to analyze the situation and learn the exact nature of the problem. He was right of course, and she forced her mind back into focus. Why did she have to be burdened with emotions? It was so much simpler before, but then she would have never experienced love. Too bad all the other garbage came with it.

What were the facts? The Lancers said their scouts had seen the Stockton Simian army on the move. Fact: The scouts were positioned to observe from an estimated five miles distance. Fact: It would take the riders three hours to reach the northern camp where Iron Eyes had been. That meant that the Simian army was probably eight hours behind them. Yes, she was focusing again and continued calculating and projecting time tables, distances and rates of travel, until she began to see the events playing out in her mind. She subdued her panic and saw a plan.

She accepted the fact that they were committed to the southern escape route because the initial escape route she planned was now cut off. She had hoped to exit the valley via old Highway 168 through mountain passes that could have delayed the enemy. Now they would have to exit the valley through Highway 190. This was the route Levi had traveled as an old man coming to Owens Valley. Unfortunately, this route was not as easily defended.

In fact it would be dangerously exposed to attacks from the San Diego Simian army since they would have to race them to the mountain pass. Once there, assuming they beat the Simian army through the pass, they could hold them off there, while the Tribe continued through Death Valley. They could continue to retreat and hold each mountain pass as the bulk retreated to the next.

She needed better intelligence data, especially from Jimmy. She needed to track the San Diego Simian army. They would be the critical link. They must reach the highway before the San Diego Simian army. Levi spoke to Jimmy, directing him to a position to observe the army as they passed. Amy's internal topographical maps provided the exact spot she wanted Jimmy to reach. From that point he would be able to see directly down the valley and able to observe both armies at the critical spots. Al refused to be left out and insisted on going with Jimmy.

She already learned from her previous mistake. They didn't have to chase after Iron Eyes like they were doing; they would simply teleport. She laughed at Levi's reaction at that thought. His startled reaction indicated that he also had forgotten the possibility of teleporting. Intuitively, she realized that Levi was more ingrained in her thoughts than he let on.

* Levi *

He sensed her confusion and stress and was puzzled by it. Amy was always so strong mentally. Why was she now stressed and confused? He

196

looked into her thoughts, many of which he could see. They were not the logical progression of calculation or recognizable emotions. There were emotions for sure, but he could not identify them. Was it anger, rage, confusion, or a combination? Could it possibly be something else entirely? She seemed at the point of weeping for no apparent reason. He sensed that Amy didn't even know. She was edgy, irritable, and ... female! She didn't make any sense and he didn't see anything to fix. He wanted to embrace her, but there was a feeling like you get when approaching a stray cat. You really don't know if it will let you pet it or eat you. He decided to withdraw and wait. Damn, he remembered his mates had acted like this sometimes, and wait was all you could do; leave them the hell alone until they wanted you.

As they jogged he was deep in his thoughts when Amy startled him. He continued listening to her thoughts, at least those that seemed rational, when she almost blurted out "Teleport." Hell yes, they could teleport. Damn, he was stupid, but he wasn't about to call Amy stupid, even though she was saying that about herself. He was honestly surprised that they (he) could make the same mistake twice. It was not to be dwelled on now.

He called the runners and Lancers to a halt, quickly telling the six Lancers and scouts to continue at a hard pace to catch up to the Tribe, explaining that his party was going on ahead. Moon and # 5 understood, but the Lancers were a little slower. Once the Lancers realized the meaning, they seemed frightened to think about the use of, what they considered magic. However, the Lancers were soon riding hard, not sure if they just following instruction or escaping the magic. Moon, # 5, and himself stood close, waiting for the glimmering air to take them, quite literally, to a spot two hundred feet ahead of where Iron Eyes led the Tribe on their march.

Iron Eyes was obviously relieved to see them and came running up. He wasted no time telling Iron Eyes the situation and the plan. Iron Eyes was upset at his inadvertent tactical error, but there was no way of knowing any different. They just hadn't expected the Stockton Simian army to start this soon. Nothing could be done about it now. Iron Eyes was pleased with the new plan to hide the slower parts of the migration such as the heavy wagons. While talking to Iron Eyes, he noticed the Owens Valley Tribe had not been idle and had completed the fabrication of many heavily loaded wagons stacked high with lances. This was a fantastic stroke of luck, but the wagons were slow. Iron Eyes ordered the lance wagons, the other heavily laden wagons, and most of the herd of cattle and sheep hidden. The drivers were instructed to take the horses into the mountain valleys and hide. The elderly and those that would slow the travel time were also sent into the mountains. All were to wait until the humans and Simians from Amy's valley were brought down. Notification to proceed would be sent through Fred. At that time all would then move on toward Barstow to meet the various other groups converging at that point. At the right time the combined groups would travel to the Mojave Desert settlement.

Since time was critical, they did not waste any more and continued the retreat toward the last and only escape route. It was well over a day's travel to reach the mountain pass, so this Tribe would not see rest until well into the night. They must not be caught in the trap.

* Amy *

The diversion of activity helped calm her confusion. Was it confusion? Hell she didn't know. She was well aware that something was not right. She was functioning on so many levels, carrying out analyses, continuing research and planning their escape and defense, but one portion of her mind kept worrying. She was worrying about everything, even trivial stuff. She was full of self-doubt, frustration, even rage. One moment she wanted to lash out and the next she wanted to weep and had no idea why. She knew it was emotions and hated them.

Levi felt her struggle to maintain and wanted to reach out, embrace her, love her, but was wise enough to remain distant. She would have welcomed his embrace, but at the same time would have radiated her seething anger. At what she had no idea. She quickly blocked those thoughts from Levi. She then had to laugh. Why had Levi referred to her as FEMALE?

At last, something to do. When they materialized in front of Iron Eyes, her attention was focused. Iron Eyes' position with the Tribe was obviously elevated. He had been one of three war leaders of the Tribe, but due to his close association with Levi, he was more elevated than previously. He was not chief, but the Chief listened and allowed Iron Eyes more authority. Levi unfolded the plan as she presented it. The instructions were processed professionally and quickly. The wisdom was obvious and they wasted no additional precious moments.

With the slower elements gone, the migration picked up speed. They would need the additional time to reach the pass. Soon, Jimmy would be in place, and she would have accurate information as to the location of the San Diego Simian army. Without that information her best estimate could be off just enough to spell victory, or defeat. One thing in their favor, timing indicated it would be dark by the time the two converging groups got within possible sight of each other. This might make the difference if Iron Eyes' group could travel at night and make the exit across open ground to the mountain pass without being seen. A mountain ridge en route would force the humans out into the open long before she wanted to and would funnel them toward the Simians for several miles before they could break east toward the pass. If they were seen or heard early enough, the San Diego Simian army would be able to intercept them, and it would be all over for the humans.

Jimmy and Al reached the vantage point she requested, and the view was precisely what she wanted. She knew it would be exactly what was needed, because she had all the geodetic survey maps and the associated elevations and X/Y axis locations of the mountain peaks. It was, however, comforting to see that the view was perfect. She opened the sensory input from Jimmy to Levi and they viewed the valley and countryside in both directions. To the far north they could see straight down the Owens Valley nestled between the Sierra and the Inyo mountains. They could not yet see the Owens Valley Tribe due to the distance. Closer, she could see the dry Owens lakebed between Highways 395 and 190. The mountain pass on Highway 190 was not visible from Jimmy's location, but she could see the area almost all the way to it.

Closer still was Haiwee Reservoir. This is where she believed, hoped, the San Diego Simian army would camp. Normally, there would be no question, since this was a main and plentiful water source. Unfortunately, water was plentiful in the Owens Valley and it was possible that the San Diego Simian army might not stop at Haiwee Reservoir. Fortunately, she projected that it would be dark by the time that Simian army reached the lake. At the worst point, the Tribe would be passing within five miles of the lake on their route to the Inyo Mountains pass. It was going to be close and dangerous.

As Jimmy turned to survey toward the south, she shuddered to see the Simian army almost directly below. Actually, they were fairly close to the predicted location. It became a matter of perspective, and this height made it look different. The Simian army was only slightly ahead of her predictions and should make little difference, as long as they camped at the lake.

There was nothing to do but wait. The day would pass slowly for the travelers; however, Levi had other places to be and it was time to re-join # 7 to liberate the Stockton Simian colony.

* Levi *

She was focused once again and sharing thoughts concerning the views coming from Jimmy. He now had a good idea in his mind how the terrain looked and the general locations of the roads and anticipated location of the Simian camp. He too had viewed the topography maps, but seeing it like this gave him a better perspective. It would be dangerous. They must travel exposed through many miles of open ground. He would be thankful for night. He asked Amy about the moon tonight. She said the moon would be out. Not quite full, but moderately bright. There would be sufficient light for the Simians to see. He had hoped for a dark night to take advantage of the Simians' poor night vision, but they would do the best they could without that advantage.

The Simian army was organized and impressive, spread out in a wave across the narrowing flat terrain. Nothing would get past them on the valley floor. The trap was closing, but not until tomorrow.

Amy estimated the Tribe had another seven hours traveling time before they would have to commit to open ground. That should be about an hour after dark. That was good.

Amy said, "There is nothing more we can do right now and it is about time for # 7 and his strike force to be at the Stockton colony. We need to go."

202

The timing, for once, was not critical, because he had instructed # 7 to wait until his return before moving on the complex. However, the timing was good for them to leave now. There was no sense spending the time running when there was something else that could be done. He nodded and said, "Okay, hon. Let's go."

Without stopping, he moved next to Iron Eyes and explained the situation and how critical it was to maintain a low level of dust and noise as they approached the valley highway exit. He, Moon, and # 5 were leaving and would re-join Iron Eyes as soon as possible. He cautioned that the party should only go into the open cautiously if he had not returned by then. Iron Eyes understood. By nature Iron Eyes was a cautious man, and those he led would be fine.

Next, he moved to Moon and # 5 signaling them to the side and away from the others. He quickly brought them up to speed with the current situation, the timing, the night approach to the mountain pass, and the approaching San Diego Simian army. They looked grave, but resolved. He then told them that it was time to join # 7 and the Sacramento complex. Moon seemed anxious for that. He assumed the Stockton Simian colony represented the only remaining Simian stronghold they knew of in California. It seemed like they were making headway, even though the Simian armies were chasing them in force, attempting to wipe them from the face of the Earth. The Simians have never understood that Earth is ours and we don't die easily.

They gathered as Amy spun her magic. He knew it was science not magic, but it seemed more acceptable and exciting to refer to it in mystical terms. Actually, to him it was magic because he didn't understand any of it. All he knew was that in just a few seconds they would be miles from here standing and looking at different scenery. Then, that is what happened. They were standing in the spot where he and Amy had first observed the Stockton Simian complex. There it was below and to the west about three miles.

This time, they had instructed # 7 precisely where to wait for them. There wouldn't be a repeat of the confusion at the Fresno complex. They rendezvous on the back side of this small mountain were they currently stood. As they descended the backside, they saw the small Simian army gathered below. He greeted # 7 but looked stern as he stared at the Los Angles Warriors. He must maintain the fear. Moon and # 5 spread out to demonstrate their lack of concern or respect for the Warrs. There was no need to delay this further and gave orders to attack the complex and kill the Warriors.

* Amy *

After passing on the instructions to Iron Eyes, Levi, Moon, and # 5 moved to the side as she prepared for teleporting. Although easier each time, it still required time to gather energy from around her. This would never be something she could do instantly. She didn't totally understand how she was able to do it. It was a product of mental energy manifested in a physical form. She had tried to

204

explain it to Levi many times, but it was something Levi would never understand. She thought about where she wanted to transport the mass she enveloped within the gathering energy and let it flow to the other location. Before teleporting she would gather a great amount of energy from the surrounding air, earth, trees, anything, living or dead. Those within the umbrella remained untouched, however. That mass was the focus of the energy. She knew the energy was powerful and transcended time and space to make the transfer possible. As she visualized these thoughts, Levi's interest perked. She realized he saw something in those thoughts that she did not and idly wondered what it was, as she began the teleport process.

The strike force was precisely where she anticipated. As expected, the Warriors were agitated at the sight of Levi and seemed anxious to do his bidding, and quickly, if it meant getting away from him. There was no purpose in delaying, so Levi ordered the attack.

The Warrs did not delay, but charged around the very rocks screening them from sight and on toward the complex. The battle screeches echoed off the mountain. The line of some one hundred and ten Warrs was disorganized as they ran. The challenging screeches were returned from within the complex, but those Warrs did not come pouring out. They were taking a defensive position at the openings. This was new. This defensive tactic would reduce the defenders' losses, but this might work to their advantage since the strike force most likely outnumbered the defenders.

Levi and his small group followed behind the attacking strike force as the Warrs clashed with those defenders at the opening. The fighting was fierce. Warrs were falling on both sides and were being dragged back allowing room for others to assume the position of the fallen, and both sides continued to dwindle. You had to admit, the Warrs were committed to the task as they continued to drive forward. Suddenly, there was a break in the line as the defenders crumbled in and the Los Angeles Warrs flooded over the break and fallen Simians. The battle then disappeared within the walls.

Levi and his group passed inside to observe the battle. The Warrs continued to clash in vicious rage and fell. The Los Angeles Warrs were winning and the prisoner guards inside came to join the battle. The four of them continued to walk into the camp oblivious to the raging battle around them. They went to the Technical Simians' stockade and opened the gates. The relief was apparent on the Techs' faces. These Techs had apparently heard of the human Levi and his Technical Simian partner. They came flooding out screeching their gratitude and talking to both Levi and Moon. The Tech prisoners now rescued were theirs to command.

She counted only ten Techs. This was the smallest group liberated to date. While she was pondering the situation, Moon ordered the Techs to pick up the swords from the fallen and kill Warriors. She was shocked, but realized what he was doing. There were only four Warriors left and three of them were from the strike force. Moon evidently wished to see just how dedicated the new recruits were. Without hesitation, the ten Techs ran to pick up swords. She knew they had little training, but the odds were ten to four. Now the odds were ten to three as the last Stockton Warr fell. Before the Warriors knew what was happening, the Techs fell upon them inflicting wounds from behind. The Warrs turned and engaged the Techs, but they were exhausted, outnumbered and wounded. Even so, the Warrs held their own against the inexperienced Techs for many minutes before falling to the overwhelming strikes. Finally it ended.

The ten Techs had fought and now turned with pride to face Moon and Levi. She sought to discover any hostile emotions emanating from the Techs, but detected nothing but calm pride in their accomplishment and wellbeing toward Moon and Levi. So now they had ten new recruits for Moon's swelling Simian Army.

* Levi *

Amy said something very profound when discussing the process of teleporting. Well, actually, it was her thoughts. Seldom did they use words to communicate anymore. Words were slow and cumbersome in comparison. As Amy described the process he saw the gathering of power. As it was described, it was a great deal of power that was gathered. He saw it as a potential for explosion. If you gather that much power how was it that there was no explosion or release of this power? She explained that it was a slow transfer of power. The power at one end was replacing power gathered at the other end. It was an equal transfer, therefore no build-up of power to be released. This had piqued his interest and knew it would occupy his mind for a long time. There was something else here that he must discover.

The battle at the complex lasted almost an hour. At the end Moon had ordered the ten rescued Techs to kill the last three remaining Warrs. He was glad Moon was his friend, because that alien mind could be vicious when he wanted it to be. Hell, almost as mean as him. He liked that idea and had to laugh at the thought. Their action showed dedication on the part of the Techs. If the Techs all fought together, they could become an awesome force.

He then turned and began walking through the complex and was surprised to hear his name being called. What the hell? It took him a minute to locate the direction of the voice. He finally located the source and jumped with both shock and surprise. Coming toward him was Johnny, the mate of one of Iron Eyes' daughters. Johnny was followed by eight humans clinging as if to his shadow. The humans could not believe that Johnny was so bravely walking toward the Simians. Johnny happily ran to embrace him. He even turned and embraced Moon also. Moon was also pleased to see him. Johnny was one of the first humans that made Moon laugh by dangling from a lance fifteen feet in the air during their first practice. He, too, often thought of those early learning days when the tribe was trying to become Lancers.

The eight humans huddled together in fear, but expressing new found hope at seeing Johnny, their friend, embrace a Simian and not being eaten.

"Johnny," he asked, "how in the world did you wind up here?" Johnny's face took on a sad look as he told of an encounter in the hills. He and his Lancers had gone out from Owens Valley over the pass to spread the word. Many of the teams had done likewise. His team had encountered a small tribe in the hills, some of which were here as he indicated to the eight other humans. They hadn't been with them long before a seven-Simian team had attacked them. He and his Lancers had been able to kill one Warrior before they were overpowered. The other two Lancers with him were killed in the charge, and he had narrowly missed the same fate. He would have been killed immediately except for the horse. The other two mounts ran away when the Lancers were unhorsed by the Warriors' swords, but his horse had been mortally wounded and fell. That is what saved his life. The Warrs had killed the other two Lancers immediately, but when he fell they went after the horse. He had been tied, while the Warriors fed on the fallen horse, then he and the others were led back to this complex. The story was always the same. There had been fifteen males captured and four females, but the females were raped and killed on the way back to the colony. Also, seven of the men had been eaten during the few days they had been captured. Levi often wondered why the Warriors did not have sex with the Simian females. Maybe Amy would know their secrets through her research soon.

Johnny had been around the Technical Simians a long time now and understood much of the language, and from communications between the guards, he learned that Levi and Moon were here. The Warrs were afraid and kept screeching "Little Demon." That was the closest interpretation he could make. That made Levi smile and Amy's eyes sparkle with humor.

Johnny said, "We heard the battle raging and when our guards left to join the battle, we knew they were losing. As soon as the guards were out of sight we humans broke down the fence to our cage to come find you."

* Amy *

She was so very happy to see Johnny coming toward them. Johnny had been one of their first Lancers from the original training. Johnny had been prominent in the training of the Mojave Desert Lancers as well. Iron Eyes had lost too many of his family, as she sadly remembered his son Wolf who had given his life in a raging battle with the Simians. He had been a brave young man and had saved many fellow Lancers in the process. Seeing Johnny now was pleasing, and she was happy for Iron Eyes as well.

It had been Johnny who came over the mountain to spread the word to the Amy's valley people, as Levi was calling them now. They did not remember his name, only that it was Lancers. Unfortunately, they had been discovered in the hills south of the colony and Johnny had been captured. He had been very lucky. She shuddered to think just how lucky. Normally the area Johnny surveyed was safe, but the mobilization of the Simian armies had changed everything.

210

Continuing through the complex, they found the females and children in the center area. She counted fifty females of varying ages and twenty-two young. The females were cautious, but unafraid. What was the mystery involving these females? Why were they unafraid? Why did they seem so remote from the activities of the colony? She resolved to direct her delayed research in finding out these mysteries.

It was now back to logistics. What to do with the females and young was now the question. There was no choice. They must be taken to join with the Simian females from the Fresno colony. It would be a couple of days travel for this latest assembly, but the gathered group, currently in her valley, was not yet in a hurry. There was just too much going on down below them on the other side of the mountain. Hopefully, it would all work out.

Levi initiated the plan. The humans, except for Johnny, would travel with the Simian females and young. The group would be led by # 7 and # 5 to her valley, who would indoctrinate the Simians en route. There were only two rules. You don't eat humans, and you war with any Simian that does. That shouldn't take long to learn, but they would have to hurry before they got hungry. Once they reached Amy's valley the humans of the group should be happy to join with the humans there.

Accessing the growing groups, they broke down to the following: In just a few days they had already liberated thirty-eight Technical Simians. They had only saved sixteen humans from the Simian complexes but had gained numbers from the various human settlements. All together the humans numbered one hundred and thirty new members to the Human/Techs army. There were fifty-five men, forty-three women, thirty-two children, and now eight more men. This was becoming a major responsibility for her, and it was worrisome. Hell, everything was beginning to worry her and she wished she knew what was causing it.

It helped to focus on things that needed to be done, and there were plenty of things to do right now. It was getting late and it would be sundown soon. It was time to turn their attention to the Owens Valley Tribe.

* Levi *

The Stockton colony was much like the Fresno colony. The Simian females and young followed Moon's instruction without fear or hesitation. According to Amy's plan, these liberated Simians would join those from the Fresno colony near her valley and travel with them to meet in Barstow with those coming from the Los Angeles colony. Damn, that had to be over one hundred and fifty Simian females.

Amy said, "It is actually one hundred and sixty-two females and eighty-seven young."

He was annoyed with the injection of exact number. Hell, who cares...it's a lot. His thought continued. The Los Angeles group was bringing their small cattle herd, but would it be enough for all these Simians. Amy reminded him that both Bob and Jimmy's groups were bringing cattle also. "Yeah, I forgot." Maybe it would work out after all.

212

He saw her grin at him even through the agony he felt in her. He wished he could help her somehow.

He worried about the humans that would be traveling with the Simians, but Johnny had been telling them how they would be safe with the Technical Simians. Johnny would be with the humans which should give them some confidence of safety. They knew they were going to meet other humans and join the combined defense against the Warrior Simians. They were also free to go, but where were they going to go? Actually, they were safer now than they had ever been, but they could go home, wherever that was. After second thought he gave them the option. Some of the humans looked at each other and opted to find their home if it still existed. He wished them well and told them where they would be if they changed their mind, and he thought they might, but it didn't really matter.

Amy said it was time to go. He looked at the sun setting in the west and realized that time was indeed short. They needed to re-join Iron Eyes. Amy commented that it served no purpose to travel with them. She said they could best help Iron Eyes and the Owens Valley Tribe by securing the mountain pass and observing the drama as it unfolded. He wondered what drama? There weren't enough Lancers to do any damage if there was a battle. He assumed that she meant the drama of sneaking past the Simians.

At the mention of the Simians, Amy opened the input from Jimmy. The Simians were approaching the lake, but they were continuing to move north. The lake was several miles long so it wasn't yet time to panic. The timing, according to Amy, was approximately correct as predicted. He wished it was a little darker which might ensure that camp would be set at the lake. As they watched, the view changed to the northern end of the valley. Fred had reached his assigned vantage point and was observing the Simian army pass by. Actually they had passed long ago and he was seeing them in the far distance. Fred was instructed to keep the assembly in the mountains until any straggling Simian patrols had passed. Additionally, they were to wait for the Techs coming from the Stockton colony. It would be necessary for them to remain there for an additional two days minimum.

They could wait no longer and called Moon. Grinning, he said out loud, "Well, it is back to just the Lone Ranger and Tonto again." Even Moon smiled at that. Damn, Moon was learning the English language well. With Moon standing close, Amy was beginning her process to teleport them to the pass, but he asked her to take them instead to Iron Eyes so they could pick up the riflemen. He said there might be danger in holding the pass, and what better way to hold it then with the riflemen. There were only five rifles with the special gunpowder Amy concocted and five humans could be teleported easily. Amy agreed.

She could see Iron Eyes' column of Lancers from Jimmy's elevated position, so she knew approximately where he was. They materialized a few hundred feet from Iron Eyes and waited for him to reach them. He quickly told Iron Eyes what he needed and Iron Eyes sent runners to fetch the riflemen. Iron Eyes had the column spread out long and hugging the mountain ridge, much to Amy's satisfaction. They had gone about as far as they could without running the risk of being seen by the Simians. They would have to stop now until the sun set and it was as dark as it could get.

* Amy *

From Fred and Jimmy's perspectives she knew the exact location of both the Owens Valley Tribe and the San Diego Simian army. The Simians were stopping now a little past where she had hoped but still near the northern end of the lake, while the Tribe was waiting patiently for night to cover their passage across the open ground toward the mountain pass.

She saw no need for Levi to travel with the tribe and intended to go directly to the mountain pass, but Levi suggested that they stop by Iron Eyes' location and take the riflemen with them. That was a good idea. It would give the riflemen time to dig in and find the best locations from which to defend the pass.

They materialized just ahead of Iron Eyes and waited as he approached. As time was short, Levi quickly explained what they were doing. Iron Eyes immediately sent runners for the riflemen, and as they waited, Levi told Iron Eyes of the good fortune of finding Johnny yet alive in the Simian colony. After the tragic loss of Wolf in the battle with the Los Angeles Simian army, Iron Eyes was very happy in learning this news, which was revealed with a single tear on his normally stone face. Iron Eyes had certainly had more than his share of losses

215

to the Simians, and Amy was pleased to be able to bring him good news.

Once the riflemen arrived with their gear and minus their horses, Levi pulled the group together as she again gathered the energy around her and pictured the precise spot at the mountain pass, chosen from memory. The opposing views superimposed then changed as they were physically teleported to the mountain. This was a first for the wide-eyed riflemen. The fear faded quickly, replaced by awe then jubilation at the realization they had experienced something that few ever had. They were all familiar with Levi, having worked closely in the night raid on the Colorado River Simian colony. Now they were again pleased with the opportunity and honor of being chosen to fight at Levi's side again.

It was still light when they arrived and had the opportunity to scout the area. She was relatively positive it would be clear, but wanted to be sure. Levi wanted them to find their defense positions before dark. The locations were spread out two on each side of the pass, with retreat access to the rear behind the pass. He positioned one rifleman at a high-point just to the left of the road in front of the pass and down about thousand feet. This location would serve to cover the rear of the Tribe as they went through the pass and double as sentry before the Tribe arrived. That had been a second thought change when she noticed there was an odd number of riflemen but a good precaution. The whole deployment was a precaution, but far better than just walking with the others.

The light was fading, and from Jimmy's location she could see the Simians lighting fires for the night. She thought it was more for sight than anything, since it certainly wasn't cold and the Simians didn't cook their meat. She knew that humans would be eaten tonight in that camp, but there was nothing that could be done without jeopardizing the entire Owens Valley Tribe. She tried not to think about it and blocked her thoughts from Levi. Levi had either not considered this or was also blocking the thoughts from her. Sometimes there simply wasn't anything to be done.

Before the light faded and Levi released Jimmy and Fred to return to their camps, she saw the Owens Valley Tribe move out across the open ground going toward the mountain. Over the next few hours they would be moving closer to the Simians as they followed the edge of the mountain ridge. At the closest point they would be within three miles of the Simians for about two miles until they were hidden again behind a mountain ridge standing between the two forces. This would be the most dangerous part of the passage, which would take place in approximately four hours. She knew that Iron Eyes would keep the cattle to the rear and expendable if necessary. A bellow from a cow at the wrong time could be disastrous, but having no food was almost as bad. For now they could do nothing but wait.

* Levi *

Amy's memory was total. She remembered everything, and this was no different. She had

217

chosen the perfect spot to materialize. They were standing in the road at the first lower pass into the mountains. The pass was not as narrow as he had hoped but was defensible with rifles as long as there was not a full suicide charge. Nothing would defend against that. This was the first logical defensible location and the riflemen's positions were chosen with the odd man assigned as sentry down the road from the pass.

He and Moon busied themselves stacking firewood and hunting. Once the Tribe made it through the pass they would be relatively safe, but hungry. He wished they had some cattle right now, but guessed they would have to wait. At least he could get the fire ready to go. Other than that, hunting was all he could do for now. After an hour he had only found and killed seven rabbits. It would have to do. Amy's ability to see better in the dark with his eyes than he was able to always amazed him. She could see the movements of the rabbits in the dark and guide his rock throwing. At times like these he felt like a puppet. Satisfied, he returned and built a small fire behind the rock, dressed out the rabbits, and started them cooking.

Moon, it seems, had been luckier, at least from his point of view. He had somehow managed to kill a desert burro. It was no horse, but guessed it was probably close enough for Moon's taste. He also imagined it would be extremely tough to chew, but hell, Moon had the shark teeth to do it. Out of long habit Moon ate his kill far from where he was cooking the rabbits.

Once Moon fed he joined him at the fire, and they talked about the planned retreat through the mountain passes. There were a number of mountain passes that could be used as defensive positions, which served their purpose. The Tribe would be able to move at an easier pace, while the Lancers and riflemen held the Simian army at the last pass. As the tribe continued to move through each subsequent pass, the defenders could withdraw and set up defenses at the next pass. Amy estimated the Simian army could be delayed for well over a week by this method, longer if necessary. Eventually, the Simians would try to go around the mountain and come in from the rear, but that was a long trip and they would be through the valley and into the next range of mountains by that time. They couldn't hold them continuously, however, no longer than it would take to completely circle the mountain range, which Amy calculated to be a week at best. They would be in the open desert then and in danger. Amy hoped to give the slower part of the Tribe time to gain distance across the desert before the defenders ran out of defensive positions. Moon saw the logic of the plan and could add nothing.

Several hours had passed since they arrived, but there was about two hours more before the Tribe was out of danger and successfully bypassed the Simian camp. The rabbits were cooked, so he made the rounds of the riflemen giving each a cooked rabbit for their supper. He had eaten two but was still hungry. For a split second he even looked at the remains of Moon's burro but quickly decided he wasn't that hungry.

When he was on returning to the fire, he heard the shots. Oh shit! What happened? He turned and ran back down the road to the sentry's position where the shots had come from. Moon was right behind him.

It had been a good idea to bring the riflemen with Levi to the pass. She wished there were more of them, but unfortunately, they had only found ten AR-15 military rifles in the hidden cache she found at the Mojave Desert settlement. The full rifle team was made up of five men each from the Owens Valley and the Mojave Desert settlements. Fortunately, they had plenty of ammunition made from the modified gunpowder she created. She also thought about the bowmen with the poison arrows. That had been very effective against the Simians. The problem with that, they would have to retrieve the arrows once fired, which could be difficult under a defensive retreat.

They had spent the hours waiting preparing campfire wood stores, surveying the area and hunting. They managed to get enough rabbits to feed the riflemen and Levi something, but not enough. It seemed they would have to wait until bigger game was found or Iron Eyes got there with the cattle. The riflemen were happy to get the roasted rabbit and dug in greedily. Levi had eaten two of the rabbits, but his need for protein was far greater.

Levi was returning from the forward sentry post when they heard the gunfire. Damn! It was far too soon. What was happening? She heard rapid gunfire for several bursts then silence. They turned and ran back toward the sentry. Turning, she saw Moon rushing to join them. They were almost back to the sentry's location when she heard more shooting. The previous shooting had come from the forward sentry's location, but she could see flashes coming from firing to the left. Levi reached the sentry's location and strained to see into the dark. What were their targets? There, three hundred feet ahead she saw two Warriors lying in the dirt. One was still jerking in its death thralls, while the other lay still. Still farther out she could see a third Warrior limping off. Scanning the area she saw no additional Warriors or movement.

Levi turned to the rifleman. The question didn't need to be asked. The sentry said he had been watching, well kind of staring out into the dark, when he saw the Simian patrol come out of the dark headed directly for him. In retrospect he realized they were headed for the road, but he would have been seen. He started firing with the obvious results. Two were down and the third wounded. He said he had also seen movement off to his left after he had fired and believed that is what the other posts had seen and were firing at. The sentry didn't know if anything had been hit there.

She was analyzing what this meant. It could only be a disaster. It depended on how many Warriors were out there patrolling and how fast the main army would react. The Tribe was still too far away and could be easily cut off. She had to know. Damn! What could she do? She felt so useless. Where and what was happening?

Levi scolded her saying, "Calm dawn and think!"

Damn! He was right. She blanked out her mind and fought back the panic. She analyzed. The Simians came out of the dark, but they couldn't see well at night. Here was the discrepancy. She opened Levi's sensory inputs and looked. It was dark, but there was a moon tonight. Suddenly she realized she saw no moon and jerked Levi's head up and saw the clouds. They were not solid and at the rate of movement, the moon would be visible again in three minutes. The Simians must have been traveling in the moonlight and now also would be waiting for the moon to come out again.

Her panic was subsiding. The shock had frightened her and the data had not made sense, which added to the sudden panic. She also realized Levi was griping at her.

He said, "Damn, Amy that hurt. I almost fell when you jerked my head up."

In spite of the situation, she laughed and said, "Oh, stop being a baby. If I break your neck, I will fix it."

* Levi *

When he got to the sentry, he was pointing. He could see two Simians down, one obviously dead and the other dying. As he peered farther out into the open field, he saw nothing but darkness. He looked inwardly toward Amy, but saw no answers there either. In fact Amy was having a panic attack. Her emotions were making him breathe hard and his muscles tighten up. These emotions were overwhelming her. It was getting bad, but she must calm down now before she flipped out. He

222

forcefully told her, "CALM DOWN!" More gently he pleaded, "Get a grip. Use your intellect and analyze instead of panicking." It seemed to work. She seemed to withdraw from everything. Her mind faded away for a few seconds then returned in focus. Yes, she was analyzing now, but he couldn't keep up.

He stood to survey the surroundings and just then felt Amy jerk his neck muscles, shooting his head up to stare at the sky. "OUCH!" He felt his neck vertebrae pop as she did that and pain shoot through his neck.

She said, "Sorry. #$^%^ ... clouds ... #$^%& ... three minutes----@#^%$."

Hell, he didn't understand what she was saying, but knew she was talking mostly to herself. That was good, because he knew she was doing something positive.

In a few minutes, the moonlight was showing on the valley below. Suddenly, he realized what she had been talking about and glanced up to see more clouds. Yes, they would again be in darkness in a few more minutes. The light would, in fact, be on and off as the clouds passed. At Amy's insistence, he returned his view to the sloping terrain below them. Yes, they could see. He could see four fallen Warrs below them. The sentry must have been able to see earlier at a greater distance before the clouds obscured the light. To their left he could see another two Warrs on the ground. Damn, he wished he had more rifles. At a distance he could see another seven Warrs gathered below, waiting and obviously wondering what to do.

Amy said it was time and he slapped Moon's massive arm and pointed down the road. They would not be seen by the Warriors as long as they stayed to the right of the road. Amy wanted them to move about a mile and a half down the road so she could see the main Simian camp.

At the speed he and Moon were traveling, it didn't take long to reach the spot Amy wanted. He understood immediately the implication of what she said next. She pointed out the Simian campfires. The blinking out of the campfires meant that the Warrs were running past the fires. In fact he could see torches being carried, which were lining up and moving toward their location. He couldn't see Iron Eye's group, but he knew it was farther away. This was a disaster! "What can we do Amy?"

* Amy *

She hadn't communicated much with Levi during her temporary panic, but he was quick to understand when the moonlight flooded the terrain. Well, flooded made it seem like there was plenty of light, which there was not. There was, however, much more light than they had previously.

She immediately saw the fallen six Warrs and seven remaining of the advanced Warrs grouped in discussion. She knew the riflemen could hold these remaining scouts, but she must know what the main Simian camp was doing, and quickly. It was prudent to assume the worse. Sending a patrol in force to guard the pass showed planning and intelligence, which was not an overly common occurrence among Warrior Simians. For whatever reason, she

224

must assume the camp would also react intelligently. Unfortunately, they could not see the main camp. It was behind a small mountain ridge tapering out into the open terrain. The remaining seven Warrs presented no immediate threat to the riflemen, since their location was known. The Warrs would not be able to sneak up undetected. As a result, she decided that Levi must be where he could see the camp and hopefully Iron Eyes' approach.

Levi ran at a fast pace even outdistancing Moon by about a third. They could plainly see the Simian army mobilizing and heading directly toward them. They were closer than Iron Eyes and on intersecting courses. More disturbing was the fact that the Simians were in a position to cut the humans off from going either direction. The humans were committed unto death, which is what would happen. The Tribe with no more than one hundred and seventy-five Lancers, in the dark, and with no charging field, had no chance at all against a full Warrior Simians army, especially since the Lancers' horses were involved in the migration. It was hopeless! She was frantic and didn't know what to do. In desperation she asked Levi for ideas. He was good at abstract thought and she was good at calculating and deployment once she had a direction, but no plan came. Levi had challenged her so many times to expand, but she saw that even Levi had no hope.

Finally in desperation Levi said, "Call ASONE."

What could ASONE do? Hell, if she knew that, she wouldn't need to call him even if she knew how. Maybe he/it couldn't do anything either, but surely something better than her. Could she evoke ASONE? Once she used fear to evoke the entity and once anger. Both had worked. She wished she could control the emotions and ASONE, but that was impossible since she had to lose herself to become ASONE. Certainly she had fear. Well, it was more hopelessness. Would that work?

His thoughts were solemn, as were hers. The situation was hopeless as it was and the desperation was raging in her. She concentrated and let the rage build. Finally, she felt the flow of energy, felt Levi becoming stronger and more prominent and felt herself fading. She said, "It's beginning."

They began to flow together, their energies mixing. They... he... she ... who was who? She was becoming someone else, then Amy was no more, Levi was no more, and ASONE was both. She no longer cared about Amy as her perspective changed.

* ASONE *

Amy was there and so was Levi. They were there, yet neither existed. ASONE was both of them, yet neither of them. ASONE was raw power and intellect beyond measure. The intellect that had been Amy was now combined with the life experience of Levi to produce a new entity. This entity was neither male nor female and had seemingly unlimited power. Amy's intellect was refined by ASONE and was able to create power from surrounding matter. Secrets of the universe were now known. Levi's memories, experience, emotions and human intuitiveness gave the entity direction. Levi could think abstractly to solve a

226

problem and Amy could provide the means to accomplish the goal. ASONE could both think and act, providing a loop of thought into action.

ASONE was aware of Moon standing beside him staring. The Technical Simian knew or felt the power now radiating from it. The Simian moved back in fear, but ASONE spoke, "Do not fear. Remain with me or risk death." Moon shook in fear but nodded and remained silent and remote.

Thoughts were clear. It must see in order to effect changes. The visual spectrum was altered and increased. It saw infrared now and other undefined frequencies of light. This was still unacceptable. Knowledge was sought for sensory input. Bats! They generated a type of sonar to see in the dark. He gathered energy and created an oscillation. It could best be described as a vibration and increasing high pitched squeal as might come from a finger rubbing the edge of a wet, crystal glass. The pitch continued to increase until it was beyond human hearing. ASONE altered the sensory receptors so he/she/it could detect the sounds. The ears were altered to more correctly determine direction. It sensed the reflection of the squeals along with the time of the reflection. The intellect analyzed and correlated the data. This information was overlaid on the topographic maps in memory. The combination of the sonar, infrared, and other light spectrums gave ASONE a very detailed view of the terrain and the Simian and human occupants.

The Simian army, even though not totally aware of what was happening, was completely mobilized now and coming directly toward the road where It now stood. Simian guards remained at the lake guarding against any passage in that direction. The humans were also coming to this exact spot, but further behind. The humans had seen the Simians with the torches and knew they were in trouble. The Lancers were being brought up from the ranks to gather at the front for battle. The Simians hadn't noticed the humans yet, but that would happen soon. The Simians were two miles away from ASONE's location, but the humans were three. The trap would be here. The Simians would have the humans trapped against the mountains with nowhere to run. Time was running out, and ASONE would have to do something soon, but what?

How could its power be used? It heard a whimper from behind and turned to see Moon on the ground. Moon was frozen and paralyzed. ASONE immediately knew it was the frequency range of vibration It was using. The frequency and pitch of the vibration was affecting the Simian's nervous center. It moved toward Moon, poured water on the ground, and quickly it made a paste of mud. ASONE then took scoops of it and plastered it into Moon's ears, then took Moon's hands and positioned them over his own ears. Moon blinked his red blazing eyes and seemed to shake his head as he recovered.

During the care of Moon, ASONE had ceased the emission of the high frequency transmission. This resumed now with more vigor and purpose. Forces were gathered at an increasing rate and channeled into the transmission. Not only was ASONE able to see the Simians, but was focusing the high pitched squeal at the advancing army. The Simians were slowing as the force directed at them increased. Stronger it grew. ASONE held arms and hands high as the forces gathered and focused toward the Simians. A blue aura grew around ASONE, like a glowing statue. The aura flowed into ASONE from all directions and channeled out in an expanding beam of barely visible light aimed at the Simian army. It was an unbelievable sight to those staring at this miracle. The Simian armies' advance ceased only a thousand yards from the humans. Iron Eyes stared in disbelief at the now frozen Simians, but he continued urging the Tribe past the Simians. It seemed like a holy procession in silence and respect; as if afraid they might wake the sleeping giant.

Moon was now active and watching, obviously aware that it was ASONE he watched and not Levi. Moon waved Iron Eyes to a faster speed. ASONE did not waver but stood in the center of the flowing glow with outstretched arms, as the Tribe began to pass. Although ware of what was going on, It was unable to break concentration. Muscles quivered under the stress and power of the forces flowing through ASONE as hours passed and the Tribe, along with the cattle, passed. Out of its peripheral vision ASONE noticed Moon signing to Iron Eyes telling him about the seven Warriors ahead and the need to hold some of the Lancers here to cover Levi's retreat.

ASONE and Moon remained behind to gain additional time for the Tribe, but the physical body ASONE occupied was failing and needed repair. It began to move slowly trying to reduce the transmission. The body failed along with the

229

transmission, collapsing to the ground and into darkness.

* Moon *

His master was transforming into the strange one again, the terrible one that saw only rage. It was the one to fear, but he knew it would not hurt him. It was not Levi anymore and he didn't believe Amy was there either. He didn't understand it, but knew something was going to happen. He knew something had to happen or these humans would die at the hands of the Simian army. When he looked into Levi's eyes he felt fear. Those eyes were so intense with power they were glowing with light. It was not the same as the last time he saw the change. This time he saw the power of the mind, intelligence, but not the rage. It was nevertheless frightening. He saw the concentration, the glow surrounding Levi, and soon felt a vibration in the air around Levi. Shortly after, he began to hear the vibration. It was getting louder and higher. It reached a pitch that became painful. The increasing strength began to affect his mind and soon he lost awareness.

Becoming aware again, he felt Levi's strength as he was held in Levi's arms. The invisible power of this small man could be felt as a presence in itself. It was as if he was weightless in the small human's grip. Levi packed something into his ears and felt the steel grip of Levi's fingers grabbing his own hands and placing them over his ears. He realized what Levi wanted and held them there. Levi resumed his vibration and he could almost see

230

the energy flowing out. After a few minutes the energy was visible and getting brighter. He felt the golden hair on his body stand and wave in the invisible flow of energy. He moved back more in fear as the glow increased. Then he saw what was happening. The Simian army was disabled just as he had been. They were still standing but not moving. The Warriors were sort of rocking on unsteady feet. The humans were unaffected by the sonic vibration and continued to come. They sped quietly past the immobile Simians taking advantage of the opportunity.

Moon became concerned as time passed longer and longer. This was a considerable amount of pressure on Levi. He remembered when Levi, in this state, fought Gord. After the defeat of Gord, Levi had collapsed from the effort. He believed that too would happen this time as well. He already saw signs of stress on Levi. His face looked distorted and bulges were appearing on his body. This must end soon before Levi destroys himself.

He rushed the tribe past and signed instructions to Iron Eyes who quickly obeyed. Lancers surrounded Levi for protection even as he was beginning to falter. Levi finally collapsed into his arms. He quickly picked Levi up and began running toward the mountain pass. Even before Levi passed out the Warriors were beginning to shake themselves and screech in anger. Their rage was obvious at having been robbed of their victory and they were determined to triumph at all cost. Moon knew this meant a suicide attack in rage. He warned Iron Eyes as they all began to run.

They had a fair lead, but the Warriors were running full-speed and without fear, stemmed from their blind rage. Moon was burdened with the weight of Levi but making good time. Behind, he heard the clash of arms and knew the Lancers were driving into the leading Warriors. He also knew the Warriors would not be teamed and careless and would fall to the first charge of the Lancers, but he dared not turn to look back. He saw the pass ahead, but it was still far away and the sound of battle was too close behind. At least the Tribe would be safe as he saw them pouring through the pass.

A Lancer charged past and connected with something running only yards behind him. Just as he was thinking they weren't going to make it he saw the riflemen poised to shoot. Only seconds passed before the firing began. All five riflemen had run forward to cover their retreat. He didn't slow but raced past. The pass was just ahead now. He was through now and ran to the side almost dropping Levi to the ground. He turned to see the riflemen backing into the pass, but only occasionally shooting. The Warriors had calmed their rage and were holding back. They had made it, Moon thought with a grin, and his master had saved them all, again.

* Amy *

Always when she merged to become ASONE, it disoriented her. As Amy, she always knew the exact time and what was happening, but she always became lost in ASONE. This was no different. She knew what happened, but had not done any of it

232

herself and actually had no control. When Levi's body collapsed, the link to ASONE was broken and they began to split. Levi was mercifully unconscious, but she felt the pain of his body rushing to her. She was trying to clear her head, but it took many precious seconds. Moon had saved them and was carrying Levi toward the pass. The battle was raging around them. She heard Lancers clashing with Warrs and shots ringing out, but the immediate problem was to repair Levi's body. ASONE had almost destroyed it. ASONE's control had been too long. Levi's mutation was almost out of control and she was desperately altering things back the way it should be. After long, desperate minutes the mutation was stopped and began to reverse. Levi would be alright now, but it would take hours to completely repair him. Hopefully they now had time.

Several hours had passed and Levi was sleeping an exhausted rest. The attack had stopped and the Tribe was resting and eating. They would be safe for at least another eight hours. It would take that long for a Simian patrol to go around the mountains to the next pass behind the humans, even if they thought of it. Their group would have to cross the valley and through the next pass before that time. This would be the nature of the retreat until they ran out of mountain passes.

She let her mind listen and comprehend the activities going on around her and on occasion would even open Levi's eyes to look. Her mind even seemed settled and calmer than it had been in a while. She rested too. It was at that precise moment that she felt IT!

What was IT? She felt a presence. It was pure hate, rage, confusion, and others unexplainable, but it was all in the form of a force that washed over her. It was living and it was strong. She sought to locate it. Laughter filled her mind, a wicked laughter that made her shrink with fear.

It screeched, "You know who I am, and I know who you are too. I have been watching you and now I know who you are and where you. I know your secrets and now you will die!"

She froze, paralyzed with instant fear, because she did indeed know who it was, for the thoughts were coming to her in the Simian language. This was the Supreme One! This was the source of all her irrational feelings of late. It had been toying with her and learning. She felt violated! She began to wonder if they had escaped the valley or if they were being herded toward it.

CHAPTER 6
(ESCAPE OR DIVERSION)

* Levi *

It was daylight and he was alive. It was going to be a good day. For an eighty-two year old man he felt good. Hell, he felt good for a twenty year old. Laying on his bedroll, not bothering to open his eyes, he was feeling the sun on his face and hearing the noise of the camp and was well aware that he had survived. He also knew ASONE had saved the Tribe as well.

He remembered what had happened. He was there as part of what was happening, but he had no control, yet was part of the control. It was like the part that is Levi now, was observing and remembering what the total entity did, yet it was he/they that was doing it. Hell, he couldn't explain it any better. All he knew for sure was that he remembered. He remembered the sheer power he felt and the intelligence. It was beyond belief and scope of what he could relate to. He was Levi and he was Amy, then they were one. ASONE had created an energy transmission that had immobilized the Simians for what seemed like hours. He remembered seeing Moon in pain and wanting to help him, while also feeling indifferent to Moon's pain. The entity saved Moon, even in its indifference. The entity had acted in the best interest of the Tribe, as both Amy and he would have done. He remembered how the muscles ached and strained right up to the point his, or the entity's, consciousness faded.

He knew that the identities separated at that point and resumed being, separately, Amy and Levi. He didn't know how he got to this place or what had happened to him, but assumed Amy had repaired him. He really did feel good. He felt so good that he had an erection, which he hid by rolling over onto his side. Maybe Amy repaired him too well. He smiled at that point, because he was feeling a little kinky. He and Amy could have sex in front of everyone and no one would know. Their love, and more precisely their sex, was in the mind. It was very real to both Amy and him, but technically only mental.

He was playful, reaching out to Amy. He touched her mind, and she his. The next instant he felt her anger.

Amy said, "Is SEX all you ever think about?"

That shocked him and his playfulness was gone along with his erection. That is something women will never understand about a man. The male libido is very fragile. It can be turned off by a wrong word or gesture and even destroyed by repetitive cynical comments and rejection. Luckily, it hardly ever happened with Amy. Actually, it had never happened before. Usually she enjoyed the intimacy as much as he, and certainly she was just as playful and romantic. Something was wrong.

She was emotional and he sought to comfort her and reach out to her. Amy melted into his embrace and wept. Wow! Something was very wrong. She ignored the obvious problem and fought to regain control of her runaway emotions. As she did, she began to share what had transpired. She began from the time his body collapsed and related the retreat to the mountain pass and how Moon had carried him while the Lancers and riflemen covered the withdrawal. She ended with the real cause of her problem, the invasion into her mind by the Supreme One. He was stunned! This was totally unexpected, but in retrospect from what they knew or had learned, the Supreme Ones were exceptional in the evolution of the Simian race. These abilities were not out of the realm of possibilities, once you considered the genetic enhancements that had been done. The applied genetic science could have jumped millions of years in Simian evolution, even though the Simian race was already ancient. Certainly Amy knew the science of genetics and these possibilities far better than he. She was, however, still in shock.

He also realized, or believed, that the Supreme One was the cause of Amy's distress of late. He asked, "Amy is this the source of your runaway emotions?" She looked hard at him as if in thought. She was not seeing him in her fixed stare. It was just a blind unseeing stare as if her mind churned over thoughts. Eyes focusing, she nodded to the affirmative. She then surprised him by smiling!

* Amy *

Still pondering the Supreme One, she became aware that Levi was awake. He was playing possum so to speak. Oh, he was a kinky one with his thoughts, and any other time she would have found the thought of having sex in the middle of the day in

237

front of the camp strangely exciting as well, but not today. She crushed his advances and desires with her words. She was sorry as soon as she said it, but it was too late. Levi's erection was already subsiding along with his arousal. She could sense his disappointment and hurt from her verbal abuse.

She felt his concern and when he reached out to her with affection she lost control. The tears spilled out and she fell into his arms sobbing. She took the comfort of his arms around her for many long minutes, allowing her pent up emotions to be released. As she regained control she began to relate the events from the time he lost consciousness. She knew like her, that he remembered what ASONE had done; it was always like a dream. You were part of what happened, while having no control of what the entity did. It was still hard for her to accept the loss of control, something totally different to her normal existence.

He listened attentively and registered incredible shock at the news of the Supreme One's contact. He was quick to realize that this was possibly the source of her emotional turmoil over the last few days. She should have surmised as much, but hearing the question from Levi made her see it from a different perspective. The Supreme One was attacking her and this was a war. This was not about feelings and emotions. It was about data, information, strategy, and finding weaknesses and strengths. It was a mental attack upon her and she now understood the game, at least the strategy of it. Better yet, she now understood how to fight back or at least defend herself. A knowing smile settled over her face as she told Levi that he was correct.

It was clear now. The Supreme One had been feeling the raw power of her intelligence and possibly reading some of her thoughts and emotions. She didn't think it was able to look deeply into her mind, only the active conscious thoughts, and even then only in part. It had been experimenting with her mind and touching it. Knowing that, she could probably prevent it, but just in case, she must only think in English and not in Simian. Hopefully the Supreme One only understood Simian. In the future, she and Levi must only communicate to the Techs in hand signs and she must think in sign language and not Simian when conversing.

Another thing, she must shut down her research with the Simian computer immediately. The Supreme One could possibly learn English through her communications and translation of language with the computer. It could be disastrous if it could read her or Levi's English thoughts. This disturbed her greatly since the research was so important to their future. She would have to plan around this problem to find an alternative way to communicate.

These thoughts were flickering through her mind, unaware as always that Levi was monitoring her thoughts. She didn't care. He was her love and soul mate, but he could really surprise her sometimes, just like now.

Levi simply said, "Do your research in French."

"What?" Of course... he was right. Leave it to him to come up with the simple solution. Eventually she could have devised an incredibly complex coded encryption network, but that would have been silly. If the Supreme One was monitoring some of her or Levi's thoughts, then alter the language. It would do him no good at all.

Actually, she processed data, thought, mostly in an abbreviated mind language, which Levi also understood. Their communications had developed over time as they interfaced. It was totally unique and completely undecipherable. The Supreme One would never understand those thoughts, but, assuming it learned, or was learning English, it might be able to see the communication thoughts in English for speech. Levi's suggestion would work here too. She and Levi could think in French and interpret directly to the spoken words. In this manner the Supreme One would only see thoughts in French, which would mean nothing to it. The problems were being solved one at a time.

Yet again, Levi surprised her, saying they should not eliminate the entire Simian and English thought, just the important information. He said some thought, especially Simian, could be an advantage, by providing misinformation. Here he goes again, with subterfuge. She was too much computer in this regard. She dealt in absolutes and truths, while Levi could be a sneaky and cagey bastard. He said it was the training as an attorney, but she suspected it was as much learning human nature over eighty-two years of life. Whatever the reason, she needed this viewpoint. So she would continue allowing some open thought to maintain the potential communication channel to the Supreme One and provide the misinformation as Levi suggested. He would have to control that part. If she tried, it would be too obvious and it wouldn't work.

Levi grinned and said, "I will teach you how to be a sneaky bastard too."

Actually, he meant sneaky bitch. So she was going to be a sneaky bitch. She liked that idea and rewarded Levi with a wide grin.

* Levi *

Sometimes Amy was too damned smart. He saw her thought patterns and realized where she was going. OVERKILL was the word. She would go into creating completely new sciences just to accomplish a simple task. There was no need to encrypt and decipher, just use a different language, which she already had in her memory. She could teach him any language in seconds and then he could use that language as if he had been raised speaking it. She seemed startled when he told her to use French instead of English. Hell, the Supreme One didn't really know English, much less French, and had no real source to learn it. Amy got a little stupid-looking grin on her face and he knew that she accepted the idea.

To be so smart, Amy still had no idea about subterfuge, misinformation, or just plain lying. He didn't believe she knew how to lie. She was, however, smart enough to recognize that he could be a real sneaky bastard and would follow his direction in that matter. He believed that the Supreme One was not under any compulsion to play fair, so why should they?

This discussion took place during the time he was waking and getting up. Only a few minutes had actually transpired, but he smelled steak and was

241

hungry. He almost dreaded sitting up, expecting the bombardment that he got. Iron Eyes was there in an instant, thanking him for saving the Tribe, and wanting to know what the plan was now. Moon was there, as always, but was asking nothing. He was there to help, but he knew Moon would want to know the plan also. Essentially, Moon knew the original plan, and was quite sure that Moon had communicated that plan to Iron Eyes already. He was also sure that Moon would have informed Iron Eyes of all the other activities that had taken place since he left the group to join the Owens Valley Tribe. He almost shuddered to think how Moon might have elaborated on Levi's deeds. Moon was becoming quite a gifted story teller and was almost single-handedly responsible for the "legend of Levi."

He gazed pleadingly at the cook fires, which brought a chuckle from Iron Eyes, who immediately called for food. He accepted the heaping plate of steak and fried potatoes from the grinning lady and quickly began shoveling food into his mouth. As always, he noticed the lingering eyes upon him from the many women of all the camps. They must think him the most eligible bachelor of the camps, but if they only knew.

Between mouthfuls, he kept the conversation simple and non-informative. He was careful not to divulge any locations, deployments, or plans. He wasn't sure just how much the Supreme One could sense, if any, but wasn't about to take any chances. At best, he feared Amy's thoughts might be detected if only due to her mental strength, but then his thoughts became Amy's at some point. It was probably overkill, but a lot was at stake here. As he was about to ask Amy about the French vocabulary, she told him it was already available to him. He turned his mind to French and behold, it was there. He was able to think, hear, read, comprehend, and speak French as if he had been born to it. In reality he had rarely even heard the language spoken in his long life. It took a little practice, but he was soon able to think in French and speak in English with only a slight delay. Oh well, he talked too fast anyway. The most amazing thing, he noticed a slight accent now that had never been there before. Amy said that would pass.

It was the mental thought in English that Amy believed was susceptible to reception by the Supreme One and not the actual mechanics of the language. So now, even at best, the Supreme One might be able to sense her thoughts in French, but would not receive additional data in the form of French words and information to correlate with the thoughts. It would not even know that the thoughts were different than the speech. It would never be able to comprehend and Amy could survive its probes.

Amy was mostly concerned with the Supreme One monitoring her thoughts and Levi's through her. She said she believed the human brain was too alien to it and would not be able to read most humans. She said the human brain was simply too weak to radiate far and also believed, it did not yet understand English. Other than Amy herself, the obvious problem was the Technical Simians. Almost any of them were susceptible to probes from the Supreme One. This was their weakness and the most probable direction of attack from the Supreme One. What could be done about this? They must keep a close watch on those Simians around them.

With this modification in thought, he began to talk about plans. Amy had a precise schedule of retreat designed to draw the Simian armies after them, then hold and delay their progress. There were numerous passes providing strategic locations to hold and retreat for fourteen days, which Amy hoped would be sufficient time delay to consolidate and organize all their forces. This retreat would take them through some very rough and hot country, but it was mostly a defendable retreat until they neared the Mojave Desert settlement. Hopefully by then, the other forces would reach the settlement and they could all join together to defend themselves at the Settlement or continue the migration toward Phoenix. Amy wasn't sure what the Simian armies would do.

* Amy *

The schedule of fourteen days was the maximum she believed it could be stretched. After that, the armies would be starving and resort to suicide attacks, which could not be repelled. She didn't want to think about what the Simian armies were eating now, and blocked the thought from Levi also. There was nothing that could be done anyway.

She hoped for a lot during the fourteen days. The Mojave Desert settlement was working on evacuation plans. The caverns were being sealed and hidden, the tradesmen were working on the new weapons day and night and wagons were being built and loaded, while others were doing the many necessary duties in preparation to leave. The Techs had taken over care of all the cattle, and had them rounded up and ready for travel. They had moved the herds close into the adjacent valley and were interfacing closely with the human residents. Many of the Techs had even joined the human workers making the weapons, which had greatly increased production. At the rate they were going, the total of five hundred spring loaded lances would be finished in ten days, well within the schedule.

Anything could happen to change the schedule, but to a certain extent, she had control. The timing of the strategic withdrawals would set the schedule. It was time to start the clock since the groups in the mountains could not move until the Simian armies were well past the mountain pass the humans currently controlled. She discussed it with Levi and he gave the order to withdraw to the next pass, a good seven miles away. The pass was narrower and a more strategic location with less opportunities to be flanked by the Simians. It was also better in that the valley between was sizable, and would allow the now combined armies of the Simians of almost two thousand strong to move into and camp. This would allow their groups in the mountains to continue through the Owens Valley unobserved toward the gathering place at Barstow.

All but the riflemen and one company of Lancers began the trek toward the next pass. It took the procession over three hours to enter the next pass, which bothered her greatly. When Levi mentioned it to Iron Eyes, he also expressed concern and vowed to speed them up. When it came time to retreat from the pass, it went without a hitch. As quietly as possible, the riflemen abandoned their post and ran for their horses. The supporting company of Lancers and riflemen all sped away toward the next pass. Levi, Moon and Iron Eyes waited to see the reaction. It took the Warrs long minutes to explore the defenses before probing experimentally into the pass. Once they saw there was no shooting, the army moved through more quickly and then flooded through to pursue the fleeing Lancers.

There was nothing more to be learned here so she teleported Levi, Moon and Iron Eyes to the second pass to watch the approach of the Lancers and pursuing Simians. They walked through the pass as the Lancers and riflemen reached them. She noticed that each of the riflemen now had two assistants. Yes, that made sense now that the duties of the riflemen had become 24 hours. The riflemen fanned out to take up defendable positions inside the pass, yet at various elevations for firing. They waited for the approaching Warrs to come within range and commenced firing. Three Warrs fell nearing the pass and the attack stopped as before. A routine was being established that should remain for the next few days. The Simians would continue to follow in pursuit, but would remain outside of firing range and wait. Yes, so far her strategy was working.

Levi was grinning and said, "Was there ever any doubt?"

As she watched, she marveled at how well the rifles with the modified ammunition were working. She wished they had more rifles, but, so far they

246

had not found additional rifles other than the ones that had been hidden in the lost cache. Granted, they had not launched a massive search, but the few that had been deployed to search had found armories empty or totally destroyed. It was as if the Simians purposefully destroyed Earth's defenses even after they were useless. Those few rifles found had been rusted and unusable. At the first opportunity she would make it a point to try and discover a new cache of them.

Levi's comment brought her back from her thoughts, and she was glad. She loved him so much. She was never alone. He was with her constantly, sharing, comforting, and even scolding her. Life would have little meaning without him, even if it were possible, which it was not. If anything ever happened to Levi she would be plunged back into her prison of darkness as before, but she would still be alive. However, life without Levi in it would have little meaning. She didn't even want to contemplate such an existence, so she simply smiled back. The smile conveyed her strong love.

* Levi *

Damn! Amy was beautiful! He knew her features were a computation of all his most desirable preferences and wishes, but still, she was breath-taking. He suddenly remembered how shocking it had been when Amy had first displayed her image in his mind. There was no chance for him. It was perfect and he loved her for creating an image in his ideal of perfection. He remembered how disconcerting it had been initially. He had even

247

asked her to distort some of the features until he could get used to it. All these thoughts came flooding back as she smiled. It melted his heart and she damn well knew it, but all he could do was smile back. She meant so much to him.

The first withdrawal had gone perfectly. The Simians were content to follow and wait for their opportunity. There was nothing more Amy and he could do for the next few days on this front, so he made some suggestions for ancillary movements. Actually, Amy was ahead of him again, but she always wanted to hear his thoughts. It seemed to give her confidence that she was thinking right. He suggested that they bring Fred or Jimmy, someone through which she could monitor, here so they could proceed on to the desert settlement. Amy said it was too early yet, because she needed Fred and Jimmy to monitor the progress of the traveling bands of Techs, females, and humans. Once Fred's group was through the valley and linked up with Jimmy's, she could bring Fred here to remain with Iron Eyes. He chuckled at the thought of Fred's reaction at having finally reached relative safety just to be thrown back into the jaws of the enemy. Yep, there would really be some griping. Amy smiled as she agreed with his assessment.

It had to be Fred because Jimmy had a team of Lancers with horses, so it was not practical to separate him from his team. Additionally, Amy shared some of Jimmy's activities over the last couple of days. Jimmy was very smitten with the shapely blonde girl of the group they were guiding, and by the looks of it, she was just as interested. The two were spending more and more time together, and it would be a shame to break up these two. He and Amy both smiled proudly at their adopted son.

They contacted Fred and gave him the go ahead to bring his group along with the cattle out of the mountains and through Owens Valley. They didn't tell him yet about moving him to the Tribe's location. There was plenty of time yet for that. Next they contacted Jimmy, instructing his group to proceed out of the mountains, gather up any stragglers they could find and wait in the valley to intercept Fred's group. Both Jimmy and Fred were pleased that the plan was going as anticipated and were anxious to get started. The Techs from Los Angeles, # 1, # 2 and # 4, should have reached Barstow by now and should be waiting. He wondered if they should go check. Amy agreed. He wondered if he should make his last suggestion now or wait until they reached Barstow. He saw Amy's eyes narrow and knew he was in trouble but started laughing anyway. Hell, Amy had already seen his suggestion.

* Amy *

Levi had good instincts, they just weren't enough. So much more had to be done. For one thing, she wanted to bring the other five riflemen from the Mojave Desert settlement. They weren't being used there and sooner or later the Warrs would make an all-out attack on the Owens Valley Tribe's defenses at one of the passes in an effort to break through. The Warrs were not overly patient and easily frustrated. She believed that the humans were safe through the next few passes because they were very narrow. However, the passes opened up wider closer toward Death Valley, and the frustration level would have risen in the Simians by then. She expected a push at that time.

There was another reason she wanted the riflemen. Levi, in his arrogance or stupidity, was suggesting that they teleport to the San Diego Simian colony and liberate that group as well. What a gutsy idea. He always stretched the envelope, so to speak, and this was no different. Judging by the size of the Simian army, the San Diego colony would probably have at least fifty Warrior Simians left to guard the complex. She assumed that there would be less threat there than the previously warring northern colonies, which had approximately seventy-five Warrs left at each complex.

At this point there were only Levi and Moon to take on the Simian guards and the odds of fifty to two seemed somehow uneven. There was the added potential of bringing forth ASONE, but the entity was so unpredictable she didn't know how to plan. Her plan could not include ASONE.

Levi was also wrong about teleporting to San Diego. They had never been there so they would have to astral project to that location to fix a target location before teleporting. While they were there they might just as well survey the opposition. Once that was accomplished they could teleport to the Mojave Desert settlement to pick up the riflemen. She had decided to take the riflemen along with them to San Diego before depositing them with the Tribe to help support their retreat across Death Valley.

Levi almost looked hurt as he monitored her thoughts, but she would never belabor the point that he was wrong. She knew he would accept the modification of HIS plan. All he really cared about was liberating the San Diego Simian colony. He was positive she would take his plan, well goal, and accomplish it her way. So, there would be no problem between them. He would remain silent now as she planned.

Levi hand signed his intentions to Moon. Even though Moon now knew there was more to what Levi called meditation, he never inquired or questioned Levi. Moon would protect Levi's body with his life. They found a secure location where Moon could watch over them and soon settled. She felt the now familiar feeling of her mind and reference rising along with the essence of Levi's mind. Soon they were soaring high, free spirits racing through the sky high above the terrain. It felt invigorating; she was free of earthly bonds. It was almost hypnotic. She enjoyed these times for the pure joy of it and for the lack of stress from constant data input. Without these distractions, she isolated herself to only the current experience through Levi's senses. She found it refreshingly quiet.

Forcing her mind back to the situation at hand, she began surveying the terrain flowing beneath them. Levi suggested that they look at Barstow to see if the Los Angeles female Simians along with # 1, # 2, and # 4 had reached the gathering spot. They would have enough time. At his suggestion she turned to the left and soared over the mountains and down into the sweltering hot, flat desert. In minutes they were circling Barstow. Everything was well.

They observed the Simians and cattle mingled together and resting in shaded areas, wherever it could be found. All looked to be in order as they turned back to a southerly direction.

She was going slower now as they traveled over unfamiliar territory. She wanted to record the roads and contours of the land in her memory banks. They flew over Highway 15 toward San Diego. As they approached, she identified the old communities from her internal maps. They passed into the city suburbs and saw no Simian colony. She made a pass over La Jolla and out over the ocean to follow the coast line. Soon they were over the island of Coronado and saw people, lots of people, an entire human community. She could not believe her eyes, well, Levi's eyes.

* Levi *

He wanted to seize the opportunity to liberate the San Diego colony while the army was away. There wouldn't be many opportunities like this. Amy knew this too, but commented that what he suggested was as insane as trying to resist the might of the Simians.

Amy said, "Think about it. Even if are we are successful, this endeavor will virtually guarantee that the Simian armies will follow us to the end of the earth. They will follow, if for no other reason than to get the females back."

Laughing, he said, "Oh hell, Amy, they are going to follow us anyway, so why the hell not try to clean out everything behind them." He knew he was overly nonchalant, but what the hell.

Amy, after only briefly chastising him, began planning. He realized then that she liked the idea too, but didn't want to show it. After monitoring her thoughts for only a moment, he also realized that it was much more complicated than he had initially thought. He knew there would be Warriors there, but he left that up to Amy to solve. That was her expertise, hell she was expert in everything.

He hadn't realized that they couldn't just teleport there. Where were they going to teleport to, who was going to lead them back, and he hadn't really thought about who could help him fight? He hadn't thought about much of anything except freeing the last colony in their part of California. He wanted to think of it as a victory, but there was two thousand pissed-off, Simian Warriors chasing them. The Simians would be more pissed when they found out that they had stolen their females. The victories could be short lived.

He wondered what Amy would come up with. It was not reasonable to believe that he could just go marching into the complex with Moon and kill them all. Even he realized that sounded kind of impossible. He saw the plan as it was developing in Amy's mind and smiled. Yes, the riflemen were a good idea, but still not enough. They needed to go to Fred's group and pick up some of the Techs. Yes, they were consolidated, and six of the original "Dirty Dozen" Techs were now together. They could pick up # 5 and # 7 to go with them to later lead the San Diego Simian females to the gathering place in Barstow. He thought it would be a good idea to also pick up Al from the group if they were going back to the Mojave Desert settlement. Amy would have read his thoughts but added, "Dawn will be worried and anxious about him, plus Al, at this point, will be better used back in his own command of the desert Lancers." Amy nodded agreement.

He began to understand just how complicated this was getting, when Amy told him that they needed to astral project to San Diego, locate the Simian colony, and identify locations where they could teleport to. Not only was that necessary, it was a very good idea, if for no other reason than to assess the strength of the Simian guards left behind.

With Moon again watching and protecting his body they were soon free and floating high. As they took off, he suggested they check to see if the group from Los Angeles had made it to Barstow. The LA group had indeed made it and was settled in waiting, so they proceeded on to San Diego to search for the Simian colony. What they found instead was a sizable settlement of humans, complete with houses, farms, small herds of sheep and cattle, and a thriving community on the island of Coronado. He was shocked!

From their vantage point he observed that the island had once been connected via a peninsula road that had been destroyed along with a large bridge that once spanned the bay. Coronado Island was now truly an island. It made sense to him now as he watched sail boats in the bay and out at sea. The Simian bodies were very dense and compact making them heavy. They had learned this when Moon had fallen in the lake trying to capture him. A Simian and water did not mix. It was impossible for a Simian to swim; it would immediately sink to the bottom and drown. He remembered how hard it had been to walk on the bottom of the lake carrying the dead weight of Moon on his back. Yes, it made a lot of sense. The humans were safe on this island unless the Simians found a way to cross the water. Obviously they had not so far. He assumed the Simians also had a strong fear of water. He knew this was a new number in Amy's equation for the survival of the Human race, and hope surged in him as he realized that other island communities might also be surviving. Hell, maybe even whole island countries survived. A vision of Japanese Samurais flashed in his mind.

This community was several hundred strong, maybe even a thousand with maybe three hundred able bodied warriors. This was a safe haven. All they had to do was get there. He wondered if this community could be the ally they sought. The Warrior Simians were an enemy to all humans, but these humans were safe at the present. Would they help? Hell, could they help? They would have to give it some thought. Amy had brought them floating low now, moving among the buildings and people of the island and he knew she was recording the area for possible teleporting in the future.

They continued the search, circling San Diego. There! Oh, that was not good. They saw the space ship in the center of a stadium. It was a large professional looking football stadium with thousands of seats and acres of parking. It looked like a fortress.

* Amy *

She realized in an instant why the humans were relatively safe on the island. The density of the Simians made their weight in water sink like a rock. There was no buoyancy in their bodies. This density would provide a natural fear of water on this world. The Simian race would never be able to swim nor could there be a defense from drowning. The only solution would be to stay away from water, which is obviously what they had done here. As she surveyed the area she wondered why the Simians had not attempted to use barges to traverse the bay or construct material over the narrow breach in the peninsula road. It did not look that ominous. She surmised that there were enough humans living on the mainland to satisfy their immediate food needs. It just seemed strange to see a safe haven for humans, when apparently the rest of the world suffered. Already part of her intellect was searching maps to identify other possible safe havens.

She stopped speculating about Coronado and proceeded to survey the area, memorizing the terrain and locations she might need for teleportation. Actually, this only took seconds since everything was total to her. Once seen, she remembered everything about it. It was important however, to make sure they looked at the areas from a ground elevation. A triangulation of any target area was necessary to insure they didn't materialize with their feet in the earth or inside a building wall.

Soon they were off again searching for the Simian colony. She gained elevation so they could survey greater area, but hadn't ascended far before she spotted it. No wonder they hadn't seen it before. It was inside the football stadium. Her records indicated that it was named Qualcom Stadium. Unlike the other colonies they had seen, this space ship had only one circle of buildings ringing it. The Simians were apparently using the stadium walls as their outer ring, which provided a quite formidable defense barrier.

The Simians were too arrogant to believe themselves in danger from humans. She knew the location was not chosen for defense. The real reason, most likely, was that this was the most convenient location to land. The terrain here was hills, mountains, and tall buildings. The ship probably had little time to choose a landing site and took the first open flat area in which to land. Unfortunately for her, the location did offer a strong defendable position. She laughed to herself, thinking they, the two of them, might just charge the fifty defending Simian Warriors and overpower them. Levi looked startled at that, but soon broke into laughter.

Levi said, "Oh yeah, just give me my red cape."

They descended to the complex and began a slow sweep around and through the compound. She had been correct about the reduced number of Warrior guards. Actually there were fewer, only forty, but the way the complex was protected within the walls of the stadium, these defenders would be more than sufficient. Within the complex they found the organization much the same as others they had seen. The Technical Simians were caged and guarded along with humans adjacent to them. There were the typical two guards for each group. The stadium had several entrances, but only one was used for access. All the others had been closed off. At the stadium entrance there were two additional guards and it would be necessary to go past the remaining Simians to reach the cages. It would not be possible to infiltrate this group unseen, as they had once done at Los Angeles. This would take some thought.

* Levi *

As Amy pointed out, the only positive thing they saw was a smaller number of Warrs, but in this fortress it didn't matter. He wasn't giving up though. He knew Amy would come through. She excelled when challenged and expanded with each new challenge to became stronger.

If he had any second thoughts about the task before them, it was gone when he saw the humans caged. In fact his blood boiled with rage when he saw human bones and left over appendages from Simian meals. There were faces still gaping in death on severed heads and bloody fingers attached to arm bones. Flies swarmed in droves. He was thankful that they couldn't smell this carnage. There had been no attempt to discard the leftovers or clean up the mess left from many meals. This was uncharacteristic of Simian compounds they had seen in the past. The guards left here must be some of the most unsavory of the army, unwanted, or chosen for their lack of conformity.

The sight was disgusting and horrible, but the most disturbing part about it was the fact that apparently the humans had been eaten in front of the others still caged. He found this to be unmercifully cruel and sheer torture to those still living. To watch their friends and relatives eaten alive, knowing they would face this same death soon. His rage exploded and nothing was going to stop him from saving that dozen or more humans still alive.

The Techs were, just as previously found in other compounds, caged and in an under-nourished condition. There were about fifteen Techs. He wondered as always, why the Warrs hadn't simply killed them. Amy said it probably was habit because they were kept alive in the event their technical skills might be needed in the future. When the Simians had first landed, Amy estimated that there had been hundreds of Techs in the original group. Over the subsequent fifty-two years of preventing the Technical Simians from breeding and killing or starving them, their numbers had dwindled from hundreds to the typical fifteen remaining at this complex.

Many of these thoughts ran through his mind, mingling with the rage he barely controlled, as they soared through the sky returning to his body. Amy could have done that instantly, but he knew she enjoyed the freedom of flight. He wasn't overly keen with the heights, but took pleasure in Amy's pleasure. He could appreciate how Amy might feel, experiencing this form of freedom after a lifetime of captivity, so he relaxed and waited.

They soared over Al and Jimmy's location and watched the migration of the group, which seemed to have grown in numbers since last observed. They were, however, progressing toward Barstow, on or ahead of schedule. Jimmy could be seen riding Thunder, the horse he had given him after his metamorphosis into the Levi of today. He chuckled thinking how Jimmy must be showing off for the pretty young blonde that had his attention. He was truly happy for Jimmy, the son he never had. He felt Amy's pride as well.

They then proceeded to the Northern end of Owens Valley to check on the progress of Fred's group. That group was also on schedule, and would make their trek through the exposed area of the valley closest to the pass in the next few hours after dark. That had been the plan. Amy was concerned that random Simian patrols might spot them before they exited the valley. He thought they were safe, but it never hurt to play it safe.

The journey was nearing its end, and he saw the first pass then the second pass with the massive Simian army spread out below. The Simians seemed content to wait for the time being, but hunger would drive them forward soon. No captured humans were observed below them, but he didn't want to see any humans because there was nothing he could do. He idly wondered if the Simians would eat cattle if they left some behind. That might hold off the hunger a few more days. He was rewarded with a smile from Amy. Yep, she liked the idea.

* Amy *

The moment she saw the outrage of human desecration and felt Levi's rage, she knew all discussion was over. Being so close to Levi, she had learned his many weaknesses. Without doubt, he would forfeit his own life to save these humans. She knew also that, unless she had a plan, Levi would simply charge ahead, forcing her to try and save his life. This was scary and reckless because Levi could get himself killed before ASONE had a chance to take over, assuming it would. Plus, there was no way to predict what ASONE might do or if it could save them. She was startled to realize that she too was referring to ASONE as a third person. It was she that invoked ASONE; it was not the other way around. If she was slow or failed to find a way, Levi would be dead and she, although alive, would plunge into darkness again. It would be far worse than before, because she would not only be in total isolation, she would be without Levi. She could think of nothing worse than that.

She told Levi that she was devising a plan and blocked her thoughts in order to hide her panic. She had no plan and was doubtful one would come easily, but she would come up with something. There were five riflemen from the Mojave Desert settlement that could be used, but they would need more. Levi had speculated that they could pick up # 5 and # 7 from the group that had now consolidated. She agreed with his thinking, but what could they do with five riflemen, three Techs, and Levi against forty Warrs in a stronghold? A comprehensive survey inside the stadium and Simian complex before finally beginning the return trip helped build data. She soared high in the momentary thrill of her seeming freedom, following the inevitable silver thread leading back to Levi's body. Again she felt the warning and comfort of seeing the silver thread spiraled out before her. Was this her clairvoyance again, premonition, or just a passing thought. It angered her that these wondrous powers of hers were so unpredictable.

On the return they reviewed the progress of the separate groups. All were on schedule with the plan. Approaching the last pass and Levi's body, she was startled at Levi's seemingly idle thought about leaving cattle behind to feed the Simian army. Damn! That really was a good idea. Levi seemed to always view life and situations a little differently than she did. Sometimes she wished she was more abstract in thought, but then most situations could be resolved with just plain old logic, calculation, research, and planning. Then there were times Levi saved them with his radical ideas. Together they had both talents, radical and calculating.

They melted back into Levi's body easily now, the focus and perspective of the senses changing minutely at the final transition. When Levi spoke, Moon jumped and turned to face him. She quickly re-established contact with her own body, well living brain, and resumed monitoring a thousand functions. The priority was to correct the mutation of Levi's body. Her internal clock indicated that they had been gone five hours. Amazing, without her internal clock, it seemed like only minutes, but judging by the amount of mutation, which was extensive, they had indeed been gone for hours. Levi's body was not in danger and would be corrected in twenty-eight minutes. She went about her work as Levi commenced giving the instructions as they had discussed.

* Levi *

He spoke, startling Moon, anxious to get everything done so they could get back to the San

Diego Simian complex. He briefly told Moon what they were going to do. If possible, Moon was grinning, apparently liking the idea. Hell, Moon now liked the excitement as much as he did. Admittedly though, this looked tough and he couldn't help but wonder what Amy would come up with for this challenge. His thoughts betrayed him. He was rewarded with a "Shithead" from Amy.

He was talking to Moon as they walked toward Iron Eyes. A serious looking Iron Eyes came forward to meet them, but still smiling at the tribe's good fortune at being alive. It had been a narrow escape, an escape that shouldn't have happened. Without the intervention of ASONE they would all be dead. Iron Eyes was more than willing to accept any instructions from Levi, Amy, or ASONE. He didn't care. Any of their instructions or suggestions was as orders to him.

Levi instructed Iron Eyes to cut out a few head of cattle and leave them behind when they made the next withdrawal. Iron Eyes stared at him for a moment and suddenly saw the purpose. He said that he would tether the cattle immediately because the next scheduled retreat would be soon. The majority of the slow traffic was already gone and the rest would start soon with only the rifleman teams and Lancers remaining to cover the retreat. He nodded understanding and told Iron Eyes what he and his group were going to do under the cover of their organized retreats. Iron Eyes looked concerned, but also nodded.

There was little more to be done here, so he explained to Iron Eyes that they were going to the other groups and begin implementation of the plan and would catch up to Iron Eyes' group at the proper time to help. Iron Eyes was to follow the schedule outlined for them. Iron Eyes acknowledged his instructions, as he and Moon moved off to the side to await Amy's teleport. They delayed long enough to contact Fred, Jimmy, and Dawn simultaneously to explain the plan, so # 5, # 7, the riflemen, and Al would be ready upon their arrival.

Amy opened the input from Fred so he could monitor what Fred was seeing. Fred realized what was happening and moved to the side and was looking at a perfect spot to teleport. That is exactly what happened. He saw the area through Fred's eyes then saw the perspective change as they materialized. Fred was actually smiling, which looked so out of place on someone as nervous and frightened as he typically was.

He went to Fred and clapped him on the back and gave him a warm smile in return. He wondered what Fred had to smile about, being among all these Simians. He had almost expected another cussing. Amy reminded him that there were other humans as well, and that Fred had # 11 and # 9 flanking him. He guessed that was enough to make even Fred feel secure.

The two Techs, # 5 and # 7, were standing apart, obviously happy to be called upon, and waiting. He and Amy talked only briefly with Fred, knowing they could speak telepathically with him anytime. Instead they talked in sign with # 9, Moon's chosen 2nd, for many long minutes. Moon also spoke at length in sign to # 9 informing him what was happening and giving instructions. The Simians used little unnecessary communications, but Moon had learned to be more open, which many times brought looks of wonder from other Simians when he chatted with them.

Soon they joined # 5 and # 7 and waited as Amy teleported them to the selected spot Jimmy was observing. Again, they were suddenly there, staring back at Jimmy. Jimmy's smile was as contagious as always. He couldn't help but laugh along with Amy. Even Moon hiccupped his laugh, which made matters more humorous. Soon even the solemn faced Al was grinning. Jimmy had such a winning and warm personality. It was amazing how he could make you smile even when you didn't want to.

He wished they could stay for a while, but there was too much to do. They collected Al and were off again spreading their atoms across time and space. He idly wondered if Amy could screw this up, only to wind up with fingers growing out of his head. Laughingly, he thought about second thumbs on his hands like a Simian. Amy stuck her tongue out at him as they materialized at the Mojave Desert settlement main camp. They found themselves standing in the middle of a gathered assembly of humans and Simians, and most of the Simians were females. What the hell?

* Amy *

While Levi gave instructions to Iron Eyes she corrected the mutation of Levi's body and organized herself. Sometimes it was disorienting to be without reference and time and it took her a few seconds to establish her equilibrium. Her brain action and thoughts were normally totally organized and the loss of control disturbed her greatly. On the other hand, she loved the freedom from the mundane. Life with Levi was not without its own excitement.

Levi was anxious to proceed and pressed her to leave. They contacted Fred, Jimmy, and Dawn with instructions, and to inform them of everyone's status, and what Levi was about to attempt. No one liked the chances he was a taking, but wouldn't voice it. She could sense the fear in their minds. Everyone knew Levi was the heart, soul, and future of the human race and, for that matter, the Technical Simians as well. They knew if Levi died it was over for them too, but there was little choice. Besides, they had seen Levi do the impossible far too many times to give up on him no matter the task or odds.

She teleported Levi and Moon to Fred's location, quickly collected # 5 and # 7 and then teleported the assembled group to Jimmy's location to collect Al. The next stop was the Mojave Desert settlement, where they teleported directly into the center of an awaiting group of Simians and humans. Levi was shocked. She had been unable to tell him what was going on. Much she didn't understand herself, because discussions had taken place while they were astral projecting and she was unable to monitor and little discussion had taken place since she began monitoring again. She only knew they waited.

She had learned from her research into the Simian computer that there was more to the Simian females than they suspected. Much of the information concerning the females was conspicuously missing and a mystery surrounded not only the females, but the recorded information as well. It was as if the data had been tampered with. She did know, however, that at one point the female population had been much more active in the governance of the Simian home world than their current position would lead anyone to believe. From what they had observed, it seemed that the female's position in the current society was to breed and nothing more. The females required nothing and even acted as if they were not intelligent, but through monitoring Dawn, she was discovering much to the contrary. She suspected that they were about to learn a well-kept secret, and anxious with the prospect.

When they materialized Dawn went to Al immediately, throwing her arms around him in a happy greeting which lasted brief seconds, but was intense.

A smiling Dawn turned to Levi and said, "Boy do I have a surprise for you."

Yes! She thought. Damn, Dawn loved suspense.

* Dawn *

She began by explaining that when they left a few days ago she had gone to spend time with the Simian females. At first, fearful, but she discovered the females were open and friendly, showing far more emotion than the males. She began teaching them sign language and soon discovered they were highly intelligent and picked up the language almost immediately. As she was talking to them now in English she was signing and the Simian females

267

seemed to be following the conversation. The females had been kept in the dark by the Simian males and didn't understand what was happening until she explained it. It was like a door opened and a different Simian female emerged. They had been successfully hiding for generations from the Warrior Simians and then the Supreme Ones, and it was time to emerge from their cocoon.

An older Simian female that Dawn had simply named Mama had established herself as the leader and spokesperson. Mama was the elder Simian female at one hundred and sixty-seven years old, far beyond the breeding age. Mama had explained that her age made her more mentally stable. When Dawn questioned that statement, it was explained that Simian females were dangerous when they were in the breeding season every seventy-five days. That was the reason the Simian males left them alone. Females possessed poison fangs under their nails for protection and could kill a male during passion or anger and passion sometimes became violent during mating.

Mama had explained that far in the distant past, before the Warriors became strong, the females had stood in the ranks of the scientists, technicians, writers, thinkers, and leaders of the race. They were the first to see the inevitable, and took precautions to protect and preserve the female race. They feared the genetic manipulation could extend to the Simian females and a new race of females could be created, such as had been used to create the Warriors. The females chose to become docile and appear of no threat, invisible if you will, to preserve their race. They did however; take advantage of the genetic manipulation to develop the finger fangs for their race. Their decision and action worked, but subjected the female race to a life of slavery and non-existence, but they had been preserved as a race. Now, like the Technical Simians, they saw an opportunity to emerge. Slim as it was, they were going to go for it. Besides, they had little to lose because the technology no longer existed to create a new genetic race of Simian females. So, they had nothing to lose and everything to gain. If the humans lost, they would be in no worse shape than they were now.

The females, after learning of the pact the Technical Simians made with the humans, quickly decided to do likewise. That is what they were doing now. Mama and a select group of Simian females had come to meet Levi and Moon. Dawn had told them of Moon's status with Levi and wanted to meet both Levi and Moon. Mama wanted to make her own agreement with Levi to join the team.

* Levi *

He was totally surprised to see those gathered, especially the females. Amy also seemed to be surprised, but he knew Amy was more knowledgeable than she was admitting. She reminded him that monitoring was cut off most of the morning due to the astral projecting and she honestly did not know what this was about. He just grinned at her. Whatever it was, it was going to be good. He waited and listened as Dawn told her story. He didn't know what to expect, but it had to be good.

As the story concluded and he heard what they wanted, he smiled. General Harkin was happy at this turn of events. He looked around at Al who was also smiling. When he turned to Moon and the other Techs he saw fear. Oh shit!

Amy explained that the Techs were probably more shocked than anything. They were not used to seeing assertive behavior from Simian females, plus they were not accustomed to associating with females in any manner, even mating. Additionally, the females were more like a separate race of Simians. The males and females only came together to procreate and their association ended there. The females had been cared for and fed, but even the Warrior Simians remained apart from them. Amy made another startling comment.

She said, "There are many more females than Techs. I wonder if they can be persuaded to fight?"

Damn! That was a good idea. He asked Moon, "Do you have any objection?" Moon only nodded to the negative. It was almost comical the way Moon and the others were staring at the females. It was almost a human emotion. He chuckled and returned to face the females, which he quickly termed (Fems) in the order of Warrs and Techs.

The Fems wanted equal status in the new world order, a position in governing, and guaranteed rights to exist. This was very much the same as the Techs had asked for. In return they offered their loyalty, knowledge, and numbers to join the ranks of the army to resist the Warrior Simians and the Supreme

One. Everyone seemed to be in agreement and Amy was grinning, so he bowed to Mama and agreed.

Mama and the other five Fems seemed very happy. Mama returned her stare to him and started signing. She was expert in her communication and very fast. It was amazing how fast she had picked it up, but more amazing, was the instructions she was now giving him! He muttered, "Damned women." He squealed as Amy mentally pinched his butt.

* Amy *

Levi was skeptical that she didn't know, but she really didn't. All she knew was that they were there. She suspected much, but had missed the final discussion between Dawn and Mama and the revelation of the Fems' hidden society. They had separated from the other Technical Simians in order to preserve their race. In this world they saw the only hope that existed, other than the slavery existence, was by aligning with the humans and this super-human Levi. The Fems, like the Techs, knew the leadership of the new order would be Levi. It was the smart assumption.

As the story unfolded about the Simian females, things began to make sense. She suspected many things, but not to the extent coming forth. It did explain why there were gaps in some of the stored history in the Simian computer. The data had been manipulated at some point in ancient history, by the females, while they were yet in a position to do so. The Technical and Warrior Simians, over generations, forgot that Fems once equaled them. The females were ignored by the Supreme Ones and the Warriors, and the female race was preserved intact by becoming breeding stock only. Since the DNA of males and females did not mix, the females' DNA remained pure. They continued to produce exact reproductions of the donor (male or female) while continuing to produce exact reproductions of females also. The race continued in the pure form.

Amy wondered what knowledge Mama was referring to and how it had been preserved through history. At the speed the Simian females (Fems) had picked up the sign language, they obviously possessed a high intelligence. Was it possible to transfer knowledge down from generation to generation by word of mouth and maintain the integrity of the data? She wondered. She would be very interested to know just what knowledge these Fems possessed.

She had to admit that hiding had been a smart move and had obviously worked. The Warriors had not seen the need to genetically alter the females, thereby creating a new race of females and dooming the old. The plan had been brilliant. The plan got even better when she realized that the Fems had done a little genetic alterations of their own by creating the fangs and poison into the Simian female race.

Somehow it seemed strange dividing the Simians into three races as if they were different creatures. Warrs, Techs and Fems, however, were genetically different. Males and females were symbiotic only in that it required both male and female to reproduce. Even though the DNA remained the pure male donor or female host, it required a male to gestate a female egg. The original male donors had been the Technical Simians, and they would again return just as it had been in times past. The circle had been completed. She found humor in the thought of how these two races would interact in the future. It should be interesting to say the least.

Mama was telling Levi that the Fem to her right was the chosen one to accompany him as Moon currently did, to represent the Fems. "What?" Oh my, Moon was instantly raging and screeching his indignation, but Mama stood her ground unflinching, and staring at both him and Moon. Moon in his rage reached out for the Fem, but the Fem countered with her claws, complete with fangs.

As soon as Mama said it, she anticipated Moon's reaction and the predicted counter. Moon's reaction was automatic and was abandoned almost as soon as his blow reached out. Unfortunately, his reaction had triggered an automatic response from the already tense Fem, and she was aimed to kill. The fangs were already extended as the Fem's arm shot out toward Moon. She reacted faster than the Fem and shot Levi's arm out to foil the blow. It was close, but the aim was spoiled and it missed Moon's arm by inches. Levi immediately stepped between the two, watchful of both directions. Neither resumed the attack, but stared around Levi with red eyes blazing at each other. Oh my... like she needed internal conflict with all the other problems.

* Levi *

When the implication hit Moon of what Mama said, he was instantly angry. This Fem was to

273

assume equal status with Moon? Hell, he would never accept that; the Fem had not earned that right. Moon was his right arm and always would be. Moon had been in awe of the Fems moments before, but now he was instantly enraged and lashed out. It was an automatic reflex, but caught him unexpectedly. In response he saw the Fem lash out in defense, or anger, as well. He didn't know which, nor did it matter. All he could see in his mind was Moon being injected with the Fem's deadly fangs. He was panicked. He felt his arm lash out and divert the Fem's strike. He was very thankful that Amy's reactions were instantaneous. If they hadn't been, Moon would be dead now. Anger boiled in him at the thought.

It had been close, but he immediately stepped between them to prevent further conflict. They continued to stare at each other, but neither had wanted the conflict and made no further attempts. Moon, however, remained angry. For that matter, so was he. This Fem had not earned the right to equal status with Moon and never would. It was nothing personal, it was simply unacceptable. Moon's position as his friend and partner was not a matter for discussion. He did realize that some concessions would have to be made though. Amy was cautioning him, but he knew how to negotiate. He explained that Moon and he were inseparable because they were friends, and not because he represented the Simians. It was the other way around. He had put Moon in charge of the Simians because he was first his friend. He stared unblinking and said, "That is the way it is, and there will never be an equal to Moon." As he was signing he noticed that Moon was calming, realizing that he too felt the same.

Mama was undaunted and signed back, "Fems are not the same race as the Techs and will not be represented by Moon. Moon does not represent or govern humans so why should he be expected to govern Fems?"

Damn, Mama was tough! He needed time to organize his thoughts. Amy was trying to help, but only presenting facts. This was not the time for facts, it was time for arguments.

He was thinking quickly and asked the name of her presented Fem. It was diversionary and Mama knew it, but answered anyway saying something roughly equivalent to a small furry animal with spots. It obviously was an animal from their home world, but the description reminded him of a movie he had seen in his youth.

Levi signed, "Bambi can represent the Fems, but can NOT assume Moon's status. That status is reserved for Moon alone and if you cannot accept that, we have no agreement." Amy was horrified at that statement, but he silenced her. He let that sink in for a moment then proceeded to point out that the humans had several leaders and none of them had a status equal to Moon. Again he let that sink in and then gave her something to save face.

He pointed his finger at Mama and said, "You will be the leader of the Fems and not Bambi. That is my authority as the leader to decide." Silence lingered for long minutes then he continued explaining that Mama would be the leader, but he would accept Bambi on some of his trips where interface with other Fem groups was likely. Bambi

275

would speak for Mama and report back to her, but Bambi would have a no rank position. He looked at Moon for approval and received a nod. After some minor discussions, Mama looked hard at the others of her group then back at him and nodded. It was over. Damn, Mama was a born leader and would govern the Fems well. He did however hope that she didn't make it a habit of arguing with him.

* Amy *

She saw the strategy as Levi argued with Mama. The fact that Mama argued was something very different. Everyone accepted Levi's suggestions as orders, but not Mama. Both Mama and Levi presented a good argument, but Levi ceased arguing and simply told her the way it was. It was sudden and shocking to her. Levi rejected the deal Mama presented. This could not be. It had to happen, and she was telling Levi this when he hushed her. She hated when he did that and felt the anger rise. What he said made sense when he continued. She had wondered why Mama had wanted Bambi to be the leader, but Mama explained that she was over childbearing age and unable to assume a leadership role. Levi dismissed that notion with a wave of his hand and told her that the rules were all different now on Earth and he was the leader and he made the rules. He said he was assigning Mama to the leadership position and that was it, end of discussion. In essence Levi also agreed to take Bambi, but without a leadership position, she was no threat to Moon. Actually,

Bambi would be useful in dealing with the other Fems, and they had plenty to deal with too.

Metaphorically speaking, she breathed a sigh of relief at the apparent solutions Levi had fabricated. Since everything was working out, she also forgave Levi for hushing her. Analyzing what had just taken place, she was impressed with all the subtle twists and ploys that Levi had successfully presented to, and deflected from, Mama. Yes, Levi was a constant source of surprise, and pride. In her happiness, she kissed Levi hard on the lips and was rewarded by a massive smile that must have looked crazy and out of place to those around him. She didn't care as she kissed him again.

Levi carried out her suggested plans, telling Mama to continue learning from Dawn and the others about what had happened, and what the plans were. He instructed her to get the Fems ready to travel. He also told her about the females from the other Simian colonies that were en route and how they would look to her for leadership. At that, Mama's ample chest and belly swelled even larger. Levi had won another victory, and Mama was his loyal subject from that moment on. Somehow though, she felt that Mama would never be bashful about giving her opinion.

Al was already taking charge and issuing Levi's instructions. The camp would be ready to leave soon, and on schedule. The timetable would allow six days. This would give the Owen's Valley Tribe time to reach them, as well as the growing migration of Simians and humans coming from Barstow. It was, however, a very short time to travel from San Diego and they hadn't even freed the Simian compound yet. It was time to go.

* Levi *

It was quite apparent that he had made Amy angry, but the timing was critical. Amy fell silent, but he knew she was deeply concerned. He had learned many tricks in his brief association with the law firm he joined right out of college. Those skills were now used and were successful in finding a reasonable solution for everyone concerned. It had been close, but everyone was happy, even Amy. He was rewarded with a very big kiss, two actually. He was aware that he must have looked stupid in front of everyone, but at that moment, he didn't care.

He began to implement Amy's plans and soon everyone was off seeing after their tasks. Now it was time to go to San Diego. Here stood his army! It consisted of Moon, # 5, # 7, Bambi and 5 riflemen. He chuckled thinking the forty Warrs didn't have a chance. He looked inwardly and sought Amy. "What is the plan, Amy?" After a pause, listening, he said, "You have got to be kidding!"

Amy's plan was actually no plan. She was going to transport them all to the front entrance of the stadium and let the riflemen start shooting the guards and continue shooting the Warriors, while him, Moon, and Bambi teleport inside to the pen and kill the guards and free the prisoners. She had no plan to escape.

Grinning, Amy said, "We will improvise."

Surprisingly, he was comfortable with her plan, and signaled the group together. As they gathered, it surprised him to notice that, except for the riflemen, whom he didn't know, his chosen allies on this engagement were all Simians. Startled, he looked around to see if the humans noticed, but no one was giving him a second glance. He assumed that they were becoming as comfortable as he was with the Simians.

Once together, Amy began to gather the energy around them as the scenery began to change. As quick as it began, it was over, and they were standing behind a wall near the stadium entrance. He looked around at a sudden gasp to see Bambi shaking in fear and shock. He had failed to warn her, and she had not known what to expect. She was screeching, chastising Moon for not telling her what they were doing, and Moon was screeching back defiantly. Quickly, he again stepped between them apologizing for not warning her. Bambi's red eyes blazed past him to Moon, but began to calm. There was obviously underlying resentment here. He would have to watch them closely. He went on telling them in their language what the plan was. All were nodding.

Moon, Bambi, and he stepped to the side and waited as Amy again began gathering energy. Bambi was much calmer as they materialized within the complex, but he was horrified! Even before they completed the teleport, he saw it was a terrible mistake. They were materializing within a semicircle of about thirty surprised Simian Warriors. Once the teleport was complete, the Warriors quickly converged on their position and

279

sixty strong Warriors hands grabbed them in vice like grips. Amy was screaming in fear and anger. It was over!

CHAPTER 7
(FACE OF THE ENEMY)

His name, roughly interpreted in English, was "Satan." The name, given by the races of his world, personified everything evil and frightening that his world offered. His unique race had been created by genetic manipulation in a Simian scientific research center eighty-three years earlier. He was one of only ten created by the scientists at that facility, but only two grew to maturity. He later discovered there were others and sought those out as well.

Discovering there were others like himself ignited anger so intense within that it never went away. Competition could not be tolerated; it must be destroyed. He personally killed six of his siblings when the assistants weren't around to protect them. Their deaths were made to look like accidents whenever he could, but one of the last siblings had expected his attack and was prepared. Satan was bigger and stronger than the others; in fact he was bigger, stronger, and smarter than any of the mature Simians he had met, even though he was yet an adolescent. When his attack had been resisted and successfully repelled, his rage took over, and he fought his way through the research assistants to break his sibling's neck.

At that time there were only three of his kind left at his facility. The fourth had previously died from a mysterious accident, which he suspected had been caused by his last victim. That was another reason to kill; it was kill or be killed. The last remaining sibling mysteriously disappeared. He later found that it had been secretly taken to another complex and hidden from him. Months later he discovered the hiding place and killed the last sibling.

Almost from his first aware thought, he had known he was special. He saw and felt things that others apparently did not experience. Those around him seemed simple and uncomplicated. They seemed stupid and barely able to function. At an early age he became aware of the ability to read the simple thoughts of those around him. Soon that became a source of fear to them, which he also felt. There was no affection to those that cared for him, and he even took much joy in punishing them. He angered easily and raged openly, often killing those around him with his mind. When he was developing, he hadn't understood how or what he was doing, but enjoyed seeing the fear in their eyes while they were dying. Only later did he discover that it was his overwhelming mental strength that was being projected to a much simpler mind unable to handle the overload.

When he was brought into the vicinity of his siblings, he always felt anger and became more livid when he discovered he was unable to mind-shock them. He did not like them! He felt their minds touch his, and he knew they were a threat to him. The assistants wasted time with them that should be spent on him. He had needs. As he got older, this resentment continued to fester. He liked being different and apart, but he needed these assistants to teach him, show him the way of this world, and to feed him. If he killed any, always new ones would come. He was still young and didn't yet know what he wanted, but he knew this would change.

When his ability to kill those like himself with his mind was unsuccessful, he began to find ways for them to die. It was simple at first, falls always seemed to work. One would trip walking down the stairs, another fell out of his bed and got its neck caught in the binding ropes, still another ate something that apparently wedged in his throat. When one would die, the assistants would be very concerned and many others of those weak minds would come and talk, but they would go away. He hated his siblings, but he also enjoyed killing. Feeding on the taste of fear and the power it generated, became a necessary nourishment, as necessary as the air he breathed or the food he ate. Feeding on this energy of fear seemed to make him stronger.

Soon after the death of his strongest brother, he dropped all pretense of hiding his powers and began to take over. There was little more he could learn from these simple beings. He rebelled at their attempt to exercise authority over him. He was stronger, far more intelligent, and destined to rule. When anyone stood in his way they died horribly. Soon all resistance to his authority vanished. Only once did they make an organized attempt on his life with weapons. He had read their simple thoughts from a great distance, and in anger, went on a killing spree. He had identified the planners and went after them. No hostile thoughts of that nature would be allowed to go unpunished. Everyone in his path was killed en-route to the mind that plotted against him. The planner was a Simian leader and

Satan walked directly into his government building killing. He used his mind to kill, but also his hands and teeth. His physical size dwarfed even the largest of the Warrior bodyguards, and he felt great exhilaration in killing them. He ripped arms and heads from jerking and quivering bodies, tossing the broken bodies aside as he continued toward his target. The leader was old and offered no challenge, not even attempting to rise from his chair. The leader was brutally killed in front of his quaking staff. Afterward, he simply stayed, beginning his reign.

It was amazing how easy it was to take command. This leader had many underlings that were only too happy to tend to him once their old leader was dead. He learned quickly from these simple minds and was amazed that they had ever been able to rule this world. The position he assumed did not rule the world, only a portion of it, which angered him. He decided he would take those positions over as well when he learned more. Learning the ways of the world became more difficult than he originally believed. His orders were obeyed instantly, but there were so many issues. He listened, watched, and learned. There were too many issues to manage and he recognized that he would need these underlings to handle the daily functions. He would manage only what he wanted to manage.

In time he learned and began to reach out his authority assuming and assimilating more and more territory and leaders. Only a few times was he challenged. When that occurred, he attacked. He was very aggressive and always immediately went to the offending ruler and killed. As in the original attack, he killed for the sport and fun. He killed everyone in sight. The minds were so easy to read. The plots, the plans, the strategies of attack were so simple and easy to foil. He always took his revenge to the top, the conceiving mind, and never left anyone alive that plotted against him. In time all resistance ceased within his territory.

He continued to mature and gain strength. His mind grew to limits the world had never seen or believed possible. As his mental reach extended, he felt the others, like himself. He thought he had destroyed them all. Where had they come from? How many were there? These questions and their existence were a source of considerable rage for him and became the focus of his thoughts. He also felt their probes as well. He could never allow others like him to survive. It was their nature to be the only one. His life became obsessed with the discovery and destruction of the others.

Minds were searched around the world and he discovered who he was and where he and the others had come from. He learned of the genetic manipulation that developed the Warrior Simians and how he and the others were an extension of that research. There were five separate land continents of their world and there had been three research facilities. They were each individually governed by the three largest governments of the world. The research centers had each developed multiple subjects, but like his center, the New Ones had begun killing their siblings.

His research center had developed ten New Ones, but only two had survived. The other research centers had begun to separate the siblings earlier and more of them survived. All totaled, he was able to identify eighteen New Ones remaining, separated across the five continents.

Unfortunately for him and fortunately for them, most were beyond his reach. He knew they were feeling the same need to eliminate each other and become the only one, but their immediate attention would be occupied warring against each other within their own continents and not be concerned with him at present. Not all had risen to the top as yet; it was a matter of time before the New Ones ruled everything. In many ways he was lucky. He had only one sibling to contend with on his continent and proceeded to the task.

The only brother to escape his center had been taken to the remote end of the continent, where it had immediately begun to take over just as he had. There was distance between them and each had sizable Warrior armies for protection. It would be difficult, but it must be done. There could be only one, and he obsessed with the need to destroy him. To feel him so close drove his rage to dangerous limits.

It took five of their years to reach his goal, but he finally faced his brother and killed him. The civil war had devastated the armies of both sides, but he had won and took great pleasure in ripping the head from his brother and taking over the entire continent. He anointed himself the supreme ruler of his part of the world. It was then that he began calling himself the "Supreme One," which was quickly adopted by the other New Ones as well. They were all called Supreme Ones by choice.

By the time he successfully consolidated power on his continent, the surviving Supreme Ones had also consolidated. There remained only five surviving Supreme Ones, one on each continent. Each one remained far too protected to reach the others. While it continued to cause him great rage, he forced himself to accept the fact that there would be five on the planet until he could find a way to kill the others.

While he waited, he set out to ensure that there would be no more. He destroyed the research center on his continent and killed all the scientists and workers that had ever been associated with the project in any way. Additionally, he killed any female that conceived one of his offspring. Unfortunately, they were few; most did not survive the brutal act of sex with him. He did not comply with the limits on sex, imposed by the females and their puny defense. Stupid females and their futile attempts to control him would never work. He simply controlled their minds and took what he wanted when he wanted.

The aggression and loyalty of the Warrior Simians pleased him, but they were even more stupid than the Technical Simians. Only the Technical Simians were capable of understanding the technology for space travel, which would be needed during the next hundred years. He had realized and calculated that the war with the Outsiders had depleted the resources of the planet and polluted the atmosphere beyond repair. Their world would die within one hundred years, and there was nothing that could be done. In order to survive, he would need the Technical Simians.

The Warriors' numbers, since the war with the Outsiders had ended, had increased and they had become powerful. That, combined with their aggression, meant doom for the Technical Simians. Without his intervention and the intervention of the other Supreme Ones, the Warriors would have taken over completely and destroyed any hopes of salvation for their races. The Supreme Ones united to this common goal. All resources, technical and financial, from all the continents were applied toward relocating the races to a planet compatible to their requirements.

After thirty years, the first migration was launched. It contained an occupation force to subdue the planet. The Supreme Ones made one error: no Supreme One went with the first invasion. Without the Supreme Ones' control, the Warrior Simians rebelled in space and took control. It was devastating to the plan. The Warrior leaders were beyond their mental control and would not listen to instruction even from them. The invasion was almost a disaster due to poor planning, but had been successful in launching the neutralizing agent against the target world's defenses. He knew that the invasion had been successful, because all defenses from the world had been neutralized.

There were to be five more scheduled invasions to the target world, which would transport the majority of the population. The intervals were to be staggered every twenty-five years, taking the time table to the end of their world's estimated existence. Since their world still had a projected life of over one hundred and twenty-five years, there yet remained a considerable future on the home world.

The Supreme Ones were not anxious to give up their control and start over, but he was prepared. Yes, he was more than ready, because he had a plan.

He reluctantly agreed to lead the second wave to the new world. He didn't want to appear anxious, although he was. He wanted this for several reasons. First, he knew the initial Supreme One that made it to the target world would have more time to establish his rule. Secondly, he knew several of the Supreme Ones had joined in a plot to destroy him. His position was envious and some of the others were combining forces to eliminate him. He would leave and let them fight for the leftovers afterward. That threat didn't bother him so much, other than the effort and resources it required to resist, and counter the plot. By offering to lead the second wave, the plotters would wait. He allowed them to think their plot was undiscovered, while planning his relocation and attack on them. There could be only one.

When word reached their world of the use of the neutralizing weapon and defeat of any resistance on the target world, he knew it would be safe to travel to this new planet. His plans were sealed then and so was the fate of the conspirator Supreme Ones. He knew he was smarter than the other Supreme Ones and was quicker to recognize the opportunity. Let the others fight over his holdings. It would keep them occupied while he planned his escape. He even felt pleasure in knowing that most would be dead when he left, and the remaining Supreme Ones would continue to fight among themselves. He would be all alone on the new planet without competition to his supreme rule.

When Satan's fleet was making their final orbit around his dying world, he launched an attack upon the three Supreme Ones involved in the plot. If possible he would have destroyed all of the Supreme Ones, even if it meant destroying the entire population and the world to do so, but it was not possible. He did not have enough destruction bombs. The bombs were provided as a means to launch an attack on the target world if needed, but he preferred to launch them against those who would challenge him, those that felt equal or superior to him, those that were an abomination. As they were leaving orbit and before entering light speed, he was rewarded by seeing three of the continents flame in instant destruction. Three of his enemies were gone forever. Now there were only two.

He regretted not destroying the entire world, killing them all. For the rest of his long life he would be haunted by the knowledge that there was another Supreme One alive, and he was not alone in his superior intellect.

It took over ten of the new world years to reach the site of relocation. It was everything that he had been told. It was a pleasant world with green continents and blue water. It had more water than his planet and Simians hated water. His research indicated that the water on this planet, while capable of supporting life, would be even less dense and therefore more suffocating. He chose a location in an apparent warm climate well away from any major bodies of water. There were two hundred ships in this wave with over one hundred thousand Simians. They would have to be disbursed across the planet, but he took twenty ships carrying ten thousand Simians to the main location with him. It was necessary to control this world, but with the major water bodies separating the continents and without the ability of flight on the altered world, it would be difficult, possibly impossible to maintain control. He disbursed the ships worldwide but kept half of the ships on the main land mass where he located. At least in this way he would maintain control of half his invasion force without dealing with the problem of water separation.

The fleet orbited the planet and identified the locations of existing Simian colonies. Many were located on the west coast of this chosen land mass. The amount of surviving Simian colonies was pathetically low. The inhabitants of this world had fought hard and well. This world's dominant species possessed strong technology which they used in defense. The original fleet of one thousand five hundred ships had been reduced to less than a hundred. What a tragedy that had been! The last resort weapon had been used in their defense to destroy the world's technology. That had also destroyed most of the Simian technology as well, but they had never intended a long term use of it. The Warrior Simians simply were not capable of using the more sophisticated technology and the Technical Simians would always be a threat to him with their combined knowledge. He was actually pleased that technology would not be necessary now. The Technical Simians would not be needed once space travel was over. Technology was gone, and he did not care, because he was smarter and stronger than any Warrior, and there was no threat on this new planet from the puny inhabitants.

In the survey he observed a major population center of the native dominant species untouched by other Simian colonies. It was an area where two major groupings of native habitats once existed. These closely distanced groupings once were heavily populated by the dominant species. Even now, although only a remnant of what once existed, there remained a large number of the species. In order to maintain the number of Simians of his twenty colonies, they would need major accessible food supplies to supplement the food supply brought with them.

He had brought breeding stock of their home world's natural food source (roughly equivalent to an earth elephant without a trunk). Unfortunately, it would take time to build up a herd large enough to feed the colonies. Unlike the original invasion fleet, he had prevented the Warriors from feeding on them to extinction, but an alternate food source would be required.

Through the initial survey of this world, he had discovered that the Simians were feeding on these natives and these two closely grouped native groupings were still abundantly populated. His plan required twenty ships and their colonies to land and surround the population centers and simply keep the natives within their established circle of colonies. In essence, imprison their food supply and feed on them as necessary, allowing the natives to tend to their own needs until needed. It was a brilliant plan, which had taken some time to locate the right native population grouped close enough to make the colonies self-sufficient and his plan successful.

The conditions were ideal. Patrols from the twenty Simian colonies maintained the perimeter and contained the humans. His rules were established. No Simian went into the clustered natives without orders and then only to retrieve live food for the colonies. He wanted the contained group to feel somewhat safe, therefore continue to plant crops and raise their own food. To ensure the food supply was never depleted, he maintained outside patrols as the other colonies had done. These patrols searched for other groups of natives. These were fed upon first and when gathered in numbers above their immediate need, were released into the contained perimeter.

Life was without incident for many years. He was calm and controlled his empire with a strong hand, but his empire was limited. Without communication, his empire stretched only as far as his ability to communicate through runners. The laws of physics on this world, thanks to the use of the Simian ray, destroyed his ability to communicate with the other colonies. This drove him into frequent fits of rage, knowing he was not in control of the entire world and vowed to find a way to establish communication.

He tried to re-establish the communication network without success. The ships and technology fell prey to the radiation from the altered mass of this world. The radiation signature of this world eventually changed any new mass into an identical state, rendering the technology useless. He had suspected this would be the case, but was angered by it anyway.

Back on his home world he had been able to isolate minds and detect their simple thoughts. After concentration and learning how to separate individual thoughts, he could systematically read minds at will. It was not a complete sharing of minds but more of a feeling or seeing the thoughts on the surface. He could not detect stored thoughts. On his home world there had been so many minds, but he had eventually learned to control distances and reached out. Perfecting this skill had saved his life more than once by detecting plots against him. Now on this new world it was much easier, because there were fewer Simians, but unfortunately, the distances were far greater establishing limits. This too angered him.

He trained his mind over the years to reach out, seeking thought, and also to project his thoughts. It was not easy, because the Warrior Simian minds were so simple, but he had succeeded in making his will known in some cases. It was slow coming, but he was getting stronger.

Two summers ago, during one of his mind searches, he had been startled, shocked, and eventually enraged to detect an intelligence in this world far above anything he had felt before. Even the Supreme Ones did not generate this level of mental activity. All his fears, jealousy, and rage surfaced again. He would not tolerate competition. There could be only one. This was an enemy that must be destroyed at all cost.

He was unable to read the entity's mind. It was foreign, alien but very intense and strong. He began

294

learning the focus of the mind. He could sense where it was originating from, but the activity was directed always toward a puny individual of the dominant species of this planet. He began searching the minds around the individual and found the mind of a Technical Simian that seemed to always be with him. Much was learned from observations of the puny human, as they called themselves, and his Simian companion. He continued monitoring this human through his Simian companion until something changed. Suddenly, he was unable to decipher the Simian's thought any longer. He could detect the mind, but it was encrypted, unreadable. This enraged him even more.

Undaunted with the loss of the Simian mind, he was still able to follow the power of the mysterious mind and the human through other Simian minds when they were available. This powerful mind worked well with the human called Levi. Together they were an incredible force. The team was definitely an enemy, well beyond just existence, which was in itself an abomination to him. They fought Simians! They fought Simians and WON!

He had watched through the Sword Master's eyes as this entity named Levi had defeated and killed him. He watched through the Simian leader's eyes as this human, with the incredible mind's help, defeated the Fort Mojave Simian army. He had tried to give instruction, but he was not yet strong enough. Later he had watched the battle between Levi and Gord. The skills displayed by Levi had been incredible, but he knew the skills and abilities were coming from the mind. He felt the change and saw the mental power as the human Levi, the puny human, changed into the most powerful creature he had ever seen. He watched through Gord's eyes as Levi slapped him senseless. He felt the powerful blows and writhed in pain as the little human broke the giant's neck. Satan experienced rage like he had never felt before. He hated this entity with a blinding fury that threatened to strip him of any orderly thought. He wanted to kill this power. He must kill this mind. He would kill this mind! He forced himself to calm and remain rational while he planned.

Satan knew about the runners sent out by Gord to consolidate the Simian colonies. He knew that Gord was aware of the Phoenix Simian colony and would be sending runners to that group. He dispatched his own runners with orders. Satan knew his orders would be obeyed without question. His orders to Gord's runners were simple, "Come to me!"

Satan had consolidated all the colonies that landed on this continent immediately upon arrival, but had not yet bothered to pull the old colonies under his wing. With the threat of this entity in the west, he now wanted to do so. He wanted the runners from Gord's colony to face him so he could experiment with mind control on them in hopes of being able to communicate orders to, and through, these runners to the old colonies.

The runners finally arrived and were brought into his presence. They were frightened beyond belief, even more so than his colonies. It had been so long since they had even heard of one such as he, much less been this close. These lives were so simple and insignificant, but he had use for them.

There were three in this patrol which served his purpose well. There were three colonies in the west. He intended to memorize the mental pattern of these simple minds and adjust the pattern of his thought waves in tune to them. He hoped to communicate to them at the distances to the remote colonies. He owned them, bodies and minds, and would do as he willed with them.

For days he burrowed into their small brains learning the simple patterns of their minds. He learned the communications centers and the receptors in their brains and memorized the patterns. He could already tune into most of the senses such as sight and hearing and sense the surface thoughts. Now he hoped to be able to give instructions. The Simians were taught how to detect his mental voice. It was crude, but somewhat effective. The simple minds were not capable of receiving much, but it would have to do. His next concern was distance. Would he be effective at the distances that would be required?

The patrol was sent back to the land by the sea with orders for each of the colonies. One would go to the Stockton colony, another to the Fresno colony, while the last, the smartest one, was sent with dual instructions. He would deliver Satan's orders back to the five generals at the Los Angeles colony, and then continue on to the San Diego colony. All three would deliver the orders to the Phoenix colony en route.

Satan continued to monitor the three Warriors as they traveled back across country. He was still able to monitor their minds, but his ability to provide information to them diminished as the distance increased. By the time they had reached the place to split into different directions, his ability to give directions was limited to their rest time when their minds were the most open and receptive. He had instructed them how to periodically stop and open their minds, but they soon forgot and he was unable to get their attention. He knew if he frightened them too much they would forget all their instructions, so he remained calm. If they could not be useful to him for communication, he would kill them horribly when the time presented itself.

His rage boiled over the Los Angeles Simian colony. The very thought of a human or a Technical Simian presuming to lead Warrior Simians and the colony was absurd. Never could this be allowed. Satan continued to monitor the Warrior generals and saw the anger building in them as well. Before the returning Warrior reached the Los Angeles colony he saw the confrontation developing between the Warriors and the Technical Simians. He was trying to push the Warrior generals forward in their defiance of the Technical Simians and the "MAN" as he was called that was with them. This was not the man called Levi, but another less exceptional; in fact this one was quite unexceptional, even among humans. Satan believed that he had been successful in pushing the generals into action. He had concentrated very hard using all the hate he could muster, which was abundant. He radiated the hate toward the generals, driving them close to killing those standing in their way.

He was incredibly angry at the absurd thought that Technical Simians could rule under this man called Levi. As he thought about the Technical Simians aligning with this human against the Simian race, he shook with rage, barely controllable. The blinding rage threatened to consume him, building to an explosive level. This pure hate radiated from him in lethal waves of energy. Those Warriors within a hundred feet of him began to quiver and fall to the ground in violent and thrashing spasms. Their bodies locked in death thralls. Those Warriors outside the circle of death quivered, but managed to run or crawl to safety. Seeing the damage he had done, he fought for control. He didn't care about the ten dead Warriors around him, but he needed his comfort and was used to being attended to. As he gained control, he smiled at the new power he had just discovered.

As the confrontation climaxed at the Los Angeles complex and the generals were about to kill those offenders and resume control, he was stunned to see Levi and the one called Moon materialize out of empty air. Anger was replaced by shock. The mind and this man had powers he could only imagine. His rage radiated out and directed his rage toward the generals. "KILL!" His mental powers transmitted orders, reinforced by the sudden surge of mental rage, reached the generals and pushed them into action.

The Technical Simians, the weak human, and the one called Levi were outnumbered by the Warriors by incredible odds. He smiled to himself thinking how easily this was going to happen. It was then that he sensed the mystical power again. This mental power grew and surrounded Levi. He could sense it more that see it. He was looking through one of the general's eyes, but sensed the focus of power with his brain. The power grew and continued to spiral to an unbelievable level. It concentrated and focused in the human, then became one with the human. The man was something new. Levi, armed only with two small knives fought through the Warriors as if they were but small children. The human killed without mercy, brutal and efficient. The Warriors' blows were batted aside as if nothing. Simian arms were ripped from bodies. It frightened him. Realizing he felt fear, the rage consumed him again. He had never been afraid of anything before. He screeched out in total frustration and ferocity. His huge black teeth chattered, chopping off a high pitched screech so shrill that his Warriors were covering their ears and running for their lives. He raged again, beat the ground, ripped doors off, kicked in one of his walls and destroyed everything within reach. Finally he shook with frustration, as his body quivered with uncontrolled fury. He had to kill this entity. He had to kill this human and the mind!

Suddenly he stopped raging, stood very still, and slowly began smiling. Satan had a plan! He knew where the mind was, and he knew how to kill both the human and the mind. It was so simple.

300

CHAPTER 8
(THE THREAT GROWS)

* Levi *

They had been in so many life and death situations during the last year that it seemed like a way of life, but this was different. For once in his life, he saw no hope. When Moon, Bambi, and he materialized within the massive group of Simian Warriors, they didn't even have a chance to react. The Warrs fell on them immediately, and they were pressed to the ground in mounds of heavy Simian bodies. The only lucky thing was that their materialization shocked the Warrs. It was so sudden that the Warrs didn't have time to draw their swords. That had saved their lives for moments anyway. He was in shock too and couldn't believe it could end so suddenly. They weren't even going to be able to die in battle. He hated that.

His mind reached out to Amy to share his last thoughts with her. He would die, but Amy's living death would continue in her dark prison. He wished they had been able to find an alternate method for Amy to interact with the world. It is strange what you think about when you are about to die, but he wondered if Amy would still be able to monitor the minds of Jimmy, Fred, and Dawn after he was dead. He didn't really understand how Amy did it or if it required his mind. He did assume his mind was required to talk to them, however. Maybe Amy would be able to continue receiving inputs. At least that was better than the alternative. He would go crazy if he had no sensory input, and it wouldn't take long. How had Amy maintained her sanity during those fifty years?

Only seconds had gone by as his mind raced, but even as he wondered about ASONE he felt the strong Simian hands moving and cold steel of short swords trying for position to stab. He knew he would not live long enough for ASONE to make an appearance.

Why was Amy so quiet? He looked and saw Amy grinning. Why in the hell was she grinning? He was about to scream at her when he felt the changes taking place. It was a feeling he knew well and knew what it meant. "Way to go Amy!" He met her grin with his own as he felt the energy gathering.

* Amy *

She knew she had made a terrible mistake even before the teleport was complete. She saw the Simians gathered in the unlikely spot to which she had chosen to teleport. The good news was that the Warriors weren't in the exact same spot in which they were materializing or the physical bodies of the two groups would or could have mingled. More likely the physical matter would have simply replaced each other. She lost her logic and screamed in panic. How could she have been so stupid?

Amy fought for control, but precious milliseconds passed. There wasn't time for her to react. She thought of assuming control of Levi's body and using his weapons, but there simply wasn't enough time for her thoughts to become action. The Simians fell on them and Levi's body was pressed to the hard ground. There must have been many on him, judging by the weight she felt. Levi wasn't even able to breath. What could be done?? Levi was saying good bye. NO!! She had learned from Levi NEVER GIVE UP. Her mind raced at the speed of light, searching. Something she had just thought, what was it? Damn! She must hurry. Think! Teleporting, replacing matter, was that it? Nothing would change if she teleported this group. They would still be on top. She saw it. It was a matter of where she teleported the group.

She gathered the energy around them, while she began modifying Levi's body. Yes, this would work if she had time to complete the task. Precious milliseconds more and it would be ready. She saw the plan register in Levi's thoughts as he felt the changes. He was laughing now as he saw it too. Hurry, she must hurry.

The dark and distorted view changed as they materialized in the lake where Moon had almost killed Levi so long ago. This was the only body of water for which she had coordinates. The only water that Levi and she had been in before. She remembered how frightened Levi had been of water, until she had adapted him with gills. He had actually enjoyed the water afterward and saved Moon from drowning just for the sport of it. He would have to save him again, Bambi too, because Simians and water did not mix. They would not be able to move due to their dense bodies.

As the air around them was replaced by the surrounding water, the Warrior's grip on Levi released as they struggled in panic for the surface.

Their struggle was futile as the Warriors fell like rocks to the bottom, and Levi scrambled to avoid being taken down with them. Levi was grinning as he began swimming around like a fish looking for Moon. They had learned that it took a Simian a long time to drown from the previous experience with Moon, but didn't really know how long it would take. To be safe, he had to hurry to save their friend.

* Levi *

He must be becoming a really weird person to laugh in a situation like this, but when he felt the changes in his throat, he knew what she was going to do. He saw the simplicity of the plan and knew it would work if she was fast enough. As the thoughts formed the question even without words, he felt the energy of the transfer forming. Then they were there fifty feet under the clear lake where he had learned to swim.

The immediate concern was the dead weight of the dense Simian bodies. Even though they had let go of him their weight was propelling him downward. The bodies were still dangerous if they forced him into the mud bottom. He pushed and kicked his way out from under them only a brief second before they hit the bottom at a hundred feet.

His next concern was oxygen. He held his breath initially, but finally succumbed to the necessity and breathed the water. As he remembered, he felt the panic and suffocation of sucking water into his lungs, but thankfully it only lasted for a few seconds. He was soon rewarded with the refreshing surge of oxygen as it entered his

304

body again. The water flowed into his mouth and lungs where somehow the water exited out gills in his neck that Amy had just installed. He didn't question it. It worked. As it had been before with Moon, the Simians were motionless on the bottom. Amy speculated it was probably some form of defense shut down mechanism designed to keep them alive longer by reducing the need for oxygen. That didn't make sense to him, but he really didn't care. It would just take them longer to drown, because they seemed comatose and didn't appear to be trying to help themselves. Oh well.

He settled on the bottom and began moving the heavy bodies until he finally found Moon. Soon he had also found Bambi. He moved them over to a rocky bed area where he could carry the weight without sinking so deep into the mud. He took Moon first, saying, "I don't know how long they can hold their breath, so I'm taking Moon first." After long, strenuous minutes he walked Moon up to the edge and pushed his head out of water. He left him on the bank so he would not have to re-fill his lungs with water. He didn't like the transition much. Bambi was lighter but not by much, and he soon managed to get her to the edge. Moon had recovered by then and was able to pull her from the water and up onto the bank.

Before exiting the lake, Amy wanted him to take a closer look at the Simians. Amy said, "I want to know, first, how many Simians are there, but secondly, I want to see the results of my hard energy transfer."

He had no idea what "hard" meant but was only too happy to swim back down. With the immediate pressure off, he was able to be a little more objective in his observations.

He had been focused before, but he now realized what Amy meant by HARD. The edges of the transferred sphere of energy had been rigid and defined. This was obvious upon closer examination. There were body pieces missing. There were bodies with missing legs, heads, or arms. Some were burned into by the sudden energy sphere, as if by a laser. Yes, he now knew what Amy meant by "hard." He was pleased that Amy saved them and was still growing in power.

* Amy *

She knew it must be uncomfortable for Levi to take water into his lungs, but more so she remembered Levi's fear of water came from a near drowning incident as a child. Once he made the transition he was fine and able to wrestle the dead weight of Moon and Bambi out of the depths of the lake. Once they were out of the water the two Simians would recover quickly, while Levi went back down to survey the damage. She had been unable to make a smooth transition. She had done it quick and hard and expected damage on the edge of her energy sphere. She counted fifteen Warrs on the bottom of the lake and extra parts of five others. Obviously it worked both ways and parts of some of these Warrs had been left behind. She estimated that twenty Warrs had been put out of commission through the hard and sudden energy transfer.

Suddenly, she remembered the riflemen and Techs they had left at the San Diego colony. "We must get back!" The Techs would be in trouble if the Warrs launched an attack now without them, and they had no way of knowing Levi, Moon, and Bambi were not inside. They may even think they were captured or worse, dead, if they heard the commotion. She hoped they were holding at that location as planned.

It was time to leave as she prodded Levi to hurry. The shithead was swimming around on his back and flipping over and over like a kid, but when he heard and saw her thoughts he sobered and headed for the surface. Moon and Bambi were waiting for him as he exited the water. As always, Moon was stone faced, but Bambi was radiating admiration and praise for Levi. She was trying to help or hold Levi, she couldn't tell for sure, but Levi had to wave her off while he leaned over and choked out the water in his lungs. Levi looked so uncomfortable during the process. She felt badly for him, but it caused him no real harm and there was nothing she could do other than modify his lungs back to accept air and eliminate the gills.

After a few moments of coughing, Levi regained his composure and was able to stand up and receive the very attention from Bambi she had been holding back. Obviously Bambi was totally converted and dedicated to Levi now. Levi was actually in pain from the bear hug she was giving him, while Moon looked on sporting a knowing grin. After a few long moments he was able to extricate himself from Bambi's attention. Levi was still smiling as he began telling them in hand signs about the twenty drowned or wounded Warrs. He went on to explain the concern about their Tech and riflemen friends back at the San Diego complex and the necessity to return as soon as possible.

During the excitement, Moon and Bambi had also lost track of the original plan, and concern registered quickly on Moon's face. Bambi too looked shocked at the information. Levi felt for his weapons to insure they were still attached, somewhat amazed that they were. He had even been swimming with the heavy weights and was silently proud of how good he was getting. She didn't bother to tell him that she had been able to modify his body buoyancy to compensate for the extra weight.

As they gathered together for teleporting, she planned. They would teleport to the entrance where they left # 5, # 7, and the riflemen. She was careful to choose a location removed from their group. She was not taking any more chances. They would decide what and where to go once she saw the situation there.

* Levi *

He saw Amy's concern for those of the group still at San Diego. Amazingly, he had forgotten them in all the excitement. He agreed that it was time to go and swam to the shore and climbed out onto the bank. This was the dreaded part as he leaned over to drain his lungs. As before, this was a choking situation and very uncomfortable while the transition took place. Also as before, it passed quickly and he was ready to go, but Bambi was very appreciative of being saved and wanted to show it. Somehow he was not overly excited with her attention and hugs. Bambi seemed mushy and he

308

was uncomfortable with her attention, but allowed it. This too was over quickly as Moon, anxious to get back to his friends, pushed them roughly. Hmm, was Moon jealous? He chuckled to himself and Amy.

He heard the increasing echo of the gunshots first as they began to materialize back at the San Diego stadium. As soon as the teleport was complete, he ran toward the sound, which seemed to be by the gate. He immediately observed the five riflemen standing side by side firing down into the stadium. Once abreast of the riflemen, he looked toward the focus of the firing and saw several Warrs, maybe six, lying along the steps. Past the fallen Warrs he could see # 7 and # 5 trying to fight their way through the Warrs. "Oh NO!" They were trying to get to where they believed Moon, Bambi, and he were. The two Techs were berserk and fighting in uncontrollable rage against six Warrs. They had obviously fought their way through several Warrs while the riflemen were pelting them with bullets. The Warrs were going down, but there were still far too many for the two Techs. "Keep shooting!" he yelled as he ran passed. He could sense Moon close behind.

His anger was rising as he ran to help. He realized that he loved these big ugly Techs and would save them at all costs if it was possible, just as they were trying to do for him. Believing Moon and he were in trouble, they were sacrificing their lives trying to save them.

Even as he was drawing his pickaxe over his shoulder to strike, he saw # 5 fall. He went down hard with a massive broadsword buried in his shoulder. He leaped over # 5 and sank the spike of his axe in the head of the Warr as it was pulling the sword free from # 5. The Warr went down taking the axe with him embedded in its thick skull. He continued over the dead Warr, throwing his weight into the two Warrs behind. It was like running into a solid oak tree. He literally bounced off withering in pain and fell back on the Warr he had just killed. He saw the two Warrs raising their swords to strike. Oh shit!

* Amy *

Amy knew instantly that it was as she had feared. The Techs had heard the screeching and squeals of victory from the Warrs when Levi, Moon, and Bambi had been captured. The Techs had gone berserk and came to their aid. It seemed like a very long time that they had been at the lake, but it had only been thirteen minutes. That seems like a lifetime in the situation they had been in, and certainly it was long enough for # 5 and # 7 to have been killed. Fortunately, their rage and the firing from the riflemen had kept them alive. Together they had survived for the thirteen minutes and even killed six Warriors, but even as she watched, she saw # 5 go down.

Rage out of love for these Tech friends had driven Levi into his own fighting rage that sometimes consumed him. He was already running toward the battle. The dumb shit had no idea what he was going to do when he got there, but she did! She would choose a much different strategy if she was in total control, but there was Levi running like

310

a wild man, which of course he was. She loved him, yet there were times she would gladly kick his ass. She could, but would not allow anyone else to do it. What could she do now? He was moving straight forward already pulling his pickaxe so she directed him how to use it. Unfortunately, the spike struck too deep and wedged in the head of the dead Warr as it fell. She had not counted on that and his momentum was carrying him forward toward the two Warrs behind the fallen one. She spurred Levi even faster and threw him sideways before the impact, but it did not have the desired effect. She had hoped and calculated that the impact would at least knock them off balance long enough for Levi to move, but the Simians anticipated the impact and braced. The impact was bone crushing to Levi. Actually she was already repairing a cracked rib before he hit the ground. She saw the swords coming down from two different angles and saw no escape. She jerked his body to the side to minimize the damage, but it seemed too little too late.

Her mind registered the fact that the riflemen's shots were sporadic now as the targets were intermingled. Their caution against shooting a friendly was commendable, but possibly deadly for Levi now. They needed a miracle now which came in the form of a screeching, raging, female Simian named Bambi. In her haste to save Levi she almost crushed him under her huge feet as she stomped her way over Levi to attack the two Warrs. The Warrs stopped in mid-swing to stare in shock and maybe some fear. It was hard to tell which element was the most daunting to the Warrs as the raging and charging Fem crashed into both of them. It was a blur as she simultaneously threw her body against them and lashed out with her claws and FANGS! Amy had forgotten about the fangs.

She watched in awe through Levi's eyes. The rage and pure hate spewed forth from Bambi. Her charge had knocked the two Warrs flat on their backs and she sat atop both of them. She was totally brutal as she repeatedly plunged her finger fangs into the necks of the Warrs. The force with which she struck was even lethal. The Warrs' eyes were already glazed over from the poison and all motion from them had ceased, apparently already dead or dying. Bambi stood, apparently now in control, to look and realize what she had done. However, she seemed unconcerned and turned to ensure Levi's safety.

Even though it was brief seconds, Levi, as was she, had been frozen in shock at what Bambi was doing, but the clash of swords brought his attention to the conflict on Moon's side. One of the Warrs had gone down and the sides were even, but # 7 was obviously exhausted and beginning to falter. Levi would have to help.

* Levi *

Even as he saw the swords falling toward him he heard the Simian female screeching out her challenge to the Warrs. This was something they obviously had not seen before, because they stopped in mid-swing, frozen. He couldn't believe his good fortune until Bambi stepped on him. It was not gentle and very painful, but Bambi was insanely oblivious to the treatment she was inflicting on him.

312

Bambi was totally focused on the two Warrs. Her attack was not a work of art, rather it was clumsy and awkward, but quite effective. She simply thundered in, battered them down with her bulk, and scratched them like you might expect a human female to fight. The difference was that human females do not have fangs in their fingers. Wow! The Warrs seemed paralyzed, either from shock, fear, or the poison. Whatever the reason, the Warrs never recovered.

He always worried about Moon, even though Amy had augmented his fighting skills through mind downloads. Still, Moon had become like his right arm and he would hate to be without him. When he looked he knew his worry for Moon was unnecessary. The odds had been three Warrs to # 7 when Moon had joined the battle, but he could see that Moon had already killed one of the Warrs and the sides were even. Unfortunately # 7 had been fighting for some time now, and he was about to collapse. He had to do something fast. His axe was still embedded in the Warr's skull, so he pulled his short sword and swung it from his prone position into the back of the Warr's leg. He swung hard and low, cutting the tendon to the foot and taking the Warr by surprise. Chopping into a Simian was like chopping a tree trunk, but the combination of strength and surprise made the Warr stumble and fall. It was dead before it hit the ground from a final desperation chop from # 7's huge sword, before he too fell to the ground exhausted.

Moon was finishing off the last Warr as he turned his attention to # 5. He was still alive, but he looked really bad. The sword was still embedded deep in his shoulder. Actually the sword was well into his chest. He had no idea what was there. In a human it would have been lungs or maybe even a heart, but not in a Simian. He remembered the Simian Amy made him dissect during which he discovered other organs were in the chest and the lungs were where the stomach is supposed to be. Amy seemed to know though. She told him to remove the sword, which he did. There was never a moan from # 5.

Tech # 5 said, "Let me die, it is the Simian way."

Levi said, "Hell no!" He didn't give a shit, # 5 was not going to be allowed to die if he could help it. Amy was agreeing also, but she reminded him that they had a job to finish here and there were other Warrs to deal with now. She said leave # 5 and # 7 with two of the riflemen to watch over them while they completed their task. He was glad Amy planned everything and worked all the details out. He hated that part of leadership. Hell, he hated it all! He didn't like the responsibility. He just wanted to kill Simians.

He called the riflemen up and gave instruction to everyone while Bambi was stripping clothing off of some of the dead Warrs to use as bandages. He had only to retrieve his pickaxe and he would be ready. Soon # 5 was bandaged up as best as could be done and he, along with Bambi, Moon, and three riflemen were continuing into the complex toward the holding pens. Amy reminded him that there would be at least four more Warr guards to watch out for. They would be no surprise to the Warrs this time so they took their time and remained alert.

314

* Amy *

It was humorous at times when Levi actually believed he was acting on his own. Of course he knew she augmented him with plans and action, but sometimes he thought he was acting on his own. She would never destroy that illusion, however, the fact was, compared to her he did not think fast enough. Not that he was slow by any means, rather her mind worked much faster than any human mind. Like now, he thought it was his idea to chop the Warr in the heel and cut its tendon to help # 7. She calculated the precise angle and force necessary to penetrate the thick hide, augmented his strength with chemicals in order to accomplish the task, and sent the ideas to his head while she simultaneously directed his muscles. By the time the ideas hit his brain he was already moving. This gave him the speed while allowing his mind to perceive that it was his plan. The blow was timed to also break the Warr's balance. It worked to perfection and # 7 had enough strength to take advantage of the Warr's diminished defenses. That was the part she had no control of, because # 7 was on the verge of collapsing, but he was successful. She noticed the last Warr's momentary glance at the falling Warr, which cost him its life. Moon seized that advantage and struck the death blow.

Once the immediate threat was over, everyone's attention turned to # 5. He was severely injured with the sword deeply imbedded in his shoulder and chest. Obviously major bone damage had occurred as well as unknown internal damage to muscles and organs. From observation, she realized that Simians did little in the way of medical treatment. This was a technology lost to the Warrior Simian and abandoned because it required acknowledging the Technical Simians, which they would not do. She was unaware of any medically trained Tech remaining alive; however, her ongoing research of the Simian computer had uncovered a massive amount of medical data. She would have to download this data into a Simian and recreate the healing ability among the Simians. This would have to happen soon in order to save # 5, but they must complete the task at hand first and free the humans, Techs, and Fems.

They left the exhausted # 7 with # 5 and assigned two of the riflemen to remain with them while the rest proceeded into the complex. She estimated there were only four, possibly five Warrs left that would be expecting them. Cautiously they continued toward the human compound. There were no guards, so they opened the pen releasing the twelve humans imprisoned. Levi talked to them and calmed them, explaining that these Simians were friends and rescuers. As expected, they were suspicious but complied totally with Levi's orders. There would be time for detailed explanations later.

The Warr guards were gathered at the Technical Simians pen. In frustration they had decided to kill the Techs before they were killed. Two Techs lay dead already as they took in the situation. The riflemen began shooting immediately. They were close enough to be effective with their shots. He and Moon charged the Warrs screeching battle cries. The Warrs turned to face the threat and in doing so turned their backs on the obviously enraged Techs. The remaining thirteen Techs, encouraged by the support from Levi's group, attacked the rear of the Warrs. Being greatly outnumbered, the Warrs were quickly overpowered. The arrogance of the Warrs never ceased to amaze her. They simply could not conceive of resistance to their will from Technical Simians or humans... amazing. Stupid is what it was, to turn their backs on an enemy.

* Levi *

He was very pleased to know that Amy had deciphered much of the medical knowledge of the Simians. She would be able to download the knowledge to one of the Simians. She would have to; Amy and he couldn't handle anymore. It must be delegated. Amy agreed and said she would choose from the new Simian recruits. That was smart, but she needed to hurry because # 5 needed help now. Well that is where they were heading anyway so it wouldn't be long.

They freed the humans without any resistance. There weren't any guards at all. He briefly explained the situation to the humans like he had done before to the other liberated groups. He enjoyed the feeling knowing they had saved lives. Somehow it seemed to make up, in some small way, for all those he was unable to help before. As was always the case, the humans were mostly in shock and starved. Mostly they would just follow him. It helped more that there were other humans besides

317

him in the group. There was time later for their questions.

As they rounded the corner, he was appalled to see the last of the guards inside the Tech pen killing them. Amy didn't understand that either, but they hadn't come all this way just to let the Techs die. Moon had already screeched his battle cry and was running, but he was right behind him screaming also. Both stopped in their tracks when the Techs in the pen jumped the Warrs as they turned to face their challenge. There must have been some built up rage, as the Techs took the swords from the Warrs and literally dismembered them. He was pleased. These Techs had not lost their will to fight.

Bambi had separated from them earlier and went directly to the Simian females. Already they were returning, with her in the lead, and witnessed the Techs defeat of the Warrs. It hardly slowed the group. There were twenty-five waddling Fems coming directly for him. There was no hint of the dim-witted appearance they had been accustomed to seeing in Fems. These were open and searching, seeking him. Bambi must have done a good job of instructing them.

They didn't have time for a discussion at this point so, at Amy's insistence, he simply screeched, "Bambi will answer all your questions on the trip." Bambi was surprised at that, but he ignored her glance and said they would be joining other colonies soon. He told them that if, after they heard everything Bambi had to say and did not wish to join, they were free to go. He shut off further conversation by saying then screeching, "We all have to leave soon."

318

Before heading back toward # 5 and # 7 he asked first if there were any trained medical technicians. There were none. Then he asked the Fems beyond childbearing age to identify themselves. Of the twenty-five Fems gathered, only five stood forward. He wasn't sure why Amy wanted older Fems, but complied. Amy selected two and he volunteered them to be medical technicians. Amy had scanned their minds and saw only good will and no hostility at all. He placed a hand on each head and felt the vibration of the download. He didn't have time to explain and hoped the Fems didn't freak out. They were wide-eyed in surprised, but didn't balk. Damn, was it that easy? Problem solved! He laughed to himself and was rewarded with a smile from Amy. He wished all their problems were solved this easily.

While he was having the discussion with the Fems, Moon had gone to the Techs. That discussion had gone as expected and the group was returning. Together they returned to where they had left # 5, # 7, and the two riflemen. It was time to lay out the plan. Well Amy, "What is the plan?"

* Amy *

It was obvious that Bambi had opened the eyes of the Fems. All illusion to the slow witted Simian female was gone. Having gone through the negotiations with Mama, Levi had no desire to have another discussion that was plainly coming, with this group of Fems. She agreed, there simply wasn't time for it now. It was better that Bambi and Mama handle that part anyway. It would reinforce Mama's

319

authority. Levi was firm and successfully stalled any immediate discussion.

The most pressing problem now was # 5's health, and she had to find some volunteers fast. She decided to use two of the Fems, specifically those beyond child bearing age. She knew that Fems went somewhat crazy during mating time and had to be supervised to prevent the Fems from killing the male with their fangs during the act. That would not work well for someone that must maintain control and help others, regardless of stress. It also had to be a Simian, because the alien nature of their minds prevented linking. Downloading or linking with another human mind would link their minds permanently and she would never be able to break the link. She could not allow another human mind to be open to her. She could maintain those she already linked, but more would possibly take her beyond the ability to maintain her sanity. With the tampering of her mind by the Supreme One, she was not about to take any risks.

She quickly scanned the five older Fems that came forward and found no hostility. Truly, all the minds seemed intelligent and receptive. She found this to be further assurance that the entire Fem race had effectively hidden, even from her probing scans. She chose two that she perceived to be more intelligent. As before, she had Levi touch the heads of those two. It was a matter of forcing her brain waves through the resistance and then writing information on their minds. She also knew that she was permanently altering the thought pattern of the Fems, but that too was good since she hoped it

would prevent the Supreme One from reading their mind.

The download went quickly and the two Fems were now knowledgeable Simian medical technicians and proficient with hand signs. It was obvious that it worked as the Fems registered shock in their eyes. The reptilian slit in the red eyes opened wide making the darker pupils appear to bug out. It was almost comical.

Levi saw it too and said, "Problem solved!"

Levi had a knack for over simplification. He was a turd sometimes, but she loved him anyway.

The plan was in place, and there was so much to do. They would have to teleport the new medical technicians and # 5 back to the Mojave Desert settlement. There were medicines stored in the cave and she had provided the Fems with knowledge of the Earth drugs as well. Infection was the main problem, but surgical tools and equipment were available there to patch bones and stitch up muscle and skin. They would communicate with Dawn and get everything ready. The newly liberated Techs would need to be indoctrinated, which would have to be done by # 7 during the trip to Barstow to join with the others. Bambi would need to bring the Fems and travel with # 7. She couldn't leave the shaken humans so they too would be taken to the Mojave Desert settlement when they teleported. "Plan? Yes, there is the plan. Now it's your turn to deliver, smart-ass. Make it happen"

* Levi *

He knew something was wrong when she called him, "Smart Ass." She meant it and was not smiling. There was a lot going on, but nothing beyond Amy's abilities, not even close. Amy should be happy since this San Diego Simian colony represented the last Simian colony in their immediate part of the country. It should be seen as a major victory, even though most of the Warrs were still coming after them. So, something else was wrong. His mind touched hers, but encountered a solid mental block in place. She seldom kept secrets and would eventually share with him, but as she said, there was much to do.

He delivered Amy's plans and rushed them all to comply. Even Bambi, who was determined to stay at his side, saw the logic and necessity and took charge of the Fems and young to comply. The Techs and Fems were departing as his greatly reduced group prepared to teleport to the quickly organized operating room being readied by Dawn.

As the group materialized outside the cave entrance, Al and Dawn, anticipating the shock and fear of the humans, quickly greeted them and shuffled them off toward the cooking area. This was one of his favorite places. He was always hungry, but it would have to wait for a while before he could indulge. The resident settlement doctor with assistants greeted # 5 and the newly trained Simian doctors and rushed them off to the treatment center. It had been close, but # 5 was still alive. Now they could only hope.

Amy suggested that he join the group of rescued humans and riflemen at the cooking area and eat before they returned to Barstow. Yeah, like he needed to be reminded. There was no way he was going to leave without visiting the food area. That got a smile from Amy. She also reminded him to re-supply his chemical vitamin pills before they left. His supply was getting low so he decided to do that first so he wouldn't forget. He never wanted to be without them again. The last time he was separated from them he had almost died without Amy's chemical control of his body.

Moon had taken off to find one of the settlement's prize sheep to feed on. No one would deprive Moon of anything he wanted, but he had noticed that lately the sheep were herded off whenever Moon was around. It didn't matter; Moon would find them. Levi chuckled at the thought. While he was alone, he detoured into the cavern to re-supply the pouch on his side, his backpack too and even the emergency pocket Dawn had sewn inside his vest. The doctors were still working on # 5, but he could not find out anything as yet, so he proceeded to the cooking area.

Eating his normal heaping portions of food, he watched the spirit slowly returning to the rescued humans. Some of the other settlement humans had gathered to talk to the newcomers and comfort them. As always, he was embarrassed at the stories being told about him and Moon. To escape the embarrassment, he let his mind and eyes wander around the camp. Suddenly and shockingly, he noticed that there were about as many Simians as there were humans in camp. Techs and humans together were working the forges and beating molten metal, assembling the weapons per Amy's design, and various other odd jobs. He even noticed the Fems involved in most activities, all except cooking. Most of the Simians close to him at some point or another had shared their repulsion of destroying meat by fire. They would never be found near the smell of cooking flesh. Well, the feelings were mutual concerning the Simian appetite of devouring raw bloody flesh, some even rank from decay.

Amy's absence of comment increased his apprehension that something was very wrong. He tried to pry into her mind, but she could be very stubborn when she wanted to be. Ouch! That got a reaction.

"Stubborn?" She said, "That's your middle name."

* Amy *

Levi made everything happen just as she planned. It was all going well, but she could not stop the irrational feeling that something was wrong. She knew the source this time, however. It was the Supreme One. That was the cause, but not as it was before. Now that she knew about the Supreme One she could block its invasion into her mind, but this was different. This was more the effect of its words. It had said he knew where she was and she would die. This was more the cause than anything else. She felt the clairvoyance of the death wish from the Supreme One. It had a plan, maybe several, and she could feel the hate even now radiating out from its formidable mind. Yes, something was going to happen and she had to figure out what. She analyzed the problem and could find no answers, but her clairvoyance continued to warn her. The clairvoyance power was a curse. It answered nothing, only warnings she could not interpret.

Levi was probing, but she kept her thoughts private. Was she trying to spare him? That was absurd since he would die if she did. She decided to share the thoughts with him. His cynical mind might even be able to see what she could not. He had taken care of the business necessities of her plan and was eating now. Why not? It was his life too. She opened her mind to him and he was quick to grasp the situation.

For a moment, he thought in silence, so deep in his mind that she could not see. When he spoke, he said he trusted her clairvoyance. He reminded her that clairvoyance had saved them several times, even if she was unable to see the whole scenario. The latest warning she received was of the rear attack from the San Diego Simian colony. He was right! Yes, an uncertain warning was better than not having the gift at all.

Levi let his legal training come forth, and his cunning. He started tossing out ideas and asking questions in general, then started answering them. How would the Supreme One attack? He already has an army after them, so what else could he do? The Supreme One had said he knows where you are. That means he knows where your facility is. How? That was a good question. The Supreme One could not read human minds. They were simply too alien, as she had learned in her experience with Simians. Additionally, the Supreme One, she believed, could not understand English. Yet! That meant he was reading a Simian mind, and the only Simian that knew where the facility was... hmm... Moon? No, that's not so. They had taken # 5 there also.

She analyzed these facts. She had linked with Moon. Doing so had altered his basic brain wave pattern, which she believed would make him immune to the Supreme One's probes. On the home world the Supreme One had controlled minds and even killed by probing Simian minds. The Supreme One would have every reason to hate Moon almost as much as Levi. The distance separation had prevented this mind control so far, but she expected it would come sooner or later. She thought Moon was safe, but # 5 was a different story, because she had never downloaded to him. If # 5 made it she would have to download something to him and the other key Simians to alter their brain pattern. When she did, she would install additional protections from the Supreme One.

So, from the mental exercise with Levi they had discovered at least two areas of possible personal attack in addition of course, to the obvious total annihilation from the Simian armies. She believed it was personal with the Supreme One, and as such, the personal attack would be his choice. The mental control of Simian minds was one form of attack. The Supreme One could direct a Simian to surprise attack Levi. The solution was to maintain a personal bodyguard team of mentally adjusted Simians to intercept any suck attack. She believed that was the solution, hopefully. The second area of possible attack might be launched on her physical body (brain). A secret army of Simians could be en route to her facility even now. Her facility was very secure, but a total, unrelenting attack on the facility might secure access. They could in time tunnel through the mountain rock. Levi thought that was a likely assumption. She had a plan. This was not the best timing, and what she wanted to do was not for this reason, but this was as good as any time to start.

* Levi *

When she opened her mind to him, he realized that she had simply been deep in thought and maybe she was trying to protect him, but Amy realized it was his problem too. If she died so would he; besides, he was devious. He grinned to himself when Amy said that because it was true. Amy was too damned honest and up front. She couldn't lie if she had to, and this inability was dangerous, because she failed to see the hidden agendas and plots. Luckily he actually was devious, cynical and many other things he cared not to think about. Part of this training came from his law school education and association with the law firm he had worked for after graduation. He remembered his grandfather telling him once that a lawyer was trained to lie in such a way that no one could tell, and answer all questions without saying anything. In many ways Grandfather had been right. In contrast, his grandfather could say much with few words.

He remembered when Amy opened her mind to him, and he had heard the voice of the Supreme One. It made his hair stand on end and a tingle crawl up his back. Even now, when he remembered it he felt the cold bite of fear. There was pure hate radiating from that mind. He was unable to sense the strength of the mind, but Amy said it was incredibly powerful. He could sense the threat in the laughter and knew it was real. So far they had been too busy to address this threat, but obviously Amy was feeling the clairvoyant warning. Amy found her clairvoyance annoying, but he reminded her how it had saved their lives on many occasions and that it was truly a gift and something to be thankful for. Certainly they should address the problem now since she was receiving the warning.

There were probably many ways they could be attacked, but of every possibility he could conceive, the likelihood of direct control of a Simian's mind close to him by the Supreme One was the most likely approach. For example, what if the Supreme One took over Moon's mind and forced him to attack from behind? He would not stand a chance. Even to think of it was hurtful. Amy put him at ease when she explained that even though she was not permanently linked to Moon through the initial direct contact with his mind, she felt that the rearrangement of his thought pattern from the link altered him. She calculated that it was just enough to prevent the Supreme One from tuning into his mind. He hoped she was right.

If that premise was true, then Amy would have to make contact with all the Simians that were, or got, close to him. Amy insisted that he also have bodyguards in addition to Moon. He didn't like the attention, but knew Amy was not flexible on this issue, so he agreed. There would be two bodyguards always near him and awake. He knew without asking that the bodyguards would be from the original group of Techs He also knew of course that she was always awake and would be mindful.

The other immediate issue was a guard for Amy's physical location. If the Supreme One had identified her physical location, which it had alluded to, then it must have learned from monitoring # 5's mind. It was too late to correct that so they must adjust. Amy believed that the Supreme One might also be able to sense her location from the mental power radiating from her physical mind. No matter, the Supreme One knew and the facility must be protected. Who could protect her location and what scheme was Amy working on? And she said she wasn't devious. Right!

* Amy *

She grinned at his thoughts. Withholding information wasn't being devious. Was it? Oh well, maybe she was. It was simple, however. She wanted to reactivate her facility and staff it with Fems unencumbered with the breeding rage. The Fems could head up her research efforts, serve as the maintenance staff and also be her private protectors. Additionally, assuming she could reactivate her facility, she could defend herself.

Her plan wasn't devious. It was, however, complicated. Her continued research delving into the Simian computer had revealed the theory and science behind the ray they had used to alter the laws of physics on Earth. The effect was not reversible for Earth. It was like magnetism, you could take a piece of iron from a magnetic field and neutralize it (revert it back to the original state), but once you put it back into the existing magnetic field it would change it back, polarize it. Earth was the altered magnetic field. Of course, it was much more complicated than that, but it was terms Levi could relate to and understand. Her plan was to alter only her facility by creating a series of reversing invisible energy fields within her facility. If that could be accomplished, she could counter the forces of the Earth that had been altered within a limited area around her force fields. This would be like taking that piece of iron out of the magnetic field. If successful, she could re-activate her facility, complete with electricity and all technology that existed there before. It would, however, be a very small portion, a bubble within an ocean of altered energy.

It was a beginning, if she could overcome the first step. She had to generate the first energy field in order to fire off the power generator. She knew how to construct the energy fields using electricity as the source, once they had electricity. Surprisingly, it was not terribly complicated. It was only a matter of altering and adding some simple components to the existing fluorescent light fixtures, altering the radiation that naturally occurs from the enclosed gasses. These could be activated in a spiraling outreach throughout the facility. As the radiation from an altered fixture activated, it would, under constant bombardment, eventually reverse the effects of the Earth's altered radiation, but only in the close vicinity of the radiated alternative energy field. It would work if every light in the facility was modified and permanently on.

The facility already had redundant electrical generation plants and emergency backup systems for everything, but no one had anticipated neutralized electricity. If she could overcome this first obstacle she believed her plan would work. A portion of her mind had been working on this problem for some time without success, but she continued to hope.

One thing was for sure; she would have to relocate some of the older Fems to her facility whether she could activate the facility or not. They would be necessary just to ensure her safety. Also, if Levi was right, they had better do it soon. Levi had more confidence in her clairvoyance warning than she did, but this ability was just annoying to her. She dealt with precise or exacting facts and figures, and clairvoyance was just a feeling, an emotion. Certainly she trusted Levi's gut feelings more than her own clairvoyant warnings.

* Levi *

He was shocked at Amy's intentions. When she finally let him look, it shook him to his bones. Damn, she was a deep thinker, and damn, he liked the idea. It would not only offer protection for Amy, it would open up new possibilities to fight the enemy. Another thing he was thinking about was that, should he be killed, at least Amy would not be a prisoner locked within her own mind. She would have her research, the facility to maintain, contact with those that were there through cameras, speakers, and printers. She would be a busy girl, and he would never have her exclusively to himself ever again. However, he had faced that when Amy had established communications with # 5. He wanted that for her, and Earth's only chance was through her. Yes, he wanted that to happen.

He found it ironic that the Supreme One was forcing this. He knocked on his head and said, "Knock on wood." What they better be thinking about was saving Amy. The Supreme One had incredible hate for Amy. Even he had sensed that, and the threat must be taken very seriously. The Supreme One must have a plan and they must prepare for any option.

Even as he was toying with the thoughts, Amy told him that it would have to keep for a few days in order to organize the migrating groups of Techs, humans, and Fems. Additionally, there was an organized retreat ongoing, the evacuation of the Mojave Desert settlement, not to mention the two Simian Armies pushing them toward the jaws of an even greater Simian army. He waited to see if Amy would say, "We have them just where we want them." They both laughed at that thought. It was amazing how they had become accustomed to death hovering over their heads like dark clouds.

As he finished eating, he noticed that the sun was setting in the west. He thought back since they left the Owens Valley tribe, remembering what had happened. Damn, it seemed like months, but remembered that it had only been this morning. He was shocked, and the weight of all the events seemed to suddenly fall on him like a bolder. He was bone tired. Amy smiled at him and said everything could wait until tomorrow. Already he was nodding and thankful as he lay down right where he had eaten and fell sound asleep in seconds.

* Amy *

She knew he was tired even before he did and calculated that all the individual groups would not all arrive at Barstow until mid-morning tomorrow. Also the Owens Valley tribe should have made a successful retreat to the next mountain pass during the night. As always, there was danger, but nothing immediate. Everything could wait until tomorrow. Amazingly, Levi laid on the ground in silence and fell asleep immediately. Those around him watched, some still in awe, but those that knew him were used to the unusual from Levi. They moved away in silence to give him his peace. The gesture was nice but totally unnecessary, because he was deep in sleep and she had taken him even deeper to achieve total rest and repair. She would have preferred a more secure place for him to sleep than the dining area, but would remain alert and could wake him instantly if need be.

As expected, Al had been busy since his return and was with Dawn only for moments at a time. Dawn however, had also been busy and continued spending her time with Mama. As a result, her monitoring had been fruitful. Mama had organized the Fems into all manner of projects. No longer were they slow and docile. Now they were dynamos of energy and production. The Fems were joining the ranks of the Techs and even the humans. The work was progressing ahead of schedule now. She found it humorous that Mama had even begun bossing the Techs around. Even more surprising was that the Techs were jumping to comply. Mama was not trying to start any conflict between the Tech's leader # 9 and herself, and in fact went out of her way to support him. Though, any Tech other than # 9 that got close to her found himself running or volunteered for some task. They simply did not know how to take her. Mama was trouble, but she liked her immensely.

Mama was the one she wanted at her facility to run the special team of Fems. She had been considering it and trusted Mama. It came naturally. Mama was strong and demanding, and that was what she needed. On the negative side, which was also a plus for this decision, Mama needed to be separated from the Techs, she was simply too demanding and abusive. They had put Mama in charge of all the Fems, which served its purpose at the time, but things had changed now. Besides, Mama's choice of Bambi would work now. Bambi had learned that she could not always get her way, plus, after they had saved her at the lake, Bambi was a loyal convert to Levi. Of course Bambi was trustworthy to the cause previously, but she was now totally committed to Levi's welfare as well. Bambi would work out well and Mama would be the protector and boss at the facility.

Her plan was defining itself. She estimated that there were no more than twenty Fems over the breeding age throughout all the Fems groups liberated. Working with this number, she was organizing duties. She would have to download human technology to the Fems along with fighting techniques and adjustments to their thought

334

patterns. They would need technicians for electrical work, mechanics, scientists of all kinds, genetic engineers for yet another project she was contemplating, computer engineers, janitors, and even shepherds for the flocks of sheep and cattle for her field. This was the field where Levi had run with Thunder in the beginning. She grinned as she remembered how surprised Levi's horse, Thunder, had been the first time Levi outran him.

She continued to plan and think during the long night. Levi had been very tired and worn out and needed the sleep. He had still been somewhat mentally shaken from the episode in the desert when ASONE channeled the vibration through him to paralyze the Simian army at the first pass. That was just two nights ago and he hadn't had a full night's sleep since. Yes, he needed his rest to settle his mind. She had already repaired his physical body, but his mind was something he had to control. Luckily, he was very stable mentally.

They were lucky and no one or nothing disturbed him during the night until the camp started breakfast. At some point, however, she sensed and smelled Moon, and knew he was watching over Levi. She could do nothing about the smell of the morning cooking. It gently invaded his brain like a raging bull. When Levi smelled the cooking bacon, he was awake and looking around. At least he didn't have to walk far for breakfast.

* Levi *

He was dreaming and he was laughing, but he couldn't remember about what. Then he was

335

dreaming about food. In his dream he smelled bacon cooking, and it smelled good. Rousing, he realized it was real. Yes, he was awake now and said, "I'm hungry."

Amy said, "So what's new?"

"Ha ha! That's very funny, Amy. You made me that way." He was on the hard ground lying underneath a table. He laughed at himself, realizing what he had done.

As he got up and sat at the table, he noticed one of the young helpers was already bringing his first heaping plate of food. As he dug in, he rewarded the girl with a huge smile. Moon, also close, came to sit and talk. He signed that # 5 was going to live, but would not have full use of his right arm and would need time to heal. He and Amy were pleased with the news. Moon said # 5 was disappointed to be alive. He would be unable to fight and felt useless.

Amy said, "That's not so. There will be plenty for # 5 to do. He can remain behind in the caverns until healed then work in my facility. He will have a very useful position working on computers, both Simian and human."

When he relayed the information, Moon seemed to smile and was off to talk to # 5 and pass on the news. Levi smiled and said, "Thank you, Amy."

Amy opened her mind for him to see her thoughts and the plan developed during his sleep. Wow! He liked it. Mama was the one for sure. He was kind of glad that Amy would be dealing directly with Mama. She was a tough old broad to deal with for sure, but she and Amy would work it out. He had a feeling Mama would like the idea of taking care of a female of importance. In fact he knew Mama would take on that job with pleasure. He also knew Amy would be safe with Mama looking after her.

Amy was shocked when he reminded her that now Mama and her whole team would be aware of her existence. For some reason she hadn't considered that, but then he also reminded her that they would always be at the facility and would probably never leave, so it didn't matter all that much after all. Actually, she would have a private, exclusive and very elite team with her. Oh shit! The team was all females, except # 5, poor # 5. He chuckled at that thought until Amy gave him a very sharp pain in the ass. He said, "Ouch! Pinching my ass is becoming a habit."

He considered Amy's plan. He had been thinking about the problem Amy described, about the energy necessary for the first step of her plan. As with many problems, he had learned to sleep on them. Many times an answer came while he slept. This may be one of those times, maybe. Suddenly, he remembered a time in his youth, before the day of chaos, when he had seen a man illuminate a fluorescent light bulb by just holding it. It was a trick, but he later learned that the man was holding it in a field of energy.

Amy had described the force field required in relationship to the energy radiated from a fluorescent bulb. If she couldn't generate the proper energy necessary to alter the Earth's energy field, maybe they could work backward from the problem. Modify the light fixtures first and then simply force the initial bulbs to illuminate by her mental energy. He didn't know how she did it; she had certainly radiated massive amounts of energy at the advancing Simian army. He had felt the energy and it had almost destroyed his body. Surely there would have been enough energy field to explode any fluorescent bulb. That was his idea anyway. Illuminate the bulbs at the generator's location through her mental energy and let the modified light fixtures provide the exact countering energy to alter the Earth's energy field. Once the generator started and electricity began to flow, she could slowly back out of the loop and leave it running. Problem solved. Maybe the merging of their minds made him smarter. He even understood what he just thought.

When he had finished running through his thoughts, he asked, "Well, will that work? Am I smart or what?" As he looked into her mind he knew it would. Her eyes were rolled back and her mind was racing. She was oblivious to him and he knew he had found the secret to the puzzle and Amy could make it work now.

* Amy *

As always she had missed his company while he was sleeping, but his dreams were always interesting, if not amusing. She actually giggled to herself to see Levi hover between dreaming and reality. She found it funny that he was dreaming about smelling the bacon cooking. He was always hungry from his body's demand for protein. This was one of the negatives from the metamorphous she had put him through and would always be a fact of life now, since his body required so much energy.

338

Such as it was, it was still amusing how Levi enjoyed eating. He took great pleasure in the act. She couldn't quite understand the pleasure he received, even though she enjoyed sharing some of the sense of taste with him. Certainly, it was a frequent topic of conversation among the humans; even Moon had once asked him where he put it all.

Another topic among the humans was Levi's apparent lack of need for sex. They had no way of knowing that Levi was very sexual, but their sharing of each other's emotions and experiences made sex between Levi and her unequaled and totally satisfying. No other woman could interest him no matter how hard they tried, which they often did. It was a game among the women. Such was the case now as the pretty young blonde brought Levi his plate heaping with food. Levi paid no attention to the almost exposed breasts as she leaned over in front of him, but he did reward her with a radiant smile that made her flesh redden. It would have hurt her feelings to know that he was far more interested in the food than her.

Moon had apparently watched over Levi throughout the night, but was in obvious distress smelling the cooking meat. Moon came to inform them of # 5's condition, which was indeed good news. She had kind of expected # 5's reaction to being somewhat crippled. It was not really in the Simian's nature to care for any handicapped, but this worked into her plans. She could use # 5 at the facility if he was willing to live with all the old females. She assumed he would. Levi and Moon thought she was doing # 5 a special favor by offering that position, and partly she was, but she was being selfish also.

Levi understood better when she opened her plan to him. He liked it, but as always he seemed to see things that she had not anticipated. His thought patterns always seemed to open new viewpoints. In many ways it was helpful and refreshing, but in others, disturbing that she could miss some important facts. Of course, Mama and crew would have to know about her existence, but she had overlooked that fact. Also, as Levi pointed out, the older Fems would probably live out their lives at the facility so it wouldn't matter much. He speculated that the group would be very elite and clannish, which was probably very good.

Levi's thoughts revealed many aspects of her plan, mostly positive, just things she had not considered. However, when he started thinking about the technical problem of reversing the Earth's altered energy field, she focused hard on his idea. Damn! He did it again. The technical considerations of her plan were incredibly complex, yet he applied a simple solution and solved the problem. The solution was not as simple as Levi was suggesting, but the approach was. Work in reverse. Yes it would work, as she saw the end results. Her mind was racing to work out the details.

Amy had long ago engineered the energy field solution. The radiation was precise and predictable. She knew how to counter react the Earth force field by altering the existing fluorescent light fixtures. It involved altering the voltage of the ballast in the fixture to increase the specific natural radiation from the gas filled tubes. The second adjustment was a coating on the bulbs that further filtered the undesirable radiation and accented the desirable radiation. This could be calculated and designed, but she had not figured out how to generate the radiation to begin with to start the power generators. Levi's approach was incredibly simple. All she had to do was generate any kind of energy to stimulate the bulbs. From that, the modified light fixtures would provide the exact mixture to alter the molecules back to the original state. It would take time; she calculated twenty hours. Could she maintain the energy that long? Levi interrupted her thought to say that all she really needed to do was concentrate the fluorescent radiation on a very small portable generator at first and get that running. Then it was a matter of increasing the number of lights one at a time until the main generator could be altered. And so on and so on. She smiled and said, "I love your mind. It is so incredibly simple!" They both laughed.

Yes, they had a plan and it would work, but it would have to be coordinated with the other activities currently progressing. She reminded him that their forces were now gathered at Barstow and it was time to referee the melee. It was getting complicated there and they must go very soon. Levi agreed and suggested that they take Mama and any other of the geriatrics team. The humor was not lost on her, but she thought they could come up with a better name for this very special team. Levi laughed and offered the name Greys. He was still joking, but she liked it.

Bringing Mama was a good suggestion. They communicated with Dawn instructing her to tell

341

Mama to put someone else in charge of the Fems until Bambi came back, and bring herself and the other older females to the main camp. Tell them they are volunteering for a very special assignment and they wouldn't be coming back. Dawn had learned not to pry, if explanations were not readily provided. She was off to accomplish her bidding.

It took Mama less than forty minutes to gather the other three as requested and present herself and the other Greys at the main camp. She was indignant, but you could tell she liked the attention. Without telling them everything and certainly not about Amy, he told them basically what he wanted and that they would be taken to a secluded place to operate a very secret and important facility. They all readily agreed. Mama even seemed particularly happy.

It was time to go, and she knew there wouldn't be much help from Levi. Oh, he would do whatever was necessary; he just wouldn't be energetic about it. The organization and details bored him, but Barstow was waiting and it needed their leadership, hers and the shithead's.

342

CHAPTER 9
(HER FACILITY ACTIVE)

* Levi *

As expected, it was a chaotic mess when they got to Barstow. When he and Moon, accompanied by Mama and the other three Fems, materialized at Barstow, the others all came running. He hated this end of the business, but Amy organized things well. Actually, she had been monitoring Jimmy all the while, but other than knowing that everything was well and everyone was alive, he really wasn't concerned or interested. He was happy to let Amy do the planning. Still, when he was on the scene, they all expected him to make decisions for them.

Bambi, seeing Mama, went straight for her. He could tell she was originally headed for him until she saw Mama. Somewhat puzzled, she turned and was reporting to Mama. He knew that Mama would pass on the changes to Bambi. He interrupted them long enough to tell Mama, "Address the other Fems as well and report the changes then gather the older Fems." Mama gave him a knowing look and possibly an aggravated one as well, as if to say, "I know what to do, Sonny." He laughed in spite of the heat that flushed over his face. Well, this is one that wouldn't bother him to make decisions.

Amy already knew that Bambi had gone directly to the other Fems upon her arrival, which had only been about three hours ago. Already they could see that the other Fems were excited and far from the docile Fems that he had seen earlier.

Damn, there were a lot of them. There must be at least one hundred and fifty Fems and about the same number of young Simians. In addition to the Fems, there were fifty-eight Techs, including eight of his original group, and hundreds of humans that seemed to have come from nowhere. There were herds of cattle, wagons and gear everywhere. It was very confusing and actually scary to think of the responsibility and organization this would require. He just turned it over to Amy by saying, "What are you going to do, Amy?"

He was barking Amy's orders and instructions to all that came around, but was having a hard time keeping up with the big picture. He just wanted out of there.

* Amy *

She really could sympathize with Levi for once. It was complicated to organize. Most of the groups were remaining separate, and no one seemed to know what to do. There was food on the hoof and plenty of water in the wells, but no one was in charge. She didn't need this. Time was too precious. She needed to put someone in charge, but whom? The obvious choice for all the Simians was # 9, so Levi sent Moon with the bad news. Even # 9 didn't know what to do with the liberated Fems, so Levi also sent Moon to tell Mama to inform the other Fems to follow # 9's orders. Hopefully, that problem would be solved since # 9 was a good organizer and firm leader.

What was the objective? The goal was to get this horde of Simians and humans to the desert

344

settlement as soon as possible. Was that so hard? Although, the problem was that they didn't have a human leader.

Levi said, "You can't have two generals for an army."

He was right of course. They didn't have to look for Jimmy as he was right beside Levi. Levi told Jimmy that # 9 was in charge of the groups and instructions would be issued through him to the humans. It would have to do. Jimmy looked apprehensive but nodded in understanding.

Attention turned to # 9, who also seemed to be apprehensive, but he soon began organizing and issuing instruction for wagon loading, water, supplies, herding of the cattle, placement of the different groups in the marching line, etc. She took this opportunity to slip Levi out of the crowd and away to the next problem.

Where was Fred? She knew Fred was avoiding Levi. For once in a very long time he was out of immediate danger and with other humans. He was no longer in constant fear for his life, but he knew that would change any minute. By looking through Fred's eyes, she located him hiding in a grove of trees nearby. Fred knew he couldn't hide from Levi, but she could tell that the momentary false well-being was comforting. She hated to spoil that, but asked Levi to speak to him and get him ready to go to the Owens Valley Tribe at their organized retreat. Levi smiled, knowing what Fred would say to that.

Two things were a certainty: They had to take Fred and the other five riflemen to join the retreat. The extra riflemen were needed to help cover the retreats and Fred was needed to monitor the situation. So far she was just hoping that everything was going well. If it wasn't, she would have no way of knowing. The other thing that must be done soon was mind link with Mama and the other chosen Fems. Mama was gathering the volunteers now so that could happen as soon as they returned back from seeing Iron Eyes.

It was time to leave and Levi was more than ready. He didn't have to be asked twice, and called Moon, the riflemen and a grumbling Fred.

* Levi *

Even Amy was ready to go; he certainly was. He hated the stress of leadership and longed for the peaceful days before this all began. That was strange. Always before he longed for revenge against the Simians and now that he was getting it, he wanted the peace. He said, "I guess you had better be careful what you wish for." Amy smiled in return.

Amy, as usual, worked everything out with # 9 left in charge and Jimmy being the spokesman for the humans. Jimmy would get a taste of leadership and would be able to openly advise # 9 of the human requirements or instructions from Amy. He should be okay. At least Amy would be able to help him if necessary.

When he called Fred and explained what was needed, Fred, as expected, was frightened and grumbling. They had long since discovered that this was Fred's way. No, he was not a brave man, but he never refused. Fred was a good man at heart and could be counted on, even if he was afraid. They were really beginning to like Fred a lot and were amused at his antics. Like now, Fred knew he couldn't hide, but there he was in the grove. He almost hated to bother him.

As the riflemen gathered with Moon and the slower Fred, they saw Bambi coming. She was not to be left behind even on this first short trip. He felt the energy pulling the hair on his arms as they began the teleport. In the next instant they were standing in the middle of the pass looking around. There were no humans to be seen! Levi asked, "What is wrong Amy?

Amy said, "I don't know. They should be here."

It was then they noticed the Simian armies between this pass and the next one in succession. The Tribe had made the next transition early. It took only minutes to teleport to the coordinates Amy had previously recorded. This time they were behind the defensive barrier of riflemen and Lancers.

Almost immediately the alert went up and Iron Eyes came running. He quickly explained that the last pass was not as defensible and the attacks were more forceful with the disadvantage, so he made the decision to pull back a day early. Other than that one problem, everything had been operating as planned. In some ways it was better, but unfortunately, they had reduced the schedule by one day. The sentries reported that the Warrs had taken the cattle that had been left behind and were, in fact, feeding on them. This was definitely good.

Iron Eyes was elated to see the additional five riflemen and was quick to assign them to the defense team. He also instructed that relief teams be assigned to the new riflemen so a stronger twenty-

347

four hour watch could be established at the pass. Levi was glad Iron Eyes was a good leader and he and Amy weren't going to have to get involved as they had with the other teams. They had enough to think about planning the overall defense plan.

Iron Eyes also accepted the assignment of Fred to his side as communication. Iron Eyes was thankful for the communication and relieved, even comforted to know that Levi could be summoned if necessary. Of course there would be little that could be done if the Warr army broke through with almost two thousand screeching giants.

* Amy *

It was not really surprising that Bambi insisted on going with them on this errand. Bambi felt like she was one of the main team now, and she was, or would be. It was a manageable size group anyway, but her comfort was soon abandoned when they teleported into an empty pass. She was immediately concerned about the Tribe but was quick to realize that they must have made the transition earlier than expected. This could have been devastating if they would have teleported into another gathering of Warrs like they had done back in San Diego. They were lucky, but it reinforced her strong desire to have communication with the Tribe. Oh well, Fred was here now to save the day. She was grinning as she shared her thoughts with Levi.

The location had been recorded from before when they astral projected through the route, so it was no problem readjusting the teleport to the now current location. It was routine and they discovered that everything was more or less still on schedule. Well, almost. They now had only eleven days instead of twelve in the passes and relative safety. Even that safety had now been enhanced with the addition of the second group of riflemen. She was comfortable leaving now, but Levi was still yapping to Iron Eyes. Sometimes he talked too damned much.

As she insisted, Levi made his farewells and they teleported back to Barstow to check on the new Grey recruits. It was as she had hoped. There were fifteen Greys waiting with Mama for their new responsibilities, but they also presented a new problem that threatened to destroy all her plans. Mama looked at Bambi and told her it was bordering on the gathering. Both Moon and Bambi looked shocked, but recovered quickly, although Moon continued to watch Bambi. Bambi turned suddenly with almost visual fire blazing from her eyes and screeched to Moon.

Bambi screeched, "It's not my time! Stop looking at me."

Moon visibly jumped and backed up, but he was grinning and so was Levi. In exasperation Amy said, "Are all males the same?"

Levi actually laughed out loud and said, "Yes."

This information shocked her too. She was aware that the gathering for mating occurred every eighty days and lasted for five days, but they had never witnessed one. Although a lot had happened and it seemed longer, it had actually been less than seventy-nine days since the last gathering. There had not been a gathering since the first group of Fems from the Colorado River Simian colony

349

females joined the desert settlement. Tomorrow would be the anniversary of the original eighty-day cycle. They had used the last gathering, when all the Warrs returned to the colony to mate, to pass safely by the Simian colony on the Colorado River.

She had learned more about the gathering from her research of the Simian computer. It was the time the Simian females came into season for breeding. She had not learned the significance of an eighty-day cycle, but assumed it must have been ingrained from moon and sun cycles on their home world. Luckily, only about a third of the females came into season on any individual gathering. The other two thirds assisted the females that were in season. They protected them from the sometimes uncontrollable passions from the males and also protected the males from the passion of the females. It was not uncommon for a female in passion to inadvertently claw and poison her male breeder by mistake. The male Simians outnumbered the females in season about thirty-five to one, which resulted many times in battle for the right to breed. This was a form of survival of the fittest to the extreme. Fortunately, in this gathering there would be approximate even numbers of males verses females, and these breeding males were Techs.

All their plans would have to be altered. She knew that the Techs would want to stay for the gathering. In reality, they had better stay, because there were no other males, but what about Moon?

When Levi asked, Moon said, "I will wait on Bambi."

This brought another blazing look from Bambi, but her comment was not intelligible... something about faeces of an unknown animal.

Moon ignored Bambi's comment and said, "We can go, but I do want the others of the original group to stay. It is time to repopulate the Tech race again."

This would also be the first time in over fifty years that the Technical Simians would be able to procreate. She understood that Moon also wanted the lost experience of sex again for his friends. It was also becoming obvious that he wanted Bambi for himself, and Amy suspected that idea wasn't so terrible for Bambi as well, in spite of the show of annoyance and hostility projected at Moon

* Levi *

He was shocked to hear about the gathering. He was surprised that it had slipped by Amy, too. She never forgets, but he remembered how stressed she had been and the pressure of leadership had been intense. She had a right to forget. Amy said, "I didn't forget, I just hadn't remembered it yet. After all, the gathering doesn't start until tomorrow."

He choked off a laugh. He could have teased her some, but decided to leave it alone.

It was actually pleasing to see the bickering between Moon and Bambi concerning the mating. Truly, he thought it was natural for Moon and Bambi to pair together since they would be traveling with him all the time anyway. He wasn't sure if Simians loved or ever mated in permanent pairs, but it seemed like they were both headed in

351

that direction, even though Bambi looked fit to kill. He thought it was humorous, as did Amy.

What would or could they do now? How devastating was this gathering to the overall plan? Certainly it would slow the Simians by five days, but would it destroy the other plans? Amy was calculating and modifying the plans as they discussed it.

She said, "The Greys should be able to leave since there would be two thirds of the Fems unaffected by the mating fury that could help with the mating."

The humans were potentially the slowest anyway because of the wagons and must leave. However, she suggested that Jimmy stay to monitor the gathering. He suspected that Amy was curious to learn about this event. Actually, so was he.

The problem that existed now was, "Who would be in charge of the wagon train since both # 9 and Jimmy would be staying at Barstow?"

Amy said, "They are already organized; just send them on their way. The Simians would catch the slow wagon train before they got to the desert settlement anyway."

He didn't really care. He was just wondering.

The instructions were passed on and the human wagon train made ready to leave. They seemed to be in a hurry to get away from the potential of raging Simian passion, and he couldn't blame them. When he notified Jimmy that he was to stay, he also cautioned Jimmy to watch from a distance and never venture too close.

Jimmy smiled really big and quickly said, "Don't worry. I'm not that damned curious."

He was worried about Amy being exposed to danger at her facility. Amy was seemingly not in a hurry. It was like other things were taking priority, but she was the most important thing to everyone including him. It was time to go and begin protecting Amy from the Supreme One. When he suggested that they go she was agreeable, but had a different schedule of events. She wanted to download her training programs to the Greys first.

She said, "It will help to ensure that the Supreme One will not invade the Greys' minds."

He knew she was afraid that secrets of the facility might be learned or one of the Greys might be influenced to do harm to one of them. As usual, she was right.

He backed his mind out of the situation, while Amy went through all the motions of downloading the programs she developed. His hands held Simian heads and he was vaguely aware of the vibrations as the programs were transferred. Amy was rattling off information about electronics technicians, electricians, research engineers, mechanical engineers, diesel mechanics, and others; but he didn't even remember what most of those functions were anymore. Amy seemed exasperated in his lack of interest, but he found that funny.

At long last they gathered for the teleport. The Greys knew what was going to happen, having seen him teleport before, but looked apprehensive just the same. He really didn't blame them. It was a smooth teleport however that materialized them just outside the main entrance, almost. The materialization never was actually completed. The scenery of the location was becoming clear then suddenly was replaced with blackness. From the smell he knew they were inside the facility. He said out loud, "What the fuck is going on, Amy?"

The answer was quick as Amy simply said, "Warrs were outside the main door."

The only intelligent thing he could think of to say was, "Oh shit!"

* Amy *

She had learned from the Simian computer archives that, prior to the genetic creation of the Warrior Simians, the original race of Simians were in fact paired for life. This basic way of life changed dramatically when the Warriors grew to competing status. The Warrs had no need or desire for companionship of a mate. They were only interested in raw animal lust and propagating the Warrior Simians as the dominant race. As the female population dwindled in comparison to the Techs and the artificially created Warrs, competition for breeding females became extremely difficult. As a result, the females were gathered and protected. This was mainly protection from the Warrs' brutality, but to a certain extent, the Warrs wanted to prevent breeding from the Technical Simians. The result was the same. The Technical Simians lost their position as the largest population and dominant race.

She believed the basic instinct for pair mating was still deeply ingrained in the Technical and Female Simians' basic genetic programming and would surface again in this pair of Simians now staring and bickering back and forth. Levi, even

354

without knowing the history of the Simian race, was quickly recognizing the humanlike emergence of courtship. Levi even found it humorous as he watched. Strangely, she also found it humorous. For whatever reasons, she agreed with Levi. These two were likely to be a pair, but only time would tell.

It was time to proceed on to her facility with the Greys. As they grouped together, she began to detail for Levi the intricate details of her plans to download information, education, and job descriptions. She had all the Greys assigned functions in her plans. All she had to do was download the information. As usual, she was exasperated with Levi. He was not in the least interested in the mundane details of engineering, mechanics and job functions.

Levi said, "I know you will make it work and control it, so why do I need to worry about it?"

He was right of course, but it really was a good plan and she wanted to share it with him and possibly get an "At-A-Girl." Oh well, that was not to be. He really could be an ass sometimes.

Levi seemed to back away from his body and allowed her mind to move in and take control. She liked the feeling of having a body, but there was never any doubt that Levi was in control and he was just letting her borrow it. His will was simply too strong. She talked through his mouth, moved his hands to the Simians' heads, and went through all the motions of her plan. It seemed to take hours to accomplish the mind modification and information transfer, but in actuality it was only eighteen minutes. The Greys were slowly realizing that they knew information they previously hadn't possessed

355

and seemed to be keenly aware of their new purpose in life. This new meaningful responsibility seemed to greatly excite the Greys. They were anxious to put their new knowledge to work, and so was she.

Levi re-joined her in his body, and she began the matter transfer. The image in Levi's eyes slowly began to superimpose over a new image at their destination. As they were beginning to materialize she sensed danger. Yes, she already smelled the strong musky scent of Simian Warriors and altered the destination. The calculations required were astronomical but necessary. She worked frantically and altered the materialization point fifty feet to the south, bringing them safely within the main enclosure. The sudden change left them standing in total blackness as the Greys began to panic. The Simian home world had two suns and three moons, which meant they were never exposed to total darkness. She had learned that total darkness was very frightening to Simians, and this was sudden and totally unexpected. Levi quickly spoke, calming them as he anxiously searched for the lanterns she guided him toward. Light was soon radiating out, pushing the blackness away. The Fems raced for the light and huddled in its apparent warmth and protection.

With the immediate problem of light resolved, she quickly began to analyze the problem of Warrs outside the facility door.

Levi broke the silence when he said, "What is that damned banging?"

Surprisingly, she hadn't seemed to hear the banging before, but there it was loud and clear. Solid and loud bangs reverberated within the massive cavern of the complex, echoing back from the distant walls and corridors. She hadn't seen the Warrs outside, only smelled them. There were many individual smells, maybe as many as twenty-five separate identifying scents. They were evidently beating on the huge metal door with heavy objects. Would that gain them entrance? She calculated and analyzed. Yes, it could work in time, but it would take a lot of energy and time. How long had they been here working on the door? She had to know and observe the damage. If they got in, they would be in trouble if not dead. Only then did she hear the Supreme One in her mind laughing. It was pure evil, and she went cold with fear.

The Supreme One screeched, "Now you die, bitch!"

* Levi *

He felt the panic and fear. "Amy, what's wrong?" She said nothing, but he felt something was desperately wrong. Amy was paralyzed with fear. He had only seen her like this once before when the Supreme One had spoken to her. Was that it? Of course, that's it! That was why the Warrs were outside hammering on the door. The Supreme One had sent them to kill Amy. Had he spoken to her again? Amy had said, "The Supreme One promised to kill me." The way Amy was acting maybe she was afraid that he had or was about to do just that. He silently screamed at her, but nothing. He screamed again, "Wake the fuck up Amy!" There was nothing but silence. Damn! What was he going to do? He didn't feel dead so he must be alive.

357

He could sense Amy and feel her mind, so she was alive. She must just be scared or in shock. All he could do was wait. Well, he had no intention of dying without a fight, so he would have to figure out what the Warrs were up to and how to kill them.

Amy usually did all the planning. He was actually surprised with himself, realizing just how much he had allowed Amy to take over all the planning. Well, she would be alright. She just needed a little time and he would get her attention soon, hopefully, but what to do now? He had a brain. He must use it now.

First, he had to find out how many Warrs were outside and what their plan was. Answering the second question first, he said to no one in particular, "Well, they are obviously trying to beat the door in." The crashes on the steel door were thunderous inside. He cautiously found his way to the source of the banging. They were concentrating on the small door built in the massive steel door of the cavern entrance. By the looks of it, the small door was losing the battle. Each crashing blow shook the huge hinges on the door. They were bending with the crashes. The door was caved in at the center, which had loosened the hinges and latch even further. The latch was strong, but if a hole could be opened in the center, the latch could be released. Already a small hole could be seen opening. He remembered how futile the steel door had appeared before when he was challenged with trying to gain access to Amy's facility. Without Amy's telekinesis, they would never have entered, but these super strength Simians were gaining access.

358

It was only by accident that they had happened along when they did. The Simians would gain access to the facility within hours had they not come when they did. Come to think of it, they might anyway. Again he screamed, "Wake up, Amy. I need you!" Nothing!

He thought. He needed to know how many Warrs there were. Suddenly, he remembered the escape hatch. Where was it? Damn, he needed Amy's maps in his mind. He began searching. As he started toward the wall he again became aware of the others. The Greys were closing around him and the light, following. Moon and Bambi were staring at him, obviously wondering what was wrong. He must look like a crazy man. He laughed out loud in spite of himself. That seemed to break the tension that had been building in him and the others. He relaxed and told them what was happening. They were serious and quiet, knowing that he would tell them what to do and provide a plan. The only problem: it was Amy that always seemed to know what to do and provided the plans to do it. Damn, he would never take Amy for granted again.

As he searched for the escape hatch he again tried talking to Amy. He said softly and gently, "Please come back to me, Amy." He thought he felt her mind touching him briefly, but she didn't respond. He was worried. The Supreme One was using terror and fear to paralyze her. He had to break the hold it had on her, but how? Abruptly, he knew how, but it seemed unfair. He told Amy, "I am dying, and you are the one killing me. My mutation is killing me and you are letting it happen. HELP! I need you to save me Amy!"

* Amy *

She seemed to shut down. She was frozen in fear. The Supreme One had invaded her mind again and filled it with pure terror. Nothing seemed to work to break the hold he had. She felt the pure evil hate and knew the Supreme One would never stop, never give up hating, and would never quit until she was dead. It was worse. She knew the hate was all consuming and total. He wanted to terrorize her and destroy her will. He wanted to reduce her to a quivering, quaking, defeated mind. That seemed even more important than even her death. The only thing that would stop the Supreme One would be her demise. It made her almost welcome death.

She was vaguely aware of Levi trying to talk to her, but her fear was all consuming. What? Levi said he was dying, but he was not dying. He was alive and well, but the words had gotten through and grabbed her attention. It was just enough to realize what the Supreme One was doing to her. Damn, her fear instantly turned to anger! How dare the Bastard enter her mind to spread fear? She felt violated! Figuratively, she shook her head to loosen the imaginary hold and to start her mind again. As she did she felt the total uncontrollable rage of the Supreme One at having lost his grip on her. It was brief then faded away. She could still sense him, but he was not in control... not anymore. She vowed, "You will never control me again!"

She was in control again and even more committed to the war against the Supreme One, but Levi was her immediate focus. He needed her and she needed him. She realized what had happened and knew what Levi was doing. She had been frozen, but her subconscious mind had still registered what had happened. The subconscious mind was always there, but since she never slept, she didn't feel any benefits from it. Now she did.

Levi was thinking well. The access hatch would be a good observation point and safe. She superimposed the maps in his mind to guide him, but suggested that he light other lanterns and leave the Fems behind to watch the door. She said, "Tell Mama to use their finger fangs to kill any Warr trying to put his hand inside the hole. Levi was happy she was back and quickly followed her suggestions. This was different. He usually showed resistance to her orders. That is why she now made suggestions. He took suggestions much better.

As Levi was providing the plan to the others, she altered the plan again saying, "Implement the conversion plan now. There is no reason to wait and every need to have the electronic defenses." That brought an exasperated look, but he began issuing the orders. All the Fems knew what to do. It had been programmed in along with the necessary skills and technology to accomplish the job, well, profession. The nonessential Fems to the facility activation need to remain and watch the door, while the others take the other lanterns and get started. Bambi and Moon seemed lost, but doggedly followed Levi as he resumed his trek to the escape hatch.

* Levi *

361

He was startled when the facility maps popped into his mind. He immediately realized that Amy was back. She was quick to open her mind to him so he would know what had happened. He had been right. It was the Supreme One, and it had almost destroyed Amy; but he could see Amy's resolve to prevent that from happening again. He said, "Good for you, Amy. You go girl!" She smiled, but was not side-tracked as she issued her orders. As usual, her plans were well thought out and focused on the immediate needs.

The electricians and diesel mechanics were off to the power plant on the upper level above them. Others were off in different directions doing he knew not what, but they looked focused. Amy would be needed to begin the process, but there was much preparation to be accomplished. Parts necessary for the lighting modification would need to be located in the supply inventory, the circuits built and installed in the fluorescent light fixtures, the diesel generators would have to be serviced and readied, and the portable generator would also need service. Luckily, the dry air inside had prevented rust from eroding the equipment. Mama and a few other Fems were standing at attention at the door waiting on the opportunity to fang any hand that came into reach. So much to do... so little time.

Amy said, "Activating the facility will allow me to develop defenses to protect us from future attacks, but we are on our own now with this immediate problem. I hope we can survive this first attack."

He knew this was his job and took off following the route visible in his mind to the escape hatch. It wasn't far, but required making several corners and corridors. He quickly found himself at the base of the ladder leading up two decks. He left the lantern with Moon as he began climbing. As quietly as possible he turned the wheel inside the hatch and opened it. Light flooded into the passageway and momentarily blinded him. He had not considered the sudden light, but he realized that Amy had or he would not have been able to see for some time. As he adjusted to the light, he cautiously lifted up over the edge. His heart sank as he saw the gathered Simian Warrs below. He didn't count them, but Amy said there were thirty. They had axes and huge hammers and were taking turns working on the door. The metal of the door was shiny in the sunlight where it had been assaulted by the Warrs. The metal was in shreds and a large pile of the metal flakes covered the ground. The door looked very weak and he wondered if they still had hours as they had hoped. They needed to do something very quickly. He asked Amy, "What are we going to do?"

He saw the intensity of Amy's mind. He had seen this before. She was calculating, planning, and yes, scheming. He suggested that they teleport and bring the riflemen here, but she opened her monitoring, and he saw that the Owens Valley Tribe was under attack at the pass where they recently had withdrawn. It would be disastrous to take the riflemen now. He mentioned the bows, but Amy reminded him that there would be no way to retrieve the arrows and they already had poison with the Fems. Nothing new would be gained. As last resort she asked him to contact Dawn and have the five bowmen at the desert settlement gather in case they were needed. She said they might help some. He started to make other suggestions, but recognized a certain look in Amy. He saw the determination and even hate for the Supreme One, and he finally saw a look of satisfaction beginning on her face. She had something! What was it? Then he started smiling as he saw what she had in mind.

* Amy *

She adjusted the irises of Levi's eyes as he opened the hatch. As expected, the mid-day sun was bright and flooded into the facility, spreading a beam of light cutting across the interior. After a moment, Levi lifted his head over the edge and looked down on the scene before them. She counted thirty Simian Warriors. They had inflicted major damage to the outside of the entrance door, far more than she had anticipated. The door still held and she hoped the hinges would continue to hold. It would be disastrous if the entire door came open. The Fems would attack but they would not have the advantage if the Warrs could use their swords. The Warrs had to be driven off or defeated, but how?

Levi had some good ideas, but none suited her needs. For their safety she didn't want others learning of this facility. That is why only a select few and now the Greys were the only ones that knew the exact location of her facility. The Greys would live here permanently so that didn't matter, but none outside the immediate circle of friends needed to know the location or the true nature of her relationship with Levi. They had taken strong measures to keep it a secret.

The butt, Levi, said, "Don't you think the Supreme One knows where your facility is?"

Diplomacy was not one of Levi's strong points, but he was right. Still, she wanted to limit those that knew. They would have to solve the problem on their own and she was starting to see a plan.

There were probably many things that ASONE could do, but she had no control over invoking the hidden monster or angel, depending on how you viewed it. So, she would have to devise her own plan. There were so damned many of the Simian Warriors though.

Even as she started the modifications on Levi's body, she received a knowing and approving smile from Levi. That was reassuring, but a totally unnecessary show of support for her plan. Actually, it was all she could think of and she had no choice. It was simple. She was modifying Levi's body into a look alike Supreme One using descriptions and memories she had seen in the minds of some of the Simians she had mind-linked with. A Supreme One had ordered this attack, and it was a Supreme One that was going to change the orders. She had no doubt that the plan would work. The Warriors were deathly afraid of a Supreme One and would follow any order from one without question. She was, however, positive that it would only work once. The Supreme One would make sure of that, once it calmed down from the initial rage. She was smiling as she shared these thoughts with Levi.

She would gain some revenge in the process. She had felt the pure evil hate and rage radiating from the Supreme One when it had invaded her mind. Now she was anxious to feel the satisfaction of causing this reaction in the bastard. Give him a taste of his own assault.

She was concentrating on the changes. It was going fast, faster than maybe she should have gone. Her first warning was the reaction from Moon, Bambi, and the other Fems. There was terror in their eyes. Even Moon was frightened and backing up to the edge of the light from the lantern. "Oh shit." Levi reacted quicker and immediately explained what was happening. They looked relieved, but remained back from Levi.

His body had grown to a height of twelve feet. No wonder they looked frightened. His height had almost doubled in less than fifteen minutes and he looked much wider and heaver. She had expanded his body density to make him appear wider, but in fact he still weighed the same. She did not have the ability to increase his body mass, only the density. He would never be able to fight like this, but that was not the intent. He was totally appearance now, but what an appearance. He looked fierce and menacing, but the most striking feature was the piercing white eyes blazing out from under heavy grayish white brows. The skin had turned white and golden hair grew profusely over his now naked body. Levi had shirked his clothes with much complaining as his body expanded and they became tight. She would have to devise clothing for him before he appeared outside. Mama solved the problem by handing Levi a cloth wrap she had in her pack. It only served to cover his waist and thighs, but not sufficient to cover his chest. That would have to do.

Levi looked identical to descriptions of the Supreme Ones she had recorded from various interviews and, judging from the reactions from the others, it must be fairly accurate. It probably would not be judged too critically from the Warrs outside. Shock should work to their advantage. It was time to exercise her plan.

* Levi *

"Damn it, Amy, give me more warning next time!" Amy had started the modifications to his body and his first warning was the tightness of his shoes and clothing. He had to scramble to get his shoes off before they got too tight. He got them off just in time to rush to get out of his leather pants and vest. He had no time for modesty and found himself standing naked in front of the gathered Simians, but that didn't seem to shock them nearly as bad as what they saw. He knew what Amy was doing, but they did not. He quickly told them what was happening, but they remained frightened, even Moon. Mama was the first to recover as she approached carrying a cloth for him to cover with. It wasn't much, but it would do as he wrapped it around his waist.

He felt very awkward in his newly-modified body. He was tall and gangly and seemed terribly weak and uncoordinated, but judging from the reaction from the others, he must look like a Supreme One. Certainly, he hoped so if this plan was going to work. From what he could see he did look like a giant Simian. This, in essence, was what he had heard a Supreme One looked like.

Amy said, "The modifications are complete and, yes, you do look like a Supreme One, and it is time to exercise the plan."

Amy told him to have Moon and the other Fems gather and be prepared to back him up as they materialize outside. Moon was fully recovered now and immediately took his position beside him. He felt the golden hair stand out as Amy energized the air around them in preparation of teleporting. He saw the scene change. They now stood outside the entrance about twenty feet behind the working Warrs. Those working did not notice them, but those to the side stared in disbelief and fear. A nervous screeching erupted from those that saw, quickly catching the attention of all the others. They turned in unison to stare in total shock. The Warrs began to jump from foot to foot indicating fear and uncertainty. He felt his vocal cords begin to vibrate and Amy's words emerge from his throat. His voice was very deep and the screeches almost hurt his throat as the hissing was added to the screeches. The combination resulted in an eerie and sinister sound. The tone was almost as fearsome as the words. He screeched, "Why do you disturb my rest?" He did not expect an answer and continued, "Leave this place NOW!"

The Simian Warriors were not overly intelligent, just as Amy was counting on and jumped in agitation and fear from foot to foot trying to leave but all going in different directions. They ran into each other tripping and falling, just to get up and do it again. He was laughing to himself in spite of the situation. One by one the Warriors were finding a route away from him in every direction possible. No two seemed to go in the same direction. Eventually, there was only one left, and when he looked again, he almost froze in shock and fear. The Warr was quivering with rage, almost uncontrollable. The pure hate radiating from his red eyes sent foreboding through his mind.

Amy said, "Watch out! This one is controlled by the Supreme One."

He could see great intelligence, but just barely in control. Rage dominated this Warrior and pure hate. He could feel it even without Amy's explanation.

He registered this in a fraction of a second. It could not have been long. Determination was there also, determination to kill him. The Warr launched a berserk attack directly for him. Amy had not expected this. He could not fight in this condition. He didn't even have his weapons. The Warr came fast crossing the fifteen feet separating them in two steps. The sword was high and swinging. He was ducking, but his new body was so blasted big he knew he would be unable to get out of its way. He could feel Amy again frozen by the presence of the Supreme One. "Damn!" They had made a terrible mistake, which might cost them their lives. They were so close now only to lose everything.

* Amy *

She was always amazed at Levi's ability to laugh in the middle of tense situations. This was one of those times. When they materialized outside the facility the shock was immediate. The Warrior Simians are simple minded and easily tricked under the right situations. This was one of those times. They had been bred and programmed to blindly obey a Supreme One, so when she spoke through Levi's mouth, the order was immediately obeyed. They ran into each other in their haste to depart. Levi was laughing at the antics of the Warriors as they bounced into each other falling to the ground and then running in the other direction. It really was comical to see. This was one emotion, humor, she actually enjoyed, and Levi was making her laugh also.

She felt it before she saw it. She felt the pure rage and hate of the Supreme One. It must have been monitoring some of the Warriors and saw everything she had done. Now its rage was so intense she felt it as if he was standing in front of her. Then she noticed the lone Warrior. He was standing rigid, but his body quivering with the barely controllable rage of the Supreme One. She warned Levi, but it was already too late. The raging Warr was charging Levi with up-swinging sword. There was no way she could get Levi out of the way quickly enough. In his present expanded shape and loose density, a sword would cut through him like a hot knife through butter. She had heard Levi use that expression before and that just about summed up the effect it would have. Levi would be dead in two seconds, and there was nothing she could do. She took control of his body and was making him duck but she could see it was already too late. All she could do was scream, "NO!"

As she was screaming she noticed movement to Levi's left. It was a flash of light reflected off metal. As the Warr's sword made its full swing at the apex, just barely a foot from Levi's head, another sword, which had to be Moon's, clashed and deflected the blow upward to send the Warr's sword an inch over Levi's head. The rest was a blur even for her abilities, but what appeared as a golden wall crashed over the charging Warr. It was Mama, Bambi, and the other Fems charging in unison. It was not pretty. They clawed and tore the Warr as they literally crushed his body beneath their huge stomping feet. She could hear black bones breaking and shattering under the attack. The Warr died a hundred deaths in those few seconds of the attack.

She loved these Simians. They had saved Levi yet again, and they had saved her as well. She wondered, "How can these Simians be so different from the Warriors?" She altered her question to herself and said, "How can the Warrior Simians be so different from the Technical and Female Simians?"

Levi had assumed she was again frozen in fear by the Supreme One, but she told him that would never happen again. He might have died, but at least it would not have been because she was frozen.

Levi laughed at her and said, "Well that's very comforting."

"There he goes again," she thought, but this time she laughed with him. Levi was hugging his friends and friends indeed they were. They seemed pleased with the attention even though he still looked like a Supreme One.

Moon had left to scout the area down the trail and returned to say that the Warriors were still running, and still running into trees. With that statement, even Moon was grinning. Somehow the black shark teeth, visible with Moon's grin, failed to leave a humorous impression with her, but the gesture was not lost on either of them as Levi returned a black toothed grin of his own.

She wondered just how long it would take for the Supreme One to be able to control its anger and then regain control of the fleeing Warriors. She had no doubt they would eventually return, but she hoped it would take at least two days. If she had two days, maybe three, she could activate enough of the facility to be able to defend herself. Was that too much to hope for? They were due a break.

* Levi *

So many times he had thought his life was over. He was almost eighty-two years old and he had lived a full life, especially the last year with Amy, and it wouldn't disturb him so terribly if he did die. Unfortunately, Amy would die too, and that thought bothered him. The human race would most certainly die without Amy, so it was important that they both live. He needed to live for Amy, the human race, his human friends and so many fantastic Simian friends. Friends like these that saved him now.

Levi was happy to see Moon and the hoard of screeching Fems save him. It must have been frightening for the Warr to see them coming. He was sure that the Warr had seen the m, but he was totally controlled by the Supreme One and he was

372

just as sure that the Supreme One was too focused to even notice anything outside its immediate target. He had seen the fixed and hate-filled stare boring into him and knew his life was over under the attack that was launched. Only the intervention from Moon had saved him which was followed almost immediately by the Greys. They ripped the Warr to pieces. The Warr was dead many times over from the poison claw fangs that were so liberally used on him, but the mass of Fem bodies stomped the body into a mass of quivering purple meat. The Fems were not terribly efficient but quite effective and totally without mercy. It was fortunate they were on his side.

He couldn't believe their good luck. Well, it was more than good luck; it was good friends. It was even more than that. It was as if these aliens were family. They were his brothers and sisters, and that was something he had never had in his long life. He loved these golden giants and felt Amy's strong affection as well. Amy trusted Moon and the original group of Technical Simians long before he ever did. He was actually ashamed that he would have let Moon drown at their first encounter.

Moon broke Levi's daydreaming as he reported back from his short scouting trip. He was saying that the Warrs were still running as individuals down every trail available and they still looked scared. Moon found that humorous as he was jumping back and forth from one foot to the other. This gesture he knew to be Moon's indication of humor. In this instance, however, Moon was also grinning. The inner lips didn't quite cover the ominous black shark teeth. In spite of himself he smiled back. It was funny to think of these huge Warrs being scared and running. Suddenly, he saw his Simian hands and realized that he was still appearing as a Supreme One. He said, "Damn, Amy! Get me out of this costume." Even as he said it he began to feel the changes moving over his body, and followed up immediately with, "Thanks."

Amy said with a smile, "Sorry. I was planning the conversion of the facility. We have to complete it quickly before the Supreme One can regain control of the running Warrs and bring them back."

That shocked him. He had assumed that they would keep running, but when Amy saw his shock and puzzled look, she explained that the Supreme One probably would not be able to gain control until the fear left the Warrs. It would most likely take some time; she hoped a couple of days to gain control of all of them and get them organized again. He hoped Amy was right. He was now focused again.

They stood together as Amy teleported them back inside the facility. The lanterns were still burning brightly inside as they materialized. The Simians were showing little fear now as they awaited instruction from him. He realized they were all looking at him and it took him a second to realize why. He was looking more like himself, just naked again. He recovered quickly and dressed, then said, "Okay, Amy, give me the plan."

* Amy *

They had to rush the conversion of the facility before the Warrs could be re-grouped. Many of her

374

team was already working on the various parts of the plan. She knew where the inventoried parts were stored for the modification of the light fixtures and this information had already been downloaded to the new Fem electrical and mechanical engineers along with their other programming. The Fems knew what to do and how to do it. She wished it was that easy with humans. Humans were so illogical and stubborn, especially Levi.

There was no known science or technology that she could use to explain to others what she was doing; however, her new knowledge and science could easily be calculated and proven. The frequency, phase, and wave density of light radiation could be altered by modifying and using the existing fluorescent bulbs. The result was to temporally reverse the effects of the Simian's ray that altered Earth radiation making electricity, among other laws of physics, inoperative.

Her modified light fixtures would reverse the effects only within the radiated light field of the fluorescent bulbs and only as long as the fixture was radiating. The counter alteration was not immediate, which meant the conversion would be slow. Each successive light fixture would radiate and alter the field of the next allowing it to then be activated.

She knew without verification that the modifications were being built and installed by a Grey team just like she knew the portable generator and main generators were being readied by another team of Fems. The Greys now had the knowledge and spare parts to completely rebuild the diesel engines if necessary. Fortunately, there also existed an electrical generator turbine powered by the same underground river running under her facility that provided her life support. Some of the basic emergency power requirements could be supplied from this source. At least that was the original design.

Those areas were being handled, but other things needed to be done. She was sharing all of her thoughts with Levi, and to his credit, he remained quiet for once. He knew she was stressed and focused, trying to anticipate their immediate needs, which were many. Many things had to be done in a hurry and not all of them could be done immediately so she was also analyzing priorities.

Her instructions were being relayed. Levi sent two of the Greys to find patching material and an oxygen acetylene torch to repair the door, two others were sent to help the electrical engineers, and another pair was sent to help the mechanical engineers. Other than the door repair, the highest priorities were those that were already in progress. She wanted the remaining few to watch after the door entrance. Nothing more could be done here and it was time to activate the facility, so they left to start the progress. Moon, Bambi, and Mama remained with Levi. She knew they would not leave him and would be his private guard. She liked the idea of their protection, even though there was little chance of any direct attack on Levi within the facility. At least she didn't believe there could be, but you never knew.

* Levi *

Amy's mind whirled like a turbine. She had explained what and how she was going to counter the effects of the Simians' doomsday ray, but he didn't understand. She made it sound simple and he was sure it was for her, but he was also sure that the rest of the world would find it incredibly difficult. He knew though that if Amy said it could be done, then it could. He smiled to himself as he remembered his contribution to the plan. Oh, it did no good to smile to himself, she saw the thought anyway and pinched him playfully. "Ouch!" When he yelled, they both laughed.

His contribution was the basic key to the plan. Amy had everything figured out with the exception of how to start the first bulb radiating. His suggestion was to use her mental energy to stimulate the first fluorescent bulb. Amy almost yelled as she realized the feasibility and simplicity of that suggestion. Amy tended to think formulas, calculations, analysis of facts, scientific procedures and the like, while overlooking the simple and abstract thoughts. He knew that even with all her mental ability, she envied him in this respect, but it seemed normal to him.

Amy reported that the plan was going forward, but made modifications, sending help to the Fem teams already working and sending yet another team to repair the doors. Amy shared the location, and he sent two Greys to get an oxygen acetylene torch and material to repair the door. That was a good idea in case the Warrs returned before they were ready for them. It would buy more time if needed. Amy believed the Warrs would return, but he was still chuckling at the way they had run for their lives from the imitation Supreme One. His humor evaporated when Amy reminded him just how close he had come to death. Yes, that was sobering.

Amy said, "It is time to start the activation of the facility."

Complying and leaving a few Greys to watch the door, he, along with his immediate team of Moon, Mama, and Bambi, maneuvered the corridors aided by the internal mental map. Soon they were entering the generator room. They saw the light long before they reached the entrance. It was a large open room and the lantern light didn't reach the far walls, making it appear even bigger. In spite of the size, it was a beehive of activity inside. Greys were coming and going, climbing ladders installing equipment, reassembling parts on the generators and diesel engines, and numerous other activities.

When the head electrical and electronics engineer saw him, she came immediately to report the status. He told Amy, "We need a name for her. Let's call her Sparks." Amy grinned.

Sparks had serviced the portable generator and believed it was ready. He told her, "Okay, let's get started." He knew this was going to take a while. Amy had estimated that she would have to hold the mental radiation of energy for at least two hours. That would put a severe strain on his body, and he was not looking forward to it. Amy told him to get comfortable, so he found a soft place to sit and held the bulb in his hands. It was a four foot bulb that had already been treated and had the electrical modification attached. He didn't know how the electronic portion was going to work, but Amy said it would. Amy had said the single bulb was enough, and it would have to be due to the energy it would require.

He laid his arms outstretched on his knees, closed his eyes, and waited. He really didn't need to close his eyes, but he hoped to sleep if he could, while Amy did her thing.

Amy said, "You're a lazy shit!"

He agreed and smiled, even as he felt the energy start to radiate through him. It was becoming hot. His hands felt the heat. He opened his eyes and was startled to realize that the fluorescent bulb was radiating and the slight heat generated is what he actually felt in his hands. He relaxed again, closed his eyes, and went to sleep. Just before slipping into sleep, he said, "Amy, do your thing." Amy didn't seem to find that funny for some reason.

* Amy *

Levi could be such a shit sometimes. This was one of those times. As the newly named Sparks readied the small portable generator, Levi sat down holding the fluorescent bulb. He was too relaxed, and she saw that he intended to sleep. She shouldn't have told him it was going to take two hours. She could use the company, but no. She grinned when she thought about how hungry he would be when he woke up, and she had a surprise for him. They packed only the old sealed packs of military rations, and Levi would be very grumpy. That would teach him. Maybe she should tell him now.

She had calculated the amount of energy. Actually, it would require quite a lot to radiate a bulb. For this reason she had asked for the small bulb as opposed to the standard eight foot bulbs. The smaller bulb however would be sufficient to alter the Earth's radiation affecting the area around the small generator. Once the generator was operating it could be used to light the first modified fixture. At that point, she could back out of the conversion operation and let the Greys continue.

She began gathering energy and directing it through Levi. The effect was immediate. The bulb jumped to life and light burst forth, penetrating the darkness around them. The Fems jumped initially, but soon were staring in appreciation of the new light source. The Fems knew what it was going to be like, but it was still shocking. It had been fifty years since any of them had seen an artificial light source.

She maintained the energy flow to the bulb for minute after long minute. It was troublesome maintaining the mental energy necessary, while controlling Levi's body as the turd slept. Many of her internal functions had to be pushed to a lower priority or stopped all-together during the process. The minutes seemed to pass even slower as she approached the two hour countdown, but finally it was time to wake the sleeping shithead.

She had been firm with Sparks. She was not to try the generator until the two hour limit had passed. Sparks had a good grasp of time and had patiently waited until the required moment. Now Sparks screeched to Levi. He quickly roused and now Amy could finally see as he opened his eyes. The bulb was still burning brightly, highlighting the features on the old Simian's face. Sparks was anxious, almost as anxious as she was. The downloading had been very effective, but the drive, motivation, and dedication came from within. She was very proud of Sparks and the others as well.

Levi gave Sparks the word and she began pulling the start cord on the portable generator. She pulled several times and nothing was happening. They didn't even hear a crackle or firing of any kind. What had she overlooked? She let her mind analyze the data. No, she had not forgotten anything. Had she? Suddenly, there was a backfire and choke sputtering before it died. Yes, the spark had worked and the generator had tried to fire. It was going to work.

She bubbled with excitement and sought Levi's mind for some praise, but he seemed so indifferent and calm. She became instantly aggravated with Levi. "What is your problem, Levi?" His reply was so intelligent.

He simply said, "Huh? What are you talking about?"

She asked angrily, "Aren't you excited? Aren't you proud of my accomplishment?" She lost her anger with his next response and realized that Levi was praising her far better than she had hoped, but she had missed it.

Levi said, "Of course I am proud of you. I am always proud of you, but I am not jumping up and down with excitement because I never had any doubt in your ability to do what you said you could do."

She felt his honest confidence and pride in her and began to beam.

He almost ruined it by asking, "Do you need to be praised for all your accomplishments?"

His previous comments were just too nice to let the end spoil it. She laughed and ignored the last comment.

Her thoughts were interrupted when the portable gas engine sprang to life and the room was filled with the sound of a combustible engine. That sound had not been heard in over fifty years. With a few minor adjustments from Sparks, the engine purred as it generated electricity to supply power to the bulb and replace her generated energy. The first step was complete.

* Levi *

He was instantly awake when Sparks screeched at him. He knew it was time, even before Amy told him. When he opened his eyes, Sparks was standing impatiently waiting for word to start the portable generator. He had barely nodded when Sparks began her routine of pulling the generator cord. It looked tiny and very easy in Sparks's hand. She pulled and adjusted the screws, then cranked it again. He sensed Amy's deep concentration on the activities and wondered why. Amy's plans always worked, so why was she so tense?

The routine continued for several minutes, and those efforts were finally rewarded with a backfire.

Amy jubilantly said, "The back fire means it's going to work."

He said, "Well, of course it's going to work." Amy seemed angry with him, but he didn't understand why. Amy asked if he were proud of her. That sounded almost like a rebuke, and he didn't like to be rebuked. He wondered why she was being critical, but decided to let it pass. He just told her, "Of course I am proud of you. I am always proud of you." She was still grumbling, but he believed that she finally realized that he was proud of her and he had simply had more confidence in her abilities than possibly she did. She could be so female sometimes.

It didn't take long for Sparks to tune the generator to a fine purring machine. The noise was loud, however, and the echo accenting the noise was disturbing. He wanted to get away from it as soon as possible. Sparks was quick to plug in the light fixture she had rigged up. The light jumped forth to radiate and fill the generator room with much more and brighter light than the single bulb he now released. Now Amy was out of the loop and the chain reaction was started.

It was just a matter of time now before the entire facility could be activated and Amy was happy. He too was happy for her, but then he was dreading the completion. He knew that Amy would be heavily engrossed in the activities here and less with him. Was he jealous? Amy was grinning back at him.

She said, "I love you too."

They both laughed. Amy told him that she would always be with him no matter what was going on here. She said she could do multiple tasks and was in truth, already doing so with the monitoring of Dawn, Jimmy, and Fred. He realized that was true, but then began to worry about her ability to do another major function, after all this would be far more involved than monitoring.

Amy said, "I will be all right."

His mind retraced to what he had said earlier and realized he was premature with his jealousy and started laughing. Amy was puzzled until she looked closer into his mind, then she blushed with embarrassment. He had realized that when he left Amy would just be an observer and not even that until the Greys had activated the electricity and installed cameras. She couldn't do anything here. They had not introduced Mama or any of the other Fems to Amy and they had established no line of communication other than him. The Fems had no idea of her existence and no real justification to activate the facility other than he told them that was what he wanted, even if it was actually Amy. It shocked him to realize the level of dedication these Fems were demonstrating. He was amazed.

Amy said, "It's not as bad as you seem to think. As soon as the facility is active I will be able to talk directly to Mama and the others and # 5 will be here as well, when he is healed. He supposed that was true, but she would scare the crap out of them if she just started talking to them. Amy agreed that an introduction was in order, but that it would have to wait until they returned.

"Huh, where the hell are we going now?"

CHAPTER 10
(THE GATHERING)

* Amy *

The facility was on its way to being activated and little could stop it now. She had programmed the Fem engineers to follow a predetermined pattern in the activation process. The first portion, after the generator room, was to work toward the doors and defensive positions. Once done, cameras from inventory could be installed inside the facility within the altered radiation pattern and focused to view outside. Holes would be carefully drilled and concealed to prevent light from escaping. Additionally, a liberal amount of insulated studs would be disbursed and installed around access doors and accessible locations. The studs would penetrate through small holes. These studs would serve as a defense parameter that would provide an electrical shock to anyone touching them, even a full grown Simian. She had many such surprises planned.

Knowing that the engineers would be completely engrossed in the activation and defense plans for many days, her only concern was the time factor for the main defense deployment. She estimated that it would take two full days, but inside defenses utilizing lasers could be established in a single day. Once activated, she could defend herself. She believed that the laser beam, once generated, would stay bound and work outside the altered field. In short, she believed a laser beam could be used outside of the facility to defend against approaching Warrs, as long as the beam was generated inside.

She needed no communications with the Fems initially to direct their activities. They would work independently, so it was not nearly as disturbing to her to find out she had overlooked a major flaw in her plan. She had failed to establish any communication links to the Fems other than through Levi. When he pointed that fact out, it was with his usual callused and crude manner. It embarrassed her. She hated when she made a mistake. This one was not that critical, however. She agreed with Levi in the total dedication the Fems had obviously given Levi, even though they knew only little of the story. They had always intended to tell them. These Fems would be HER team. It was part of the plan from the beginning, and the single main reason they had chosen the elder Fems. These Fems would live here permanently. This is why it took her so much by surprise.

The problem could easily be rectified, but it would mean stopping their work. This was not an option right now; besides, they were preprogrammed for the next two days and far beyond. She and Levi had other pressing tasks to take care of right now anyway.

They had so many battle-fronts and tasks that needed to be coordinated. Their forces, both human and Simian, were in the process of gathering and traveling to the desert settlement. Well, the Simians were having their own gathering right now also, which needed to be explored. The Simian gathering was occurring at both Barstow and the desert settlement within the Simian colonies. Unfortunately, the Simian armies did not have females and would not be stopping for any gathering.

The humans were moving toward the desert settlement, but at a slower pace she was sure. Jimmy had remained behind with the Simians so she had no monitoring capabilities of the advancing humans. She just hoped they could hurry, because the Owens Tribe was continuing to slow and stall the advancing Simian armies, but they couldn't hold them for many more days. They were running out of passes. The schedule was too close and so many things could go wrong and probably would.

Levi told her, "Think positive."

He was right. She became negative far too frequently, but they did need to leave and address the other requirements of their various groups and commands.

Levi refocused her attention and direction again by saying, "I'm hungry and sleepy!" She had been so engrossed she had forgotten that Levi and the others hadn't eaten or slept in eighteen hours. Levi could eat the packed K-rations and she would take pleasure in his discomfort, but she couldn't give the Simians Army K-rations. Other options were required. They had cattle in her valley only a few miles from here that had been left there to support the food requirements of this group, so she suggested to Levi that they, being careful and watchful, round up a few head of cattle and bring them inside the facility. Firewood would be needed too.

Levi just gave her a hard stare and said, "I know what to do and you don't have to tell me to be careful or how and when to cook my food."

Yep, he was hungry, tired, and grumpy.

* Levi *

He wasn't going anywhere until he had eaten and slept and let those desires be known to Amy. She didn't require sleep or food, but he and the rest of them sure as hell did. Sometimes she forgot that fact. He didn't detect any emergency in Amy's thoughts that would require immediate attention so he balked. Besides, he was not about to eat those damn old army rations no matter how good they were for him. He wanted meat and he knew where to get it.

He was tired and grumpy, but even so, he would have been aggravated just the same with Amy's mothering. There she was telling him where the cattle were, like he wasn't one of the group that herded them there. Then she was telling him to be careful, like he would never have thought to watch for the Warrs they just ran off. The idea to bring a few head of cattle back within the complex was a good idea, but he really had it when she told him to bring wood for a fire. She was smothering him. She was acting like he couldn't think for himself, but he wasn't stupid. In spite of his aggravation, he grinned when she stuck her tongue out at him.

It was a short trip to Amy's valley and Moon, Bambi, Mama, and he soon had some cattle back within the complex. The cattle weren't anxious to enter the dark cave-like entrance, but after some prodding they finally entered and the doors were resealed. He didn't blame the cattle so much. He didn't like the darkness, damp and stale air, and the eerie echo noise coming back at him. Hell, the cattle might improve the smell inside. If the cattle only knew what fate awaited them, they would be even more frightened.

The Simians soon stopped their work to eat. He was thankful that the Simians dragged their kicking and bellowing victims back out of sight. He heard tearing of meat and breaking of bones even at that distance. It still brought back bitter memories, but at least the victims were not human.

He knew many of the Fems would be back to work soon, working in shifts throughout the night, but not him. It took him longer to build a good fire and roast a rump. He ate his fill and even indulged in a canteen full of wine. The combination of food, drink, and a warm fire soon had him comfortable and sleeping.

He felt much better when he awoke in the morning. Amy was ready and waiting for him and he was happy to see her. He also noticed that Moon, Bambi, and Mama had bedded down surrounding him protectively. What a comfort. With Amy, and these Simians he was as safe as if he was in his mother's arms. Amy answered his unspoken question.

Amy said, "You have slept for ten hours, and it is 8:00 am."

He was, however, still hungry. He sat up and reached for the remainder of the roast. This would do. After a quick stuffing, he was also ready to leave to visit the other parties, but for different reasons... he wanted more and better food. He was ready to visit the desert settlement and their twenty-four hour kitchen with slabs of bacon and piles of eggs. He wondered if they still had any coffee recovered from the hidden supply cache Amy discovered. Amy was openly laughing at him now and he said indignantly, "Well, you made me this way with your infernal modification!" She continued to laugh and he soon joined her.

His movements soon aroused the others, and their screeching began almost immediately. He quickly reminded them of the Supreme One and their need to use hand signs to communicate. That too had been part of the programming download. Truth was: Levi actually wanted the quiet. Even though his vocal cords were modified to screech the Simian language, it still offended his ears when he spoke it. Amy said it was psychological, but he didn't care.

She laughed again and said, "In the facility with its thick mountain walls, and since the download modification of the Fems' brain waves, I am fairly positive that the Supreme One cannot monitor these Fems."

Again he said, "I don't care!"

Exasperated she said, "Okay! We can go to the desert settlement first."

Now he was happy.

* Amy *

Sometimes Levi could be pathetic when he whined. Sure, his metabolism required massive amounts of protein, and his hunger was excessive,

390

but she believed Levi had always liked to eat, and this was just a good excuse. At any rate, she relented and decided to take him to the best food, the desert settlement. They had to go anyway at some point to check on the progress of the new weapons. They might as well go now, but she wasn't about to tell Levi. She wanted him to think she was doing it just for him. The smile and mental embrace was worth the slight deception.

As she was about to ask Levi to gather the group, he amazed her again.

Levi said, "Instead of waiting to tell Mama, just download the information about you and the Simian computer language to her. It wouldn't take long, and Mama can explain to the others."

What a great idea, abstract thought! She wished she had it. She responded calmly saying, "I was just about to ask you to call her for that very purpose." If he grinned, she couldn't detect it.

All of Mama's questions were answered in the download, and Levi was right, it didn't take long at all, and best of all: now she would have communications here while Levi was gone. She had known that the Fems would do a good job of activating the facility, but now she would have some control and direction. Even before establishing communications with Mama, she knew that Mama was extremely happy, but now she beamed with pleasure. Amy sensed that it was the association of females. Mama was even happier to be elevated to the position she now held, and the worth and importance of her position included protecting the female brain behind the man called Levi. She couldn't directly read Mama's mind, but

391

she sensed the general thoughts. If Mama was happy before, it was not nearly as happy as she felt right now.

Mama no longer followed Levi around with the others. She had a new purpose and was already headed down to the tenth level to establish direct communication with Amy through the Simian computer. She knew Mama would have to be refocused to concentrate on the activation of the facility, but it was only right to let her make her introduction directly. After all, it was going to be a very long and close relationship.

Levi was right with his assumption. There were many stressed activities and dangerous situations among the different groups, but there were no immediate emergencies. The Owens Valley Tribe had successfully retreated to the next pass, and with the five extra riflemen, they were keeping the Simian armies at bay, so far. She hoped their luck would hold out through five more passes and five more days.

By monitoring Dawn, everything seemed to be on schedule at the desert settlement, but Dawn wasn't every place Amy wanted her to be. So much could go wrong there.

Jimmy's monitoring of the Simian gathering was very revealing. She had already suspected and now verified that Simian mating was very rough and dangerous for the participants. One of the newer Technical Simians had been accidentally clawed in the mating and died. The act of mating, as observed at a distance, appeared to be more rage than sex. She was glad that they had warned Jimmy to stay far from the participants. He had willingly complied.

With their continued direct involvement no longer required at the facility, she was ready. Levi, Moon and Bambi grouped together and she began the teleport process. The transfer went with ease. The views changed, one fading, while the other materialized. Soon they were standing at the kitchen in front of startled humans and some Simian workers.

* Levi *

He had been thinking about the problem of communication for Amy. He thought it was funny that Amy had overlooked a problem with Mama. Actually, her mistakes made her more human, but it bothered Amy a great deal when she made one. She believed she was much more than human and, in fact, was, but she rejected much of the characteristics of humans. She could not accept human faults. Well, it didn't bother him to make a mistake, so let him be the bad guy.

There was no reason for Amy to suffer with lack of communication. It was simple. There was no need to take all the time of explanations, questions, justifications, and history. Mama and the Greys didn't require these things anyway. They were obviously totally committed to the facility and to him. They had already proven that with their willingness to do whatever was required to activate the facility. The Greys were already accepting the responsibility without even knowing how important it was to both the Simians and humans. It was amazing.

He just stated the obvious without any hint of emotion, challenge, criticism, or implied fault. He said, "Instead of waiting to tell Mama, just download the information about you and the Simian computer language to her. It wouldn't take long and Mama can explain to the others." There was silence for a few seconds before Amy admitted that she was planning on doing just that. He blocked his thoughts as he felt Amy searching. He did not make it obvious that he was blocking. He disguised the block as being busy and occupied with other thoughts. He had learned how to do that and believed that Amy did not suspect. The thought he blocked was the laughter at her statement. He knew she had not even remotely considered that option, but would never admit it. She accepted the idea and had saved face. He had succeeded and the problem was solved without embarrassing Amy. It still amazed him how smart Amy was, but she had little common sense.

Mama accepted the download and information with much jubilation. It was obvious in her excitement that she relished the new tasks and responsibility. With some regret, Mama dropped him like a hot rock and was off to established communication with her new idol. Mama had a new purpose.

Finally, Amy was ready to leave, so he called Moon and Bambi for the teleport, and they were soon standing in the desert settlement kitchen and he was very happy. After the shock of seeing the group materialize at the settlement, the kitchen workers quickly smiled at him and began preparing food. Moon took Bambi off in the direction of the sheep pens. Levi grinned as he realized Moon was going to introduce Bambi to the delicacy of sheep. He grinned even wider knowing that soon Al would be coming, asking him to try and control Moon at the sheep pens. There were some complaints that Moon had been taking some of the prize breeding stock, but no one had ever complained directly to Moon. He smiled to himself at the thought.

Word spread fast throughout the camp that he was here, and as expected, Al and Dawn were headed his way. Actually, Amy announced them first. He was happy to see Al and happy that Al still seemed very happy with Dawn. His friendship with Al was mutual, but Al seemed all business this time, which suited Amy fine. Al reported that the camp was almost ready to move.

Al said, "Everything that can't be moved is already hidden in the caves, wagons are filled to the brim and three hundred and fifty of the new weapons are finished." The latter was said with a grin.

Levi knew what he would be doing after he ate, and Amy was more than anxious. He assumed the news was good and reflected a knowing grin back.

Al turned somber at his next subject. He reported that the Simian gathering at the settlement was disturbing and the noise and screeches were constant and frightening. Most of the humans had pulled back from the Simian community out of concern for safety, and were all hoping it would be over soon.

Little work was getting done by the Simians and it was slowing them down. Al wanted to know if anything could be done. Between bites he said, "I am not really sure, but I doubt it. Not without losing a hand or a head."

* Amy *

Levi's appetite was real. He needed the protein for the accelerated metabolism, but times like these she found boring and a waste of time. Unfortunately, she had no choice. She wished Levi would eat the K-rations. They were much better for him, but she had to admit the taste was not that good. Oh well, she would live with it. Levi was eating his fill when she saw that Dawn and Al were coming. They were still a ways away, but she could see Dawn's trajectory and knew the destination. She told Levi. Levi stopped eating only long enough to hug them as they arrived then resumed eating, knowing that Al would give his report.

She expected the concern and fear from the Simians Gathering, so this news was accepted in stride. Al got her attention when he mentioned that there were three hundred and fifty of the new weapons completed. Actually, they were slightly ahead of schedule. She had just lost her focus with so much going on. Yes, the weapons needed experimenting, and the assigned humans needed training too. Unfortunately, the humans that were going to use them were still en route from Barstow.

The new human fighters were the mostly new and untrained humans that were recruited and others that freely joined the caravan as they evacuated the mountains ahead of the Simian armies. Both the Owens Valley Tribe and the desert settlement were already trained and experienced in the horseback lancer method of fighting. This had been very successful to date. The problem was that they had no more horses to support a new Lancer army. The new army must be able to fight from the ground against Simians, which could easily be suicide. This new weapon was designed to even the odds against a Simian Warrior. She hoped it would, and was anxious to see the weapon tested.

She decided they would stay in this camp for several days and wait for the humans to arrive. There was danger everywhere, but nothing that required her immediate attention. However, it was true that she had no idea how any of them would live past next week. It was overwhelming.

The desert settlement population, complete with its Simian population, the humans, Simian Females, and the Owens Valley Tribe, would all converge on this spot in five days followed closely by a horde of angry and driven Warrs. This would be one hell of a massing of allied forces, but they were still hugely outnumbered. She was trying to formulate plans, but nothing seemed to give her any hope. All they could do was retreat in the direction of the Supreme One and hope the two Simian armies didn't launch an all-out attack. She believed that was the Supreme One's plan: drive them into the waiting Simian armies in Texas. Their choices were to die in five days or put it off until they reached Texas, some choice.

None of these problems were explained to Levi, but she knew he saw much of it in her mind. He was very sensitive of spirit, but would never admit it to himself, much less to her. He was macho! She grinned in spite of her stress.

* Levi *

He wasn't quite sure why and really didn't want to know, but they didn't make their rounds to all the groups. They stayed at the desert valley settlement for the next few days. He rested and ate his fill. The only really productive thing they did was experiment with the new weapons. They were very good, but too slow for him. He was strong and didn't need the extra features built into the weapon, but he saw the worth for others, humans mostly.

It was a spear basically, but much more. The spear point was spring loaded in the shaft and additionally, the shaft held an air chamber. When the spear point was loaded into the shaft and the chamber pumped up five times, it posed a formidable weapon. A thrust and impact against the target released the tensioned spear point with lethal power against a Simian. It could penetrate the thick and heavy hide of a Simian and reach organs. It could kill. The only problem was that it required reloading. The spear point required a manual spring push reset by the operator until it caught, and then required five pumps on the handle. All this took time. This was unnecessary time for him, but he could see where it would be an excellent weapon for a man of normal strength. Amy developed a fighting procedure that would allow for staggered attacks then retreat for resetting the spear. If she said she could do it he believed her. It looked as if they would find out soon enough. They seemed to be surrounded by Simians and therefore far too many opportunities to test the weapon.

Al liked the weapon and assigned some of his Guard to train with them. He only wanted some ready teachers from his group to learn and be able to train those new human recruits en route to the settlement. Actually, the Lancers were proud to be Lancers and, honestly, were quite good at what they did. Too bad there weren't more horses. The Lancer picked up the fighting procedures Amy designed very quickly. It was clumsy at first, but soon smoothed out. Amy had each team consisting of four members. There were two on the front with loaded spears constantly, while the other pair was behind reloading. When the front discharged their spears, they would immediately retreat to the rear to be replaced by the fresh and loaded spear pair. It was not terribly efficient, but would be effective if they could get under the Warr's sword. At best, the odds of four humans to one Simian were still less than even, but at least it was a way to fight back.

On the last day of the Simian gathering they decided to visit the colony. Amy was still curious and he had to admit so was he. He assumed that it was lots of raw violent sex, which was exactly what they saw. They watched a Fem come in heat and mate. Fems were holding the arms of the excited Fem to prevent her from clawing the male, while the male took her violent and rough. Other Simian males remained close to prevent the male from killing the Fem in his agitated condition and were obviously ready to take their turn. The Fems' passion for mating wasn't constant, but evidently came in daily cycles throughout the five days and lasted for about an hour. When she cycled into heat it stimulated the males within her scent range and drew them to action. During this hour she mated with several males until her urge was satisfied. Afterward, they lay spent on the ground heaving in huge volumes of air. It was beyond just rough sex.

It was at this occurrence that they saw # 10 coming toward them. He liked # 10. This Tech had ingratiated himself at the battle of Black Bones Valley, as everyone now called it. This Tech had been made to stay with the wagons during the battle and had become very agitated and angry at being left out. His actions had made it possible for the Owens Valley Lancers to join the battle, but # 10 had not liked being left out. He had always like # 10 for this dedication, which was one of the reasons he had been chosen to rule this Simian colony.

He was smiling at # 10 as he approached. He was truly happy to see him. As # 10 neared, Levi was still smiling when Amy screamed alarm. His muscles suddenly tightened as Amy jerked his body to the side. Even as he was trying to help Amy move his body, he saw the short sword swing from around behind # 10. He saw the rage burst from the Simian's eyes and knew that # 10 was not in charge of his own mind. The intelligent mind controlling # 10 anticipated the move and was already swinging down where Levi's body was moving to. It was too late. He felt the impact of the sword hit his right shoulder, just missing his neck, but ripping down through his chest. He wondered in amazement if his heart was on this side. The agonizing pain radiated through his body and paralyzed him. His mind was swimming into darkness, as he wondered what would kill him first. His last thought was of Amy and how happy he was that she would remain alive through her activated facility. As he sank into blackness, he said, "I love you Amy."

* Amy *

The weapon was all she had hoped it would be. She had designed it from inventoried parts stored in the caverns. The parts consisted of stainless steel hollow shafts, hardened steel spikes, steel springs, gas chamber and pump, plus a vast assortment of other pieces and parts. A man could set the spring and charge the gas chamber with five short pumps. It wasn't that time consuming as Levi was complaining about. It was a dangerous use of time but necessary. The attack and impact of the power spear against the target released the spring and gas pressure. The combination of the concentrated release of power was sufficient to drive the eighteen inch spike through the dense hide of a Simian to reach organs.

Levi said, "This can kill!"

He was right, IF they could deliver the power spear on target. That was the main concern, kill and not be killed.

She was happy that Al seemed to take over the training of the power spears. She liked Al as much as Levi did. He was a natural leader. She knew the new recruits would be ushered into Al's army. It was an ambitious move on Al's part, but she knew that was not the reason. Al simply was a military leader and that a general was needed now.

Al picked a special team to learn the power spears and teach others. The training went well and she had to make only a few corrections or suggestions. She had laid out the basic plan of a four man team, which Al accepted and perfected. The training would go quickly as soon as the recruits arrived. It would have to be quick with the Simian army in hot pursuit. It would probably have to be learned as they traveled east.

Wanting to learn more about the gathering, she suggested that they go and observe the mating. Levi seemed curious as well. They discovered that Levi had been right, it was just rough sex. There was no romance or courtship. It was just copulating. The Fems had to be held to prevent them from killing the mating male and the males had to control each other to prevent harm to the Female. A Fem in season mated five times during the gathering. She came into heat for an hour each day, which aroused the males and brought them running. There was some competition between the males as to who would mate, but with the Techs it probably wasn't near as violent as Warrs would have been. This must seem civil compared to what it had been.

She wondered how it had been before the Fems' genetic alteration producing poison fangs and the mutation of the Tech genetics into the Warrior Simians. She was positive that the Warrs had greatly affected the mating habits of the gathering. She was positive this is where the Warrs prevented the Techs from mating. But, this gathering had no Warrs. The male genetic donors were all Technical Simians at this gathering. This Tech mating had probably not happened in over fifty years. The mating was rough, but she had to wonder how much rougher it might have been if they had witnessed the far more violent Warrs. The thought was enough to make her shudder.

She felt something was wrong. Was it that old clairvoyance feeling? Was it that? She never knew. She considered it a curse more than anything else, but it was there, nonetheless. Was it something that was going to happen or was it something happening now? She was looking around for something out of place. All she saw was # 10 strolling toward them. He was not rushing and looked peaceful and happy. Actually, he looked pleased to see Levi. She continued to look through Levi's eyes at the surrounding peripheral in hopes of seeing anything out of the ordinary. Levi remained focused on # 10 much to her unease. The feeling was getting stronger. What was it?

She almost missed it, but suddenly # 10's gaze turned from friendly to icy cold. His eyes suddenly turned solid red and rage shot out toward Levi. The Supreme One had hid its control until the last possible second. The power necessary to hold back that level of rage she now saw must have been incredible. She cursed the ability that gave her warnings, but without details. The sword was already swinging from behind # 10's back before she saw it. The momentum was established and had been hidden from her. The Supreme One had planned well. Even as she seized control of Levi's muscles jerking him to the left and away from the projected slash, she saw the fallacy of her plan. That move had been anticipated. It was too late. All she could do was put an extra twist, which prevented, barely, a blow to the neck planned to sever the head. Instead, the sword blow struck Levi's shoulder and down into his chest. She felt his pain and felt his mind fading into darkness.

If # 10 had severed Levi's head, she would not be able to save him. As it was, she could repair the damage if Levi didn't lose too much blood. Already she was repairing bone, vessels, and tissue, but the sword was still embedded in his chest. Worse, there was no one to protect Levi and he was at # 10's mercy, which it didn't have. She had made the very mistake she said she would never do. She left Levi without any bodyguards. Even Moon was off about his own business. All his bodyguards were at the gathering, for all the good that would do now. The Supreme One could have taken over any of them, since she had not yet modified their brain patterns according to her own plan.

Her mind was racing to find an answer. She could still teleport even with Levi's eyes shut, but to where? Who could react fast enough to save Levi? Fred was not close to any warriors and he couldn't help. Dawn was in the kitchen area and separated from Al. Jimmy was asleep. Frantically she sought an answer. All her searching took only a tiny fraction of a second, but she found the answer while # 10 was trying to pull the sword form Levi's chest for another strike.

The only solution she could think of was daring. She concentrated hard on the transport location. She had no coordinates nor could she see the location. She gathered energy and transferred the mass of Levi and # 10 into open space high above them. There was no danger of teleporting into rock or earth, only open space. She opened Levi's eyes as they materialized in air. They immediately began to fall. As they did, she saw # 10 let go of the sword handle and begin to drift away as they both fell. The sword was still embedded in Levi's chest and blood was flowing from the wound. She also realized with a sickening feeling that the energy around Levi was constantly moving and it would be very difficult to gather the necessary energy for another transfer. So much was wrong.

Frantically, she tried to seize energy around her, then realized she needed to gather energy from below so they would fall into the space. With that recognition, she completed the transfer. As Levi began to fade, she saw # 10 continue to drift away toward the ground rushing up toward them. She could still see the rage and hate in the Simian's eyes. She was thankful that # 10 would never know what happened, and she hoped that the Supreme One would feel the pain of a crushing death. The seething rage of the Supreme One could still be felt as # 10 disappeared from site.

Levi materialized near the kitchen in a cloud of dust as he hit the ground. There was no way she could cancel out the total falling energy exchange. The fall was equivalent to a fall of about ten feet, but was loud enough to make a commotion and attract everyone's attention. Levi fell in front of Dawn with the sword still protruding from his chest. She used Levi's mouth and yelled for them to pull the sword out. Dawn quickly seized the huge sword handle and with others helping, wrenched it out.

Time was short as she began to close the wounds around the sword slash. Luckily, Levi had been good about taking his chemical vitamins, and she had complete ability to control his body. She felt Levi's body being lifted and she presumed that they were taking him to the camp medical facility. She again opened Levi's mouth and asked for Moon and Bambi, knowing that neither of them would leave his side for more than a few minutes at a time during his recovery.

It wasn't long before she heard Moon rushing to Levi's side. The sounds were easy to identify from the heavy thuds of his feet and angry low guttural screeches escaping his mouth. She could tell he was very agitated and angry. Using Levi's modified vocal chords, she screeched to Moon telling him that it was # 10 at the colony. Moon left Bambi to guard Levi and was off to the colony. She knew what he would find, but she had to be sure.

With the sword removed, allowing her to repair his injury, she would have him up and going again in less than two days. He would need to replenish his blood supply, but she could assist in that process. He had been very lucky.

* Levi *

Was he detecting some sensation? Was there something coming out of the darkness? Yes. He was aware of something, a feeling. It was getting stronger. Pain! His body shuddered with pain and he shrank quickly back into darkness. He was vaguely aware of conscious thought and pain reoccurring on several occasions, but he always retreated back to the safety of darkness. Each time of awareness was longer before retreating. Finally, he realized he was

406

aware of noises, smells, sounds, in addition to the pain. The pain was almost bearable now, but just barely. He heard Amy comforting him, telling him he was alive and would live. What had happened and what was she talking about? His memory was coming slowly. Suddenly, and with great agitation, he remembered the sword and pain!

Amy quickly calmed him saying, "You're safe now, my love."

He relaxed in the comfort of her words and slept, a deep sleep.

When he finally awoke fully, he felt the bed, heard the noises, and inhaled the antiseptic smells of what must be the medical area. He knew he was safe. His mind was trying to remember what had happened. He remembered thinking he was dead. He was at the Simian gathering and # 10 was approaching, then suddenly attacking him. The wound had been inflicted by # 10. He remembered seeing the rage and hate in its eyes. There was no doubt that it had been the Supreme One controlling # 10 even before Amy told him. Amy relayed what had happened after he passed out and the death of # 10. He was truly sorry to hear that. He had liked # 10, and he would be missed.

It had been a brilliant plan for Amy to implement, working alone, and knowing her, it probably surprised her as well. Thinking about it now, he realized that had she teleported anywhere else, the reaction time would not have been sufficient to prevent # 10 from making another swing with his sword. That would have definitely been fatal. Teleporting into empty space had allowed shock and gravity to separate them and had certainly saved his life.

He blocked his next thought from Amy. He knew she had saved his life and was thankful and knew also that she had done what she had to do, but wondered if she might have been able to save both of them. Amy loved the big boy as much as he, and felt her pain at the sacrificed # 10. He didn't want to hurt her more, so he blocked his thoughts. What if she had teleported into the lake? Would they have been able to save # 10? No, that was a stupid thought. It would probably have killed them both. He would not have been in any condition to pull himself out of the water, much less # 10, assuming the Supreme One left him. No, she did the only thing she could, and brilliantly too. He let her see the last thought and was rewarded with a smile.

Slowly his eyes opened to the outside world. No one noticed at first as he looked around. He was in the medical area surrounded by medics and nurses. He smiled to himself knowing how surprised they must have been to see him heal in front of them. He should be dead. Anyone else would have been.

Amy said, "You are mostly healed now. Your muscles, bone, and skin are repaired, but your blood supply is very low. You need more time for that to be replenished."

He told her, "I'm hungry!" Amy laughed with pure delight.

Moon noticed him first and screeched in astonishment and alert. Everyone jumped and saw Levi awake. There were so many waiting to serve him. He felt humble to be admired so much, but he was hungry. He announced, "I need food!" Surprisingly, it was Bambi that rushed off toward the kitchen area to get food. Her desire to help him overcame her repulsion of the smell of cooked or cooking food. He appreciated Bambi.

He appreciated Moon, too. He believed that Moon must be upset for not being with him when he was needed, and knew Moon would be even closer in the future. He also realized there would be no more personal independence, that Amy would have bodyguards around him always. One thing that he would insist upon immediately, well, after he was able, was to contact the original Techs, his friends, and modify their brain patterns so the Supreme One could never take control of them. He didn't want to lose any more of them. They had lost far too many already. Seeing his thoughts, Amy agreed that would be the first thing on the agenda, and most were already en route to them now as fast as they could travel. It would happen soon.

* Amy *

The repairs to Levi's body were well underway, and he was out of danger. Levi's strong will to live made him fight to regain consciousness, but when he emerged from his deep repose the pain sent him back into the safety of darkness. Each time he emerged staying longer until finally, he remained conscious, although very drowsy. Eventually, he fought the panic of his memory, but she was ready and calmed him. His mind and body jerked awake at the memory of the attack. It returned in sketchy

409

pieces until his memory fully returned and she was able to provide the story of what had happened.

She relayed the report made by Moon. At some point Moon had returned and told Bambi what he found. Amy knew he was reporting to her and that she would hear what was said to Bambi. He had found # 10 lying in a crumpled heap, very dead. Moon had talked to some that had seen what happened and was able to piece together the total story. He was sad to find # 10 dead, but would not have hesitated to kill him personally had he found him alive. She was sure Bambi thought Moon was acting weird, reporting everything to her, especially when he said that he would now put # 9 in charge of all the Simian colonies including this one. Bambi couldn't care less, but then Moon was reporting to Amy and not Bambi. She appreciated the report and so did Levi.

Levi still thought he could block his thoughts, and she didn't want to destroy that illusion. It did hurt her to think about the loss of # 10, and she would feel even worse if she discovered that there was a way she could have saved him as well. Luckily, Levi, with his uncanny ability to see a situation, could not come up with any other solution that would have allowed her to do so. She felt some relief with that thought. She also agreed that the original Techs would need to be modified as soon as possible. She didn't want to lose any more of them either.

Levi was also right about his suspicion. He would lose his personal freedom and definitely would have bodyguards watching him at all times from now on. It amazed her that she had allowed it to go on this long. It was her fault. She should have had bodyguards on him permanently since they discovered the existence of the Supreme One. Levi was, after all, the Supreme One's prime target and the main route to her. There was nothing it would not try in an attempt to kill Levi, and she should have realized that fact and reacted sooner.

Damn! Even in Levi's diminished mental state he thought well. Abstract thought ruled. She was so envious. She could perform multiple tasks, hundreds of calculations simultaneously and could take complicated and interfacing situations to logical conclusions, but sometimes the innovative ideas eluded her. This was one such time. Levi had monitored her thoughts and suggested that they should go to the original Techs and not wait for them to come to them.

Levi said, "Why wait and give the Supreme One the opportunity to take over another Tech? Do the unexpected and go to them. That way the Supreme One would not have any warning and probably would not have the opportunity to invade another mind."

He was absolutely right! It was so simple. Why hadn't she thought of it? Maybe she would never know or reach that level. Maybe that might be good. Levi did think weird sometimes. At any rate, she would comply with that suggestion and told Levi, "We will do just that after you have eaten and you're able to travel." He grinned at the thought of food.

Bambi returned from the kitchen quickly with three plates of various foods for Levi. In addition she balanced a large pitcher of milk for him. Even this action on Bambi's part was commendable. Levi accepted her offering with great enthusiasm and dug right in. His body needed the nourishment, and he ate like a starving man, which he was. All gathered were used to seeing Levi eat, but this was a feat even for Levi, and they watched in silence and amazement as he devoured the food. He even asked for more. Normally, it was impossible for a human stomach to hold that much, but she was breaking the protein down quickly and distributing it throughout his body to replace muscle mass she had depleted while she was repairing his wound. Her chemical language was working quickly controlling these functions.

During Levi's rest, she had been monitoring their communications team, especially Jimmy. He had remained with the Simians at Barstow for the gathering. Through his observations she discovered little or nothing new concerning the mating ritual of the Simians. Perhaps there was more affection at this location and possibly a sign of some gentleness. Additionally, she observed that # 9 had mobilized the Simians immediately after the gathering and the entire combined Simian colonies were being rushed to the desert location. In fact they should arrive by tomorrow.

All the groups were coming together, converging on this location, all except the Owens Valley Tribe in the mountains, but they too were running out of mountain passes and would be converging on this location within days. The grouped humans from Barstow had arrived yesterday while he was in a coma. As expected, Al had immediately taken control of them and started

412

their training on the new weapons, which were now complete. They had been totally absorbed into the community and assigned duties. Al was a good organizer and she was thankful for that.

* Levi *

He liked the food at the desert settlement. They knew how he liked his food, LOTS! He relished the large platters of bacon and eggs, ham steaks, beef steaks, lamb shanks, sausages of all kinds, fried potatoes, turkeys, and anything else that was handy. The cooks, as usual, had prepared and provided these favorites to him in large quantities. He was happy to see Bambi bring the platters, as unusual as it was to see a Simian around, much less carrying cooked food. He was glad that Bambi had gone for his food because she was carrying much more than a human could have carried. He did not wait to question Bambi, but accepted the food and hungrily dug in. He was vaguely aware of stares, but he could care less what they thought. He was hungry and for some reason Amy thought it was funny. He took enough time away from eating to tell her, "Shut up!" She only smiled more.

No one bothered him while he ate, and Amy was able to bring him up to date concerning all the activities of their armies as monitored by their communications team. Little new or out of the ordinary activities were occurring. That is to say all was still on schedule, whatever that meant. As Amy indicated, all the groups would be grouped here by tomorrow, with the exception of the Owens Valley Tribe. They would be here in three days followed by the combined Warrior Simian armies. She really didn't have much of a plan after that other than head east, and that would only work if the Simian army held back an attack and simply herded them, but another factor in this equation was that the Phoenix Simian Colony was directly in front of their herded path. She believed this would be the case, and he agreed. They would have to play it by ear from that point on.

During his two days of darkness, Amy had been busy. She had maintained almost constant communication with Mama through the Simian computer. Amy said that she had to make Mama go sleep and rest. Mama was just too excited and very aware of the importance of her position. The other Greys pushed themselves to the point of exhaustion as well in an effort to activate her facility, but they had made significant gains toward completing the task.

They had managed to fire up three of the four diesel engines powering the electrical generators, thus guaranteeing more than enough electrical power to supply the facility. He suspected that the designed power capacity was probably enough to supply electrical power to a medium size city if necessary. The Fems had also completed the conversion of the light fixtures on all topside levels. More and more of the complex was becoming active. Amy had directed the installation of additional fixtures through the main utility corridor leading down to her physical location. This had effectively converted the connecting communications cabling down to the communication computer that had interfaced her

414

with the outside world. After repair and re-booting of the main computer system, she had completed her physical communication link outside her physical dome for the first time in over fifty years. He sensed that this did mark a major moment in history for Amy. They switched from BC (before communication) to AC (after communication).

He could see much of the outside data she was monitoring and it seemed strange, as if a third party was now in their heads. Amy was receiving inputs from some cameras throughout the activated floors, allowing her to begin to direct some of the activities of the Fems. She was good at giving instructions, and the Fems didn't seem to mind Amy's directness. Mama simply obeyed without question.

Her immediate concern had been the defense of the facility, which he absolutely agreed with. Through the Simian computer, she had directed the installation of cameras to view the outside through holes prepared in the doors. With the activation of the cabling route, she was now able to view much of the top floors and now the outside. Additionally, at her direction, lasers were installed at strategic locations within the activated portion of the facility and at the doors directed toward the outside though firing slots. She now had total and sole control of the laser movement and firing sequence. He was very thankful for the lasers, but wondered where they came from.

Amy said, "This was a research facility, but was also a military installation. Many things were stored in the underground warehouse including a large supply of hand held and wall mounted remote controlled laser weapons."

She explained that they had been inventoried and used in high security areas like this one. That got his attention! He asked, "Can the laser weapons be used outside the altered environment inside the facility? Are there rifles inventoried in this facility that can use the modified gun powder? What else is inventoried here that can be used against the Simian Warriors?" He was bombarding Amy with questions and saw that Amy was surprised and looking at him with a strange expression. What had he done? He vowed to learn diplomacy.

* Amy *

She designed a simulated voice generator capable of the high frequency screeches of the Simians. Since all the Fems had been mentally altered it would be relatively safe and easier to revert back to the Simian language. She would be able to direct her audible instruction anywhere through the facility by utilizing the intercom and loud speaker system. Once the main floor modified lighting system and door defenses were installed and activated, she instructed Mama to reassign one of the electrical engineers to construct the simulated voice generator. A list of inventoried parts was printed out for this purpose. She liked having printers, plotters, and access to data previously lost in the main storage computer. It was definitely a new beginning.

By the time electrical communication was established from her physical location to the top main floors, the simulated voice generator was complete. Units built by Simians had a tendency to be bigger than her design due to the size of their hands and the huge double thumbs. This was no exception, but she was happy to have it. It didn't take much time for it to be built and installed, which also pleased her greatly. It was amazing how she was becoming accustomed to emotions and even looking forward to many of them, but not all. Emotions were still a weakness.

Levi was excited when she told him about the laser weapons inventory and his quick mind jumped to use of the lasers outside of the facility. He was obviously hoping to use the portable laser rifle in their army, but she had already dismissed that idea. She too had hoped for that, but once the lasers were removed from the altered environment of the facility, the physics of the required electronics ceased to work. She had considered numerous options, but there was nothing she could do about it. They were useless outside the facility. The Fems, however, could use them if necessary to repel a breach of security within the complex. Her preference, however, was to control all lasers personally and make available the laser rifles as last resort. She realized that she probably was paranoid but she certainly had cause.

Levi's mind jumped to inquire if there were any military rifles in storage. They had been unsuccessful in finding any additional rifles in working condition other than the ones in the secret cache, which were still in the storage grease. All others found had been either rusted or destroyed by the Simians. Yes! She searched her files and found twenty-five AR-15 listed. She immediately dispatched a Fem to search the storage area. They had been stored in the weapons locker and the report was bad. The barrels were rusted and unusable.

Levi was not up to his norm yet, but they had to leave soon to catch the Techs before they arrived at the settlement. Levi was finished eating. It had only taken him an hour of solid eating to get full. The stares had finally stopped and most were wandering off. She helped him digest his food and relax for an hour before she told him it was time to go.

Levi said, "What?"

She responded by saying, "Hey, shithead, it was your idea to go to the Techs and if we don't go very soon, it will be too late. They will be coming into camp before morning."

He just grinned and said, "Oh."

* Levi *

In spite of having his head almost cut off he was feeling pretty good. The food was great, and since he hadn't eaten in a couple of days, he had been weak too. Now he could rest and recuperate. He had a good excuse didn't he, although no sympathy from Amy? She said it was time to go. That surprised him for sure until Amy reminded him that it was his idea. She was right too. They had to alter the original Techs before they arrived here. Amy wasn't the only one that got premonitions and he had one about this. He suspected that the Supreme One had already picked out his next target and was waiting for them to arrive. Of course it might not be one of his original group, but then that wouldn't matter so much once he had his bodyguards. Yep, it was time to go. He felt good anyway. Just as they were about to go, it happened.

Amy's activity at the facility was different than when she monitored Dawn, Fred, and Jimmy. He was only able to see what Amy directed toward him. He was thankful he was not able to see this direct monitoring. It would have driven him insane. He was, to a certain extent, able to observe what was going on at the facility, at least when she communicated. Somehow her thought pattern was a little different, but he could follow it, especially once she activated the speech communication. He followed that without much effort, probably because Amy was using language thoughts to activate the speech generator. That is how he knew about the second attack on the doors. Amy announced the attack!

When Amy focused on the cameras facing outside, he was able to see them also. The Warrs had returned armed with a form of a battering ram. It was held by eight Warrs on each side. It was fortunate that the Warrs had delayed this long, because this method could really work to batter down the door. Now it was too late for them with this kind of attack, assuming the lasers and electrified defenses worked. He saw the laser cameras and noticed the insertion of a cross hatch on the screen. There were two crosshatches actually representing both lasers. Amy had activated the lasers and superimposed the target aim of the lasers on the video. He believed that she did this for his benefit, because she certainly didn't need it. Her internal calculation would compile all the data inputs and compensate all variables without needing the actual compiled video.

The Warrs were approaching the door with the ram when Amy opened fire. The laser beams shot and interlaced across the space and into the Warrs. The thin red lights cut like swords through the Warrs. The beams cut through everything in its path, severing arms, legs, heads, and even the battering ram as they sliced across the space. He saw no Simian blood, only black sealed and smoking wounds as they fell jerking and kicking to the ground. The cuts were so sudden the arms and legs continued to move even after they were severed from the bodies. Damn, these were some strong lasers and awesome weapons. This was incredible. The Warrs never had a chance.

There would not be another direct attack on the doors. Of that he was quite sure. At least the Supreme One would have to get some more Warrs, because these were all dead or out of commission. Some had run, barely missing the instant death, but he suspected they would not come near this place again. Regardless, the Supreme One would never give up. They would have to consider well just what options might be used, for there would be more attacks. To that he was also sure.

After the attack Amy said, "We must hurry and meet the Techs en route before dark."

She wanted them all to be awake. She suspected that it might be easier for the Supreme One to take over Simian minds when they were asleep, so she wanted to catch them before they made camp. It sounded logical to him and he stood to comply, which startled everyone. Oh well.

420

Moon and Bambi remained close to him as he began to leave the medical area. The medical attendants still looked at him as if he were a ghost or maybe even a super being. Both opinions bothered him. He felt simple and liked it that way.

Amy told him, "Get real."

He chuckled out loud as he left the area.

He told Moon and Bambi that they were leaving. He received a nod but no questions, and as he went to gather his pack, weapons, and belongings, he noticed that Bambi and Moon took turns leaving to gather their packs. One of them was always at his side watching. So the protection begins. When both Moon and Bambi were with him again, he looped his arms through theirs and led them off in the direction of the caverns to find a clear spot from which to teleport. Moon and Bambi took the gesture in good humor. They seemed to like the show of affection and even smiled at him. Amy was almost overwhelmed by the sudden show of affection from him and the big brutes. He could see tears welling up in her eyes. Oh well, he did love them. So what if he showed his feminine side? He was picking up emotions from Amy now, strange since she had never really shown many. They grinned at each other knowing that Amy knew about love.

* Amy *

She saw them coming over the rise about two hundred feet from the door. The Warrs were coming fast carrying a section of a tree trunk approximately twenty-five feet long and two feet in diameter. It

421

had been tapered on the front and covered with steel. She realized they had been lucky that the Warrs had taken the time to build this tool. The Supreme One had been busy. Had they come even four hours earlier before the lasers, communication, and the speech generator were established, it would have succeeded. It might still work. Her defense system was yet untested. She gave warning to the Fems through her newly activated voice generator. The Fems jumped from both the warning and her speech and retreated from the door.

She activated the twin lasers installed on either side of the main door. It took her only seconds to calculate the interface of the video and target focus of the lasers. Levi was very anxious and troubled so she opened her data inputs and simplified the video data for him. The sixteen Warrs were positioned equally on either side of the tree trunk holding handles attached along each side. They carried it easily though the weight would exceed a ton. The momentum of the weight and the strength of the Warrs would generate a massive force against the steel door. If they connected with the small entrance door, the force would break through, and a breech in the defense there would be devastating.

She fired the lasers and was rewarded with a focused narrow beams of bright red light. Her worries were relieved when she saw the beams, but her relief turned to horror and shock when she saw the results. The laser beams were extremely powerful and cut through the Warrs with extreme ease. Body parts fell to the ground or complete bodies fell or exploded. Smoke traced itself across the Simians. The trajectories of the beams were made, and she couldn't alter them due to her momentary shock. She realized that she wouldn't stop it if she could. The Warrs had to be stopped and stopped they were. With some sadness, she realized too late that the attack had been stopped and it wasn't necessary to kill all of them. It seemed strange to be merciful with Warrs after all she had seen, but it was horrible to witness. The death or dismemberment was instant and terrible. Thankfully however, some of the Warrs managed to dodge the beams and escape.

Levi was extremely happy at the carnage. It seemed to satisfy his thirst for revenge; certainly he was pleased with her defense. His jubilation only lasted a short time as he then looked solemn. This jolted her back into perspective and asked him, "What?" Levi just said that this defense was extremely powerful and as such, the Supreme One would not make this mistake again. They had better be on guard for what other options might be available. He was right of course, but then the Supreme One might just figure that as well and believe that we would never expect him to attack here again.

Levi just grinned at the thought and said, "Look who's getting devious now?"

Maybe she was learning how to be devious, but during the attack she had discovered a fallacy in her defense. They might have been in trouble if the Warrs had attacked after dark. She had no lights outside and would have been blind. She had already decided to add infrared heat detectors to the video cameras. That would allow her to detect a night attack in progress. That would thwart the frontal attacks. She would have to review the building and engineering schematics of the facility to research other directions or methods of attack, and of course, continue to monitor the cameras. The research would take time.

Levi was looking suspiciously at Moon and Bambi. He knew they would be guarding him so she wondered why he looked that way.

He just said, "I know. I just can't believe I need a guard all the time."

She responded, "Shut up!" He started laughing and cuddled up close between Bambi and Moon and slipped his arms through theirs as if to escort them to a ball. It was a rare form of visible affection from Levi. Even Moon and Bambi responded in kind, which was even rarer. It touched her emotions to see these three locked in embrace, such that it was, but how she wished she could join them in the embrace.

They continued on, with arms locked, in the direction of the caverns to a place unobserved. They released each other as she gathered the energy. This group had teleported so many times they knew and could anticipate the energy surge and transfer. As usual the golden hair stood out as the air energized. The transfer was smooth and they appeared about two hundred feet in front of Jimmy, who was in the lead with # 9 jogging beside his horse. As had been typical of the original group of Techs, most were gathered together in a loose group. Out of the original fifteen Techs liberated from the Los Angeles Simian Colony, only nine remained alive and eight of them were here. The migration slowed, and they approached along with Jimmy.

When they were altogether Levi used sign language and, reluctantly, asked for volunteers to be his body guards. As she expected, they all volunteered. She had decided to use them all as necessary, but the first bodyguard team would consist of three members, # 7, # 11 and # 1. Tech # 7 owed Levi his life several times over and had reason to be even more loyal than the others, who were already totally committed to Levi anyway. The choice of # 1 and # 11 was totally by chance. They were chosen mathematically. When Levi groaned at her reasoning she said, "Well, they are all loyal and competent, so I picked odd numbers." He just laughed.

They were all happy when he told them they all would be his chosen and quickly gathered for his blessing. After holding each head in a ceremonial form, he assigned the three chosen for immediate duty.

* Levi *

Amy was very sure of these Technical Simians and took the opportunity of this ceremony to transfer and augment other vital information into the chosen ones. She downloaded fighting abilities, but admitted that she didn't transfer it all.

Amy said, "Moon is still superior in skill."

Levi grinned. Amy actually was becoming devious.

She just nodded and said, "Maybe."

He laughed then and said, "Mysterious too." It was her turn to laugh.

Amy also downloaded other skills and talents as well. He waited to hear what. Finally his patience ran out and he said, "What?"

She responded with," You will see in time."

"Damnit, Amy, your starting to aggravate me!" he barked. That didn't seem to bother her as her thoughts moved on to the next subjects dismissing him. "Damn!" He wondered what she had done, but resolved himself to the fact that he would only know in time, as she had said.

The Techs all soon responded to the downloads by giving him a knowing look and nod as if to say, "I have it now." Amy had transferred knowledge to all of them about the immediate assignments of # 1, # 7, and # 11 being the initial assigned guards. He was thankful that he didn't have to explain that one. None wanted to be left out. Amy also transferred all the assignment and task instructions and he didn't have to pass on anything. They already knew about # 10, what had happened, how it had happened, and now they knew what the blessing was and why. They all acknowledged # 9 as the new leader of the combined groups of Simians and common colony.

He could see that Moon had been watching the Techs closely looking for any signs of the Supreme One attempting to control any of the minds, but, as they had hoped, they apparently headed off any attempts by not waiting for them to come into camp. They felt relief now with the downloads complete. Hopefully, these minds were now protected from control. The Supreme One would have to find another way now.

Jimmy had waited patiently for the information transfer, but now made himself known. He was smiling as always when he approached. It was always an infectious grin that made you at ease with him. He was truly likeable. He wanted to know what was going on. Levi began to bring him up to date, but decided to do it mentally and simultaneously with Dawn and Fred as well. Why not? They needed to know too, and this would save time. Amy provided the information on the status of affairs and focused the telepathic transmission to the group. Jimmy seemed satisfied and he, along with the other communication team members, now knew more than most others. He knew that the team would relay most of the information to their affiliated group, with the exception of the obvious sensitive information. He liked having communication and especially being able to distribute information universally.

As they were gathered, Amy expressed concern and warning.

She said, "I feel the Supreme One. He is here with us. He is very quiet and trying to be invisible, but I can still feel the hate slipping out, barely under control. He is in control of someone close, but I can't identify who!"

She seemed so calm, but for once he was scared. He had an enemy close and didn't know where to look. With the pain of the last attack so vivid in his mind, he had fear. Being killed so many times was getting to him. Amy was mostly quiet, but tried to calm him.

Amy said, "I'm watching everything and everyone. Just stay alert."

Now that was useless information. He could not be more alert.

He used the established code word (Snake) for danger that had been established in Amy's procedures downloaded into the Techs. Per the procedures, # 1, # 7, and # 11 jumped to surround him and form a defensive parameter around him facing outward. The inner circle also included Moon and Bambi. Outside the immediate circle the other Techs formed a secondary parameter. There were so many Simians in the colony. All they could do is watch. The surrounding Simians noticed the threatening posture and spread out giving them plenty of room. They sensed the danger and moved to avoid it.

"Let's get out of here!" he barked. The outer parameter of Techs spread out to cover their retreat. As they did, he felt the vibration of energy grow warm around them and the view alter. Amy was taking them back to the desert settlement. No sooner had they materialized at the settlement then Amy reported.

Amy said, "The Supreme One is still with us!"

CHAPTER 11
(THE TRAP TIGHTENS)

* Satan *

He was livid with rage! He hated this living mind with every breath that he took. Every thought was of the destruction of this alien mind. He hated the power of this mind, and it was incredibly powerful. It was almost a match to his own mind, but not quite. It reminded him of his siblings from the home world, which he destroyed. There were possibly two left on the home world, but they too would die soon along with the planet. This mind must also die. His body shook from this rage as he thought about the mind. To make matters worse, this creature was female. Females were good for nothing but sex and pleasure. Each defeat at her hands made him even angrier and more determined to kill her. Nothing would stop him from this goal.

In one of his more rational moments he had transferred control of his massive colony to his first in command. His first in command was smart, smart enough to stay away from him. He respected that. Satan knew he would kill his first in command if he remained close, so he had sent him away. Control could be taken back anytime he wished, but the colony needed supervision and he would only kill anyone that came close to him. His immediate needs would be taken care of without the colony. He maintained a large personal staff to take care of his needs and females for his pleasure. Of course, they would die when he finished with them. He would not allow another Supreme One to be born. There would be only one Supreme One on this planet, him.

In spite of the anger and rage boiling inside, he had grown in power. This alien mind had challenged him and made him expand his mind and learn new abilities. This was good, but the fury she had generated in him had threatened to destroy him. He realized it was not the mind but his own limitations of self-control that threatened him. It had forced him to exercise control, learn and expand his abilities. His days were now spent searching and reaching out with his mind to touch and monitor or take control of other Simian minds. They were so simple, and it was becoming easier to span the distances, but the alien Bitch had managed to place blocks on many of the runt Simians. He could not see into their minds now. Those minds now seemed alien like the little animals (humans) that lived on this world, but there were some that he could touch that remained close to the animal. There were still many others of his race that he could gain information from and use for his purposes. It had taken him much practice to reach this level, but he was pleased with his abilities. Unfortunately, the simple Warrior mind was not capable of much, but enough. They could kill!

His attempts to control the alien female mind had been repelled, so far. He had gotten close several times and he might yet destroy the mind directly with the power of his, but each failure sent his temper out of control. Even though he failed, he had felt the fear and terror he generated into the mind and enjoyed the taste of her fear.

At first the mind had been open and he entered silently. The mind thought some in his language, and he learned much from her conversations with the animal. He studied the thoughts, and when he had learned all he could, he attacked.

The attack was sudden, striking with a mental blow. Her mind froze in fear, but she had somehow countered his power and eventually broke his hold. This happened twice, and she had escaped from his grasp both times, much to his distress and severe frustration. He had learned she was frightened of failure and actually cared for the lives of the animals, and even the runt Simians. This made her weak and vulnerable. He also felt the symbiotic relationship with the human animal. This was her main weakness. When he destroyed this Levi, the mind would also be lost and helpless.

Satan's attacks would be two-fold. First, he would attack and destroy the symbiotic animal and break her link to the outside world. Secondly, he would capture her physical brain hidden deep underground. He intended to imprison her mind and torture her just for fun throughout his lifetime. He would kill her will and punish her. That remained his goal, even though his previous attempts had failed.

Through long mental practice, he had perfected the ability to transmit his mind over long distances. He could transmit his thought and control to almost any Simian at will. Through one such Simian mind he had seen her physical location and the physical shape of the mind. The shape of the shiny, round mind was indelibly imprinted in his memory and haunted him day and night. It became the target of his hate. He hated this image with a force never before experienced by him. It consumed his thoughts and focused his almost uncontrollable rage.

Even without the Simian mind he occupied, he would have been able to locate her by homing in on the strength of her radiated mental power. Actually, he could do little else. Her force was distracting and became a constant reminder of his hate... hate so intense that it demanded the bitch must die!

Once he physically located her, he dispatched thirty Warriors from the Phoenix colony to the mind's location with instructions. Satan was not directly controlling their minds, only personally instructing them. When he had seen the alien mind using telepathic powers, he was determined to do the same. Over time he had perfected his own telepathic ability. If the Witch could do it, so could he. He was determined to do everything she could do.

The first physical attack was launched against the underground complex. He believed the underground complex was deserted except for the mind, and he wanted to capture and control her. The Warriors had almost succeeded in entering the complex, when a Supreme One materialized and frightened them away. For a few seconds even he believed it was a Supreme One issuing orders, but he quickly realized it was a trick of the Witch. He tried to control the Warriors, but their minds were too simple to accept his instructions. The Witch instilled fear in the Warrior Simians, and they fled in panic. They were weak and would die for their cowardice. Through his rage, he successfully took

432

direct control of one of the Warriors and launched an attack on the false Supreme One. He did not understand how, but he sensed that it was the same animal which he sought to kill. His attack was sudden and had the Levi animal within inches of death when the Warrior was overrun by the runt and females of his race. The fangs sank deep and the pain was excruciating. He quickly withdrew his mind when he felt the stampede of the females stomping the life out of the Warrior. He vowed to kill the first female Simian he saw.

Satan went insane! Again he tore through his compound in a hysterical rage, ripping through anything in his path. The screeches reverberated through his colony as a warning to all. It was unnecessary. The inhabitants had long since deserted his immediate area. This only inflamed his insanity more. He ranted on for over an hour venting his anger against walls and structures. By the time he was back in control, everything in the vicinity of his control center was in shambles and he was exhausted. It took him a day to recoup.

He continued to watch and learn the Levi animal's routine. The Witch had the power to jump from place to place with small groups, and one of the places that the animal seemed most comfortable was the gathering of humans and runts in the desert. This is where he would launch his second physical attack.

He chose his target carefully. It was one of the runt leaders that seemed to be close to the inner circle. He knew he would eventually have an opportunity to be face to face with the animal, so he waited.

433

He couldn't believe his luck when he saw the Levi animal coming. It was alone and totally at ease. Satan's controlled Simian approached slowly and friendly, hiding his sword behind him. The animal was almost within grasp, but he felt the aura of the Witch as he got closer. His hate betrayed him in the last seconds as he swung the sword from behind. He knew he had him though, even as the animal made an attempt to move. He felt the joy of feeling the sword sink deep. As he felt the jubilation of his victory, he felt an energy force surround him. Suddenly, he was high in the sky falling. He didn't care; it was not his body. All he wanted to do was kill the animal. He tried to reach out, but in the free fall they drifted apart. Then abruptly the animal was gone and he was alone, falling, watching the ground race toward him. His mind was still with the runt Simian when the body smashed into the ground. The pain was incredible before his mind was able to vacate.

The pain combined with the anger of yet another defeat from the female mind set his rage at an extremely dangerous level. Satan emerged from his quarters launching into a rampage of violence and murder. He screeched his rage and delivered his wrath on anything or Simian he saw and ripped them limb from limb. HATE! Loathing of this enemy ruled him for many long minutes before he regained control. Luckily, most of the colony's Simians had already given the Supreme One's quarters a wide berth, but there were an unfortunate few that had drifted too close. Five Warriors and two females were decimated in this rampage. None had seen Satan or any Supreme One go on a rampage this severe.

The only thing that calmed him was the belief he had killed the animal, Levi. He didn't discover he remained alive until two days later. By that time he had calmed enough to hold back the rage and develop another plan.

It took another day of searching to find the deserted Warriors and, even then, he only found seventeen. Since only sixteen were needed for his next plan, he destroyed one Warrior as an example to the others. He concentrated his mental energy and quite literally exploded its brain. He wished he could do that to the Witch, but her resistance was too strong.

When the Warriors again approached the metal door to batter it in, he saw the red beams of light decimate the Warriors. Satan didn't care about the Warriors. He was going to kill them anyway, but how could this be? They had technology!

This technology was lost over fifty of this world's years ago. He remembered lasers, but they had become ineffective when the radiation bombarded upon this world. He had been happy to lose the technology. It made the Simians stronger because of their size and superior strength. Technology had been useless, but now this Witch had re-established technology. His rage was temporally replaced by deep concern and worry. If she had technology like this, his armies would lose the advantage. He was losing again and was losing his battle to control his rage. How could he think? His body shook with rage. He screamed with the incredible pressure of his hate and rage. There was nothing left to destroy and no one to vent his anger upon. He wept in frustration of his helplessness and his inability to kill anything or anyone.

He vowed then to use the entire Simian population if necessary to destroy the Witch and the Levi animal. He estimated that he had over one hundred thousand Simian Warriors around this planet he could use and he would sacrifice them all just to kill the Witch, technology or not.

Realizing the incredible advantage in numbers and strength, he calmed some, then even more when he thought of the next planned personal attack.

He had already invaded the Simian's mind of his target and was watching closely. He had even been transmitted from one location to another with the inner circle. This even occurred twice. Satan smiled when he remembered his plan and how it would feel when he completed what he planned. It would be so rewarding and he would win.

* Amy *

She felt a wave of pure hate sweep over her, touching her mind, threatening to freeze her in fear. Only the Supreme One could hate that much, but they should be safe. Levi was surrounded by only his body guards and trusted ones. Could the Supreme One have taken over one of them? How could that be? She didn't stop to try to analyze it. She notified Levi and he reacted immediately. They had prepared for just such a moment and the code word "Snake" was given. As per the plan and download, the three assigned guards (# 1, # 7 and # 11) surrounded Levi, Moon and Bambi. The

436

remainder of the guard team surrounded that inner circle in a defensive perimeter. She could still feel the energy of hate, but masked so that she could not tell exactly where, only that it was close. The outer perimeter of guards spread out while she began the emergency teleport.

Her target location was the desert community where they had been. Whatever happened, this was as good a place as any to deal with the problem. She was quite proficient with teleporting now and required little concentration anymore, and that was good because her mind whirled. In the fraction of a second for the teleport she analyzed data. She knew who it was now. She had made a terrible mistake and now it might cost someone's life, someone important, maybe even her own and Levi's. Could anything be done at this point? The Supreme One was in control of his chosen target and had to know she was probably now aware, but he might not be sure if she had identified which one it was. This might be an advantage. She was cautioning Levi as he monitored her thought, "Don't give it away." Could Levi tell the others without the Supreme One hearing or knowing? Yes, Levi could tell them in French. All her downloads had included French. She had wanted the Simians to understand spoken French as a means to transfer communications under just such a situation. She had no idea it would ever be needed and certainly not minutes after the download, but need it they did. The only one that would not understand the instruction in French was the lone Simian she had failed to modify with a download. How had she made such a stupid mistake?

As they materialized at the desert settlement Levi began giving her instructions in French. He announced as if talking to no one in particular, but desperately intended to be heard by his Simian team.

Levi spoke in an even tone without any alarming emotions, "Do not look at Bambi, but she is the one under control of the Supreme One. She does not understand French so act normal and stand still while Moon and I lead Bambi past you. When her back is to you, grab her arms so she is unable to use her fangs then pull her to the ground. We will help once you have immobilized her arms."

Acting as if he had been daydreaming, he screeched and motioned Moon and Bambi forward. Amy knew Bambi would follow closely to Levi and attack as soon as she could get in a good position. Levi was careful to keep Moon between them and moved fast for the first few steps. Bambi quickly followed, focusing on Levi's back as she left the guards behind.

From behind, Amy felt the hate burst forth, along with a screech of rage. The screech was cut short by a muffled grunt. The timing had been uncomfortably close. The Supreme One, through Bambi, had been close to success. Levi and Moon turned to see the three Simians wrestling Bambi to the ground. She was screeching in rage and frustration and fighting like she was mentally disturbed, which she was. She was bouncing the three giant Simians around like children, but they held on tightly. Moon quickly joined his team to hold the screeching and kicking Bambi. Levi dispatched workers for rope and stakes and she was soon bound to the ground tight.

The Supreme One could destroy Bambi at any time he wished, or he could simply withdraw from her brain. She did not expect Bambi to survive any willing retreat of the Supreme One. Severe pain or death might make him withdraw, but he probably knew that they would not inflict pain on Bambi nor kill her. The Supreme One simply waited and spewed out its hate in the form of stares and verbal abuse. He called her Witch and many other words she had no idea what the meanings were. She was probably lucky. Certainly he was not calm as Bambi continued to fight her restraints and screech insults at Amy. She was considering options for saving Bambi or maybe even killing her to put her out of her obvious misery when Levi got her attention.

Levi asked, "Why can't you do a download to her now?" Damn. It was certainly an option and a simple one in his mind, but not that simple in reality. If she linked with Bambi's mind she would be linking with the Supreme One. What would happen? Could she resist his rage and insanity, or would it destroy her?

The Supreme One had been in her mind at least twice before, and she had been frozen by fear both times. She almost lost her mind to him. Both times Levi had shocked her back into control. It was a very dangerous option that Levi had presented, but possibly the only one that might work to save Bambi. When the Supreme One decided to leave, it would surely destroy Bambi upon its leaving. If it could be driven out, Bambi might survive. She knew she must try.

When Levi saw her thoughts and the potential dangers to her, he changed his mind. He did not want her taking chances, but just like Levi would have said, "There is no choice." She had to try. Amy knew it was going to be rough being so close to the center of hate and was analyzing data in hopes of discovering a defense. It was not enough to try and block the hate energy. If the wall collapsed the sudden shock could destroy her mind. She had to counter the hate with the opposite. Her defense would have to be love, something she had only learned during this last year. However, she had learned it well. Levi was her love, the center of her being, her everything. When she thought of the word love she remembered the poem in Levi's mind, the poem he had written for his first love, the poem that had made her understand what love was.

LOVE

What words do you use

When I LOVE YOU is not enough?

Love is only a word,

A word to express what you feel,

A word to express a wealth of meanings, feelings, emotions

Can it be done with a word? I think not!

It can mean many things to many people

But what does this word mean to me?

I love you

When we are together

You fill my heart

You make me happy

You make me soar to heights I have never been

We are one

Complete

You fill an emptiness
An emptiness which only you can fill
An emptiness which comes when you are away.
Love is addictive,
An addiction for you
The addiction of needs, wants, desires
As a drowning man for air
As a starving man for food
As a thirsting man for water
As a freezing man for warmth
As a blind man for sight
And as I for You
When I say I LOVE YOU
I want you, need you, and desire you
To smell you and fill my lungs with you
To taste you and fill my body with you
To drink you in and fill my need
To feel your warmth against me
To see your beauty and feed my starving eyes
You are my air, my food, my water, my warmth, my light
My everything!
MY LOVE

Yes, Love would be her light in the darkness of his hate. Was her love stronger than Satan's hate? It had to be.

* Levi *

He was very concerned when Amy told him Bambi was the one possessed. Oh shit! Amy cautioned him not to react and then revealed her plan. He liked the idea of informing the others in French. French had been his idea anyway. Amy already had French in her language banks, so it was now a standard part of the download. Now, when they spoke in French the Supreme One was not able to monitor their conversations. It was a good thing French was a standard part of the downloads considering this situation. Sometimes they got lucky, but not often.

He initiated Amy's plan and, as always, her plan worked, but he had a hard time turning his back to Bambi knowing that was what she was waiting for. As he walked away he half way expected to feel Bambi's finger fangs sink into his back. Amy had told him before that the venom was extremely poisonous and quick. It was so quick that he might die before she could reverse the effect. Luckily, the plan worked, and he sighed in relieved to hear Bambi's grunts as the Techs took control and subdued her.

Levi noticed that Moon was really upset with what had happened to Bambi. He suspected that Moon was far more sensitive than he previously believed. Moon could show affection and had in fact demonstrated friendship and loyalty toward him. Levi enjoyed and liked this quiet friend. Yes, Moon had emotions and he strongly suspected Moon had developed great affection, maybe even more, for Bambi. Moon was holding Bambi's head, keeping it from thrashing and staring down at her with deep concern. Levi's and Amy's heart poured out to Moon, not to mention Bambi, whom they had also grown close to. Bambi was in major distress and totally at the Supreme One's mercy, which did not exist.

442

His mind raced and, without considering the implications, he asked, "Can't you down load and link with Bambi now?" He saw her fear at the thought. She was afraid to link with the sinister mind of the Supreme One, which in essence is what it would be. He quickly saw the fallacy of that approach. Amy would have to face the evil one alone, and she might not be able to return from Bambi's mind. Amy could be destroyed along with Bambi. He could not stand that thought. If Amy died he would also die within hours from the mutation of his cells, but that was not a concern to him. Amy was his sole interest. He tried to guide her thoughts away from that option.

Amy was not having it and said, "I am going to link with her mind and try to drive out the Supreme One."

He knew that tone. Amy could be so stubborn sometimes. No, she could be positively bull headed. There was nothing he could do, but to say, "I love you Amy." He then placed his hands on Bambi's head and waited.

* Amy *

Amy's mind forced itself through the barrier of hate too easily. But she realized this too late as the energy of darkness and hate made up of pure evil closed around her like a vise. She knew the mental signature of the Supreme One from before and expected it, but somehow the feeling this time was much stronger. It was probably because the Supreme One had completely invaded Bambi's mind and had transferred more of his mind into her

443

brain than any time before. His mind must be incredibly powerful at the source, which was hundreds of miles away.

Amy held the aura of the hate back with concentrated mental energy, but the force surrounding her was getting stronger and closing tighter. She sensed the depth of the fury and insane intensity of hated for her. It was unimaginable. It was a turbulent black sea of tentacles reaching out to her, surrounding and holding her, tightening and pulling her in.

She could sense Bambi's essence, but so very weak. Bambi's mind was merged with the Supreme One, but totally submissive. Amy realized that, even if she was successful in driving the Supreme One out, Bambi would be mentally altered and easily subject to the Supreme One's future control at will. It might not be possible to salvage Bambi. There simply might not be anything left to salvage.

These thoughts came in microseconds as the evil trap slammed shut. She was losing the mental tug-of-war and felt the dark energy compressing down on her. As she was being closed off, she heard Levi's voice and saw a faint light deep in her mind. Although dim, Levi continued talking, reassuring her that he was with her.

Levi said, "I love you Amy. Don't leave me. Come back."

She felt Levi's love, a very dim light in the pitch black depths of the Supreme One's hate. She saw the blackness withdraw slightly from the faint light. Amy concentrated on the glow of Levi's love and felt it reaching out to her, calling her. She loved him so!

444

She remembered how she learned what love was, her first warm feelings, and how they grew. She drew on her internal love and need for Levi. Life was not something she wanted without him. She lived to please him and to share life's experiences. She thought of how complete and together they became when they made love. Although mental, it was as real as any two physical bodies. They were one body and soul merged together in their love. Their love fed each other.

She felt the glow inside her mind mixing with Levi's expression of love. She loved Levi even more for providing the focus. She concentrated on that focus and felt the glow grow stronger. The light grew and began expanding, forcing the darkness back.

The pitch black was receding from the light, exposing a storm of red lightning bolts flashing within. Even though the darkness was withdrawing, she felt the surrounding rage grow and expand in strength becoming uncontrollable. As it increased it became dangerously unstable. The Supreme One's mind was about to explode from the enormous level of pure evil hate and rage being generated. Her love continued to reinforce the glowing light pushing the darkness back even more. Suddenly, the darkness vanished and she was free. Her mind was incredibly weak from the effort, but she was free.

It took her several long seconds to gather her wits again, but her first act was to mentally embrace Levi and kiss him. In between kisses she said, I love you too, Levi." Levi was all smiles. He had obviously seen into her mind during the mental battle with evil and was breathing a sigh of relief also.

Her next action was to check on Bambi. Bambi's mind was still intact but shaken. Amy quickly downloaded the previously prepared information into her still shaken mind, permanently altering and protecting Bambi's mind. She did some special variations to alienate her even further from Simian thought patterns. Hopefully, the Supreme One would never be able to return to this mind, and Bambi might even demonstrate some human qualities as well. That should be interesting.

One side effect of the battle within Bambi's mind: her existence was no longer a secret to Bambi. She had witnessed, up close, the struggle for her life and now knew who Amy was, partly anyway. Since Bambi knew, Amy added information about her within the download. Bambi now shared her secret with the other elite, and joined her exclusive club.

* Levi *

He was unable to stop Amy from trying to save Bambi. All he could do now was try to help. He moved Moon out of the way and held tightly to Bambi's thrashing head. The link with Amy was strong, and he tried to enter into Bambi's mind along with Amy, but his mental strength was not enough. He was repulsed immediately by an evil blackness as dense as steal. He was able to monitor some, but the pure hate drove him back. Amy seemed to be captured, trapped instantly by an enclosing wall of pure black hate. He had no idea what it was, but he knew it was evil. He could sense it. The link with Amy allowed him to see through Amy's mental eyes from within the imprisoning circle. Amy was there battling with the monster for her life, and she was strong, but as incredibly powerful as she was, she was losing. Levi feared for her and tried to figure out how to pull her out, but she couldn't hear him. He screamed, but he knew the sound didn't penetrate the wall of blackness. He saw the barely perceptible light within begin to grow and felt Amy draw strength from him in some way. He let his love flow out to her. She could take anything from him. Certainly, he had lots of love to give. The battle raged for strength of will. It was a battle of light against darkness, good against evil, love against hate, and life against death. The light slowly began to burn brightly and Amy suddenly won the battle, and the darkness vanished. He was both relieved and proud, so very proud of Amy. After a few seconds, he said, "You did good, Amy. I am so proud of you."

She was mentally weary and exhausted after the battle. He had never seen her this way before. Amy must have expended incredible amounts of energy resisting the black and evil opposing powers of the Supreme One. It must have been extremely hard on her, but her face spread wide, grinning and radiating back her love and caring for him. He welcomed her back and embraced her.

Moon touched him on the shoulder to get his attention. He came back from where ever he had been. It was like a daydream, but Moon's touch startled him back to the here and now. He looked up into the deeply stressed face of Moon and smiled.

The smile told it all and Moon's relief was very visible. Moon undid Bambi's restraints and took her in his arms and held her close. Bambi was terribly shaken but alive and apparently whole. She seemed to welcome his attention and made no effort to move from his arms. It was a tender moment that he had never seen in a Simian before. Amy said those features were mostly only inherent in the Technical Simians and, even then, very latent.

She added, "The downloads make a difference too." Amy was grinning.

The ordeal was over, and his bodyguards resumed their position around him. With the crisis over, the formation was much looser and more relaxed than before. It was, however, a gentle reminder that things would never be the same again and he had lost some of his freedom. Amy was quiet and seemed to be resting so he did what came naturally. He led his bodyguards toward the cooking area for food. He knew they didn't like the smell of cooked food, but he figured if he lost some of his freedom, they would have to smell his food. They might as well get used to it, because he did like to eat. He chuckled to himself at his own joke.

* Satan *

His trap was almost complete. The Levi animal was standing in front of him. All he had to do was take two quick steps and sink the female's finger fangs into his back. He could taste victory and was already smiling. He made his move and leaped forward raising the hands to strike. No sooner than he started the leap, strong hands grabbed his mental

448

target's arms and hands. He felt heavy arms wrapped around him and pulled him, thrashing and screeching, to the ground. The female was weak and couldn't break loose. The other runt Simian joined with those that held the feeble female. He fought against them to no avail. Rage took him as the victory escaped him. The arms and legs were bound and the female was spread out, secure and helpless. His mind tried to reach out its rage and hate to touch the animal and crush it, but there was no opportunity. He hated the animals of this planet and the alien minds which he could not reach. His rage grew and the body shook, but the body was useless. He calmed some, realizing that they could do nothing to him. He forced himself to remain calm and observe as the hate simmered inside him, barely in control.

The Witch had weakened. She had feelings for the Simian female and wanted to save her. How stupid that was. He would never be so weak. There would never be any saving of this Simian female. He would destroy her viciously, while they watched helplessly as her brain exploded. He waited to see what the Witch would do. He could not believe it when he saw his chance. The mind was going to try to enter the female's mind and save her. The Witch was going to extend her mind into his. His hate had allowed so much of his mind to be transferred into the Simian female, and the Witch didn't realize how much power awaited her there. This degree of his transfer made him strong in this mind. He could capture her essence with the power of his mind and crush her. He waited.

He allowed the Witch to force herself past the barrier of his mind. Once she was well inside he slammed his mind shut around her. He had her in the trap. The hate and stored up rage gripped her. She was strong, but his mind was stronger as he tightened the force around her. Her essence was warm as he began to crush her. His stored up hate was being released on her, and her resistance was giving way. Victory was within reach. The more he compressed her mind, the hotter it became. The heat grew as her mind started to collapse more. The heat increased, and it began to fill him with pain. The heat intensified and the pain was becoming unbearable. Something was wrong.

He felt himself losing to the heat of her mind and his rage mushroomed more. His hate held the heat as his physical body shook with the effort. He felt his physical brain start to quiver from the intensity of the effort and pain, which shocked him as he began to warn. He quickly withdrew from the Simian female barely in time to save himself from destruction. As his body collapsed to the floor, he vowed to use every last Warrior to destroy the Witch.

* Amy *

Her mind had grown in the experience, expanding her capabilities. If she hadn't, she would have died. She was no match for the evil power of the Supreme One, but she had learned to adjust, devise and use other strengths to combat the hate. Amy had also learned that the power of love was greater than the power of hate.

450

What would ASONE have done? ASONE would have been useless in that same situation. There didn't appear to be any love in ASONE. He/she/it would probably have killed Bambi to eliminate the threat. It was impossible to know what ASONE might do though. It might have used powers she was yet unaware of to battle the Supreme One, but it was hard to believe that it would have cared what happened to Bambi or been able to use love as a weapon.

Exhaustion was a new experience and she was really tired. She even considered sleep, something she had never done before. That of course was impossible and unnecessary, but the concept was appealing. The battle had made her mind totally concentrate on a single objective. Her mind was absorbed on the defense and finally offense using the only weapon, her mind. Her mind had completely shut down all other functions. This was a first time for such disruption, but although the battle seemed like a very long time, it had actually only lasted one hundred and twenty seconds. It was now time to get back to work. Many things needed doing and time was getting short.

As she refocused on life, she laughed in Levi's inner ear as she saw where he was headed. Unsupervised, he always headed to the food. Levi didn't think that was funny and grumbled a few choice words. Although the words were grumpy, Levi was far from angry. She could tell he was happy to be able to banter words again, so she complied and called him, "Shithead!" Yes, everything was back to normal.

Her resumed monitoring revealed that Jimmy was very concerned, as were the other guard team and the entire combined groups of Simians and humans who had now merged. They communicated to all the team at once to let them know about the latest attack on Levi and what had happened, reassuring them that everything was all right. Jimmy had been frantic even before the emergency teleport and extremely concerned about Levi. Jimmy and all the other Techs had been looking at each other trying to figure out which one was possessed by the Supreme One and wondering if Levi was safe. Jimmy was totally attentive, listening to Levi's explanation and was signing to the others as he listened. Everyone there was relieved. Fred and even Dawn had been totally in the dark since this episode began. They were both shocked about the attack and relieved to know that Levi and Bambi were fine.

The communication team, as always, informed the leaders of their respective groups. Fred told Iron Eyes who in turn passed on the information to his groups. Dawn was grabbing Al and pulling him along as she was telling him. What was ironic was the fact that they were less than a thousand yards from Levi as the internal battle was raging. After Al heard most of the story, he was then pulling Dawn along. In fact, as Levi was taking in large bites he was watching Al and Dawn approach. There was concern on their faces.

Levi simply held up his hand and said, "I am fine."

They continued to quiz him, but little more was discussed. A knowing look from Al revealed that he knew the battle was mental, and Amy was the warrior. Levi nodded his head as if to say he was correct and everything was well. Al knew Amy was the source of Levi's life and their success to date, and looked relieved and grateful.

The combined groups of Technical Simians, females, wagon train, and humans traveling from Barstow should arrive tomorrow on schedule. The advanced human fighter trainees had arrived two days earlier and were already in training with the new weapons. Hopefully, they would be trained by the time they were needed. Iron Eyes' delaying army was at its last pass and would be speeding toward them by tomorrow. The combined armies of humans, Technical Simians, and the Females would be ready to move out in two days. She had no idea what to do now. All they could do is head east toward another trap.

* Levi *

He seemed to be much more personally in contact with the Greys at the facility, well mostly with Mama.

Amy said, "It is because I use language to activate the facility's voice circuits for two-way communication. This energizes a more active and prominent part of my brain and makes our telepathic link more pronounced."

He seemed understand this entire portion of the two-way communication through Amy's brain. He was thankful that it was not continuous like hers. He had a tendency to forget sometimes, but Amy's physical location was at the facility and naturally

453

the link to the Simian computer there provided the communication she received directly from the facility. This included the computer keyboard and data monitoring. Whatever the reason, he followed the language thoughts as Amy spoke and received this communication.

Mama was well along with the conversion of the facility. It should be completed in a few more days. Once that was accomplished, the plan was to install more lasers and cameras to expand Amy's ability to monitor the complex and defend herself. Unfortunately, Levi was unable to see the monitoring unless Amy chose to share it. That part was very much like the links to the humans she was monitoring. Amy said the Fems would then start on the clean-up and activation of the remainder of the complex. Amy was still very secretive as to the purpose of the activation of the facility. He had assumed the whole project was for defense, but he now suspected she had much more in mind.

Amy said, "It is not a secret. It is just not worth spending time thinking about right now, because we have to concentrate on surviving the next few days. It won't matter if we die before any research begins."

That was true. Amy could worry about it, but he had enough to worry about right now.

Amy's priorities were in the right order for sure. Survival did seem to be the most important goal, but as yet he had not heard a plan as to how they were going to accomplish that. He honestly didn't think she had one.

Amy, reading his thoughts, said, "I already told you I have no plan. All we can do is head east and hope for an opportunity that we can take advantage of. I wasn't kidding. We need a miracle."

Levi was angry with that retort and said, "Well, make one happen! Get mad and come up with something!" He said it out loud and probably a little too loud. That drew an angry look from Amy, but it quickly softened then drooped in despair.

Her only comment was, "I will try."

He was instantly angry again and said, "Don't even go there! Think and get hold of yourself. We aren't dead yet. Just tell me what you need, and we will come up with something."

She thought for a few seconds and said, "A miracle. We need a miracle to outrun the Simian armies and to gain us time to attack the Phoenix Simian colony."

Levi actually sat down hard in shock when he heard her. He bellowed, "What?" That came out loud and firm to the amazement to those gather around. Al, Dawn, and even Moon jumped in surprise and looked around trying to figure out what and who he was talking to. Levi just smiled and waved them off as he resumed his conversation with Amy saying, "I thought we were talking about just surviving, not attacking?" Amy was serious.

Amy said, "We are being forced, herded actually, toward the Phoenix colony. If we are not killed by the two Simian armies pursuing us first, we will surely be crushed between them and the Phoenix colony. If we are to survive that crushing vise, we must eliminate the Phoenix Simian army."

He saw both the logic and futility of the situation, but, as always, he never gave up. "All right," he said, "let me think." His mind raced, searching for ideas. It was impossible. It must be impossible because Amy didn't have an answer. Well, she had a partial idea, just not a sane solution. Take first things first. What could they do to delay the armies behind them? As he began to throw out ideas, Amy responded to each.

Amy responded, "No, there are no more suitable passes to block. It is mostly open desert. Yes, there are some obstacles such as sand dunes that would pose a major problem to them, but it would be a major problem for us too if we took that route. No, there are probably no lakes to speak of. From what I have seen of the increased flow and higher level of water in the Colorado River, I suspect that through the years the dams have all collapsed from uncontrolled seasonal floods. Yes, the river might present a barrier to the Simians, but the Simians could cross where we do on the highway and we could never hope to hold them there like we did at the mountain passes. The Simians would never allow the rifles to stop them this time at close range. They would see us escaping and simply charge the bridge."

Suddenly, he knew what to do to solve the first part of the plan.

* Amy *

Damnit, he did it again. Levi was silent for a moment after she told him about crossing the river at the bridge. Then suddenly he said, "We can blow the bridge up after we cross." He didn't have to explain what he meant. Everything clicked. The altered laws of physics on Earth had made

456

gunpowder useless until she had discovered the element that had been changed and modified the formula to compensate. That had provided the ability to make the gunpowder for the guns that were now being used in Iron Eyes' retreat through the mountain passes. That formula could now be used to make explosives that could be used to blow up the bridge behind them.

As she was telling Levi again how smart he was to have come up with that idea, she was already devising a plan. She had grown accustomed to Levi's spurts of brilliance, and it truly was a great idea, but he was such a shit about it. He knew it was a good idea and acted like it was so simple. That aggravated her, because that seemed to imply that she wasn't smart. She praised him anyway and commenced to implement the plan.

If the bridges were down behind them, she didn't think the Simians would try to forge the river, even though the depth might allow them to cross in places where the water was not over their heads. The denseness of a Simian body would take them to the bottom or make them sink into any mud that they might encounter, but the best deterrent was the justifiable fear the Simians had for water for those very reasons. Yes, that plan should work, but it was not that simple. First, they had to get their migration to the Colorado River and across the bridge without being killed by the Simian armies. Secondly, they would have to make the explosives and come ahead of the migration and plant the charges on the bridge. In addition, they would have to blow up more than one bridge or the Simian Armies would simply move up or down the river to the next available crossing. If that were the case, it would only slow the Simians down and possibly not enough to help. Finally, they would have to figure out a way to defeat the Phoenix Simian army that was surely waiting for them to come into a trap. That in itself was a seeming impossible task.

Even as they were discussing the use of gunpowder, she was already relaying instructions to Mama in how to make and package the required explosives and other additional surprises that she thought of on her own.

There was a large inventory of raw material at her facility and it was only a matter of following the formula. Only she had the formula because she chose not to allow anyone to know the mixture of chemicals, even Levi. This was for his protection. She wanted to control who knew and who could use guns. Anyone with a gun was equal to Levi, even with all his skills, and doubly dangerous if the Simians were able to discover the formula. She chose to share it now with Mama for several reasons; Mama was at her facility and would probably be there for the rest of her life, Mama and her information were personally protected by her new developing defenses, the Grays should all be immune to the probing mind of the Supreme One, and most importantly, there was an immediate need. Need demanded that the secret come out, but the formula should be safe.

She immediately saw that Levi heard her communication with Mama and he was all smiles. It was his turn to phrase her.

458

Levi was smiling as he said, "Damn, Amy, that was a brilliant additional twist. I wish I would have thought of it." Then he laughed.

He could be such a shit sometimes, but he could also be so sweet, too. She liked the appreciation. It was, after all, a good idea.

* Levi *

He saw the information flowing to Mama and he was pleasantly surprised. His surprise grew even more as he realized the shocker Amy was planning. He had not expected such immediate attention to the solution, nor had he expected Amy to divulge the secret of gunpowder. He did, however, understand Amy's logic. She had a safe house now where she could function through Mama's team in relative safety. He realized suddenly the other reason Amy wanted the facility active. Much could be possible through the activated facility. He just hoped they lived long enough to see the fruits of her plans and efforts.

The following day Iron Eyes's advanced wagons and slower traffic arrived at camp from the northern end. Their trip had been hard traveling through Death Valley. He remembered his trip through this hell hole and they were not fond memories. He was a frail old man at that time of his travels toward Amy's facility and his rebirth, but, even today, he would not welcome a return. Iron Eyes' party was tired, but they would see little rest. They had arrived only hours after Jimmy and the last group of Techs and Fems from Barstow. Only the Lancers and riflemen were left to hold the pass for as long as they safely could. When the Lancers and riflemen withdrew from the last pass, they should be able to outdistance the Simian armies on horseback. That was the plan anyway. If the Simians weren't starving by now, it just might work. Amy had better have a plan before the Simian armies caught up with them in the open desert.

Al was organizing the evacuation of the desert settlement scheduled for morning. Amy had provided the marching orders and Al was busy delegating duties and assigning marching locations. The first deployment included half of the desert settlement Lancers, which would provide the advanced security for the migration. The wagons, human females and older children, the new groups of humans joining them, and the bulk of the desert settlement would follow this advanced force. The first two groups had already left and would move as fast as the wagons would allow. Unfortunately, due to the shortage of horses, the wagons were being pulled by cattle, which made them even slower. The trailing groups would follow in the morning, but would be moving faster and soon catch up.

The elderly, most of the smaller children of the desert settlement, and even those of the incoming group were assigned to the caverns. They could live in relative safety inside the caverns for an extended period of time.

The caverns had its own water supply and food stored. In fact, all the chickens were stored inside. This underground facility would be maintained and guarded from within. The steel doors were impenetrable, especially protected by the cross bows. Cross hatch firing slots were installed in the

460

massive doors at the original installation. In anticipation of a possible long siege, Amy had designed a disposable one-shot arrow with a steel tip that could be used at close range by the crossbows. These arrows had been built in quantity, dipped in poison, and stored awaiting need. Armed with these, the elderly, mostly formally Guard members and tribal Warriors, would be able to defend and hold the caverns. Amy had everything of value stored there and hoped to be able to return to the settlement after the crisis was over. He hoped they lived to worry about this problem.

The main progression would be led by the total combined force of Technical Simian numbering about two hundred. This was a sizable force, but for the most part, they were still untrained. They would, however, be training as they traveled. Some of the original Techs were now dispersed among the gathering of Simians working with their kind to teach them as much as possible as fast as they could. It would be some time before they could hold their own with a Warrior Simian, but maybe they would get lucky.

Following the Techs would be the combined female Simians and young. There were many, probably around three hundred Fems. They would take the center position in the procession. The Fems had the ability to defend themselves with their poison finger fangs, but they wanted to do more. They wanted to fight the Simian Warriors. They had been oppressed for far too many years, and they wanted the humans to win. They now had their freedom and were determined to keep it. Unfortunately, they were not trained for organized battle. Amy admitted there could be a use for them at some point. She just didn't know quite how to use them yet.

Next in order was the livestock herded by their Simian overseers followed by the recently recruited and trained human army of five hundred carrying the new spring loaded weapons. They were slower because they were on foot. This force would have to be used sparingly in battle for just this reason. Once engaged with the Simian army they would be committed to battle and could not retreat. They would be the final line of defense.

The remaining half of the desert settlement Lancer army would bring up the rear defense. When the Owens Valley Lancers caught up they would join the defending Lancers. There would be only 450 Lancers to face the almost two thousand screeching Simian Warriors racing to engage them. Even with delaying action, it wouldn't take many days for them to catch up. Levi looked at Amy's image in his vision and asked, "Do you have a plan?"

* Amy *

She had given it much thought since they had set out on her plan to migrate east. Essentially, they had little choice. They would not be able to defend and hold against this massive Simian force. They were being driven east and she had so far just been defensive. It had worked and the bulk of the members of her followers, well Levi's followers, were still alive. So, her plans had been successful to date, but she dreaded the confrontation with the two

Simian armies because she didn't know what to do to hold them off. Defeating them was out of the question. They were simply too powerful to fight, not together anyway. Even if the Simian armies separated, a single Simian army a thousand strong on the open desert would be a major problem. She had hoped something would develop in their favor, but so far nothing had materialized in the form of help, plan, or hope. It was her secret so far, but Levi knew her desperation and was trying to help. Unfortunately, he didn't have any good suggestions either. She was doing all she could do.

Once all the stragglers from Barstow made it to the settlement, she dispatched Al and Dawn to join Al's Lancers at the front. Al could think on his own in case of emergencies and Dawn would be there so she could monitor the situation. Jimmy was assigned to the rear guard Lancers for the same reason. Fred was still with Iron Eyes and would remain with that group so she could monitor their progress also. Communication wasn't the problem. She just didn't have anything to say.

It was time to use her powers in astral projection again to view the Colorado River bridges and devise a plan for their escape, should they get that lucky. If luck was with them and they escaped over the river, they would also need to locate the Phoenix Simian army. It seemed strange to escape an impossible battle just to launch into another impossible battle, but that was what they were planning. She agreed with Levi's comment, "We don't stand a snowball's chance in hell if we get caught between the three Simian armies."

Levi was more than ready, however, and told her, "We have no choice Amy. Let's just make it happen. I am already getting bored with inaction anyway."

She responded, "Boredom is better than death." Levi didn't respond, but she could see that the point was made. She wished he could carry some of her stress and growing responsibilities. He just looked at her and grinned, while reading her thought. Levi totally understood the gravity of the situation, but was trying to keep it low keyed.

Levi didn't have to look far for Moon. Moon and his bodyguards were always there now and Bambi was back at his side again also, looking none the worse for the mental assault she had been through.

Levi told Moon, "I am going to meditate for a few hours. Will you watch over me?" Moon knew instantly what that meant and nodded in understanding and affirmation. Even Bambi nodded conspiratorially. Moon then hand signed to the others of Levi's personal guard to explain what was about to happen and what was expected. With Moon watching, Amy knew Levi was safe. Levi found a comfortable shady spot out of the burning desert sun and was soon relaxed and ready.

It was becoming easier to project their essence from Levi's physical body. Levi could completely relax now and allow her to draw his active mind away with her. They released their hold on the physical body and slowly drifted away like a cloud. Once separated, she took physical control, such as there was, and they floated up and away from his body. She quickly surveyed the immediate area and saw that Levi's body was safe before proceeding.

This was one of the few things she really enjoyed, the freedom to float, fly, and soar under her own control. It was like she had a body of her own and flying was the ultimate thrill to her. She controlled her urge to revel in this comfort and continued taking them higher. They began to see the desert terrain rushing below them as they sped forward. They were reaching the river even before she realized it. She quickly began to slow and circle the river. From the coordinates of her stored geodetic survey maps, she judged their location was just north of the old city of Needles, California.

They veered north and surveyed the river to Bullhead City. She identified two bridge crossings, a railroad trestle and a dam that could possibly be used as a crossing. Farther south was and additional railroad trestle and bridge at Topock. This was not looking good. This was a lot to blow up. Traveling south again, they identified Parker Dam, but it was breached and was useless as a crossing. There was another bridge and railroad trestle at the City of Parker. This site was the preferred crossing location if they had enough time to reach it. If they could cross there, it would draw the Simian armies away from the prolific river crossing area around Interstate 40. If they could draw them south, there was only one location they had to worry about, and that was Blythe. She assumed there would only be a single highway and railroad crossing there. These could be blown up without much problem. There would not be another river crossing area all the way to Mexico.

She turned her attention east toward Phoenix. The terrain was very much like all the other desert terrain they had already traveled over. With the exception of the green river area, all was barren, and rocky, but broken up by random hard rock mountains and rolling hills. She could see the high mountains and forest area of Levi's home just past Phoenix and began slowing. She had been following Interstate 10 and was shocked to see the Simian colony in the distance. It was settled alongside the interstate. She slowed quickly and circled the colony. It was as large as Levi had said. She estimated that the colony had over eight hundred Warriors. There was little good news to be had on this trip, even worse; it looked like the Simians were mobilizing. There was no doubt where they were going.

* Levi *

He was accustomed to facing death. He and Amy had faced it almost daily for well over a year now and they were still alive. By all rights they should be dead many times over. So why was she worried? Amy was incredible. She always came up with something, a plan, new power, or a miracle. ASONE was a miracle, at least it seemed so. When Amy had failed, ASONE came through, but ASONE was unpredictable and no plan could be made to utilize him/she/it, or whatever it was. Too bad they couldn't counsel with it now, but no, ASONE only came seemingly at the point of near death. Could they count on this entity in the upcoming battle? There was no way of knowing, but one thing was sure: they had no choices.

He knew they had no choices, but if anything were possible, Amy would find a way. He had more confidence in Amy than she did herself. He trusted her with his life, and if they failed, at least they wouldn't have given up and would go down fighting. Amy seemed a little upset that he seem to take everything so lightly, but the goal was to give her confidence. He told Amy, "I don't mind dying, but while I am alive, I want to live to the fullest without fear." She was solemn, but seemed to accept that.

Amy surveyed the bridges and he saw a plan developing in her mind. This was her expertise and she was good at it. They accomplished two things during the out of body projection. First, she had a partial plan and secondly, they discovered the Phoenix Simian Colony. Sadly though, the Warrs were coming to meet them. Well at least they wouldn't have to search for them. That was probably an advantage. If the Simians came to them, as opposed to going to the Simians, Amy may be able to stage some defensive surprises. They would need some.

As they settled back into his body, he felt the welcome comfort of feeling his heart beat again. The welcome rhythm let him know they were back and he was alive. Opening his eyes, he saw Moon staring at him and saw relief in Moon's eyes to see him back. He wondered if Moon had watched him this close all the time they were gone. Moon and the others had probably stood guard like this for several hours. He winked at Moon and said, "I'm back, my friend." Moon returned a toothy grin and relaxed, releasing the tight security he had established around Levi's dormant body. As he resumed operation of his own body, he wondered how long they had been gone. Time always seemed to stand still, at least they had no concept of time while in a projection.

Amy, in response to his thought said, "We have been gone for five hours and twenty-two minutes." He had no idea it had been that long. No wonder he was hungry.

There was no estimating how long it would be before he had a chance to eat again, so he took off for the camp galley.

He was half way there when Amy said, "The galley is closed. They have already packed up and are en route with the migration."

He thought to himself, "Damn!" He was going to have to eat those terrible government rations, and he hated them. Amy just grinned. He fooled her though, because he wandered through camp looking for a private meal, which he finally found in the Lancer camp. They had plenty and were happy to share. He looked at Amy and winked. Again she grinned. At least she was a little more relaxed now.

After his meal, he had a good night's sleep for a change and assumed that his guards took turns standing sentry. He had given up trying to get them to relax. There was little danger now, but Moon would just say, "No!" when he asked him to relax. Moon was completely loyal, dedicated, and was his friend, but Moon would not take any shit from him. Secretly, he liked that. Moon had been the only one that remained close after ASONE had emerged, and

468

Moon had earned a place of respect and honor in his heart. Moon would always be his number one, his Tonto.

The camp was a beehive of activity in the morning. Everyone was either packing or already moving out in their assigned order. After the Lancers left, his small group was the only ones left. Amy wanted to be the last to leave to make sure all was in order.

Three hours after sunup and no one was left in the camp but them. The camp was totally deserted and the caverns were sealed up and looked deserted just as it was intended to be perceived. There was nothing left to do here.

Levi then looked to Amy and asked, "What are we going to do now?" He was shocked when she responded.

Amy said, "The explosives are ready to be picked up, so we will go to the facility."

Mama had been busy! Now he was anxious. A new arsenal of potential weapons was available, and the sooner they were in the hands of those that could use them, the better he would feel. He didn't wait to be told and called his group together to teleport.

Even as the energy was gathering around them, he heard the communication going out to Mama telling her, "We are on our way." He had missed Mama's communication to Amy, or possibly Amy had just been monitoring through the internal cameras. He corrected his thoughts. The communications were generated from Amy at the facility and not the other way around. He was so used to thinking that Amy was with him, but physically her brain was there. It really didn't matter, but he sensed that his perspective switched for a moment. It quickly changed back, and he refused to accept that Amy was not with him. It didn't matter, because Amy was with him in every other way, and that would never change. Amy flashed a happy smile that told him she liked the way he thought.

* Amy *

Stress was clouding her thoughts and making her miss things she should not miss. When Levi bedded down for the night she came to him. Levi was happy and so was she. They spent a relaxing night in each other's arms. They made love and renewed the closeness, the oneness that had suffered with all the activity and stress of the last few days. She was still with him as he awoke in the morning. They kissed, and she returned to her visual image in his head. Oh, to be a real woman of flesh and blood and life. She really couldn't complain because Levi and she were closer than any couple ever before and shared more, even the other's thoughts.

Levi scrounged around and found a real meal. She much preferred that he eat the K-rations, but Levi hated them. She believed that it was mainly because she wanted him to, but she suspected it was the rebel in him also that said, "If it is good for you, it must be bad." She had to admit that real food tasted good, and she enjoyed the pleasure also, but Levi loved it too much. He used and needed much protein, but if she didn't control the storage of the fat he consumed in the process, he would be very

470

obese. The K-rations provided the protein without the fat and made her job easier. She had to agree with Levi though, the taste wasn't all that good. Levi grinned at that thought.

After his meal the group gathered and teleported to Amy's facility. Mama had indeed been busy. The explosives were ready and the grenades also. There had been two cases of hand grenades in the ammunition store room. She had instructed Mama to modify the formula in the powder and fuse and re-pack them. They were rusty, but the mechanisms were intact. She had instructed them how to clean and lubricate the grenades, and theoretically, they should now work. Two cases would not last long, but they could be used in a dire emergency. But then again, it seemed that everything was a dire emergency.

When Levi and his guard materialized within the facility, Mama was waiting. Mama had already stacked the explosives, fuse wires and grenades, and although friendly, was making it obvious that Levi wasn't needed at the facility. Mama had her contact directly and didn't need Levi for much of anything. Amy and the facility was Mama's whole life now. She felt Levi's face turning red and flushed.

When he thought about it, he said, "Well, that is one less problem for me to worry about."

Amy laughed and said, "For you to worry about? I am the one worrying with the problems." She was right of course, but Levi was the one that had to deal directly with the people and Simians. At least Mama was not one he would have to deal directly with now.

There was one problem that Mama had, though. They had brought # 5 with them to leave at the facility. Since his injury, he was useless in battle; but he was still the best Simian computer engineer available. Even with the injury, # 5 was still able to function well with the Simian computer. There were still multitudes of information that required sorting, translating, interpreting and transferring to her now operating external data banks. She still remained hopeful that additional Simian technology could be discovered that was unaffected by the altered world outside the facility. Since the Simian computer technology remained functioning, she believed other Simian technology might also be usable, but so far none had been discovered.

She had prepared Mama, and # 5 would be accepted, although grudgingly. Levi felt pity for # 5 and his plight, but Amy said, "It will be all right." Mama understood that # 5's expertise was necessary and she would in time accept him as a member of her team. The opportunity to be useful again was welcomed by # 5 no matter what the conditions were. He remained passive and unthreatening, anxious to be accepted.

Moon, as always, was unaffected by Mama's demeanor. He had little respect for her anyway. After all she was only a Fem in his mind. She cringed at the thoughts that must be running through Moon's mind. Moon only wanted to leave the facility. Moon was, as was Levi, uncomfortable within the echoing corridors of the facility. The facility appeared to be now well lighted and bustling with activity all around them, but the feeling of a tomb was still strong in their minds.

472

Moon and the other Techs quickly gathered up the packages and stood waiting. There was no communication between Levi and Mama. Levi simply grinned and waved good bye as Amy began the teleport.

* Levi *

Amy said, "Everything is on schedule more or less." The Owens Valley Lancers were, however, charged by the Simian armies and had to retreat sooner than she had hoped. Sadly, they also lost four of the riflemen and irreplaceable rifles before they could get mounted and escape. The Simians seemed to have had all of the delays they wanted and were willing to sacrifice themselves to destroy the enemy. Possibly, they were out of the cattle that were left behind and were starving, but more likely the Supreme One forced them to charge. When she opened her monitoring to him it was easy to see what was going on. Fred continued to look back over his shoulder every few seconds and the Simian armies could be seen pouring through the last pass. In Fred's vision could also be seen most of the Lancers behind him. Fred seemed to be leading the pack in the retreat. There was little danger of the Simians catching him. If it wasn't so serious it would be humorous. Bravery was just not one of Fred's best traits, obviously, but he seemed to excel in riding fast.

Amy said, "The delaying action at the passes cost the Simians in dead Warriors and bought precious time for the rest of our group." The riflemen had killed at least fifty-five of the Simians,

473

while defending the passes. That was significant, but insignificant compared to the overall army's size. With the momentum of the Simian armies, if they continued at the current pace, their scheduled evacuation time would be cut short.

Amy estimated the time and said, "In three days, at this pace, all forces will merge just short of the river. That will be disastrous if our forces get jammed up trying to cross the bridges."

They should have started their forces a day sooner, but it was too late to worry about that now.

Amy teleported them forward of the human and Simian exodus to the Colorado River to begin work on the bridges. They started on the biggest on I-40. They had to destroy a four lane bridge at this location. Moon didn't understand the concept of explosives and Levi tried to explain, but Amy did not have the Simian vocabulary needed. It was an obsolete word that hadn't been used in either language for fifty years. Finally, he grasped the idea with shock and treated the explosives with much more care. The team learned fast as he passed on Amy's instructions as to where to place the charges and how much was required.

Amy said, "The explosives are very powerful and somewhat unstable, so be very careful."

Yeah, right. That was something he didn't need to be told. The thought of what explosives were capable of made him very uncomfortable. The bridge was left intact in the event the exodus could not reach the bridge further south.

They had used up much of the explosives on this bridge. Amy decided to do the target crossing bridge next in the event that they ran out of explosives. To be safe, Amy instructed Mama to make more explosive charges from the supplies on hand in the facility. He thought that was a good idea. They spent the rest of the day planting the charges on the bridge and railroad trestle at Parker. By evening it was finished and they were all tired. There were enough explosives remaining to do some of the other northern crossings, but they decided to teleport back to the exodus camp for food and a good night's rest before starting on them. That made him very happy. He chuckled at the thought of Moon and his small group raiding the sheep herd tonight, but they had to eat too. He would hear the gripes in the morning.

He had a pleasant evening visiting with Al, Dawn, Jimmy, and many of the other senior leaders. To some extent they were overwhelmed with questions, but mostly he was able to give them confidence with his answers, even though he had little. All they could really do was follow the plan and hope for the best.

In the morning after another good breakfast they made another teleport stop to see Mama and gather more explosives. Mama had worked her crew through the night and had some ready, not enough, but enough to help. Mama was a real asset, and they owed her a lot, but that didn't mean he would be nice to her.

* Amy *

Mama was anxious to help and turned all attention to the request for more explosives. Unfortunately, the supplies and materials required

475

were running low. The facility had not been designed as a military arsenal, but did stock many items and supplies. Fortunately it did have enough raw materials and supplies to make the explosives so far. The necessary supplies were now gone and Mama had done all she could do. They would have to use the remaining explosives sparingly.

It was a fast trip and the packages were quickly gathered, but as they were beginning the teleport, Levi again waved good bye and even bowed grinning to Mama.

Levi gave his parting insult saying, "Thanks, Mama, it took you long enough."

Mama's red eyes could blazed in aggravation as they faded out of the facility. Amy said, "Stop being a shit, Levi. Don't aggravate her. Mama is on our side." She realized that Levi was only playing, but Mama would find a way to get even. Amy was certain that Mama accepted Levi as the leader and would never threaten any physical harm to him, but Mama also believed she knew who the real power behind Levi was. Mama would continue to play with his mind just out of spite and maybe fun. It was humorous to watch the two of them banter. A secret friendship and closeness were developing that would not be shown outwardly, especially to each other. This could get interesting.

All the charges were set on the river crossing at the other chosen areas, so she teleported the group to the Bullhead City area to place charges over those crossing. She didn't think there were enough charges to blow up all the locations and decided to just start at the southernmost crossing and move north until they ran out. The first span was a small bridge that she hadn't noticed before, but it didn't take many charges. This was the first crossing that could not possibly be required for their needs. It could be blown up now. As she was instructing Levi to light the charges, he surprised her again.

Levi said, "Leave it and blow it up when the Simians attempt to use it. We can kill Simians when they try to cross it."

It was risky if the charges didn't explode when they were set off, but it was a good idea. "What if it rains?"

Levi replied, "This is the desert. What are the odds it will rain over the next two days?"

This was true, but did she trust the charges to work? Yes, they should work, but she trusted no one but her and Levi to set the charges. Levi knew it was a good idea, but waited for her to agree, which she soon did. There was no need to tell Levi that he would be lighting the fuses. He had been reading her thoughts.

They proceeded on to the other highway bridges and set the charges. The fuses were gathered and of identical lengths so that the explosions would be set off simultaneously as much as possible. They had some charges left to put on the railroad trestle, but probably not enough. She hoped maybe enough to do the job. They had to leave the dam. It would require many charges to destroy the dam. It was already damaged and had water flowing over the breech, but it could be crossed if the Simians were brave enough. Moon didn't seem to have a problem working around water, but then he had survived drowning twice before by being pulled out by Levi. The other Simians were more nervous, but followed

Moon's example. She hoped the Warrior Simians were more frightened and would not attempt to cross the water. Only time would tell.

They finished out the day and teleported back to the night camp just in time for supper. They were closer, but not close enough. By monitoring Fred, she knew the Owens Valley Lancers were passing the desert settlement. They had rested last night but kept heavy watches. The Simian armies had stopped to rest but were up early and coming on strong. The armies would be hot on their heels by tomorrow evening. Time was short and she relayed that information through Levi for them to make a very early start, in fact she wanted the wagons and slow traffic to start again after their meal. They were in the most danger. Al realized that it was more serious than he thought and passed the word.

* Satan *

It had taken him days to recover from the ordeal, and he was weak. In his weakened condition, there was little rage. Hate still seethed deep inside, but it was under control and, for once in a very long time, his mind was rational. He had to search for servants to serve him, and he was aggravated, but none were destroyed. The captains were sent for, and he suffered through endless hours of reports and problems. His leadership was necessary to correct many of the power struggles that had developed during his absence. These he quickly resolved by killing two of his captains. After he was firmly in control of the situations, he ordered his number one to lead eight thousand of the consolidated colonies' Warriors west to destroy the human and runt armies. He ordered their immediate departure. His number one wanted to dissuade the Supreme One, but knew better. After only a brief battle within his own thoughts, he did as he was told. Satan was pleased that he didn't have to kill him. It would disrupt the chain of command again.

He could only be rational so long, and as his health improved, his rage grew. The Witch had won again and had almost destroyed him. Even the thought of her and her victories over him set his fury churning. He must control his rage and complete his goal of her destruction so he could resume his life again. It would end soon. He was turning all his armies against her and the war would end quickly and totally with the absolute and utter destruction of the human and runt armies. He would spare the females, but only for the continuation of his species.

He had perfected his ability to jump from one Simian mind to another. The result was total control. His mind could monitor any Simian mind that had not been altered by the Witch. Additionally, he could communicate directly into that mind or control it. His communication ability was virtually limitless. The Witch also had a communication network, but it was limited to only a few. He would take them out and she would lose the communication ability. He would make that a high priority after he mobilized the armies in the south. He had a surprise for the Witch.

CHAPTER 12
(UNEXPECTED HELP)

* Levi *

They were up early, even before the sun was up. Al had already roused the camp and was preparing to mobilize the exodus. There was little for him and Amy to do now but stay with the group. The Simian armies had stopped the pursuit late in the evening in favor of sleep and Iron Eyes's Lancers had done likewise, but Amy said they were leaving now with the Simians in hot pursuit. That would put Iron Eyes catching up around noon with the Simian armies two hours behind. The timing would be very close. He didn't have to push Al. Al read it in his eyes and started barking orders. All groups would be merged in seven hours.

It was decided to leave Dawn with the forward group in order to follow the progress, while Al would take his Lancers back to the rear to meet the Simian armies.

Amy said, "The timing sucks. We are going to have to cross the I-40 Bridge at Topoc. There is not enough time to follow the river down to the next bridge."

That increased the risk of having the Simian armies move north along the river instead of being drawn south as their plan hoped. The advantage was that the wagons could cross quickly four abreast on the large bridge. That would help.

There was no need to go to the rear. All they had to do was wait and the rear would come to them. So he waited and ate the damn K-rations. He said to Amy, "Are you happy now?" They were both grinning. They were enjoying each other while they could, wondering if they would be alive after today.

The only plan Amy had involved organization. Fred would stay with Iron Eyes, and that Lancer group would remain to the northern side of the advancing combined Simian army. Their purpose would be to charge outward from the human and Tech ranks along the northern side pressing the Simians inward toward the center. They would circle back and repeat the charge again if possible. It would be suicide to attack directly into the ranks of the Warriors. Their target was any Warrior that advanced too far away from a common defense. Judging from past experience, there would be many, but Amy's main hope was to prevent the enemy from spreading out and hopefully pull in.

Al, with Jimmy assigned to him, was to do the same along the southern side. Together they hoped to compress the enemy army into a letter V, forcing the Simian attack along a narrow line. The Tech armies would be split similarly on the north and south sides of the V closer in, forcing the, hopefully, narrow point of the attack into the human army with the spring weapons. He said, "We need to give them a better name. How about... "

Amy interrupted him by saying, "Infantry!"

Oh well, that was as good a name as any. He would stand with the Infantry, and she would command from there.

They didn't hope to win against the odds, only hold the Simians as they made a tactical retreat

481

across the bridge. She hoped the Simian Warriors would take precious time to plan an attack and organize. Every minute increased their chances of survival.

It was a hot and dusty day on the desert with no shade. There was no way to relax, so Levi, Moon, Bambi and his Tech guards began to walk slowly along the route and allowed the progression to pass them by. After three hours of breathing dust, the Infantry caught up to them and they fell in line with them. It was comforting to see five hundred Infantry grouped together as they had been instructed to do. The human army looked bigger because of the two hundred extra replacement humans trained to pick up the spring weapon of any fallen combatant and re-join the battle. It shocked him to see them. He said out loud to no one in particular, "Where did all these humans come from?"

Small bands of humans had been joining the various groups all along the route. Amy suspected that the news had spread by word of mouth, probably originating from the Lancer teams sent out months ago to do just that. The word must have continued to spread about the Simian resistance, because there were groups of humans that had come over a hundred miles just to join. Their hopes rested with this pocket of resistance. It was live or die for all of them.

The Tech army had already split up, led by # 2 on the north and # 4 on the south side. The Tech groups took up loose traveling positions behind and at the north and south ends of the Infantry, while Al and his Lancers could be seen in the distance moving into approximate position in the progression along the southern side of the projected enemy route. Amy's organizational plan was being implemented. Jimmy had done well spreading the word to all the captains, and the formation was impressive. Their army was beginning to look formidable, and he was beginning to feel hope.

By midmorning, they could see the Owens Valley Lancers approaching off into the distance. The cloud of dust was visible first, then the horses and riders took shape. They were riding at a slow trot, but still coming on too fast. The walking progression of Infantry, Techs, and stragglers was still ten miles out from the bridge, and the pursuing Simians were obviously ahead of schedule.

Amy said, "Fred is still scared and is at the front looking back."

This time there was no humor detected. When Amy opened the image, he could clearly see the Simian Warriors moving at an accelerated pace. The dust generated from the massive Simian army formed a storm cloud drifting high into the air. His recent illusion of hope shattered.

* Amy *

The formation of her organizational plan was taking shape. The brunt of the Warrior charge would hit in the center against the spring spears. The weapon would kill a Simian, but the momentum would hit the standing humans in force and head on. If the momentum was not slowed it would be disastrous. The Warriors would hopefully be compressed and dense as the V narrowed. She hoped the closeness would, in itself, slow the

483

Warriors. If that didn't slow them enough, she had distributed the modified hand grenades, all twenty-four of them, to some crash trained Infantry to be used if absolutely necessary to slow the Warriors even more.

Her mind was active but she had done all she could do and could think of nothing else. Levi, as always, seemed confident in her abilities, but that was disturbing. She was not perfect, only human. She did gain some comfort from his calmness, even though she knew Levi was hiding his fear. Levi would die before he dared show fear. At any rate, all she could do now was continue the retreat as fast as the combatants could travel.

As instructed, Dawn was positioned close to the bridge so Amy could maintain visual contact with the crossing progress. The wagons' procession was still five miles from the bridge, but the horses and cattle, used to pull some of the wagons, were being driven hard. Time enough for rest after they crossed the river. Their army would have to fight a retreating battle for at least these last five miles. Could they do it? They would soon find out.

The battle lines began to slowly form as the Simians neared. She was pleased to see that the Simian Warriors slowed as they neared, moving into a closer group as she had hoped. Sadly though, the horizon was filled with them. She released her fear as she said, "There are so damn many of them."

Levi quickly retorted, "Hold on to your confidence, honey, and keep thinking of ways to destroy them."

He had so much confidence in her. How could she let him down? What will he think of me if our armies are destroyed? How could he think that I can win this battle much less the bigger battles to come?

She could save Levi and herself and a few select others by teleporting out, but she knew he would not want to live with that memory; and he would hate her for saving him while all his friends and trusting followers died. No, she could never do that. What could she do? She had to use her mind. Where was ASONE when you needed it? What would it do? Really? Even ASONE would never be able to defeat this massive Army by hand to hand combat. Well, maybe ASONE could paralyze them like before, but where was the bastard? She did not have the power to duplicate that feat alone. No, that wouldn't work. It would paralyze the good Simians too.

Her mind was doing a thousand things as she was within herself in thought, but her mind followed the many levels of her monitoring. They had continued their retreat for another three miles, but the Warriors were closing in and engagement would begin soon. The wagons were approaching the bridge, but sickeningly slow. She calculated they would have to hold the enemy for an hour and ten minutes over the scheduled travel time previously calculated. They would have to continue the retreat as they fought, making quick retreats and stands to stop any momentum the Warriors might gain. It was a dangerous strategy, but had worked in the past, according to her recorded military history.

Two more miles and the enemy was engaged. Iron Eyes's Lancers had taken position and spent well deserved and cherished moments in rest, but as the moment came they charged a glancing attack on the north edge of the advancing Simians. It was successful in its purpose. She counted ten Warriors down from the attack and no Lancers. The dead Warriors had been too aggressive and ventured out too far from the pack. They paid for their mistake, but the advancing Warriors saw the mistake and pulled in to offer a compact wall. The Lancers didn't press the attack and continued in their patrol of the edge. The Warriors didn't pursue them as they seemed focused more on the human army in the center. The Warriors decided the humans would be a much easier target to attack and continued in their route. So far the plan was working.

Shortly after the first engagement, Al's Lancers launched an attack following the same strategy with identical results. The Warriors were moving forward and coming together as they entered the V. The Warriors continued forward toward the human target. As planned, the outer edges encountered the Techs commanded by # 2 on the north side and # 4 on the south. The momentum kept the Warriors coming forward, but the outside met motivated and trained Techs now skilled in fighting. The Techs held their ground standing side by side and protecting each other. The defense was to their advantage and prevented major losses. The Warriors seemed stunned that the Techs were formidable. The Warriors had given little respect to the Techs, which cost them in numbers. Warriors were going down on the perimeter. The position of the Techs was not head on, therefore the effectiveness of their defense served to concentrate the Warriors more. The Warriors were becoming compressed to the point the inner bulk was beginning to stumble, trip and fall. They slowed, but remained focused on the human targets.

* Levi *

He liked the organization Amy had deployed, and it seemed to be working. Amy had opened small windows at the edge of his visual range so that he could see what was going on through Jimmy, Fred, and Dawn. This was something new, but he still had trouble viewing them. His mind developed vertigo if he tried to follow them. He found that he could view them separately by directing his eyes to the source he wanted to see. He realized that it was only possible with Amy's help. She was detecting the view that he wanted to see and bringing it forward. He wondered why she chose this particular moment to provide this new ability to him. He liked it though.

Amy said, "No reason. I just believe that you might like to be able to monitor all the sources during this battle and it is easier and quicker for me to provide it automatically in this way instead of you having to ask. That would be distracting and I want to concentrate on the battle."

Levi said, "Yes, thank you."

He was worried about the Techs and the Infantry. If the Warriors decided to turn on the Techs, they would be overrun. So far though everything was going according to plan, but then the plan was to drive the Warriors directly into the Infantry. Damn! What would happen? Could they hold the initial clash? They would know soon and he wouldn't have to see it though other's eyes, because they were charging straight at him. If the Infantry didn't hold, he would be the next to fall. The Infantry was continuing a moving retreat, but stopped just before the Warriors made contact. Those were the instructions he had given them: stop and plant the spring spear in the ground, aim it so the Simian would run into it, and release the spike trigger. The Infantry was three deep so if the Warrior diverted the spear, hopefully the second one would engage. Amy had said, "The Warriors will have little respect for humans and even less for the spear. So, they should charge right into the spears." The spear would have to be withdrawn quickly, while he moved to the rear to reload.

Amy had been correct. The Warriors charged into the spears with little respect, thinking they would be able to push them aside with their weight and dense skin. Shock instead could be seen on their faces as the spikes drove deep. Few of the first rank of Warriors survived the charge. The spears worked perfectly and the human casualties were light. Maybe seventy-five Warriors went down. The spears were long enough to out reach the sword strike, but a few swords connected with the spears and knocked them aside. The second rank of Infantry leaped forward to drive and release their spears before those Warriors could draw back the spear. "Well done, Amy," he barked. Even in her concentration she gave him a quick smile, but it was short lived.

The momentum of the Warriors was stopped as they gained respect for the shiny spears. The Infantry retreated leaving the second and third ranks of Infantry braced for another attack, which did not come. During the pause, even those ranks of Infantry withdrew toward the retreating army. The Warriors seemed to be deciding how to change their attack. When they came forward testing the humans they were met with brandished spears and released spikes. Again many went down, but the Warriors were learning. Next they came cautiously fencing the spears away from harm. The Infantry continued to retreat faster, drawing the Warriors ahead recklessly. The Infantry took advantage of any too aggressive Warrior, but there were few kills.

The Infantry held the initial attacks that bought precious time for the fleeing exodus. The timing of the retreat was critical. If they held too long there was danger of the sides bulging out and changing direction of the attack. They had to continue to keep the Warriors moving forward for the grazing attack on the sides to continue to work. So far the sides had not seriously been tested. The Warriors' attention continued to be focused on the retreating Infantry and the prize of the fleeing exodus seen in the distance.

The next attack came suddenly after they had conferred among themselves. There was a leader issuing orders and that Warrior seemed strangely familiar in its action. It was hopping around from foot to foot screeching in rage.

Amy said, "That is the Supreme One in possession of that Warrior."

He never gave up, but in its rage had made a mistake. They heard the instruction. He ordered the Warriors to charge and continue despite the losses and to use their weight to propel them though. Levi had dreaded that option. The Warriors charged in a

489

very narrow point at the waiting Infantry. At the point of attack the first five out of the six Warriors went down, but the momentum carried the dead Warriors forward with assistance from pushes by the trailing Warriors. The humans went down under the pressure and weight of the falling Warriors. The attack did not stop but continued in a constant wave of Warriors. The Warriors were dying, but the humans were also, and a breach in the line widened as the Warriors sacrificed themselves. Men ran forward in an attempt to stop the Warriors, while others still scrambled to grab the fallen weapons. The Warriors were running over the tops of the fallen Warriors and leaping onto the waiting spears and into the ocean of humans. The breach in the line widened more as the Warriors poured through.

* Amy *

She detected the aura of hate first then she identified the source. The Supreme One was here. He was directing the Warriors on the front lines. He had taken over one of the Warriors and had no difficulty commanding over the other Warriors. It was as if the Supreme One was there in body also. She heard the commands screeched to the hoard of Warriors. They were to sacrifice themselves to break through the human lines. He said he would destroy them if they didn't. She saw the insanity of the instruction, but saw the likelihood of success. They built a bridge of dead Warriors that they quite literally charged over. She told Levi, "Call a retreat!"

490

This he immediately did, but added, "Throw the grenades!"

As the Infantry pulled back, some could be seen tossing something and explosions erupted in the ranks of the charging Warriors. The charge ended abruptly as Warriors fell from their injures, but six of the valuable grenades had been used. One of the explosions erupted next to the Supreme One and he fell gripping his stomach. His screeches of pain could be heard over all the others. Amy then realized how the other Warriors knew it was the Supreme One. It was the voice, tone, and commanding screeches.

As the Warriors regrouped without leadership, the Infantry continued the retreat without immediate pursuit. Daring humans could be seen running forward to retrieve the valuable spring spears and help the injured to the rear. The Techs and Lancers followed the pace, while maintaining tight control of the edges. They had held and gained forty minutes for the exodus, but it was not enough. The wagons were now crossing the bridge, but it would take another thirty minutes before the armies could cross. They continued to retreat waiting the next attack.

The fighting retreat continued without any major breaches over the next few miles. As they approached the bridge it was no longer necessary to hold the sides in, so she sent orders through Levi to Jimmy and Fred for the withdrawal of the Lancers. The Lancers broke ranks and made a wide circle around the battle and rode across the bridge. They regrouped on the opposite side of the bridge in approximately the same position as they had previously. She didn't expect the Warriors to cross the bridge, but the Lancers would be in position to continue the defense if necessary. The Techs followed the Lancers and formed in the inner V of the defense. The target of the bridge kept the attacking Warriors gathered, anticipating a crossing. All that was left was the Infantry bringing up the rear. The battle was intense, but the Infantry held.

At the proper position she told Levi, "Light the fuse." She had calculated the explosions to miss any humans, but in doing so would allow some Warriors near or on this side to get across ahead of the explosion. She also knew they would be dispatched quickly. For once the odds would be on their side. The moments were tense as they waited.

The bridge was packed with Warriors when the explosion erupted. The results were better than she had anticipated. The entire bridge almost vaporized under the Simians leaving over a hundred screeching Warriors tumbling into the river. They fell fast, hit hard, and never came up. There were twelve Warriors remaining, scrambling up the falling bridge on their side, but they never recovered their footing before they were attacked and killed by the Infantry. She could sense and also hear the new possessed Warrior on the other side venting his rage at the sudden loss of his victory. The Warriors on the other side were running up and down the banks seeking any crossing, but never venturing into the water, just as she had suspected.

The exodus of humans, Technical Simians, and Simian Females was, more or less, intact and still very much alive. They had escaped yet another destruction at the hands of the Warrior Simians and their leader, the Supreme One. They had survived only to face another Simian army racing toward them. The casualties had actually been light, considering, but very costly, especially the last casualty.

* Levi *

Damn, Amy had planned it well. Had the bulk of the Warriors been able to spread out, the raw volume of them alone would have overrun their army in short order. As it was, the bulk of the Warriors were bunched up in the middle waiting for their turn to fight. By positioning the defendants as she had done, she had kept the battle front very reduced, thereby improving the odds.

They were breathing a sigh of relief when he sensed Amy gasp. Something was very wrong. She mentally grabbed his mind with shocking force and told him, almost forcing his mind to send a message to Jimmy and Fred telling them to run to the protection of the humans and tell Al and Iron Eyes that they were in personal danger from any Simian other than the original group. The message went out immediately. Since most of the original Techs remaining were with him, there weren't many available. He remembered the small monitoring windows in his vision and looked to see Fred already running and Jimmy was looking around, but finally took off running. When he looked for Dawn's window, it wasn't there. What was wrong?

Amy said in answer to his mental question, "She is dead! The Supreme One killed her."

He didn't know who he felt sorry for most, Dawn or Al.

He quickly realized that all the communication team was in danger and that is why Amy was frantic to get them protected. The Supreme One could take over almost any Simian now at will. He had gotten very proficient with his abilities to possess Simian minds and was becoming very dangerous in that way. He wished he or Amy would have considered that possibility of the communication team being a special target. Everyone was a target. Had they suspected, they might have saved Dawn. With all that had gone on, it was no wonder they had missed a few possibilities.

Amy said through her tears, "I should have thought of it."

She seemed terribly sad and burdened and he could see tears in her eyes. He said, "My love it is well to grieve for her. She will be missed, but you carry no guilt for it. The guilt is the Supreme One's, and when we survive our ordeals we will get revenge for Dawn." He saw a determination to survive settle over her sweet face and knew she would be alright. She just needed to target her anger and release any guilt. She couldn't think of everything.

Once Fred and Jimmy made contact with Iron Eyes and Al, they took immediate precautions for their protection. When she saw that they were protected, Amy's attention turned to a more permanent solution. They would need a bodyguard and she wanted at least one of their Tech team on each one. Levi directed Amy's communication to both Fred and Jimmy informing them to have two

Infantry assigned to each of them as well as # 8 and #13 respectively. Iron Eyes and Al sent runners to collect the bodyguards, but as soon as Al passed on the instructions he turned to Jimmy.

Al asked, "What about Dawn?"

Jimmy knew Levi was monitoring and when he didn't receive a response he told Al, "I really don't know."

Al looked deeply into Jimmy's eyes with those deep blue penetrating eyes and saw only honesty. He dropped his stare and took off at a run to find Levi. Levi was not very far from Al's location and dreaded the job he had to perform.

Moon, Bambi and the other personal guard saw the distress in him. Moon was disturbed, knowing something was wrong when everything should be fine. They were all safe on this side of the breached Bridge. Nothing should be wrong. Moon's hands flew through the air asking what was wrong. Levi focused his attention and looked at Moon and told him as Amy had revealed Dawn's memory. Dawn had been positioned on the east side of the bridge monitoring the crossing as she had been assigned. All of the Simian Females had crossed with the exception of a lone Fem. She looked to be laboring with an injured foot.

As the Fem approached Dawn signed to her asking, "Do you need any assistance?"

As the Fem got close she suddenly lunged at her and sunk her finger fangs into Dawn's chest. Dawn's vision suddenly blurred and then blacked out. She had died in two seconds. He was thankful for that at least.

Moon was furious. He hopped from one leg to the other screeching blasphemies to the Supreme One. This was the maddest he had ever seen Moon. If there were one human other than himself that Moon truly felt a liking for it was Al and Dawn. Other than him, Dawn was the first human Moon had really interfaced with and had been around much. This was when she was nursing Levi back to health from the Simian sword that tore through his body. Moon felt that Dawn had helped save his life during that time and was thankful. Since Al was his personal friend and Moon was his constant companion, the two had by exposure interfaced and become friends. So it would be doubly hurtful to Moon.

After his initial outburst, Moon soon calmed and screeched, "I will find # 8 and # 13 and explain their responsibilities."

Moon took off at a lope and was soon lost in the crowd.

As he was watching Moon disappear, Al entered his vision coming straight for him. Even in the distance he could see Al's piercing blue eyes boring into him. He hated having to tell him, but Al obviously already knew. He was just seeking confirmation or some outlet to vent his anger.

* Amy *

She didn't see it coming. If Levi had been closer she might have been able to sense the Supreme One, but the link with Dawn was not that strong. Dawn saw the Fem in apparent distress and, being helpful as she always was, moved toward her

496

to help. When the Fem lashed out Amy felt the pain of the fangs and severe burning of the poison. It shocked her senses momentarily and brought her to a stop for a few seconds. The pain was excruciating, but it only lasted intensely for a second. After that all sensory inputs faded out and she knew Dawn was dead.

Her only thought then was to save Fred and Jimmy. Levi was quick to catch on to the gravity of the situation and opened his mind for her. Get them to safety first was the primary priority. Luckily, they were both assigned to the Lancer groups and were not currently exposed to any Simians, but no one would notice if a Tech or Fem came into their group. The paths of the races were always crossing or in many cases, they worked together. Jimmy and Fred did what they were told without question and were quickly surrounded by alert humans. The permanent body guards were also quickly established.

There was almost a confrontation when Moon came to deliver # 8 and # 13. The Infantry assigned to Jimmy were new recruits and their instructions were as she had given, protect Jimmy from Simians, but being new, they were unable to recognize the allowable Simians. As Moon's group approached Jimmy, the Infantry started to attack them. Moon was quick and diverted the spear thrust. Moon was unharmed, but momentarily angered. He quickly realized what had happened.

Jimmy was screaming to the spear men saying, "Whoa, these are friends!"

There were apologies, but Moon ignored them and left # 8 to his new duties. The Infantry would soon learn the sigh language or find themselves ignored.

There was not a repeat at Iron Eyes and Fred's location. Fred was actually enjoying the attention, but didn't like the reason of the attention. He didn't like being a chosen target. Fred and # 13 had spent a lot of time together and had become friends so he was pleased with the choice. They were soon hand signing, catching up on the situation and the battle that had just occurred. When Fred asked, Moon told him about the death of Dawn and why the need for the bodyguards. Fred was sad at the news, but thankful he was alive and protected.

As she watched Al approach, she was sad, but thankful that it was Levi's eyes that Al was staring into and that she was invisible. Levi did not look away and met his stare. A world of communication passed between their eyes. Levi opened his arms to Al and met his embrace. The stone hard Al broke down and sobbed in Levi's arms. They wept together for several long moments.

When he was able, Levi held him and said, "I am so, so sorry, my friend. There was nothing I could do. Just know that she died very quickly and didn't suffer."

Al stepped back and looked quickly into Levi's eyes with an unspoken plea.

Levi quickly answered the unspoken question and said, "No, she wasn't violated. It was poison fangs."

Al looked relieved. He didn't ask more about Dawn's death.

Al only asked, "Where is she now? I want to bury her."

498

He told him and left Al to his private moments. Levi knew what it felt like.

She realized that she had tears in her eyes and hate in her heart. She would avenge Dawn if it were the last thing she ever did. Already she was working on plans to strike at the Supreme One. How arrogant for him to feel so safe. She would make him lose his illusion of safety somehow. Why should she and Levi always be the ones being attacked? Sometimes the best defense was a good offense.

Levi broke into her thought saying, "The Simian army is moving up river toward the other crossings."

Indeed they were. It was time to teleport to the upstream bridge. They gathered their team and removed themselves from the crowded area. Soon she felt the electrifying surge of gathering energy through Levi's body as she prepared to teleport.

She was thinking how her ability to gather energy and project it to new locations was becoming routine now. In response to her thoughts Levi's was wondering how the teleport was actually done. She tried to explain it in simple terms, "It is swapping energy. More precisely, it is replacing energy and matter from one location with another. I take energy from the target location and replaced it with the energy I gather from the beginning area. This swap makes the transfer seamless and smooth. In the process, I surround the matter of those being teleported in a bubble of that energy."

Levi asked, "What if you just sent energy to the new location?"

She explained, "There isn't room for that energy. That space is already occupied. If energy wasn't swapped, there would be a clash of energy and force an eruption as energy compressed and expanded. The energy binds matter and, if suddenly altered, could violently alter the affected matter. The vacuum of energy created at the sending end would possibly be as forceful, but in an implosion as energy tries to suddenly fill it. To put it bluntly, we would die in the transfer."

Levi was very silent, but she knew he was thinking of something and she couldn't read it in his mind. What was he up to?

* Levi *

He wondered why he had never asked Amy to explain how the teleport process worked before. Really, he didn't have to ask; when Amy saw his unspoken question, she began to explain it. It seemed interesting and logical the way she explained it. It worked and seemed safe and that was the main thing. He sure didn't want to be in the middle of one of the other kind of teleports with energy eruptions. It didn't sound pleasant.

They materialized at the east side of the Topoc's railroad trestle. As he looked around to orient his bearing, they could see Warriors on the other side loping toward the trestle. This crossing was close to their bridge crossing, which was one of the reasons Amy's choice crossing was much farther south. She had hoped to draw the Simian armies away from the additional available crossing north, but it wasn't totally unexpected and they were ready.

They waited in seclusion while the Warriors scrambled across the trestle. At the halfway point he popped his Zippo and lit the fuse. For the most part, the burning fuses were smokeless and the Warriors had no warning. When the explosion occurred, thirty screeching Warriors clung to the sides of the trestle as it slowly fell sideways into the river. Only half of the explosives detonated for some reason. He assumed the fuses on the one side had gotten wet or damaged in some way. The half that did explode seemed to do a sufficient job, but the trestle was still somewhat intact, just in the water. Most of the Warriors lost their grip on the trestle as it hit the water. They disappeared under the water and weren't seen again; however, six Warriors remained holding to the wreckage and soon began climbing along the trestle in both directions to escape the water. The two Warriors that made it to their side of the river were met by # 1, # 7 and # 11 and quickly killed before they could get their footing.

This was the first time Moon was not at his side, and he would hear about it from Moon too. He and Amy both grinned at the thought of the aggravated Moon shaking his long finger at him. He could see Moon in Fred's monitoring window, having delivered # 13 for his new duties. He said to Amy, "Maybe we should head off the scolding from Moon and bring him here now." She grinned. He felt the energy gather and soon the startled Moon was standing near looking around trying to figure out what had happened. Moon saw him and started shaking his finger at him anyway. It was comical to watch but reassuring to have him at his side again. Bambi even shook with laughter, which brought a surprised look between him and Amy. Bambi seemed more relaxed and almost human.

Bullhead City would be the next target with two bridge crossings, a railroad trestle, and a dam that could possibly be used as a crossing. It would take the Warriors about three hours to reach the crossing. After the explosions of the last two crossings, Amy was skeptical that any large numbers of Warriors would be exposed again on any single crossing. He agreed and suggested that they go on ahead and blow them then move on to take care of business.

They gathered and teleported to the Bullhead locations and blew them. When the Warriors reached those locations they would have to turn back, especially when they saw the exodus moving south, which the main Simian army could now see.

Through Jimmy, they instructed that a Lancer team be left behind to watch the rear, while two Lancer teams move forward to survey the advanced route. Jimmy was instructed to take the point so they would know instantly if danger approached. The wagons took the road that led them out of sight of the river so many of the men on foot were instructed to follow the river edge as much as possible and stay in sight of the Simian army, thereby continuing to draw the Simian army south. Amy was still worried about the Simian army finding a route across the river toward the north. The Davis Dam, just north of Bullhead City, was the most likely weakness. Although breached, it offered only a fifteen foot gap. They had tried to blow it up and increase the opening, but the dam was thick and they didn't have enough explosives to make much of a difference. The only good thing was that the bulk of the Simian army seemed to be heading south following the exodus.

They should be safe while they traveled along old Arizona highway 95 south following the river toward Interstate 10, which would take them to Phoenix. Amy said it seemed aggressive and even insane to head toward another hopeless battle. It was like they were picking a fight, but really they had no choice. They had to take on the Phoenix Simian Colony while they had an opportunity to catch them alone. They could not fight in both directions against those totally impossible odds.

It was only traveling time for the next two days, so Amy suggested that they teleport on to Parker and the next potential river crossing and wait on the Simian army to try to cross. He wanted to give them hope that there might be a crossing and then take as many Warriors as possible. It was conceivable that these Warriors may yet be unaware of what had happened at the northern crossings. He goaded her a little. He wanted to kill Simians, not just aggravate them. She had reluctantly agreed and they had teleported to the railroad trestle. She let him have his way, but only partially.

Amy insisted that they blow the trestle saying, "There is no sense in taking too many chances."

He didn't argue. After the trestle was blown, they teleported to the bridge and made camp. They would wait on the Warriors.

* Satan *

503

He was furious again and screeching. Luckily he could vent his anger through the Simian he possessed. The withdrawal through the passes had delayed his vengeance. The frightened Warriors were unwilling to die, so he started killing them violently. He used the occupied Simian to direct his mental energy and focused on an offending Warrior and turned his brain into mush. It was messy as the brain exploded, but the Warriors chose to take their chances in battle instead of facing his wrath. The forced attack broke through the pass, but the Witch had withdrawn. All that was left was the retreating animals riding other animals. These were the ones that carried long spikes that could kill a Warrior. The Warriors followed, but the animals remained out of their reach. They continued to follow. He knew they would lead them to the main animal gathering.

On the second day he spotted them. They were gathered for battle and waiting, but continuing to move away. In the distance he could see the river. They were headed for the bridge and if they crossed, his army would be forced to fight through the narrow crossing. It would be a defense like the many passes where they had been held. He screeched in anger as he forced his army forward. The animal riders were on the sides picking off the lone Simians that broke ranks, but no matter, his target was in the center where all the animals were. He ordered them forward between the runt Simians. His anger raged again as he saw the mistake. As the Warriors engaged the animals, the small spears the animals used killed the advancing Warriors. What had the Witch done now? He hated her with every ounce of power he had. He ordered the Warriors to build a bridge of bodies, their bodies, to breach the animal ranks. They must defeat the animals on this side of the river.

He calmed as Warriors charged over the fallen Warriors. The breach was made and he was rejoicing when the explosions devastated the charging Warriors and stopped the momentum. He lost control of his anger just as the body he was occupying ripped apart. The pain drove him out. Suddenly, he was back in his room reeling from the pain. Rage consumed him. Where could he attack? He sought out and found another Warrior and returned in time to see his army advancing across the bridge. Rage turned to glee as he saw the mistake the animals made. They had failed to set up a defense, and he screeched at the Warriors to seize the advantage. The bridge suddenly collapsed beneath the Warriors and they plunged into the deadly liquid. The fear of water in himself prevented his immediate release of rage, but only momentarily.

The Witch Bitch had done it again! She had escaped to the far side of the river that now protected them. Somehow the Witch had harnessed power to destroy the bridge and make bombs. He calmed his mind; there must be a victory of some kind. Suddenly, he smiled and vacated the Warrior. He moved his mind into a Simian Female on the other side and sought and found one of those animals, which the Witch communicated telepathically with. He found the female and approached slowly and lashed out. He took the life easily and quickly. The victory was his and the Witch had been hurt. He sensed the pain radiating from the alien mind and took pleasure in this partial victory. He also felt the pain of the Witch and rejoiced in it. He wished he was in a male body so he could violate and degrade her, but there was little he could do in this female body other than kill her. That would have to do, and it was enough. He was beginning to win.

He was moving the nearest colony of Warriors toward the animals and they would catch them on the open desert. To sweeten the victory, the southern colony army approached. The two armies should unite before the battle was met. There were no other places the animals could hide. He would find a way across the river, even if he had to build his own bridge. Soon the Animals would be caught between four Warrior armies and they would be crushed between them. The Witch would be last and he would kill her personally, after torturing her for years. He would get his revenge.

* Amy *

Before she allowed the macho shit to talk her into leaving the bridge intact, she insisted on taking the others out. They teleported to the railroad trestle and set off the charges then they went on to Blyth and blew those two up. With all crossings eliminated but this one, they waited at the Parker Bridge for the Warriors to arrive. Through Fred, she was able to monitor the progress of the Simian army. As expected, they were pacing them on the other side of the river waiting on an opportunity to cross. The Simians were obviously not familiar with the potential crossing areas like she was through her stored topographic maps.

While they waited, Moon found a cast net somewhere and started throwing it from well up on the bank, but it was sufficient to net some fish. Levi saw what Moon was doing and quickly started helping him. Together they soon had a large stash of catfish and stripers. She was not aware that Simians liked fish, but indeed they did or they were just hungry. The Techs were eating raw fish like a human would eat shrimp. Levi cleaned three nice size catfish and spiked them over a fire, while the Simians looked on in repulsion. He ignored them, grinning.

Levi said gleefully, "No K-Rations tonight."

Levi was soon full and sleepy. It had been a very long and eventful day and tomorrow promised to be eventful as well. He needed his rest and she encouraged him to get a good night's sleep. She had plans to consider. How could they defeat a Simian army?

Throughout the night that old enemy of her mind was haunting her again. Something was very wrong, but as always, she did not know what it was. It was just a premonition (clairvoyance) of something that was going to happen, something ominous. How could it possibly get worse than it already was? Whatever it was it would be soon. She searched her mind for something she might have overlooked, but could think of nothing.

As the sun rose, Levi was awake and eating cold fish. He was studying her expressions and realized something was wrong.

507

Finally he asked, "Clairvoyance again?"

There was no hiding it, so she nodded.

He asked again, "Do you know what it is?"

Again she nodded but in the negative.

He thought for a moment and said, "Let's go find it."

That seemed over simple, but it seemed the appropriate action. They had a day to kill anyway so Levi called Moon and told him he was going to meditate. Moon didn't quite understand what astral projection was, but did understand that Levi and Amy were absent from the body and when they returned they had new information. He knew they went somewhere and that they trusted him with their protection. Moon would die before he let anything happen to Levi's body. They were safe.

As a safety precaution he gave Moon his Zippo lighter in case the Warriors came before they got back, then settled down in the shade under the bridge. It was cool there and relaxing. Levi was calm and ready to be taken away in spirit. They were soon beginning to slowly drift out of his body. With Levi now accustomed, it was now relatively easy for her to pull him away from his physical existence. They drifted up as she took control. She normally loved the feeling of freedom and control, but she was so worried about her uneasiness that she couldn't enjoy this momentary freedom.

She slowly turned south to survey the locations of the Simian armies. Almost immediately she noticed that the Simian army was only making a show of following the migrating humans and Techs on the other side of the river. The Warriors were spread out for miles along the river edge giving the impression that the whole army was there, but there was no depth to them. Out of site of the humans, the outside ranks were turning outward and circling back wide. They were being lulled into feeling safe, while the Simians were circling back to make a crossing. She sped north following the progression of Warriors. As she flew over the terrain she could also see the Lancer team racing toward the migrating exodus, obviously trying to inform them of the breach. She had made another mistake. They should have left Fred behind to provide instant warning instead of having to wait for the Lancers to ride back and report.

As she continued south approaching the bridge and trestle, all was in order. They remained destroyed just like they had left them. Farther north she saw the Warriors pouring across the damn. On closer examination she saw that the Warriors had built a small bridge over the breech. They had transported beams from the destroyed railroad trestle and laid them over the break in the dam. It was not pretty, but it did its purpose. It would take some time for all the Warriors to reassemble on the east side, especially since there were so many still moving south in the apparent facade of following the human migration.

There was no purpose in staying in the area longer. They had discovered what they needed to know. She estimated that the Simian army would be three days behind them. They would have to make the best of the situation and use the time wisely.

Her sole intent now was to find out the whereabouts of the Phoenix Simian army. She soared higher to gain viewing distance as she sped south and east. It didn't take long. She found them following Interstate 10 east of a mountain range running north and south through Arizona. It was a natural barrier that committed the Simians to following Interstate 10 through the mountains. They had to either attack or rush past them, but that would only put three Simian armies behind them and they could never hope to out-distance them. Maybe Mexico wasn't such a bad place to run; they were too slow and the Simians were too damn fast. It would never work.

She was convincing herself to attack the Phoenix Simians when she saw a dust cloud farther south. She turned to see what it was. Oh NO! It was another Simian army!

Levi said, "Holy Shit!"

He had a way with words, but that was her sentiment exactly. The Simian army was coming north on an intersect course with the Phoenix Simian army. They were in deep shit, as Levi would say. They would be caught between four Simian armies, like one wasn't enough to wipe them out. In deep depression, she turned and headed back toward Levi's body.

* Levi *

When he saw the fourth Simian army his heart sank. Well, it would have if he had brought it with him. He laughed at his own joke, but only half-heartedly. It was too much to ask of Amy. A battle with four Simian armies was far too many to even think of surviving against. His mind said it was all over but the dying, but it was against his nature to ever give up. NEVER EVER give up, so what could they do? Amy was quiet, and he understood why. She felt hopeless like all of humanity had felt since the Simian invasion, but it was a new experience to her. He let her have her space for a while as they headed back toward his body.

Amy became focused again as they settled back into his body. Yes, breath and heartbeat were welcome again. He did not open his eyes yet, waiting on Amy's comments. Amy knew what he was doing and was slow to respond, but when she did she seemed urgent.

She said, "We must speed the migration along and bypass the route of the Phoenix Simian army before they can get ahead of us. We must inform Al and Iron Eyes to have some of the Lancers double team the wagons and speed them forward."

Levi softly said, "We will have to let Iron Eyes do that." He didn't have to add, "Because Dawn is not with Al." Her beautiful green eyes filled with tears at the thought of Dawn, but she helped him send the instruction to Fred to speed everyone up. They gave Fred just enough information to get them excited, but not enough to cause mass depression. He and Amy would carry the depression for everyone.

When he opened his eyes, Moon was staring at him. Moon must have been able to sense the essence of his mind return. Whatever the reason, Moon was waiting on him to respond. He explained what was happening and about the fourth Simian army. Moon's eyes turned suddenly solid red indicating anger or maybe fear.

Moon said, "Where did they come from?"

He had no idea and Amy certainly didn't. They had many times discussed surveying the country and identifying all the Simian Colonies, but something had always come up to take priority. He was wishing they had made the time now.

Amy surprised him by saying, "We need to send for Al. He needs new responsibilities to occupy his mind. We need to link with him and make him the communication link. We need to replace Dawn and it makes more sense to communicate directly with the commander anyway. In fact we really need more communicators, but I can't handle another."

As always, Amy was right.

He saw in Fred's monitoring window and realized why Amy was thinking about Al just now. Fred had reported the instruction to Iron Eyes, but had continued on and found Al and was giving the same instruction to him. Levi could clearly see Al in Fred's view, and Al was clearly not himself. He looked distant and somber. As soon as they had sent the message they could see and hear Fred asking Al to report to Levi. Al focused and walked out of Fred's view.

The migration was already approaching the bridge so it was a fairly short trip for Al. He was there in less than thirty minutes, dismounted, and lazily walked toward him. At seeing him he was pissed. Al was normally a very professional and respected leader, but now he was acting like a spoiled child. Of course, he had been deeply in love, probably the first time in many years, and had suffered a tragic loss, but life must go on and Al had major responsibilities that must continue. Levi said,

"Damn you, Al. You better snap out of it and quit thinking of yourself. Your settlement needs you now and you're letting them down. You are letting the damn Supreme One win." Al's eyes narrowed and Levi felt darts of hate and anger shooting at him. That was just before Al leveled a solid right fist at his jaw.

Amy had automatically tried to move him out of the way, but he held still. He knew it was coming and deserved it, but something had to bring Al out of his depression. It just might help... Al had to hit something and release some tension. Damn! For a moment he wished he would have allowed Amy to move him. It was a hard punch and knocked him off his feet and onto the rocky ground. He didn't try to get up but just lay there rubbing his jaw and looking up at Al. Moon screeched in alarm and was about to attack, but he held him back with a wave. Moon was puzzled but stopped. He did, however, remain close.

Al stared down at him, boring into him with those damn penetrating blue eyes of his for long moments. As Levi watched, Al's hard eyes began to slowly relax and his clenched fists slowly opened. Suddenly, Al grinned as understanding settled in his mind. Soon they were both laughing as Al held out his hand to help him up. Levi said, "Damn, Al, you hit hard."

Al said, "Thanks, my friend. I will be all right now. I will mourn, but you shocked me back into my senses." He added with a grin, "Is a punch in the jaw all you wanted?" Amy was laughing with them now.

He brought Al up to speed and told him more about the situation than any of the others knew. Al could handle it. It would probably be a blessing to take his mind off his own troubles. Al turned grave at the information and realized now why Amy was rushing them. Al saw it was imperative to escape the Phoenix Simian army and was about to rush back to speed them along when Levi said, "Wait. We need one more thing from you. We want to link with you." Al stopped in his tracks, turned, and stared again into his eyes. He said nothing, but the wheels were turning in his head. Al needed no explanations what this meant.

Al simply nodded and said, "Why not?" and waited.

Levi reached out his hands and held Al's head. He felt the heat in his hands as Amy connected with Al's mind.

* Amy *

She liked Al and took the opportunity of the link to transfer a wealth of information into his mind. Al was now an expert in many fighting techniques in addition to speaking several foreign languages including the Simian sign and speech. Al had learned the sign language and understood the spoken (screeched) Simian language quite well, but now he had a commanding control. Al would discover the many things she had given him in time, but even now he looked wide eyed with the realization of many new abilities. He shook his head, smiled, and took off to carry out his duties. She was happy to have this friend better equipped to

514

survive, not to mention the communication ability to replace Dawn. Already she was monitoring him.

With the new threat and change in plan, there was no longer time to wait on the Simians on the west side to approach the bridge. There was no surprise to be had. She told Levi to go ahead and blow the bridge so they could lead the migration that was already approaching. He nodded and walked to the bridge and struck the Zippo. The bridge blew up thirty second later as planned. The Simian army could not know their ruse had been discovered, but she knew now that it had been anticipated. They were only teasing her to keep her stationary, but they would have no way of knowing about her astral projection abilities. There probably weren't all that many Warriors left anyway. Most would have already left on schedule to return north. She would have played right into the hands of the Supreme One had they not astral projected. The ruse almost worked.

They had already notified Jimmy of the new threat and dispatched him and his team ahead to locate this new army. Jimmy was as shocked as they had been, but he was confident in Levi's abilities to save them. She hated the burden of responsibility Jimmy and the others gave her, but Levi took it in stride. He cheated. He was as bad as the others in his confidence in her. How could she deliver their salvation? Levi had someone else to look to as the savior of the human race, and it was her.

The wagons were moving faster with the extra mounts hooked up to them and the teamsters driving them hard. She calculated that at this speed they could easily get past the route of the Phoenix Warrs.

Not only must they get past the Simians, but they must get a substantial lead to give her army time to attack the new threat, and this they must do. She committed the army. They had to take a chance and leave the wagons unprotected, so they issued the instructions to the communication team. Her plan now was to position the army as they had been before at the bridge. Organize them now and move them intact toward the Mexican Simian army. The armies were rushing into position even as she watched.

She calculated the speed and directions of both her, well, Levi's army, and the advancing Simians and had already chosen the battlefield. Once she knew the exact position of the Simians from Jimmy, she could adjust the speed accordingly to deliver both armies to the chosen location at the same time, which was seven miles away. It was a flat plain and no cover for the Infantry, but the Lancers could maneuver well. She had more Lancers than any other group so she was building her plan around them.

She just hoped they didn't run out of lances. She had lost track of the inventory of lances, but didn't think any large amount had been used in the battle so far. This coming battle that she must launch would, however, greatly deplete their supply, and there were more battles to come if they survived this one.

Instructions were sent to Mama along with detailed plans for building the lances. Mama would know that the lances would be high priority or she wouldn't be asking. The problem was time. It would take days to make them and she only had hours. Just

516

for clarity, Amy told her she needed them very soon for battle.

There were plenty of trees in her valley and the Greys were much bigger than humans. They should be able to handle the hard heavy work better and faster. Because of concern for the Fems' safety, she didn't want them to venture too far from the entrance of the facility and her ability to monitor and protect them with the lasers. Luckily, there were lots of trees close to the entrance. In fact she had already started measuring them for lances and began cutting them with the door lasers. She could personally help this time, and it felt good. It was wonderful to have an active facility to supply for their needs.

Jimmy made contact with the advancing army and they were right where they should be for her scheduled battlefield. She could see the dust and the individual Warriors in the lead.

She noticed immediately that the dress for the Warriors, although uniform, was different. These Warriors wore what looked like straw woven, wide bill hats and the torso was covered with a loose light brown, woven cloth blanket over the shoulders that hung down past the waist, front and back. There was a hole cut in the center for the large head, and the front and back were tied on together on the sides. The dress was so different that she believed that this colony must be from a far distance, probably deep in Mexico, with little, if any, interface with other Simian colonies, in this part of the world anyway.

The Warriors were spread out and not tightly clustered in teams, which worked to her advantage.

She issued instructions, and the battle front changed. The Lancers were told to spread out and not to force the Warriors into the V, instead draw the Warriors out farther. The way the Warriors were advancing would allow a Lancer battle and that is what she wanted.

* Levi *

He could see the new threat in his monitoring window and knew Amy was worried. He could understand why. Too much was against them. He told her, "Hell, Amy, we never had a chance from the start so don't worry about losing. I am surprised we got this far. We wouldn't have if it hadn't been for you. Just do the best you can." He realized he was sounding defeatist and was doing it on purpose to take the pressure off her and force her to get focused. Sometimes she got so negative.

Amy retorted somewhat angrily and very colorful, "Kiss my ass, Levi. I am not giving up and I never will again!"

Levi burst out laughing and said, "That's my girl." He was rewarded with a look of exasperation when she realized what he was doing

He liked her plan. It was simple, attack and retreat, drawing out the Warriors while other Lancer teams attacked them from various angles. Hey, it was so simple maybe it would work. There were, however, lots of Warriors to kill.

Amy said, "We are almost to the battlefield."

They had been traveling due south along Highway 95 for most of the day and it was boring. The road was so straight and the scenery unimpressive and barren. The line of road looked the same mile after mile and seemed to disappear from sight far in the distance. The only break in the scenery was when they had passed through a town called Quartzsite at the intersection of Highway 95 and Interstate 10. He found it funny because there was only a sign for the town, but there was nothing there. That had been the only bright spot, such that it was, in the boring march.

For a change he could see a turn in the road ahead.

Amy said, "We will turn through a pass up ahead and move into Kings Valley."

That was the chosen battlefield. It was hidden from the Phoenix Simian army coming down Interstate 10 and the pass could be used to hold that army should the Supreme One notify them of their location. Amy figured the odds were 50/50. It just depended on if and where the Supreme One might be occupying a Simian mind. If it was in her group he would even know the battle positions of the armies. For this reason they delayed giving instructions until as late as possible and only then it was the bare minimum. This was another reason Amy was depending on the human Lancers for this battle.

After two more miles traveling at the same speed, they turned left and went through the pass. They had been giving instructions along the way so by the time the army reached the pass it was strung out in a long narrow procession that prevented them from forming a bottle neck and allowed them to pass quickly through. Once through the pass, the commands quickly reformed on the other side to face the new threat, which was highly visible now and not very far away. The Simian army was still very much like they had been, disbursed across the battle field. At least something was going right.

The valley was not really a valley; it was open desert between mountain ranges. It was dry, dusty and barren. It looked like just more desert, which it was, but there was lots of room for the Lancers to maneuver. It was perfect for a Lancer battle and they would need all the luck they could get.

He had been looking through Jimmy's eyes, but the view through his was now good enough. Jimmy had done all he could do. As he looked at Amy with the unasked question in his mind, Amy nodded and they sent Jimmy a telepathic message for him and his group to re-join his command, and as always, he and Iron Eyes were to stay to the rear and observe and issue Levi's orders. Again the look of resentment, but he did as he was told. They sent identical messages to Fred and Al. Initially, Al was immediately angered and resentful with him interfering with his leadership, but he quickly calmed as he realized that he now carried more responsibilities than he had before. Fred was with the Infantry and it didn't bother him to remain a safe observer. Levi said, "That was a hard sell." They both laughed.

As the armies approached, the Lancers rode wide to the outside. The overeager Warriors advanced outward to engage them. All along the edges the Lancers met the Warriors. These Warriors had not yet seen what a Lancer could do and remained arrogant in their attack. That proved to be costly as many fell to the lances. As always, the

Lancers charged the lone Simians and many Warriors fell dead with more than one lance embedded in its chest. Maybe twenty died in the first charge, but the Warriors quickly fell back and regrouped into their teams. Afterward, the Warriors advanced in aligned teams, far more organized, and at a slower pace. He thought that was unusual for the Warriors to learn so fast. They just weren't that quick.

The second charge paralleled the Warrior line in a glazing attack. This proved to be disastrous as the Warriors struck unexpected from behind. After the Lancer picked his target and was focused on the one, a Warrior would rush out from behind to strike the horse in the rear, sending the horse and rider to the ground. Both horse and rider were struck down quickly. In some cases the Warrior that rushed out was struck by the Lancer following, but the exchange was costly. They quickly broke off this method of attack.

* Amy *

The first charge worked well taking out twenty-one Warriors. Levi saw the Simian organization change, but he failed to see the screeching commander issuing orders. There was no doubt that it was the Supreme One. The organized Warriors did the unexpected defense that cost them fifteen Lancers and horses. She recalled the charge and directed them to the end. Here the Lancers did not have to follow the full advancing line, only the corner. They were exposed to attack only at the initial contact point. The strategy worked, and the end Warriors were falling to the lances. Again the screeching Warrior reorganized and the end fell back inward forming a wide angle providing less of a target. Already she could see the entire Simian army forming an octagon of sorts. Nowhere was there an easy target, as the Warrs remained tightly clustered. She continued the Lancers in a looping circle constantly passing safely by but close enough only to attack any Warr that ventured out too far. It was a standoff as the Simian army slowly advanced toward the Infantry and Techs.

This was not going well. She did not want a ground battle. The Simians greatly outnumbered her ground troops and would slowly eat their way through the lines. Damn! She saw the Simian front line strengthen and spread out forcing the ends out. The obvious intent was to face as many Warrs as possible against the human Infantry and Techs. That ploy would work. She adjusted the Lancers to move toward the front in an effort to hold the Warrs' line in, but as the Lancers attacked the front she saw her mistake. The rear of the advancing army mushroomed out to spread the lines wider on both sides. The inner ranks emptied to fill and strengthen the outer lines that were folding out and circling the Lancers. Virtually all the Warrs could now face an enemy. Now the Lancers would not be able to circle the ends and attack the rear without allowing the front line to continue to spread out. Already her Infantry was spreading too thin for an adequate defense and some were falling to the Warrs' swords. The Simian strategy was brilliant and she admired the planning and execution, even as she realized her army was doomed and would be defeated. The major casualties had not yet started, but there was nothing she could do to stop it.

She exchanged knowing looks with Levi. Much was said between them including their profession of love, but "Never Give Up" also came through loud and clear. She had learned that lesson from Levi many times and was now second nature to her. She would never give up, but she didn't know what else to do. The Infantry was tightly clustered behind the front lines as was the Techs and they were fighting hard. She screamed in Levi's ear, "Where is ASONE when you need him?" How could she bring him forward and what could it do? If she only knew she would try it. As she was literally having a fit, Levi said, "Look!" She let her mind see where he was looking, and she couldn't believe her eyes.

Charging in from the rear was a huge army of Lancers. Yes, they were Lancers equipped just like theirs, complete to the same size lances and carried the same way. The horses were charging into the rear of the Simian army and the Warrs were not in a defensive position for a rear attack. Screeches of pain echoed from the rear as the Warrs began to fall. The Lancers were charging down the center and turning in both directions along the back lines. There were hundreds of them and she was excited. This was one time she enjoyed emotions.

As the Warriors turned to face the new attack, she quickly instructed her lancers to charge the inside of the line of Warrs to catch them from both sides. Working in unison from both sides, the Warrs were confused and didn't know which way to face. They were falling to the lances on both sides of the extended wings of Warriors. Hundreds of them fell from the attack and the extended wings were soon decimated. Much of the front center ranks of Warrs turned to reinforce the rear, allowing the weakened front lines to be overrun by the Techs. The Techs were without mercy and killed, venting years of built up hate. She watched in awe.

As the combined Lancers slowly sawed through the overextended ranks, the Infantry advanced taking many of the Warrs in the back. The tide of battle had suddenly turned overwhelmingly toward her side. The Warrs began to compress inwardly trying to protect themselves, but Earth's armies continued to advance sawing into the Warriors. Suddenly, she laughed as did Levi, as the Fems, not to be left out, charged past the Infantry flying into the remaining Warrs with hand fangs lashing out. If possible, the Warriors seemed more shocked at seeing the charging Fems than the armies. They were unaccustomed to seeing Fems attack and most didn't even try to defend themselves. The battle was over in minutes and they were victorious. She had never believed in luck, but now she even believed in God because this victory was nothing less than a miracle.

CHAPTER 13
(THE RANKS GROW)

* Mosley *

Mosley was an oversized bully, accustomed to getting his way. He ruled his followers with a winning smile backed up by force of will and strength. In many ways he ruled over his community much the same way as any Warrior Simian leader might rule his colony. He was, however, a very likable man when he wanted to be, and he wanted to be most of the time. He enjoyed being liked until he was angered. When that happened, his rage was notorious among his followers and many had seen and felt his wrath personally. He did not have a reputation of being cruel, however, and was fair as long as they did things his way when they were told. Mosley enjoyed the role of leader and did not delegate or share his authority. He was the unquestioned leader and liked it that way.

Mosley now led an army of Lancers equipped very much like the original Lancer team that visited his community. Several Lancer teams had been sent out after the battle of Los Angeles to spread the word of hope and recruit help. One of these teams discovered Mosley's community deep in Mexico. This team had described the battles and what was occurring in California and their successes against the Simians and about the need to consolidate to protect the human race. Mosley was interested for two reasons. First, his community was now in danger and secondly, he wanted to increase his kingdom and control to include those remote armies and grow in power.

Mosley knew about Simians, having once lived in New Mexico in his late adolescence living in constant fear of the Simians. He had seen them in action far too many times. His parents and only brother had been killed by a roving Simian team, and he had watched helplessly from seclusion, while they were mutilated and eaten. Even at that early age he was huge like his father, but it made no difference. He hated them but there had never before been a way to fight back or even survive against the Simians. After his family had been killed, he decided to gather as many humans as possible and find a better location free from the Simians.

His huge size and dominant presence inspired a fearful confidence in others, which he used to recruit. Many of his fellow blacks joined him, and they traveled deep into Mexico where he finally found a safe haven free from the wondering Simians. There he continued to gather the native Mexicans and Indians to his community. Over the years, his community became prosperous. They developed a permanent community complete with farms, ranches, and working trades. They were relatively safe at their location and had remained so for many years as his community flourished, but after ten years of safe living, they were now encountering more and more Simian patrols and many of his foraging teams were being attacked or not returning at all. His safe community was no longer safe and all he had built was threatened.

To discover the source of the threat, he had sent out scouts to find the Simian colony, which was finally located two hundred miles north of them. It was a new Simian colony, at least it had been built within the last few years. His community had prospered for many years since he brought them together under his leadership, but the Simian colony was now a major threat to him, and he knew it. As luck would have it, a Lancer team, which is what they called themselves, arrived with their stories and obvious skills, and he convinced them to stay and train his men. The Lancers were reluctant at first, but he forced them to stay. He smiled and promised to take his newly trained army to help the Lancer's settlements. He meant it because the Simians were a threat to all humans no matter where they lived. He was, however, more concerned with the threat to his community and how he could use the remote Lancer army to help him.

Mosley had hundreds of men he could train and an abundant supply of horses. He also had the means to make the lances. Once he saw how the Lancers operated, he believed he could probably train his men himself, but there was no real need. These Lancers had the skills and sported Simian trophy teeth to prove it. He looked upon these trophies with envy and wanted some of his own. He pledged he would have some also and soon.

The visiting Lancers finally agreed and began training his men. The Lancers were indeed good, and his men learned well. He personally even accepted their training, which was egotistically uncharacteristic of him. It was going well. After long weeks of training he now had over a thousand trained Mexican, Indian and black Lancers of his own, a stockpile of lances, and transport wagons. He even copied the two wheeled fast attack wagons. He was ready and could launch a war of his own against the new Simian colony.

Just when he was considering launching an attack, he got word from his scouts that the Simian Warriors of the new colony were mobilizing for war. Mosley was confident that he could at least put up a fight to protect his community now if the Simians attacked. He had been lucky so far that the Simians hadn't attacked before he had an army. Now he could fight back.

His scouts were watching constantly, but the expected Simian attack did not come. Finally word came, the Simian Warriors were moving north instead of south toward him as he had expected. He said out loud, "What the hell is going on?" There was obviously going to be a battle somewhere and if it was against humans, he might as well join it. If the Simians defeated a human army then he might be the next target. Whoever it was the Simians were going to attack might help him dispense with this threat. He quickly mobilized his army and followed the Simians.

It took his Lancers five days of hard riding to catch up to the Simians, but his army could move faster on horseback than the Simian Warriors could on foot. Once they had the Simians in sight they followed just out of view. He trailed and waited to see where the Simians were going and what awaited them.

Curiosity got the best of him after a couple of days, so he sent his scouts out to circle ahead of the

Simians and discover their destination. After six days of trailing the Simians, his scouts returned and reported that there was a large migration of both humans and Simians moving toward them. He was puzzled by the fact that Simians were apparently allied with humans until he remembered the Lancers mentioning what they called Technical Simians among them. One of these Simians called Moon was reported to be the constant companion of the human leader they called Levi. It was all coming back to him now. He had a destiny with this Levi.

His scouts reported that the migration was made up of a large contingent of Lancers, human Infantry carrying spears, and Simians, which were formed in battle ranks with the Lancers positioned on both sides. He didn't know what they were doing this far from their home, but this had to be the human army the visiting Lancers had talked about. The scouts also reported that the Simian army and the migration knew where the other was and headed directly toward each other. The scouts estimated that the two groups would meet head on in about a day. If this army was to join the certain battle to come in time to make a difference, it was time for him to act.

Mosley ordered his army to close the distance between them and the rear of the Simian army. Once the Simians saw the humans in front, he believed that they would be so focused that his army could advance on their rear undetected. At the least, even if they were detected, it would split the Simian army in two directions. That was the plan anyway, and it seemed reasonable.

The battle was in full force by the time his army crossed the last hill. As he observed the battle he saw the plan of attack by the Simians and the plan of Levi's defense. The defense was working until the Simians started spreading out on both sides. He saw the defense finally falter and fall back and start to crumble, but it was sweet from his point of view. The Simians had their back to him and they had spread out far too thin to defend from a rear attack. He ordered his Lancers to make two continuous charge runs down the middle and out to both sides along the extended Simian rear ranks. He had just learned this tactic by watching the defense of the Lancers. The strategy had worked for a while, but the raw numbers of Warriors and the way they deployed had finally destroyed the Lancers' defense.

His glazing attack was sudden and totally unexpected and cut along the rear of the Simians like a saw through wood. He was puzzled to see the other Lancers immediately deploy to attack the inside of the wings in a mirror attack to his own. That change had come very quickly, and he wondered how orders were issued so quickly. Whatever the reason, he was pleased.

The battle was winding down fast as he personally joined the battle. He intended to make a kill so he could wear a trophy black Simian tooth. He was not attached to a team, so he joined one that was making a kill. He screamed for the Lancers to move while he charged and sank his lance into a dying Simian. He quickly retrieved a lance and joined another team finishing up a kill. After three such charges he saw that there wasn't much left to do, so he regained his observation post to watch the end.

The overall effect was decimating to the extended enemy ranks and the Simians' defeat was quick. Mosley sat his mount and watched in awe as the human Infantry, Technical Simians, and what appeared to be Simian females finished off the remainder of the Warriors gathered in the center. Both armies killed the few remaining Warriors and began to group again. He then led his army forward in an impressive show of force toward the center area where he could see the established control and obvious leadership location.

As he got closer, he saw his visiting Lancers and trainers of his army sprint forward toward their friends. The Lancers rode directly toward a bronzed man of superior size and development. This must be the leader called Levi. He rode directly toward him. It was time to take control.

* Amy *

They had survived again thanks to the unexpected help from the human Lancer army. Where did they come from and how was it that they looked and fought like her Lancers? There were many questions running through her mind as the group approached. When she saw a three man horse team break away from the ranks and race toward her, many questions were answered. This was one of Iron Eyes' Lancer teams. She recognized them almost immediately. This was one of the teams that had been sent out to recruit new humans to their cause. They had obviously done a great job of

531

recruiting and training also, and she was thankful to see them and their army.

The Lancers rode up to Levi and reported, "Mosley, the army's leader is coming."

They seemed nervous to be trying to say more than that in the few words they had time to report. They shook Levi's hand and, seeing Iron Eyes approach, ran to him and embraced him and reported in.

Her attention was instinctively drawn to the approaching man on horseback. She could tell he was a big man that dwarfed the horse he rode, and that would be hard to do since he rode a large draft horse that looked like it should be pulling a Budweiser beer wagon. She wondered where he got it. It was the only kind of horse that could have carried his massive bulk.

When the rider dismounted, she saw that big wasn't the word to describe this man; Mosley was huge. This huge black man would tower over most all humans and even some Simians. She estimated that he stood well over seven feet and weighed in the neighborhood of three hundred and eighty pounds of hard muscles. He was a very muscular and impressive man. His arms were huge with bulging muscles as were his legs. His hands were large and wide with long thick fingers. The skin was very black, both naturally and from exposure to a harsh tropical sun. The hair on his head was long and woven in many small braids down both sides of his face and back. The braids did not appear to be neat nor clean, but functioned only to keep his vision clear.

As he came closer she caught his scent. He had a nasty body smell, and it appeared that he washed seldom. There was no hat and scant clothing. His vest, open in the front, appeared to be made from a large snake skin that covered his shoulders and torso. Loose leather shorts covered half way down his thick thighs. His big flat feet were covered with leather that wrapped around his lower legs to above his calves in an old Apache style legging. This man Mosley seemed to want to intimidate those around him in his dress by exposing his massive muscles. It worked, as most around him stared and seemed openly awed by him. It was clear that Mosley used his size to his advantage to control those around him.

As Mosley approached Levi, he held out his massive hand and flashed a gleaming smile, but she could tell the smile was for show. Mosley had an infectious grin that inspired confidence and trust or indicated cunning. It was hard to tell just what the case was since he was obviously very intelligent. The grin was most pronounced with the contrast of perfect pearl white teeth against his deep black rugged face. Additionally, the whites of his eyes shone brightly in his dark face, further augmenting his smile. Only part of Mosley's awing presence was due to his towering height and massive bulk.

Mosley towered over Levi, but Levi was not intimidated. She was proud of Levi for standing up to him. Levi was chuckling inwardly and it was obvious that Levi was street wise to Mosley's demeanor and intentions. Levi reached up to take Mosley's extended hand and was greeted with a bone crushing grip. She had anticipated this and met his force with equal strength, which seemed to make Mosley's eyes open wider in momentary shock and the grin was gone. As the pressure increased it was met with countering pressure until the silent contest slowly ended in a draw. It would not be good to soundly defeat the man until it might become necessary. There was no sense in antagonizing him. Mosley was very strong and would have crushed the hand of a normal human.

Mosley released Levi's hand smiling and said, "It is a good thing I came to save you."

Levi smiled in return and said, "Your saving is not finished yet. We have another Simian army pouring through the pass to our rear. Please take Fred with you, and I will be giving instruction through him for the battle, but we don't have much time for discussion. Deploy your Lancers along the left side of the pass there." Mosley was shaken to discover there was a new threat and the uncertainty of the situation made him accept orders without any open questions. Oh, he wanted to challenge Levi, but Levi had taken charge and this was not the time. Mosley was unaccustomed to taking orders and his smile was gone. He looked around and even stared at Levi for a long minute, but Mosley was confused and had no idea what to do so he finally turned to his horse and rode off to deploy his Lancers as instructed.

She felt Mosley boring a hole with his eyes into the back of Levi's head, but Levi had turned from Mosley, totally ignoring and dismissing him.

Levi told her, "Mosley has no choice. The Simian army is as much a threat to him as they are

534

to us. He is in danger also and knows it so he will comply."

Levi was right in his assessment, but she was still awed by Levi's bravado in taking control of the situation. This was something she had never seen in him before and was surprised and respectful.

Fred was trotting along beside Mosley like a small child, followed closely by his Simian and Lancer bodyguards. Fred was talking nervously fast. She heard Fred telling him that Levi communicated telepathically with him. He was not necessarily being informative but rather making sure that Mosley knew that the instructions were coming from Levi and not him. Fred was visibly frightened of Mosley, maybe even more so than the Simians. That information brought a momentary startled look from Mosley, but he quickly resumed his almost embarrassed walk back to his horse.

* Levi *

He saw the giant coming toward him and immediately recognized Mosley for who he was. Mosley was a bully, and he had been dealing with bullies all his life. This one was no different, just bigger. Of course, a giant like Mosley would probably know no other way of acting. The size alone would give him the confidence to assume leadership in most any situation, but thanks to Amy, Levi was not the weakling Mosley might take him for. Mosley was human though and he and his army had saved them. They were not the enemy and Mosley was not an evil man. This was obvious. He was just a bully and would take over command if he let him, but that could never happen. He might welcome that, but Amy was needed in this leadership role and could do far more than Mosley could ever hope to do.

He found it humorous when Mosley gripped his hand. He found it funny because, had it been someone else, this simple bully's ploy would have worked, but he met his force. There would be no need to outdo Mosley. Levi wanted Mosley to accept him as leader freely and not because he could out grip his hand. They must have these combined forces to survive, and there was no time for lengthy discussions. Mosley would know this as well, so Levi took command. Mosley would learn soon that he, well Amy, was the unquestioned leader by virtue of ability.

Mosley, out of surprise and shock, accepted Levi's orders and left somewhat shaken, but resumed his composure in the comfort of his own army and started issuing the necessary orders to his army. He resumed his comfortable dominant position at the head of his army and led them toward the assigned position.

Levi noticed that Moon had stood quietly beside Levi, as was his normal position, and watched the brief exchange between them. Moon had watched Mosley intently looking directly across at the human of almost identical height. Mosley may have even been slightly taller. Mosley had looked directly at Moon only briefly, but had he looked closer he would have noticed the warning of Moon's full red eyes blazing. Mosley's bullying could easily have ended there. As big as he was he was still no match against Moon.

536

Levi laughed at Moon and told him, "Everything will be fine. Mosley will be all right. We need him and his army.

Moon nodded and signed, "Why didn't you replace him as leader? I don't like the dark human."

His reply was honest when he said, "The army does not know me and might not accept me yet as their leader. They will, hopefully, in time, but let's hope there will be no need to face that issue. Mosley doesn't deserve to be taken out. He has built his army and has done a lot of good this day... he saved us. He is just a little over aggressive right now. I can handle him and he will work out well. We just need to convince him." He laughed then and said, "Besides it might not be that easy to take him out."

Amy consolidated Iron Eyes' and Al's Lancers along the north side of the pass, with the standard position of the Infantry and Technical Simians grouped in the middle. Mosley's Lancers were in position as well and seemed to be taking his instructions through Fred. They had a very impressive army now and Amy's strategy was flawless and simple.

She said, "We will slow and limit the Simian's access through the pass with the riflemen and take those that come through out. The trick was to allow only a small amount through the pass and let them enter far enough that the following Simians were also through the pass and committed when they saw what was happening. If they see what is happening, they might stop and their plan would be foiled. It was a brilliant plan and should work.

As Amy said, "Divide and conquer.

The Phoenix Simian Army was only now approaching the pass. They were not yet pouring through the pass as Levi had told Mosley. Levi had stretched the truth just a little, but then he always seemed to have a different view point from hers and truth and accurate facts didn't always come out of Levi's mouth. In contrast, her opinion was always based upon fact and truth. That brought a muttered, "Shithead" from Levi, but he was grinning because he knew she was right.

The riflemen were positioned and instructed to only give sparse gunfire, only enough to defend themselves and slow and limit the volume of Simians coming through the pass. They were not to stop them completely as they had at the other pass campaigns. Al had the clearer view of the pass and she could see the plan working. The Simian Warriors were compressed in the center of the pass flowing through in a narrow stream. The way they were grouped it would have been impossible to miss hitting a Simian if the riflemen fired into the mass of Warriors. As it was, the riflemen fired on the edges of the flow and mostly only those Warriors that tended to expand out from the small river of Simians. This tended to force the edges inward and maintain the choke on the flow. So far it was working.

The instructions were given to hold the attack until they received the word. The long flow of Simians was almost in position. She would hold the attack until the Simians made the last turn in the pass and their view became blocked from those behind. It was almost time to give the word, but she knew something was wrong even before she saw the raving Warrior in the lead pack screech orders reversing the attack. Damn Satan! He was constantly interfering now at will, and attacking individuals. She knew there would be more casualties directly from him. What could they do?

For the moment, they would have to regroup and alter the plan. Levi was quiet, but she knew he was following her thoughts and they matched with her. Since the Simian army pulled back out of her trap they would be searching for other passes and there were several. They didn't have to be in a hurry to press the attack. All they had to do was wait for the other Simian army to turn east along Interstate 10 route they had just come. She knew without doubt that Satan had already given the orders to the combined Simian army to alter their plan. Damn him! They would be caught in another trap.

Her mind was racing, searching the topography maps for routes and passes. There was one pass, but it was a single road and over the mountain. No, that would never do with the wagons. They would have to continue southeast and intersect Interstate 8 east and turn up Highway 85 toward Phoenix. Of course, this would put them directly facing the combined Simian army that had been chasing them. Could it get any worse?

Levi said, "Of course. We could head east and face ten thousand instead of only two thousand."

The shit was actually smiling at that revelation.

* Levi *

539

He didn't see it as soon as Amy, but it was soon obvious. The plan wasn't going to work. The Simian army turned around and ran back out of the pass and trap. Damn! He felt Amy's anger toward the Supreme One, who had obviously seen her trap and prevented it from happening. He also knew as well as Amy that the Supreme One was now projecting into a temporary leader of the combined Simian army in the rear changing their direction east to circle and catch the human army in his own trap. He saw Amy's modified plan, which seemed to be no more than to travel back just to face the old trailing army again. This time the Phoenix Simian Army would be pushing them from the rear toward Phoenix. This was not a plan. It was insanity and simply organized suicide. The only positive was that they would have a couple of days of travel before it was exercised. Without much thought he spoke to Amy out loud, "You have a couple of days to think of something to save us." Amy was not smiling or responding. There was a dangerous look in her eyes that seemed to be aimed directly at him. Yep, he had pissed her off, but that is when she does her best planning.

This enemy was getting far too good at projecting his mind into other Simians and interfering. The odds were already impossible, but the Supreme One was constantly projecting himself into any available Simian regardless of which side, to spy, interfere, control and kill almost at will. It was far too difficult to cope with both problems. Something had to be done. They had to attack the Supreme One and make him more interested in protecting himself than waging a personal war against them. It would be nice to kill him if that was possible. That would even some of the odds. Hmmm, he liked the idea. At least they could go out with a bang anyway and maybe take it out with them.

He imagined the Supreme One feeling safe thousands of miles away surrounded in luxury and protected by a massive army. In his arrogance, he would never suspect an attack on his person. Well, no one would, not even him. How could they attack? He hoped Amy would take up the planning, but she waited and listened to his thoughts with apparent interest. He felt appreciated so he continued.

He suspected that the Supreme One would have to leave his body unprotected as he projected his mind. It should be like when he and Amy astral projected. The Supreme One's body must be vulnerable at those times and evidently that was often, at least he assumed it would be since he seemed to be manifested in the battles almost continuously. Amy was listening and not disagreeing. Actually, she seemed very interested in the idea and he could see her nodding as he made his assumptions. If they could catch him so occupied with his mind projected, he might be able to be killed. But how could they kill him? They were occupied too in a fight for their lives, and what were they going to do anyway, teleport into the center of ten thousand Warriors?

Maybe it could be done. He was smiling now because he knew what and how to do it. Just when he was most proud of himself he noticed Amy's frown. What had he missed?

* Amy *

He was doing good right up to the last. She wanted to see his ideas because he brought a new dimension to the equation. Abstract thought still remained elusive to her and she wanted to see what he was thinking. Attack? Yes, that was a good idea and one she hadn't considered. Levi was right. They seemed to be constantly on the defensive and her archives of war strategy taught that a good offence was the best defense, but this was something out of the ordinary. His idea was very sound, however, and his reasoning was mostly accurate too. But, to launch any kind of attack would require them to astral project or teleport to the Supreme One's location. That was something the Supreme One would detect immediately. She knew he was far more sensitive to her mind than she was his. He had located her easily, even at the extreme distance of their separation. If she projected anywhere near his location he would detect it immediately and they would be in danger of a counter attack. She was also fearful of his powers if they were physically close. His powers were formidable even at these distances. Levi was right though. The Supreme One would be vulnerable while his mind was projected.

She was about to discourage Levi's plan, but froze in instant amazement at his last thought. She was almost afraid the developing idea would vanish if she interrupted him. Damn! That was a good idea. Could it work? She would have to analyze it more and consider the details.

Further consideration would have to wait while the retreat was organized. They both emerged from their temporary planning and issued the necessary orders. Retreat was in order and runners were sent from Al to notify the riflemen to remain in a defensive mode for a defensive retreat like had been employed through the many passes where it had been successful. She knew the Simian army would not press; they did not have to. The Supreme One had a plan that was working. The delaying action would only work for two days, which was the time required for the Simian army to circle the mountain range to the south. The riflemen would have to be gone by then or risk being caught in the trap. So, they had two days to travel east and plan what actions might be available to them.

The wagons had continued east during the day and would have camp and food ready for the army when it would finally reach them. At least that was covered, but there were other things that needed to be faced as well, and it was coming at them now in the form of a ranting and bellowing Mosley. She had temporally forgotten him, but with the apparent failure of the Simian trap and additional orders to move east, Mosley was threatened and probably saw his opportunity to challenge the leadership.

* Levi *

Amy warned him stating, "Mosley is coming."

He had missed it. It still amazed him how Amy saw more through his eyes than he did himself. He smiled at her and winked. She just frowned and said, "Shithead!" He knew this conformation would

543

come at the first break in activities, but he hadn't expected a break this soon. He hadn't considered what to do. He had better figure it out quickly while the huge black man pounded his way toward him.

Mosley had been taken off guard by the circumstances as he seized control the way he had done previously. Mosley had time to regain control of his momentary confusion and loss of self-confidence. The humiliation set in and he was now angry. Mosley was angry, but wisely waited for both armies to reach them. He obviously wanted all to see him take control so he would not be disputed as leader.

Amy was sober and said, "This is a dangerous situation developing."

He saw that she was worried that the two armies could possibly turn on each other in defense of their leaders. That would be an insane development when the human race was already in jeopardy of extinction. He thought quickly as Mosley approached.

There was no avoiding a physical conflict. That was Mosley's nature. Wisely, Amy cautioned him not to allow the confrontation to become Human against Simian within their own ranks. Just in time he screeched a warning to Moon to back off. Moon was already stepping in Mosley's path with obvious intentions of killing Mosley. Even as he screeched to Moon he could see the total red eyes staring hard back at him. He quickly explained that he must handle this himself and it must remain between humans. Moon stared at him and slowly the eyes relaxed and some of the red disappeared. Mosley had seen the exchange, but he had hardly slowed, only veered in a wider circle around Moon. These two would never like each other.

Mosley looked around to make sure everyone was watching. It amazed him that Mosley was not thinking out of anger as it appeared, but obviously out of cunning, and he was calm and calculating as he stepped within reach. He saw it coming and deftly rolled with the punch just out of range. If it wasn't so serious this could be fun. The huge man fell to the ground from his momentum. He was swinging from the hip one second and the next he was flat on his face in a plume of dust. He was up instantly and this time he was very angry. Again Levi waved off his bodyguards and friends who would have jumped in. A spreading and gathering circle was forming around him and Mosley as they faced each other.

He held his hands up in a gesture to wait and said, "What is this about? We need to talk." Mosley flashed a cunning grin showing his white teeth. They looked almost as ominous as the black-toothed grin of a Simian.

Mosley simply said, "You dared to give me orders. I will not take your orders. I will be the one giving them." At that he attacked again.

* Amy *

Levi was getting more perceptive, or maybe she was realizing it more; but Levi had noticed the cunning of Mosley. He had planned it just right, and she didn't know how to advise Levi. The situation was very volatile. There might not be a winner. Either way was a loss. Mosley could not be allowed

545

to win. That would destroy any hope, such that there was, for the human race. If Levi won, which he would, how would Mosley take it? What real incentive did the Southern army have in following them into certain death? They were not yet the target of the Supreme One, but they would be sooner than they would hope if Levi's army was destroyed. The Southern army was needed, but why would they stay?

Levi said, "Amy don't underestimate the human spirit, but help me win NOW before he kicks my ass!"

He was laughing as he said it, and he was right.

Mosley was charging Levi now, and he was embarrassed and pissed at having missed the first attempt and taken a dive into the dirt. He was unaccustomed to failure. She was thankful that Mosley was not using any weapons. He obviously didn't believe he needed any. His arms were outstretched in an effort to grab Levi in a bear hug that probably could crush any normal human. She timed the strike and Levi hit him dead center in the middle of the face. It took some reinforcing of his arm and hand bones, but the crashing blow made Mosley's eyes roll up in his head and he collapsed in a heap on the ground. One blow and the fight was over. She had considered making the fight more even, but decided that a decisive win would establish stronger leadership.

Levi rolled Mosley over and made him more comfortable while he was unconscious. As he rolled him over she noticed that several of Mosley's teeth fell out. That was unfortunate, but nothing she could do now. Moon noticed the teeth also and picked them up.

Without emotion Moon signed, "These teeth are unimpressive, but we can put them on your necklace."

Levi found this shockingly funny and was having a hard time holding his laughter. She of course could and was laughing hysterically at the irony of Moon's statement.

Mosley was the sole leader, so there was not a second or third in command to assume control of the Southern Army, so they waited for Mosley to wake up. This he did slowly. He had been loaded into a shaded wagon and was being attended to by some of the medical technicians. The blow had been hard, and it took several hours for Mosley to regain consciousness. Even then he was content to remain in the wagon thinking about his next actions.

As they traveled to camp, Levi was still laughing at Moon's comment and what had happened.

Levi said, "Damn, Amy, that was a hell of a punch.

I didn't even get to work up a sweat."

She sheepishly agreed, "Yeah, that might have been a little overkill."

* Levi *

He was as worried about keeping the armies together as much as Amy. Hell, a few hours ago they hadn't even known of their existence and their very lives remained because of them. It was a relatively new idea and problem trying to keep the

547

armies together. It was especially troublesome and difficult to concentrate when Mosley was dead set on kicking his butt. Even as he and Amy communicated, Mosley was charging him. Amy needed a reminder to pay attention to the immediate concerns of saving his ass.

Amy was concerned about trivial things like defeating Mosley in such a way as to save face for him, but she must not have given it enough thought, because his defense was a single full powered straight right hand into Mosley's face. Pow! It was right in the kisser, and he went out like a light, so much for diplomacy. He felt the impact all the way back to his shoulder. Amy had obviously reinforced his bone structure for that blow. He guessed maybe she did have time to think after all and wondered why she took this particular tact. He did, however, express his surprise to Amy, and they both found it humorous.

He was well beyond believing he had much control over the moves and tactics of his fights, knowing that Amy was the inspiration behind his movements. He did want to keep up the illusion, but did enjoy a good fight though and this was not much of one. One blow and it was over. What shocked him most was the surprise and awe that showed on those gathered. He was somewhat accustomed to seeing it from those of his own group, but those of the Southern Army seemed overly stunned at their leader's defeat. He tried to ignore the looks and spent his time trying to comfort Mosley. He had him loaded into a wagon and signaled the armies to continue east. There was no argument.

Moon was pleased with the results. His eyes were now completely normal for a calm Simian. Moon wasn't terribly concerned about keeping the armies together. His primary interest was more protective. Moon would never have allowed Mosley to take over under any circumstances. He felt Moon pat his back and seemed to actually smile at the outcome. Moon actually picked up Mosley's two front teeth commenting about them being added to Levi's trophy necklace. This struck him funny and sent him into hysterical laughter; which he tried to control. He and Amy were laughing together as they continued east.

It was a good thing that they had brought sheep and cattle, because there was nothing to be had for food along the way. The Simians had already packed off the few horses that had been killed in the battle, but that was not nearly enough. He wondered how long the food supply would last with both armies consuming them.

Amy said, "The Simian herders have more than enough. They brought them all."

What bothered him more was wondering what the pursuing Simian armies were eating.

Amy quickly said, "Levi we can't think about that right now. We have to concentrate on surviving ourselves right now."

She was right, of course, they couldn't save everyone, but he still remembered seeing Mr. Henderson ripped apart and eaten alive in their sight. So many humans had died at the Simian's hands, but Amy was right.

It was almost dark when they reached camp, but the campfires were going strong. Food was ready for all. It was not a balanced meal, but nourishing with lots of meat. He sent instructions for his army to mingle with the Southern army during the meal and evening. It was Amy's hope that the Southern army would learn more about the nature of the enemy and battles that had taken place. At least they would seem united in common goals and help with the necessary job of uniting the two armies.

* Amy *

Once they reached camp, the leadership group gathered for their evening meal. The group was becoming fairly large, but it was becoming a ritual that continued as it grew. It was instrumental in keeping communications together and goals focused. She asked Levi to send a runner to invite Mosley. Since he had no commanders he was the only source of communications from the Southern army. If they got past tonight she hoped to convince Mosley to establish some commanders. It would be devastating if something happened to Mosley. He would have to have functioning commanders just that they had no real authority. They could be identified in time, but time was a luxury they didn't have.

Mosley soon joined the group and Levi stood to greet him and extended his hand in greeting. Mosley appeared reluctant and confused but accepted Levi's hand. The grip was cordial this time. As they had planned, Levi acted as if nothing had happened and thanked Mosley openly for saving them. He spoke so all could hear, praising their action and making him and his army the heroes of the day. As he spoke, he made the hand signs for the Simians to follow explaining to Mosley what he was doing. Even the Simians nodded agreement. Levi made the introductions of those gathered to Mosley. Iron Eyes was introduced as the commander of the Owens Valley Army and Al as the commander of the Desert Settlement Army. Moon and Bambi were introduced as commanders of the Technical Simians and Fems respectively. All thanked and praised Mosley for his help. Even Moon was appreciative, though reluctantly. She hoped Mosley would see the sharing of command.

Mosely puffed up at the praise, but remained somewhat subdued and silent. He was not smiling and from time to time his tongue could be seen absentmindedly exploring the gap from his missing two front teeth and his swollen lips. She sought any indication from Mosley's mind, but detected neither hostility nor any friendship either. Levi invited Mosley to sit by his side so they could discuss the situation. The huge man took the offered seat as discussions among the group began for the upcoming next battle. Levi went into great detail, obviously for Mosley's benefit, since the others knew about the Supreme One's involvement and what awaited them. Mosley was all business now and listened intently as the narrative was delivered.

When Mosley heard the plan he stood, pain forgotten and bellowed, "You are all fucking crazy. You're going to get killed... all of you, but I am getting the hell out of here and head home."

Levi sensed her panic and said, "Hell, Amy, I would do the same if we had a choice."

Although Levi secretly agreed with Mosley, he continued with the argument saying, "You won't be safe there long if you leave. The Supreme One knows you and your army exist and when he finishes with us he will come after you. The Supreme One would never leave an organized army behind. Besides, we stand a better chance by sticking together."

Mosley countered by saying, "I don't disagree with the fact that we are better off together, but the route south is open. Why not head south and pick our own place to fight?"

Levi paused his argument to allow her to answer that one. She had no facts to substantiate, but her premonition screamed of danger to the south. It was too obvious. It was an open door, an invitation to a worse situation. The Mexico Simian Colony had been brought to fight. How many other Simian colonies might be in route or waiting?

As she communicated this to Levi, the look in his eyes narrowed.

Levi said, "Damn, Amy. When were you going to tell me this little tidbit of information?"

Just as sharp she snapped, "Well, it was never part of my plan to go south so why should we worry about it?"

Levi took out his anger on Mosley and said, "You stupid bastard, let me do the thinking! If you go south tomorrow you and your whole army will be dead within two days in another Simian trap. The Supreme One is everywhere and anywhere organizing his armies to kill us. That is an obvious trap!"

552

She marveled how Levi could stretch the truth even though it was probably true. That did sound convincing and Mosley was confused again, but made one final comment before he sat down. She shuddered when she heard.

Mosley said, "We don't have a damn chance if the Supreme One is that powerful. As long as the Supreme One can continue to operate freely like that, no plan will work."

Levi's next comment shocked her even more.

Levi said, "I will take care of the Supreme One tomorrow."

* Levi *

Mosley had no idea what he had gotten into, but he was quickly learning and he didn't like it. It was more than he had bargained for. He even agreed that Mosley was right. It did look hopeless, but they had little else to do but continue. Mosley was no longer the confident man that had ridden into battle today. He was afraid, possibly for the first time in his life, and looked it. He had beaten Mosley soundly, but that was not the fear he now saw. Mosley was afraid of the hopeless situation. He believed Mosley was secretly relieved that he was not in charge now, because he didn't know what to do. Hell, he didn't either, but he hoped Amy did.

One thing that must be done now was to set the Supreme One back and get him out of the battle. Mosley had been right on that point. When he said that he would take care of the Supreme One tomorrow, Amy went visibly white with shock in his vision. She had obviously planned every emotion into her holographic view. He was a little shocked at that visible reaction, but concentrated more on Amy's always intelligent verbal reaction.

Amy blurted, "What the fuck?"

Grinning, he responded saying, "Your language is becoming very colorful, Amy."

Amy responded by saying, "Fuck you, Levi."

He laughed out loud, startling those around him.

He sat back down and began to eat again, letting the conversation continue around him while he laid out his thoughts to Amy. He had been thinking about it since the bridge. When Amy had explained about soft and hard teleports he saw the potential for a powerful weapon and explained it to Amy. It could be a double edge sword by teleporting energy from one location to another in the so called hard teleport method. As Amy had described it, there would be an implosion at one end and an explosion at the other. It was simple. Do a teleport without being in it. Implode in the middle of the Simian army and explode at the Supreme One's location. It could possibly kill a lot of Simians and also the Supreme One. Amy's expression changed to one of deep concentration. He knew he triggered her to analyze the potential. He wasn't totally sure that it could be done, but in simple terms it seemed reasonable. He was positive that it was much more complicated than that, but he had successfully challenged Amy.

Al startled him back to the external world. Al was telling him that they were getting low on lances. Damn. Where were they going to get lances? All of a sudden, he remembered Amy telling him that she had sent communication through the facility computer to Mama to build more. When was that? Amy didn't respond and he didn't want to interrupt her calculations. No matter. They wouldn't need them for a couple of days and that should be enough time for Mama to complete the task. He would have to remind Amy when she returned from her internal mental concentration.

Amy's comment was short, "I am always here and it's being taken care of."

He noticed that Moon and Bambi were in a heated argument and listened more closely. They had dispensed with hand signs and were screeching at each other. The others had ceased talking and all were looking at Moon and Bambi. Moon apparently had been criticizing Bambi for the Fems joining in the attack and Bambi wasn't taking it. She was saying they were part of the "New Order" and had as much to lose as the rest and intended to fight for their rights too. Moon was about to counter when he screeched. It was not much of a screech since Amy had not modified his vocal cords, but it was enough to get their attention. He went on in sign language telling them to stop. He saw Moon's point. The Fems had not been part of the planning and they had acted independently and uncoordinated, which could have been disastrous. He explained that Moon was right, but it was his fault for not including the Fems in the planning and attack. He promised to include them in the future. That seemed to satisfy both, but the red eyes were still blazing at each other. He suspected it was more competitiveness between them or possibly the result of the relationship developing between them. They were constantly together of late and even now they remained together in spite of the argument. He smiled inwardly, but he was starting to miss Moon's close company. Oh well, Moon was still close and he had the constant annoying presence of the body guards too. He was never alone.

Tomorrow would be another busy day so he dismissed himself from the group and found a place to sleep. He would need the rest and he had been getting far too little. Even as he left, his entourage followed to bed down circling him. It bothered him but was learning to ignore them some.

* Amy *

She saw his plan even before he laid it out and it was a good one. It was, however, far more complicated than he presented it. For one thing the smooth teleport or hard, as Levi had called it, was for a reason. Levi's body was required to manipulate the transfer of energy and she was not sure if his body could handle the massive forces that would be required. Even if it could, she knew without calculating that they would not be able to do many without serious damage and major time for repair. A normal teleport took time to allow the flow of energy both ways, but in a sudden or hard teleport it was done instantly. That is what caused the implosion and explosion. It would require a long time to build up the forces and energy to affect the sudden teleport and require a sudden release of energies. On the plus side, she would not have to pull energy from the receiving side. This would be good because the Supreme One could probably detect the energy and be warned. This would require complex calculations to determine if it was possible.

Another problem Levi had not considered was this action would require a teleport from and to remote locations removed from Levi's physical location. She had never attempted this before. Always she had focused from one end or the other. Levi had mentioned the time they had teleported Fred directly to them. That was his justification and logic for the plan, but he failed to realize that they had been at the receiving end. This too would require extensive calculations to determine if it could be done. She was sure that it could, but not as easily as Levi made it sound. He always took a simplistic approach to her abilities. He simply didn't understand or was just pushing her to excel. It was probably the latter which made him a bigger shithead.

Another problem was that she didn't have an exact location for the Supreme One. She felt his power center, but she could only get close without having actually seen the location where he was to gain the coordinates.

She was quite sure there were many other problems associated with this new weapon and she would be at it for a while. She had lots to consider, and just look at the butt. He was sound asleep. With Levi asleep, she would have all night for her calculations so she began the repairs to his body. Levi had been good about taking the chemical pills so his body had reserves for her to work with to communicate to his cells.

She also sent communications to Mama to check on the status of the lances. Actually, she spoke to her through the voice communication of the facility this time. Mama was up and her crew was still working. Mama reported that many lances were already ready, but she needed another day to have the full supply. She was very pleased with Mama. As she was about to stop communication Mama reported that she was also working on something else and hopefully it would be ready when she came to get the lances. She was surprised and asked what it was.

Mama said, "I would rather show you after I run more tests. I'm not sure it will work until then."

She was actually smiling thinking about how Mama was thinking on her own. She was curious and loved it and was very pleased for sure. Knowing Mama, it would be good and probably worth the wait.

Everyone had taken Levi's lead and settled down for the night. She could smell and recognize the body guards, Moon, and Bambi. She did not detect Iron Eyes, Al or Mosley and assumed they had returned to their armies. All seemed to be in order so she returned to her internal thoughts.

Just before she returned to her calculations she thought she would attempt to try and locate the Supreme One and get a closer location. His presence was always somewhere lurking it seemed, though weak. She sought his location by narrowing her field of direction, opening her senses and mind, and homing in on his slight presence. She knew the approximate location, but not the exact location. Distance and bearing was becoming clearer and his presence was getting stronger. She found the Supreme One in Texas somewhere between Dallas and Ft. Worth. The coordinates were becoming more definitive.

Suddenly, she heard Him. He was laughing, almost sneering. His voice formed in her head, and he was hissing. It reminded her of a snake. His familiar mental power surged in her brain and she cringed from the sudden pain. She hadn't expected this and was unprepared for his attack. His power sought to again destroy her, but she did not freeze with fear like before and threw up her defensive blocks to prevent his attack. It was so sudden that his mental energy was boring into her, stronger this time. His power was growing. Slowly she narrowed the entrance and began to repulse his energy. She sensed that he saw he had failed and felt the evil, unrelenting hate. He was no longer laughing.

Satan screeched, "You dare to seek me. You will die Witch. I will destroy you. Even now you are being encircled by six thousand Warriors and within two days you, your pathetic runts and animals will be crushed between them. I can tell you now because there is nothing you can do about it and no way out. You will die!"

That was the last she heard as she successfully completed closing off the entrance to her mind, but the hiss lingered in her brain. She felt fear, but she had not frozen in panic as she had done before. She was determined not to let him panic her again.

Satan had actually revealed his plans and they confirmed that Simian armies were in deed south of them. She had been right, and what Levi told Mosley was correct. It was even more hopeless than before. Satan had also been right. There was nothing she could do about it.

559

* Levi *

He woke refreshed and hungry. Amy was quiet, so he left her to her thoughts while he sought out the cook wagon. It wasn't far and he had his fill, which was a lot. He noticed that the body guards were taking off one at a time to feed also. Everyone was ready and the migration had already begun toward the east.

He stood silent for a while and finally he blurted out in his mind, "Well, Amy can we do it?" Amy was smiling and he knew the answer, but he waited to hear it.

Amy said, "We are going to try, but it is going to be hard on you, Levi. I mean really painful. Do you still want to do it?"

"Hell, yes!" was his only reply. At her bidding, he called the Simian group together; the humans had all joined their armies. She had targeted the Simian armies grouped behind them at the pass. She said they were about one thousand strong and were probably grouped together and should be an easy target. Possibly, those numbers could be diminished if this plan worked.

Once they were together, he felt the familiar tingling of energy as his hair stood out and his vision became blurry. Soon the double images were superimposed then finally replaced with the vision at the new location. He felt the temperature change first. He didn't know how much the change was, but it was a few degrees colder. They were on the top of the mountain a few hundred feet higher in an open flat area as they materialized. Though cooler, it was still summer hot and Amy directed him to a comfortable location a few yards away in the shade of a boulder. It was surprisingly cooler in the shade as he leaned up against the cool stone. She wanted him very comfortable because, as she had warned him, it was going to be painful when she released the energy.

He told Moon, Bambi, and his body guard to stand well away from him and tried to explain what was going to happen, at least what he hoped was going to happen. He wasn't sure they understood, but they followed his directions anyway. They knew something important was going to happen and spread out to watch the view of the gathered Warriors below. Moon remained a little too close, according to Amy, and he had to ask him to move more saying, "Thanks, my friend, but you need to give me a little more room. It is for your protection. I will be fine." Moon nodded and moved back more.

He was directing his gaze at the massed Warriors below. There was a rolling sea of them congregating at the entrance of the pass. He wasn't sure, but he thought they might be massing for a rush at the pass. Maybe their timing was better than he had hoped. He sensed the Supreme One was again involved in the movements of the Warriors. This could be good too, knowing the Supreme One might be projecting his mind at this very moment. Amy nodded in agreement.

Almost immediately he felt the tingle of energy. Somehow it was different this time. The tingle did not build. He seemed to feel energy moving through him but not building around him. Amy was concentrating hard, and he didn't want to distract her so he remained quiet and tried to remain calm even though his body was becoming hot. Pressure built in two directions. The energy seemed to build outside his body flowing out of him. The pressure continued to build. It was beginning to feel like it had at the bottom of the mountain lake, like tons of water were pressing down on him. Pain from the pressure was increasing faster and faster. It was becoming unbearable, and just when he thought he could take no more it changed suddenly for the worse in the opposite direction. He screamed out as his body flared with the instantaneous release. The pressure was there one second and gone the next, making him feel like he was exploding. The pain was intense and he seemed to black out. It must have been only for a second, because he saw and heard the implosion. It was a loud pop and a circle of about two hundred feet in diameter appeared in the middle of the gathered Warriors. They seemed to suddenly compress to the center and disappear, leaving a dust cloud and empty space. It was incredible to see in spite of the pain surging through his body.

The last thing he remembered was screaming and falling over. He had no idea how long he was out, but when he did wake he was lying stretched out flat on the ground and a very concerned looking Moon hunched by his side rubbing water over his face. He felt like shit, but the pain was bearable. Amy was also looking concerned in his view monitor, but he knew she would not have gone beyond her ability to control and repair his body. He was weak and light headed and was content to just lay there. After a while he mustered up enough energy to say, "Damn, Amy!"

She was smiling now and said, "I told you it was going to be painful."

* Amy *

The calculations were complete. She had run various scenarios and had decided on exactly the right combinations of data. Levi's body was the determining and limiting factor and weakest link in the chain of events that must take place. Always before, the process of teleporting had been easy and smooth in comparison to what this would be. It was going to be painful, and Levi would have to make that decision, because he was the one that must endure it. He accepted his role as she knew he would. After all, it was his idea and he was selfless. Of course, she could quickly repair his body if she didn't destroy it beyond the point of no return. That was the basis upon which the calculations started. She would restructure Levi's body to be denser, in an effort to minimize the damage, but even then his body would, to a certain extent, try to explode with the release of the energy.

The site of the implode was an easy choice. It must be within the Simian ranks, and there were plenty within easy reach. Once Levi had eaten, it was time to begin. She teleported the group to a vantage point above the pass and prepared to do the hard teleport. This was the easy part. All she had to do was direct the energy for the short distance. The explosion end would be for a much longer distance and unobserved and un-confirmable. The coordinates were established for the Supreme One, but the blast would be approximate only due to her inability to visually verify and adjust.

She began the process by gathering energy all along the teleport route. It began slowly building for the eventual immediate release of the energy. The energy must be built as strongly as possible. The process she developed would build pressure constantly pressing on Levi as it increased. The pressure came because she was not swapping energy, only building to the maximum. Levi's body must match the pressure, but more importantly his body must be able to withstand the sudden release. As the pressure increased, she made Levi's body denser to counter the pressure and make it harder to pull his body apart with the release. It took a while to build the pressure on Levi's body to the point close to collapsing, but she managed to ready enormous energies. The twin coordinates were established, and when she was ready, fired the transfer. The stored energy sucked at the established point within the Simian ranks to be released at the directed target. As she observed, the sudden energy and matter attraction within the ranks of the Simians collapsed into a sudden implosion pulling everything within its grasp including several hundred Warriors. All matter within the target area was suddenly gone, leaving nothing behind. Whatever was picked up there was simultaneously deposited at the far end with equal but opposite force. She could only imagine the carnage as the matter was suddenly forced to combine and compete for space at the other end.

With the sudden release of the pressure and energy, Levi's body tried to explode, but she held his body compact to counter the release. Timing was important as she slowly allowed his body to expand and relax without exploding as she frantically repaired the damage. At some point, Levi mercifully blacked out from the pain. It was several minutes before he regained his senses. By that time, a very concerned Moon was tending to him.

After a few moments, Levi was able to sit up at her urging. She was anxious to see the Simian army down below and the results of the implosion. As it came into view, the circle of devastation was still empty. None of the Warriors had ventured into the area, and it appeared that they never would. As tight as the Warriors had been bunched, the teleport must have included three hundred or more Warriors. They would all be dead now. There was no question of that. The implosion alone would have turned them into unrecognizable mush, while the explosion at the other end would have blown the mass of bone and flesh over a vast area far exceeding the origination space.

The second thing she noticed was that the Warrs seemed disorganized and confused. They were leaderless and beginning to fight among themselves. At least it was obvious that the Supreme One was not present. She desperately wanted to know if the second part of the plan had been successful as well, but she was weak also from the ordeal and didn't want to risk another mental confrontation with the Supreme One in her weakened condition. If he remained alive, he would detect her searching.

* Levi *

He remembered it all. It had worked, but it took much more out of him than he would have imagined. He was tired and weak, but made the effort to explain to Moon and the others what had happened. Moon realized that Amy had done something through his body, but was concerned about him. He must look terrible, judging by the reaction of Moon and the others. He tried to reassure them, but probably did a poor job of it. All he wanted to do was rest, and that is exactly what he did. He rolled over and went to sleep.

He must have slept several hours, because the sun had moved past its zenith and the hot afternoon sun had found its way into his eyes. Amy was telling him that his body was repaired. He just winked and stood up and stretched. Moon and the others were instantly up and ready for whatever was required.

Amy said, "We have a day of rest. There is nothing we can do but travel, but we can teleport ahead to the interstate and wait for them if you want."

Those were welcome words. Even though his body was repaired, he felt mentally tired. That implosion had been an awesome weapon, but he knew they wouldn't be able to do that often. It was just too draining on him physically and mentally. He wondered what it did to Amy, because she looked tired.

Amy smiled and said, "Well I would welcome a day off too, and besides that I have been missing you."

The later she said with a twinkle in her eyes. He couldn't resist the tease and said, "Hmm, you must be horny." He saw her face scrunch up in a frown.

Amy said, "Shut up!"

He also saw the twinkle in her beautiful eyes remain. He was happy all of a sudden and couldn't keep the smile off his face.

As he gathered his pack and pickaxe, Moon, Bambi, and the others gathered their belonging. They didn't need much communication. Moon had learned his way long ago and moved to stand by him, ready for the teleport. In spite of himself, he was a little nervous thinking of the last teleport, but this one was smooth and they were soon standing on top of the Gillespie Dam. Amy explained that she had to get a little farther than she had intended because she didn't have stored coordinates any south. He was glad though. This area was more hospitable than the area the armies were traveling through. There was a small lake backed up against the dam and the air was cooler. This would be a nice place to spend the night. The only problem: he was getting hungry. Amy laughed at him and playfully called him a loser.

He signed to Moon telling him that they had time and would camp here and wait on the armies to arrive. He was beginning to wonder what they were going to eat, but noticed that, while the others gathered firewood for the chilly desert night, Moon produced the small throw net from his pack. "Way to go Moon," he signed. He was rewarded with a black toothed grin.

By the time the fire was going, Moon had a sizable pile of catfish. He picked three large ones, cleaned them and had them spiked over the fire in short order. Fish would taste good again tonight. It was too bad they didn't have more of a variety. Amy just laughed.

He walked around while the fish were cooking and found an orange tree growing in what appeared to be someone's back yard at one point. The metal fence post were still standing, but little remained of the house. At least he would have some dessert.

The rest of the evening was calming. He had his fill and they all talked about simple things: about their home world, what it was like, they even talked about the future like there would be one, and how the Technical Simians, Fems, and humans would coexist and prosper. He and Amy talked too, sharing thoughts and remembering happy times. They didn't discuss any problems nor talk about tomorrow and the problems that might arise. It was relaxing and very calming. He forgot about sex and slowly drifted off into a restful sleep.

* Satan *

He was feeling good about himself. His strength and abilities were increasing. The Bitch had forced him to grow and learn new abilities. The ability to take over minds was now easy and distance was becoming less of a problem. He was operating on many fronts now, closing in on the mind and her toy animal. The animal and runt armies were trapped. The combined armies of the west were moving toward Phoenix under his direct leadership. Each time the Bitch had killed his occupied body he had moved into another. The Warriors knew when he was there and were able to recognize him in any form. His increasing mental essence radiated out from the occupied body. He would issue commands and move on to the next location to occupy yet another leader. The Phoenix Colony was approaching the pass through which the enemy had fled, while the southern army closed in to attack from behind. Two other southern colonies were moving north also. As back up, he also had ten thousand en route from his complex. He had been forcing them to march at an accelerated pace to combine forces and converge on the enemy. They would have no chance. The enemy turned to drive directly toward the closest army. So his victory would come early.

He had learned to control his anger by directing his mind into the battles. Focusing thus, his anger was delivered to the army. They were more afraid of displeasing him than anything the enemy could deliver. This was no difference as he joined the southern army and took direct control of the battle. He had learned never to underestimate the Bitch. That mind was strong and planned well. She was also very lucky in discovering weakness and taking advantage of any opportunity. It was very personal, and it would be him against her, and he didn't care how many he lost to get to her or the animal she worked through.

The battle was joined and she was good at planning. Their defense held as the battle raged, but he saw the weakness and forced his army wide to disburse the riding warriors. Yes, they were collapsing. He had them now. It was just a matter of time, but suddenly out of nowhere another enemy army attacked from the rear and then his army was at the disadvantage. Damn her! His army was destroyed and he raged. He stood in the middle and screeched his defiance. Soon his humiliation was worsened when a female of his race sank her finger fangs into the body he occupied. He felt the pain of the poison and his screech of defiance turned to one of extreme agony. He fled the body and returned to his own body, screeching his renewed rage.

He had learned so well to project his mind that more was gone than remained, leaving his own body immobile while he was gone. When he returned fully, he launched out in rage. His body shook and his hate was out of control. There was little left to destroy within his personal compound, so he went into the open compound to find something to vent his anger on. He lashed out at the first Warrior he saw and ripped him to pieces, throwing arms and legs in all directions and taking some of the larger parts and tearing them apart, tossing them to the ground, and stomping on them. He was like a child having a temper tantrum.

The rage continued to burn, consuming him still. He looked around, but all the other Warriors, having seen this anger before, were running. He saw with frustration that he would not be able to grab another so he directed his mental rage toward a fleeing Warrior trying to capture his mind. Due to his extreme fury, the attempt went uncontrolled and what resulted was a blinding fireball of energy

570

shooting out from his head. It shocked him and he immediately calmed, watching the red fireball racing toward the fleeing Warrior. It struck the Warrior in the back, engulfing him in flame. Death was instantaneous and reducing it to a charred heap of black dust. He launched another and another with his will. After a few seconds he began smiling knowing that he had evolved again in strength and ability.

After he settled down he realized his energy was exhausted from the frenzy and power expended in the form of the fireballs. He was too tired to project himself to force the next engagement, so he decided it could wait until he rested. He sat and leaned against the closest structure so he could study the results of his new power and was soon sleeping.

It was morning when he finally awoke. The fireballs had drained his energy more than he thought. He remained where he was and projected his mind to the next closest army. He sought out the leader and took control of his body. The army at the pass had done nothing and he was angry. Screeches began to reverberate within the walls of the pass and Warriors were hopping from leg to leg in fear as they recognized him. He didn't care how many were killed and ordered an attack. As they gathered their strength to launch, sudden crushing pain gripped the body he was occupying. It lasted but a brief second before there was no longer a body to occupy. Simultaneously, his quarters exploded. As he watched, the structure he normally occupied disintegrated and he was pelted with rocks, dust, and something wet. As he wiped it away and looked he saw that it was body parts and blood. Something terrible had happened, and he felt the rage building again as he realized it was the Bitch. As the fury began to build his mind suddenly realized that he had been the target. Shock and fear replaced the building rage. He also realized that he was under attack, and it had almost worked. Had he not fell asleep outside his quarters the explosion would have killed him.

His immediate reaction was to run and distance himself from where he had been. He realized that the Bitch could find him and attack again. He would have to keep moving his location. This time the rage was building slower, and he was rational. The war had reached him personally and his strategy would need to be different now, but he was even more dedicated to killing the Witch. Fear settled into his mind, knowing he could die from these attacks from the Bitch Witch. Now he had to destroy her for his own defense.

CHAPTER 14
(NEW WEAPONS & HOPE)

* Amy *

Levi was sound asleep and safe for the moment, so she completed everything that could be done. Levi's body was repaired, details for the migration were worked out, and plans to retrieve the lances were scheduled for tomorrow. This was the time she normally became absorbed in Levi's dreams, but not tonight. She was overly worried about their future. She laughed to herself when she wondered, "What future?" Everything was hopeless. What possible chance of survival did they have? It was only a matter of time before they were crushed between unbelievable numbers of Warriors, yet she continued to lead them toward that certain death. The anger flared in her thinking, realizing how she was doing exactly what the Supreme One wanted and expected. They were puppets in his game.

This reminded her of the attack she launched on the Supreme One. She didn't have high hopes of killing him with the teleport explosion because of her random guess as to his exact coordinates, but she might have gotten lucky. Her curiosity compelled her finally to try and seek him out. Cautiously, she focused her attention toward the east searching to sense him. From her past mental contacts, she had learned to fear his ability to mentally attack her mind, so she went slowly. She was somewhat surprised that there was no detection of him. The search was narrowed and focused while she slowly removed the blocks protecting her mind. There was no sensing of his mind anywhere around the coordinates she had used for the attack. Could they have been lucky, and he was dead? She was allowing herself to get excited as she continued the search, widening the scan pattern. She almost missed it but there it was. There was disappointment initially that he was still alive, but the Supreme One was still there and still alive. He was quite some distance from where she had attacked, which was why she hadn't detected it earlier. He was also subdued and seemed weaker.

She felt the pure hate swell as her mind touched his, but it was masked with something else. Fear! It felt fear. Incredible! She didn't kill it, but they certainly had scared him. Her blocks slammed closed, but the expected mental attack from the Supreme One did not come. It was almost like he was trying to hide from her and remain invisible to her, but as the Supreme One realized he had been discovered, the rage exploded out. It screeched blasphemes and called her names she had no idea what they were. She did understand the meanings of Witch and Bitch and took joy in his verbal rampage. The joy came from the realization that the Supreme One was on the defensive. Suddenly, she realized that he believed she was capable of attacking him again. Even as she listened she detected a change indicating that the Supreme One was moving again.

He had no way of knowing just how difficult it had been to accomplish the original attack and that she wouldn't attack like that again. Levi's body could easily have been destroyed, and she would not take that risk again. The Supreme One could not know that yet. Without further attacks he would in time realize this, but right now they had a temporary advantage. He would be so busy trying to protect himself that she doubted if he would risk departing from his mind to take over another Simian mind. He would need his entire mind to detect her probing.

Without his direct leadership they still had no chance against the raw numbers of Warriors coming at them, but still, there was a temporary advantage to be had. What could she do with it?

* Levi *

He was instantly awake! This was unusual for him in several ways. Usually, when he woke he was grumpy and had always been slow to awake, taking long minutes to clear his mind and rouse his body. This morning he was fully aware and alert. Amy must have prepared him, but why? He sought her mind and found her extremely excited. Was this good or bad? He waited.

Amy said, "We are going home!"

She let him look into her mind and he saw the encounter with the Supreme One. Amy didn't have to explain it to him. He saw the advantage as well, but why did Amy want to go home?

Amy said, "I am just tired of being routed and controlled. We can change the game and just hope for an advantage."

She shocked him with her next statement or maybe it was a question.

Amy said soft and meek, "Levi." This was followed by a long pause. "I don't know what to do."

575

Oh, that ripped at his heart to hear her say that. He wanted to help her, maybe relieve some of the stress from her if he could. She was, after all, carrying the weight of the world on her shoulders, literally. The very fate of the human race, not to mention alien races, depended on her. So like a typical male he wanted to solve her problems, when he probably should just listen. Maybe he could do both.

He listened while Amy described the hopelessness of the situation. Amy explained how massive Simian armies were coming at them from all directions and there was nowhere to run. He didn't ask any questions, just acknowledged her appraisal of the situation. The only good thing that he heard was that the Supreme One seemed to be on the run and probably wouldn't get involved for a while. Yes, that was an advantage. He said, "Well, at least we did what we told Mosley we would do. We took the Supreme One out of the equation, at least for a while." He almost detected a smile.

After she stopped talking he said, "Amy, I love you. If we must die let's go out with a bang and together, but let's go out on our own terms, not the way the Supreme One wants. I agree. Let's go home... to your home. Let's try to get these friends back home then, Amy... ... let's take the Supreme One with us! Let's go kill him." Oh, that did it. Amy started smiling.

It was like the pressure all fell away from her. She now had an obtainable goal and she started planning and sharing.

The weakest link in the encircling armies was back the way they came. There was only one

Simian army back at the pass they just left, and it was now reduced by about four hundred Warriors from the implosion, riflemen and battle. This army was the only one standing between them and home, assuming the combined Simian armies continued east along Highway 10 trying to intercept them. The Simian army behind them should now be spread out in the valley they just left. If they timed it right they just might catch them by surprise since the Simians expected them to run. The Supreme One, in all likelihood, would not project himself into this battle for fear of being caught and attacked again. They just might have a chance in this battle.

Now he was getting excited. It was early and the sun was just rising, but he woke Moon and the others telling them, "Get up we have a battle to fight." There were no questions and they hurriedly readied themselves.

He began to stuff himself on the remainder of the cooked fish. There was no telling when he might be able to eat again. Moon and the others, seeing his intent began feasting on the remaining fish.

As he ate they sent the telepathic messages to Fred, Jimmy and Al preparing them for the coming battle. Soon they teleported to their armies and were met by the leadership, even an attentive Mosley.

* Amy *

The mountain of stress on her fell away. Levi had given her purpose again. They would take out the Supreme One. It was possible, maybe. Certainly they had more of a chance of doing that than they had against the Warrior armies rushing toward them from every direction. They would most likely die accomplishing it, but at least they would never give up and without the Supreme One the human and alien races might have a chance. Without the Supreme One holding the Warrior colonies together and directing the war against them, possibly their friends could find somewhere peaceful to hide and live. She remembered how the humans were living in peace on Coronado Island, because they were separated by water. Possibly other places like that could be found.

The immediate task right now was to engage the Phoenix army chasing them. They were lucky in that her army had spent the night at a very strategic location. Out of habit she had chosen a defensive location. The terrain was a series of small mountains jutting up out of the desert floor. Well, not really mountains, but more like hills of sharp, rocky points of sufficient size and position to force the Simians to funnel between them at a single place. The small mountains were also large enough to hide her army to either side of the rather large pass between them. She had her plan.

As they materialized at the army's location Levi was met by the leaders. Levi wasted no time in greeting. She had revealed the plan and as usual, timing was critical. Levi started issuing instructions. As was the case at the last engagement, Al's and Iron Eyes's Lancers would be working together on the north side and Mosley's Lancers on the south. The plan was simple. The Lancers would take position behind the small rocky hills and hide and wait. The Simians and humans would proceed some distance and serve as bait to draw the Warriors through. Once the Warriors passed the Lancer's hiding position they would attack from behind with a grazing charge along both sides. It was a good plan except for one thing.

Al was trying to interrupt, when Levi held his hand up and said, "I know Al. You are almost out of lances. Just get in position and I will deliver them to you." Levi then asked Mosley, "How are you fixed for lances?"

Mosley looked around in thought and said, "Maybe just enough. We weren't expecting to fight a war."

At first she thought Mosley was going to be difficult, but she scanned his mind and found no major hostility. That was just Mosley's style.

Levi instructed Al to cut out a couple of empty wagons and unhitch them. Al looked a little dubious but issued the orders. Levi wondered to her if she was sure she could teleport two wagons. She assured him that she could do it and gave him a big smile. In reality, it was a lot of mass and area to teleport. She would have to spread the sphere of energy wider and take a little more time to insure their safety, but it could be done. Mama had been notified and was standing by outside the massive doors to load the wagons with all the lances she had completed.

As was always the case, time was critical. They had previously dispatched Jimmy to the pass to monitor the approaching Simian army and she could see them nearing the pass and already compressing toward the pass. When she shared this with Levi he quickly dispatched the Lancers so they could be safely hidden before the Warriors got too close. The

579

Tech, Fems and humans were also hurriedly prodded on their way east. She didn't want them too far distance so the approaching Warrs would be focused on them and not exploring the surrounding area.

Suddenly, Levi and his small group were alone and they surrounded the two empty wagons waiting to teleport. How common this was becoming to be so complex. Oh well, there wasn't time to consider it now as she began the teleport, wagons and all.

* Levi *

He was all business as he met his leaders and immediately laid out the plan and instructions for battle. He was pleasantly surprised that Mosley accepted his instructions without resistance. In reality, he was a little surprised that Mosley was still there. Mosley must have believed him when he said Warrior armies were waiting south. Amy didn't know with absolute certainty, but it was sure a safe bet.

This was the exciting part when there were things to do and imminent battle. It was not so much that he wanted battle anymore. It was more that he did not have to deal with the mundane crap of organization and logistics of details. He was not that lucky as Amy reminded him that they were dangerously low on lances. Damn, without lances there would be no defense or battle. Already Al was trying to point out that fact. "Yeah, yeah, okay, Al." He saw that Amy already had a plan for that too and gave Al the instructions for producing two empty wagons.

580

Al gave him a weird look at that, which probably mirrored his own look of surprise as he realized Amy intended to teleport wagons to Mama's location. Strange that he thought of Amy's facility as Mama's. Thankfully, Al complied after only the brief look of shock. Al figured out quickly what was going to happen and jumped to the task.

With the approaching Warriors so close he slapped his hands together and barked, "Let's go, everyone! We don't have much time." They were gone in an instant to implement the plan.

Amy was ready, so he called his group close around the wagons and quickly felt the familiar tingle of energy. It felt stronger this time and seemed to take a little longer, but they were soon standing with the wagons outside the big steel doors of the facility. Mama was all business. Almost all the Greys were there and they were already holding arms full of lances, which they immediately began loading into the wagons. He was impressed. Mama always impressed him, but he wasn't about to let her know.

It only took minutes to complete the task and as the Greys backed away and the energy began the tingle he said, "Hey, Mama. Is this all the lances you made?" He enjoyed playing with her and was rewarded with deep red flashing eyes burning a hole through him. Immediately, Amy was laughing.

Amy said through her laughter, "Mama was ready for your jibe and communicated through the intercom system and asked me to give you a message. Mama said, "I have twice that many lances. Why didn't you bring more wagons?"

He felt his face flush with anger, but was soon laughing with Amy. Damn, Mama got him again.

They materialized behind the hill even ahead of Al and his Lancers. It was so smooth; the Lancers didn't even have to change direction. The progression just passed the wagons and lances were transferred to the smaller attack carts. Al was smiling at the efficiency of the restocking and gave him a look as if to say, "Why did I doubt you?"

He was a little concerned that the Supreme One might get curious and get involved before the battle started. He suggested to Amy that she might seek out the Supreme One again and keep him worried and moving. Amy thought that was a good idea and mumbled something about him being a devious bastard. Maybe so, but it should work to keep him out of the way and on the defensive. A little reinforcement couldn't hurt.

After a moment's thought Levi said, "Hell, I wish we could teleport him a grenade. That would really keep him running."

* Amy *

It was humorous to watch Levi and Mama insult each other. She could see that Levi actually liked Mama but insisted on always pushing her. It had been instant affection from a distance. It was probably because Mama was tough to deal with and also because she was so different than everyone else that seemed to almost worship him. Levi didn't like being worshiped. Mama was the only one he could meet on even terms. More surprising, she detected affection from Mama, too. These two truly liked

582

each other, but would never let the other know. When Levi, the shit, threw out the insult as they left, Mama was so quick to get back at him that it was apparent that Mama was prepared for it. Mama had the intercom connected to her computer voice interface and was ready. It didn't matter what was said, it was the way it was presented through her. Even with the stress of pending battle she found it extremely comical, especially with Levi's reaction. It was good for him to get some humbling disrespect.

After Levi calmed down from his comical reaction to Mama, he refocused on the problem at hand. He was deep in thought for a while then suggested that she seek out the Supreme One to keep him on the defensive. She wondered why she hadn't thought of it. It was a great idea if for no other reason than to ensure the Supreme One did not directly get involved in the leadership of the army. She hadn't really considered the fear factor it would invoke. The Supreme One and fear hadn't been words used together in the past.

She let her mind reach out. He would, of course, be trying to hide after the last attack and contact, but he was especially tricky. As her mind scanned the area of her last contact, nothing was detected. Her scan, as before, began to widen and canvas the area in the direction he had been moving. Nothing! Hmm, the Supreme One would be tricky and she wondered to herself what the least likely direction he would have gone. She knew instantly and turned her scan back to the main complex. He would assume that she would continue searching in the direction he was last detected. Yes, there he was. He was a few miles on the other side of his original location and trying to keep a very low mental activity. He detected her instantly and his abhorrence exploded out in a burst as if he had been holding it in and her contact was the needle prick on the balloon. The pure hate flared, but she was ready and he had no effect on her. His energy was expanding in all direction so it wasn't an attack directed at her, but more of a release of tension. Again, he was cursing her, but at the same time she detected he was moving again. He would be distracted for some time. It was safe to launch the attack, but Bambi interrupted her thoughts.

Bambi said, "You promised that the Fems could fight, but again we are excluded from the battle."

Levi was looking into her mind and reminded her, "Well, we did promise."

The Fems were not trained nor did they have weapons. Well they did have the poison fangs, but what good would they do against swords. She knew she would have to give them some role and there were several hundred of them now. She needed a plan, and it came to her instantly. It was so simple, and it would work, too.

Levi was wide-eyed when she shared the plan. Oh, he liked it, but it would take some explaining as to how it would have to be implemented. He actually sat down on the ground and motioned for Bambi to join him then began to share the plan with Bambi and Moon. They sat for a long time as Levi went into great detail as to exactly how the Fems' involvement would have to work to be successful. Even Moon was giving a toothy grin.

* Levi *

Amy was not receptive to allowing the Fems going into battle, but they had promised Bambi and the Fems. Amy was going off about there being no weapons, but he reminded her that there had been weapons laying all over the battlefield from the last engagement and the Fems had picked them up. Amy's look was a combination of frustration and exasperation.

Amy said, "That may be so, but they have not been trained and don't have a chance against a Warrior."

He was about to comment when he noticed her deep in thought and saw a sudden smile spread across her pretty face. Oh yeah, she had something. As he saw the developing plan he was totally amazed at her strategy. She was now waging a battle of brains. This battle suddenly switched from open confrontation to subversion and trickery. It was brilliant.

This would take some explaining as he sat with Bambi and Moon to go over the plan. It must be executed with precision, but both Bambi and Moon saw the brilliance of the plan. When he was sure they understood the concept, timing, and illusion that must be accomplished, he smiled and let them go to their armies.

After Bambi and Moon had left, they contacted Al, Fred, and Jimmy informing them of the change. They were to wait to attack until given the word. A premature attack would destroy the illusion and surprise of the plan.

Everything and everyone was falling into place. The chessboard and pieces were set up, so now they waited for the Warrs to make the next move. Amy wanted to teleport to a high position. That sounded good to him and they were soon standing on one of the numerous hills looking down at the battlefield. It was always exciting watching one of Amy's plans being executed.

He watched the Warrs pouring through the gap onto the battlefield. The Warrs could clearly see the human army and migration in the distance moving away. Closer, however, the Fems were clearly seen being surrounded and herded by the Techs. The Fems were obviously resisting the Techs and trying to escape around and through the Techs. Some were succeeding in escaping and fleeing back toward the Warriors. The Techs appeared to be slowed by the resisting Fems, which drew the Warriors toward them even faster, tasting victory. As the Warrs closed, the Techs appeared to abandon the Fems and ran. The Fems apparently from observation were seizing their opportunity to escape, running toward the Warrs and passing into the Warriors' ranks for protection. Soon, the Fems were distributed throughout the Army. When Amy gave him the word he let out a loud screech echoing over the combatants. This was the signal coordinating the Fems to attack the Warriors.

The Fems attacked in unison on as many Warrs as they could reach. They were without mercy and most of the Warrs never realized what happened. The battlefield was covered with kicking and thrashing Warrs dying in agony. Those Warrs that were missed in the initial attack bolted in horror and ran back toward the pass, but the Lancers were there already charging them. The battle was over very quickly. It was beautiful to behold.

He watched the Lancers run down the escaping Warriors when he noticed movement among the Fems. He squinted his eyes trying to see more clearly. To his amazement the Fems were bent over apparently digging out black Warrior teeth. Damn, he couldn't believe his eyes. Everyone was getting into the act of wearing trophy teeth.

* Amy *

The plan was simple, but there would have to be some acting. It was necessary to stage a scene for the Warrs, but it wasn't that difficult to stage. When the Warrs came through the pass, they would see several things to focus their attention on. The human targets would be seen in the distance, which would be their primary target. The second thing they would see would be the Tech and Fems. It must look like the Fems were being forced to go with them. Without the Supreme One, this army would have no way of knowing otherwise. The Warrs would justifiably think the resistance and struggle the Fems were putting up was the reason the Techs were so far behind. It should also spur the Warrs on faster to seize the opportunity to attack the Techs.

The plan was working to perfection, and the Warrs recklessly charged. She didn't want a solid wave of Fems running back, so she had planned a continual escape flow of the Fems. They were running back in small groups looking pleased to be rescued and seeking the protection of the Warriors. The Fems had been told to move into the Warrs' ranks and go as far back as possible. So, by the time the Techs broke off running, most of the Fems had escaped and were running back towards the Warrs.

The Warriors did exactly as expected. They were mean, vicious, and deadly, but they were also predictable. The Warrs were puffed up in pride at being the Fems' saviors and welcomed the gratitude the Fems were giving as they mingled into the herd of Warriors. Once all the Fems were within the ranks, Levi screeched out the signal. Almost as one the Fems found their targets. It was such a shock that most of the Fems had a chance to claw more than one Warrior. The Warrs realized their mistake and tried to run, but to get out of the pack they had to pass by other Fems. Few except those in the back escaped the attack and fled back toward the pass, but the Lancers had been approaching from their hiding place and met the disorganized fleeing Warrs. It was a head on charge and the Warrs were so afraid of a rear attack from the Fems that they continued to run directly into the lances. The whole battle was over in minutes with no casualties at all on their side and total destruction of the Simian army. She was elated with the outcome.

Bambi had personally led her army of Fems. Amy had seen her in the foray personally killing two Warriors and now she saw her taking her trophy teeth. The other Fems were quick to emulate her. Levi was shocked, but it actually made sense. The Fems were part of them now and were entitled to their reward. They would stand as equals now, and rightfully so.

Jimmy had been sent with the Infantry as a monitor, and now they sent him communication notifying them of the total success of the battle. They also told Jimmy to turn the migration around and head back toward the pass. Now they were going home.

* Levi *

Jimmy was very happy with the outcome and was blaring and signing at the same time to everyone telling them of the great victory. The armies were jubilant and cheering. They didn't have to be told to return. They were already turning, anxious to see the results. There hadn't been a lot of time to explain the plan to the armies, so some of them were just now learning of the change in plans and sudden victory. It really was a surprising victory to everyone, even him, and he was part of the plan. It had been so easy, but then they had Amy to plan. He knew Amy saw his thoughts, but she made no response. Her mind was deep in thought. He said, "What's wrong?"

Amy gave a nervous smile and said, "We outsmarted ourselves. We blew up all the damn bridges." In spite of the hopelessness of the situation, she grinned.

Damn, she was right! The only bridges over the river were further south or way to the north. Levi said, "So what are we going to do?"

Amy said, "Nothing has changed. We are going home. It is the only direction we can go. We will just have to make that SOB ASONE save us again."

He laughed out loud and said, "Sounds like a plan." He looked around, but no one had heard him. Good thing, they would think him crazy.

As they teleported down into the battlefield, Bambi approached them. Bambi had that Simian smile on her ugly face as she swaggered toward him with those broad hips. She was pleased with her Fems, and she had a right to be. Moon was also approaching quickly, and when he saw Bambi, he looked relieved. Neither he nor Moon had liked the idea of Bambi leading the Fems into battle, but Bambi had not given anyone a chance to stop her and no one tried. It would have been useless.

Moon was praising Bambi and the Fems and this time Bambi accepted his praise and attention. Moon even uncharacteristically embraced her. What was more surprising was Bambi let him... how interesting. He and Amy looked at each other and smiled. Something was developing between them.

He looked across the battlefield and noticed that Al had already ordered the swords picked up. Also, all the separate armies and groups were falling into the proper marching order. They were all starting to operate without having to be instructed on every point. Things were getting better, but he spoke too soon as the leadership was converging on him. Even Mosley had given up all pretense of resisting his authority. They all stood there waiting for instructions.

Amy had nothing more to say. She was actually off in her own world listening to music and reading poetry. So in lieu of other instructions, he just informed them that nothing had changed. They were going west and home. They understood the

590

unspoken meaning. If they were going to die, then they wanted to die at home.

Mosley asked, "What about me and my army?"

He understood what Mosley meant, home to him was south. He said, "Mosley we want to thank you and your army. We would already be dead now without your help, but going south is impossible for you right now. There are Simian armies south. I think you need to stay with us until we get over the river then you can head home. I will show you where to cross back over behind them if necessary." Mosley nodded understanding. He knew the Simians would come after him next. It was just a matter of time, but they had families. Levi understood his desires for him and his army.

Without input from Amy, he issued the orders sending everyone back the way they had come. He told them they must move fast to get back past the Hwy 10 and any potential of being intercepted by the combined Simian armies following that route.

As Al and Iron Eyes were about to leave they paused and looked at each other and came closer. He was shocked when they both put their hands on his shoulders and told him thanks. They explained that there had been no hope before they met him and Amy and now they had been able to fight back and even win some incredible victories. Their lives had meant something and wanted to thank him and Amy. They said they would not have had it any other way and if they died now their lives would have had purpose. It was all he could do to keep from bursting out in tears with the emotions that swelled within him. All he could do was nod and embrace them and say, "Thanks." As they were walking away he heard Mosley ask them who Amy was. Oh well, it didn't matter anymore.

* Amy *

Her self-contained mental capacity was virtually unlimited and now with the addition of the electronic computers and storage capacity interconnected into her physical brain, her capacity was truly infinite. With all this capacity she was still unable to save these wonderful people and aliens.

She had been rereading the stored literature of the ages in the outside storage computers. She had reviewed them before, but now with her new knowledge of emotions, she saw them with a completely different understanding. She now knew the joys of beauty, smells, tastes, sounds, pride, bravery, friendship and, yes, love. Also there was the negative side of emotions such as worry, anxiety, fear, hate and now hopelessness. She had experienced them all and could now more greatly appreciate the recorded words of the masters of the ages. They had captured thoughts, feelings and emotions that she had previously not recognized and was now experiencing.

She was listening to Mozart, Tchaikovsky, Bach, Beethoven, and many others just for the pure joy of listening. Her preference gravitated to the more complex music with its many facets and octave levels of interlacing and complex pitches, tones, and instruments. Rap was not to her liking, seemingly having no purpose or music content, but some country music touched her emotions. She was finding philosophers such as Plato and Socrates

592

profound. Paintings of Rembrandt, Renoir, Da Vinci, and many of the old masters were now incredibly beautiful. But, it was hard to interpret or understand any of the abstract works of Picasso. That bothered her. Abstract thought and obviously art still escaped her understanding. Poetry, with its rhythm and meter, was enjoyable and she was finding it pleasurable and gratifying. She found herself experiencing laughter, tears, sorrow, excitement, joy, pride, and love.

When she heard Iron Eyes and Al express their thanks she shared Levi's soaring emotions. She was experiencing many of these emotions now as she realized that their armies would not hesitate to charge and fight against overwhelming odds, even unto death. It made her think of a poem by Alfred Lord Tennyson, "The Charge of the Light Brigade." She now shared an edited version with Levi.

The Charge of the Light Brigade
By
(Alfred Lord Tennison)
Their's not to make reply
Their's not to reason why,
Their's but to do and die:
Into the valley of Death
Rode the six hundred,
Boldly they rode and well,
Into the jaws of Death,
Into the mouth of Hell
Rode the six hundred.
While horse and hero fell,
They that had fought so well
Came thro' the jaws of Death,
Back from the mouth of Hell,

All that was left of them,
Left of the six hundred.
When can their glory fade?
O the wild charge they made!
All the world wonder'd.
Honour the charge they made!
Honour the Light Brigade,
Noble six hundred!

Their armies would make such a charge if asked to do so. They would not question and they would do and die just like the poem said. She was so proud of them. Her only thought was that if they failed there would be no glory to be remembered. There would be no one left to remember the glory and honor of these brave men, women, and loyal Simians. All would be destroyed.

Levi shared these thoughts with her and the macho shit actually wept in silence. Why do men try to hide their emotions?

His body shook with the silent sobs, but managed to say, "Shut up!"

She did just that since she felt much the same way.

* Levi *

He was also wondering why men were embarrassed to cry. He had been raised that way. It was the Indian way not to show emotions, which somehow made you less of a man. Men were supposed to be strong. Amy knew his every thought, so it was useless to try to hide it from her, but old habits made him who he is. She knew how he felt, but he still didn't want to admit it so he

594

responded the only way he could by telling her, "Shut up!" The humor was not lost on her.

He suddenly asked, "Amy, do you love these people as much as I do?" She was quickly searching his mind, but he had blocked his thoughts.

She thought for a moment and said, "Yes, Levi. I love these people. Why do you ask?"

He ignored her question and asked, "Amy, do you love me?"

Her expression was of shock and said, "Of course I love you, Levi. I love you with all my heart. Why do you ask?"

He realized that Amy was at her weakest moment emotionally, and this was his best chance to do what he wanted to do. He swallowed hard and plunged forward blurting out, "Because if I die, I want you to live on for both of us and help these people." It would be hard for her to say no. It wasn't fair to her, but she had the ability to live on through her facility and be able to communicate through the computers and # 5 and Mama. She would still be able to help their friends in many ways should he die.

He had been thinking a lot about it since they made their pact to die together and try to take the Supreme One out with them. He didn't want to die, but after all he had lived a long life and it was a fairly sure bet that the Supreme One would try to kill him when they met, even at the cost of his life. The Supreme One was over twice as tall as he was and many times his weight. Even ASONE might not be able to defeat it, but if the Supreme One managed to kill ASONE, Levi's body would die, but Amy could most probably survive. She would wake up back in her facility. Amy would not want to live if he died. He knew that, and she could easily end her own life in the now active facility. It was unfair to ask, but he did ask.

Amy burst into tears and said, "Damn you, Levi!"

After a moment he softened and smiled then said, "We have come through a lot so far and maybe we can again, but promise me you will live on if I die. Please, Amy, for these that we love."

Amy continued to weep but managed to sob out, "I promise."

Amy withdrew her mind in silence and disappeared. He knew she needed time to think and get control of her emotions, but he had accomplished what he hoped to do.

With Amy alive, the human race and alien friends stood a better chance of surviving, assuming they were able to kill the Supreme One. As long as it was alive there was no doubt that he would never stop his attacks. Without the Supreme One the Simian colonies would soon lose interest in destroying them and revert back to life in their own colony area. Of course, they would still feed on humans, but California and Arizona were now mostly clear of Simians Warrior colonies and would make an excellent base of operation from which to grow. Amy's facility could be the center and controlling base of the future and she could provide the leadership necessary to continue the fight. It could all work if Amy was alive.

* Amy *

Damn Levi. He knew how to work her and manipulate her, and he wasn't playing fair. He used her love for him to make her promise to live on. Oh well, she didn't always play fair either, like now. She had no intention of losing Levi. She had a secret and a surprise and it was almost time to tell him, but she wanted to use her advantage to accomplish what she needed to do and that was clean up lots of loose ends. She spent her quiet time planning and organizing.

She had a plan. The most important thing to accomplish right now was to get their armies on the other side of the river and the quickest way was to cross the remaining bridge south at Yuma. The only problem was that her clairvoyance told her there was another Simian army approaching from that direction, but what she had just learned from Mama would, hopefully, solve this problem. She had felt hopeless just minutes ago and now she was full of hope and planning.

She broke her silence to ask Levi to send a message to Jimmy to take an advanced scouting party south to monitor in that direction. Levi, as she had hoped was only too anxious to comply. He was pleased to see business as usual, and Jimmy was pleased to comply.

The migration was mostly through the pass and she issued instruction to have them turn south. She believed the combined Simian army that had chased them across California would still be headed east along Interstate 10 trying to cut them off, and it would take them a few days to realize what had happened unless the Supreme One dared to intervene. The Supreme One would get brave again once he realized she wasn't attacking again. His rage would soon win over his caution and quickly resume his relentless attacks. She hoped they could retreat back across the river before that happened.

Levi was curious and searching her mind, but hadn't questioned her yet. This was good. She asked Levi to call Mosley, Fred, Moon and Bambi for a plan she was laying out for them. On second thought, all the leaders should be there to hear the plan. Everyone needed hope.

She wanted Moon and Bambi out of danger for what she had in mind next, but this plan would require them anyway. There were two Simian colonies from which they had destroyed the Warriors and the humans, Techs and Fems needed to be liberated from those colonies. The Fems had done such an exceptional job in the last attack that she intended to teleport a Fem of Bambi's choice into the Phoenix complex to recruit the Fems for an internal attack on the remaining Simian guards. She would have to trust this to happen because she had no way of monitoring. The liberated group would then have to find their way to Yuma to join up with the rest.

Unfortunately, she did not have any coordinates for the Simian colony close to Mosley's area. Her intent was to send Fred, Moon and Bambi with Mosley when he headed home and let them infiltrate the group and recruit the Fems and Techs for an internal attack there as well. This operation would be much more complicated because she was unable to teleport directly into the Fems. If things went wrong Moon and Mosley's army would be there to take the Warriors out. Mosley's army would have them vastly outnumbered and could kill them if he could lure them into the open. Hopefully, that would not be necessary. Fred would be there to translate and monitor the situation.

After the Fems and Techs were liberated, Mosley could take any saved humans with him and the Fems and Techs would return with Moon, Bambi, and Fred to join up with the others at Yuma.

While this was going on, her plan involved forcing a retreat of the pursuing Simian armies, then taking the battle to the Supreme One. The Supreme One must die, or all this was in vain.

* Levi *

He was feeling very optimistic with Amy's new confidence and attitude. She had emerged from her silence totally charged. He saw and listened to her plan with great interest and complied quickly.

He quickly dispatched Jimmy to the south and gathered the leaders. Amy had not shared all her plan yet, but he informed everyone of all the details Amy had laid out. He did not even try to present the plan as his this time. He openly referred to the plan as Amy's plan now. There were a few questioning looks, but mostly he realized that everyone now knew who Amy was. It was such a relief not to have to fool them anymore, and he was so proud of Amy. They listened and nodded their approval as hope soared through the group.

Everyone knew their responsibilities, and Bambi was quickly off to find her volunteer. Amy said they would wait until she teleported Bambi's choice of Fem into the Phoenix colony then they

599

would go to her facility. He was anxious and kept asking to know what surprise Mama had come up with.

Amy just smiled and said, "You will have to hear it directly from Mama. I promised Mama that she could tell you so she could rub it in a little."

"Damn!" He had no doubt Mama would do just that and almost shuddered at how Mama would make him eat crow, but her idea had better be good. Amy was smiling and laughing, realizing the same thing. Oh well, he had asked for it.

It had been another busy and long day, and he was hungry. His sense of smell was excellent, and it wasn't long before he found food in a passing wagon. He walked along beside the wagon eating his fill and didn't care that it was cold and tasteless. He noticed smiles and even some of the women found more for him. All the time the wagons and procession continued south.

Soon he saw Bambi and another Fem approaching and stopped and waited. Bambi was happy and introduced her volunteer. As always the Simian names were complicated. When he asked what it meant Bambi tried to explain that it was an animal from their planet. It was orange and jumped instead of walked. He held his hand up and pointed to the new volunteer and said, "I will call her Jumper." Bambi grinned, knowing his habit of renaming those around him. Bambi explained to the Fem that it was a sign of respect, which made her beam with pleasure. Bambi continued to explain that Jumper understood the plan, was very persuasive, and very appreciative for the opportunity. His only comment was to say, "I think

Jumper should hide her two Simian teeth before we send her." It was said with respect and a smile, but Jumper was quick to realize that was good advice. They all smiled then. She removed her tooth necklace and said she was ready. She was taking a big chance, and he loved her for it.

He gave her a big hug, then stepped back and watched the shimmering air take her away. All they could do was hope for the best now. The commitment was made.

Amy said it was time to go to her facility. He had mixed emotions. He was anxious to find out what Mama had come up with, but knew she was going to rub it in, a lot. Moon, Bambi and his bodyguards wanted to go. There was no real need for his safety there, but he liked their company and soon they would be off on their own missions. He motioned them to him and waited as Amy began the transfer. Soon they were standing inside the massive open area just inside the main doors. He was immediately shocked. No longer was it a dark and depressive tomb. Inside was bright and clean. Of course, it would have to be bright, considering how it was necessary to alter the environment back. He had just kept the old image of his last visit.

Everywhere was a beehive of activity. Incredible! Everything was working. A fork lift was stacking crates off to one side and noise from a hundred activities was echoing in the facility.

Amy suggested that they go below and as he started walking toward the stairs she changed his direction toward the elevators. Well, damn! He had to admit this was totally unexpected. It was like it was before the invasion with complete technology.

The only difference, there were no humans. It was all Fems, Greys actually. Still in shock, he entered the elevator and pushed sub-level 10 as Amy suggested.

As the doors shut, silence again greeted him. He felt the long ago familiar and unaccustomed sinking in his stomach as the elevator dropped beneath his feet. He felt his stomach sink again as the elevator stopped and the doors opened on the 10th floor. His shock continued as he stepped out into a sanitary white, well-lit corridor. Amy led him down to the left toward the center circular internal structure, which he remembered was where Amy resided. He opened the double doors and saw Amy as if for the first time. The center of the circular white structure was Amy, a brilliantly shining, silver, circular dome ten feet in diameter and standing five feet tall in the center. He remembered that Amy's brain was four feet in diameter surrounded by three feet of solid lead. Off to the side, looking somewhat out of place, stood a square metal desk with the Simian computer setting on top. His attention immediately turned to # 5 sitting at the desk working his big fingers over the glass dome of the computer. Wow, so much had been happening outside that he had forgotten about the facility and what must be going on here. This was Amy's other life.

He screeched, "Hey, # 5. How's it going?" The Tech was instantly up and embracing him. Ouch! He was obviously healed from his wounds and very glad to see him. They signed together for quite some time, but # 5 became quiet as someone entered behind him. It could be none other than Mama.

He turned to see Mama standing behind him. He grinned in spite of himself and gave her a big hug. He hoped it would put Mama off her obvious intent to put him in his place, but that was not to be. Amy was just smiling enjoying his discomfort. He took the time to call her a "Shithead." That only made her smile bigger.

Mama said, "I am glad you are here. I am going to save your sorry butt again."

He laughed out loud and said, "How are you going to do that?"

Mama said, "We have developed a portable self-contained environmentally altered laser that we can take outside of the facility to kill our enemies the Warrs."

He wasn't quite sure, but he thought his jaw dropped to the floor and he said nothing, letting that sink in. Finally he offered an intelligent response, "No shit!" As soon as he said it he regretted it, because Mama was beaming from his reaction. Oh well, if it was so she deserved her moment in the spotlight.

His mind was racing with the implications. He remembered the devastation the door lasers had spewed forth at the attacking Warriors. It had been total and absolute destruction, and if they had the ability to take this power outside the facility to the Simian armies, it would definitely change the balance of power. His response increased in IQ when he said, "WOW!" He wanted to know all about it.

Mama enjoyed the attention and praise and began to elaborate on the details. She said she got the idea when the lances had to be cut and prepared, and he had given them little time to do it. Amy had used the door laser to cut limbs within reach of the laser, and she had realized that the work would go much faster if they had a portable laser to take into the forest. They had begun work on developing a portable laser then. They had, in fact, built a very clumsy, awkward portable laser, which they used to make the lances, but it took some time to re-engineer a functional laser. The laser itself was fairly small, but they had to build an enclosed altered environment around it, which took quite a bit of space. A portable generator, storage batteries, and an enclosed lighting system had to be built. She motioned him to follow her into the workshop, which he quickly did. He was like a puppy following the food. He no longer cared that he was doting over her and her invention. He had to see it.

Amy was as curious as he was. Mama had done this independently of Amy, and she was very proud of Mama. Amy was observing everything, but realized she was pouring over the design. His assumption was that it would be efficient and would do the trick.

He was shocked again when he actually saw the unit. Damn, it was huge. No human could use this. It was made for a Simian, and a strong one at that. It was designed to fit over the shoulders and balanced over the front and down the back going down to the waist. It must weigh over three hundred pounds. The Fem he had affectionately named Sparks was there and demonstrated how it worked. Sparks stood up through the head opening lifting the unit on her shoulders. The actual laser was enclosed in the right oversized sleeve and designed to swiveled from side to side and up and down. Amy said the design was very good, but he was becoming skeptical.

* Amy *

She was enjoying Levi's discomfort under Mama's obvious pride in her accomplishment. As Sparks demonstrated the unit and Mama continued to explain the unit, she was pouring over the designs. It was, in fact, quite impressive. The inside of the totally enclosed unit was coated with a very reflective material that would reflect and redirect the modified light throughout the inside to insure the altered environment was maintained. The outside was made of a moldable plastic like material that must have been from a Simian formula, but it was dense and reflective in both directions. It functioned to repel bombardment from outside as well as reflect internally. She truly was impressed. She vowed to return to her research of Simian technology as soon as possible.

Levi rightfully noticed that only a Simian could carry and use the portable laser, and Sparks apparently had volunteered for the position since she was the one demonstrating its use. I guess Levi now had another member to his group. They had only completed one so far, but one was all they needed. So, there would only be one Fem added. The thought of another member of his team brought a frown from Levi, but no comment. Levi believed his entourage was already too big.

Amy read his thoughts and concerns and explained that part of the designed body armor enclosure included chambers that held the propane fuel. The obvious disadvantage was the power source, which would have to run continuously outside of the facility. There was enough fuel to keep it running for about eight hours, but extra propane tanks could be carried outside the unit. She calculated that the energy drain of the laser would be the major limiting factor. According to her calculations it could be used continuously for only a minute before it required recharging, but the laser could be used in short bursts to extend the life of the laser blasts. The exact timing would require detailed calculations once she had all the information, but it was an extremely formidable weapon they could use.

Levi was smiling like a kid with a new toy and actually so was she. They were very pleased with Mama and her team. Levi swallowed his pride and thanked Mama, but on second thought he got a sly grin and said, "Why did it take you so long; we could have used it sooner?" She cringed knowing the bickering between them would never end. Honestly, it was fun for them and both must look forward to the next confrontation. Mama ignored his question, but she knew Mama's insult would be returned in kind and probably even more insulting. She laughed. Moon and Bambi were enjoying the verbal bantering, but stayed out of the conversation.

She told Levi that they would stay here tonight in the resident quarters and he could actually shower and sleep under clean sheets tonight. It had been over fifty years since he had slept in a bed and was smiling at the prospect. He would, however, have to cook his own meal in the cafeteria. Levi even liked that idea. This was a completely different world; modern, clean, and comfortable.

It was getting late, but there were two additional matters that needed to be taken care of. She asked Levi to help her download additional information into Mama.

Levi quickly grinned and said, "Hey, Mama. Amy wants to download more information into your head. I guess you're not smart enough."

Mama hiccupped a laugh and said, "No, I think you are not healthy enough. Amy wants me to research your DNA."

That got his attention. He looked into her mind, but she was just grinning. She then added, "I want to try and stabilize your mutation so we can have a son." His mind shut down, but she could see a smile on his face. She had hoped he would like the idea, and he obviously did. Levi hated needles, but she didn't think he would put up a fuss now when she told him she needed blood for the research. He just nodded and held the grin.

She had been thinking about this for some time, but until her facility was fully operational she did not have the means. Now she did and he was here and available, so this was as good a time as any. To accomplish the research she needed hands and fingers to do the tedious physical labor required. This is where Mama came in. Mama could do the work and she could supervise, look over her shoulder as it were.

Levi asked her out loud and smiling, "Do I have to TOUCH Mama?" Again, everyone was laughing.

Quickly, Mama shot back, "Hey little human, remember that I get to take your blood. I can think of many ways to do it."

The laughter was becoming hysterical now, and Moon and Sparks were shaking with their hiccups. Levi was also grinning as he placed his hands on Mama's head. She had prepared many levels of information to download. All the research on DNA and the new knowledge she developed through the years of isolation were downloaded, along with her stores of medical knowledge. It was a good investment in Mama. Mama had demonstrated that she could think on her own and would be a welcome assistant. After a few moments Mama's eyes opened wide in understanding.

After a few moments of enjoying the new information, Mama turned and left down the hall mumbling something about it being her turn. She soon returned with a large glass vile and syringe. Levi lost his grin immediately but submitted to Mama's directions. The big chicken had to look away as Mama drew his blood for storage. It would have to be divided up into small samples and quickly frozen for the many future tests. Mama was off to her tasks and it was time for a quick meal and bed.

* Levi *

He was liking Mama better all the time. She didn't take any crap from him, which was refreshingly pleasant. Try as he might he couldn't best her, much to everyone's amusement. As they were wisecracking back and forth Amy shocked him senseless when she told him she was trying to have a child with him. He hadn't thought much about it since Amy told him about his mutant DNA, but when she mentioned that they were trying to stabilize his DNA, it all made sense. He liked the idea right up to the time Mama came at him with that big needle and a smile.

Afterwards, he was led to the cafeteria, which was loaded with equipment and supplies. It was sanitary, but reeked of the smell of raw meat. After rummaging around, he found lots of stored can goods ranging from ham to yams. He was smiling as he opened a few cans and found the food still good after all these years. All the modern conveniences worked. Cans were opened with an electric can opener and the food heated in a microwave. This was great. He stuffed himself with a variety of vegetables he hadn't had in years. Amy was enjoying his reaction and welcomed his choices of food. She even commented that it was all good for him. That may be, but mainly they just tasted good. When he started nodding off Amy spoke over the speaker telling Sparks to lead Levi to the sleeping quarters. It was all so strange to him.

He felt like he was in a different world and time, but enjoyed it immensely. The quarters were clean and cool. It took him a moment to recognize the sound of the air conditioner but finally identified the low hum. He stepped back in time over fifty years and was giddy with the sensation. The bathroom shower was very inviting. It was a large shower with dual massage shower heads. The water was hot and he watched the steam rise. His cloths were off in seconds and enjoying the refreshing hot water massage on his shoulders. Oh, he could get used to this! There was soap and shampoo, which he used liberally. When he finally came out his skin was wrinkly and pink, but damn he felt good.

The next sight was even better. There was the large bed with clean white sheets and big fluffy pillows. Beside the bed on a table was a bottle of red wine chilling in a bucket of ice. It just didn't get any better than this. As he poured a glass of wine, he noticed new clothing lain out on a chair beside the bed. There was a pair of new jeans, actually the name brand Levis. He laughed as he remembered his father telling him that he had gotten his name from the Levi jeans. There were also a T-shirt, new army issue boots, a leather vest, socks and even underwear. Now that was something he hadn't worn in years. He said, "Wow, Amy, you thought of everything." Her smile and wink said everything. This was going to be a great night.

After he finished a few glasses of wine, he spread out on the bed. It was so comfortable after sleeping on the ground all these years. He pulled the sheets up over his naked body to his neck and just enjoyed the feeling but quickly threw them back as Amy slipped into bed beside him and cuddled close. The cool sheets contrasted wonderfully to Amy's warm soft body. Yes, this was going to be a wonderful night.

* Amy *

It was good to see Levi happy, and it was indeed a wonderful night for both of them. She had planned it with Mama and for someone that acted like she didn't, Mama cared so much for Levi that she went out of her way to make it special. Simians had little use for hot water and the conveniences of the facility, choosing to sleep most anywhere, but Mama made sure the water was hot and the quarters were spotless. She found this ironic since hygiene was not one of their strong points either.

She remembered how Mama had resisted cleanliness initially, but Amy had insisted that anyone working in the lab be clean and exercise a strict sanitary discipline so not to contaminate the research. Mama had reluctantly submitted to her wishes, but her idea of sanitary was hardly more than a good hosing and blow drying. She had given in to Mama to some extent. It would have to do, but accepted nothing less that completely sanitized equipment. Remembering this made Mama's efforts even more surprising and it was appreciated.

Mama had readily complied with her wishes concerning Levi. The quarters were spotless, the water was hot and steamy, and the towels and sheets were clean. Mama had even found an excellent wine in the storage cellar and had it chilled. Levi was shocked and surprised all at the same time, but found the experience wonderful as did she. He had forgotten how it had been before the fall of civilization, but it all came back quickly and she could tell it was enjoyable. This pleased her greatly.

For a computer, she was totally aroused. She found that funny, because she had learned how to love physically and please Levi completely, not to mention satisfying herself like she was quite sure no female had ever been satisfied. Their love making was a true joining of minds and bodies, even though her body was in their minds.

When he woke in the morning, he had a big smile. They had made passionate love and slept wrapped in each other's arms throughout the night. As enjoyable as the night had been, morning brought back the weight of responsibilities and it was time to get back to work.

Jimmy had reached the objective just south of the Yuma Interstate 8 bridge and, as expected, a large Simian army could be seen in the distance. The timing was bad for their migrating armies, but she had learned to expect bad luck. The Simian Warriors would reach the bridge before her armies, but she had half expected it and was included as part of her plan.

Thankfully, the Supreme One had not ventured out from his protective defense and was still evading her probes. She had, however, sought him out during the night and had located him. He seemed to be constantly changing direction, but a thorough search had located him moving west again. She was not sure if he had detected her probe since she had only gently probed. She had all night so she hadn't been in a hurry, and she hadn't wanted a negative confrontation to spoil her fantastic night with Levi. She felt that the Supreme One believed himself safe for the moment and hoped it lasted a while longer. She needed time to complete her plan before any forced conflict with the Supreme One.

Levi was relaxed but sensed the stress return to her, and he was ready to implement her plan. Levi was so trusting that he hadn't even ask what the plan was. All he wanted was to be pointed in the right direction and to have a sword in his hand. She chuckled at his bravado.

She had already messaged Mama, and as they emerged from the elevator and headed for the front door, Sparks met them at the elevator door already fully equipped in her Super Simian costume of molded plastic and laser. It looked bulky, but Sparks moved with ease and apparently without straining. Moon and the others were already gathered and waiting as they approached.

Moon gave him a knowing mischievous look, but said nothing. Understandably, everyone looked kind of solemn now they were facing more battles today. Somewhere along the route someone had handed him a bucket, of all things, full of various foods. Hell, he didn't care what it was. He was hungry and started eating large handfuls. She couldn't help pointing out how uncouth he was. He just grinned but kept eating.

As soon as they were all gathered by the massive front doors, she began the transfer. All comfort and conveniences were left behind as they materialized in the morning desert heat at the east end of the Yuma bridge. She could see that Al, Mosley, and Iron Eyes were organizing to engage the quickly approaching Simians. It was understandable but not to her desire. She wanted the approaching Simian grouped together. They quickly issued a change of orders and positioned her armies behind her with instructions to hold and push the migration on over the bridge. They could see the movement of the armies to comply and a long string of the migration move forward and turn for the bridge. Seeing the lack of readiness of the humans spurred the Simians on toward their position at an accelerated rate. This was her intention, and this was the moment of truth.

Levi stood in the front to present himself as the target. The Simians seemed to know who he was and focused their attack directly at him, serving to congregate the Simian into a compact group. Sparks stood ready, and as if reading her mind, nodded to Levi. They waited until the group got within a hundred feet then Sparks released her power. Suddenly, there was a bright red light shooting out from her laser, cutting a horizontal narrow slice across the approaching Simians. It was horrifying to witness the Simians falling all across the line still kicking as if running, but the top half was wide eyed and falling without legs or lower bodies. Shock was still registering on their faces. The lethal beam did not stop with the first layer of Simians, but seemed to dissect the ranks many deep. It was as though the severed bodies presented no resistance at all to the lethal red beam of light.

Sparks showed no emotions or mercy as the angel of death. She brought the beam back across the still charging ranks cutting another swath of death deeper into the ranks. It was like cutting swaths of wheat with a giant scythe, but in this case it was the scythe of death collecting souls. Screeches of pain could now be heard emerging from the separated bodies on the ground, while the legs continued to flail, going nowhere. Smoke rose from the severed bodies as the scent of burnt flesh reached Levi's nostrils. She tried to stop Sparks, but her shock kept her paralyzed from action. Soon it was no longer necessary as the laser went silent with the depletion of the charge. Sparks was still trying to fire at the fleeing Simian Warriors, but the laser was dead. Hundreds of Warriors fell in seconds, and the remaining Warriors were running for their lives back the way they had come. The battle was over.

The sight she had witness revolted and nauseated her. If she had a stomach she would be retching. The Warriors had been totally committed to their destruction and would have shown no mercy had the roles been reversed. She kept trying to tell herself that, but this was totally brutal.

Levi had been frozen in shock too, but he came alive with anger directed at her.

Levi was screaming, "Stop it, dammit! Don't feel sorry for them. They came to kill us and eat us, too. Not one of these Warriors is worth the life of any one of our friends. Remember Mr. Henderson, Wolf, and Dawn. These savages killed them. Get over it. This is a good thing, and we are now winning."

He was right, of course. Yes, he was right, but she also felt the horror he was feeling also. He wasn't nearly as tough as he made out. Still, he was right in what he said. This was good and maybe salvation for them. Unfortunately, now that she had a chance to analyze what had just happened, this could have just as easily been a disaster for them. The laser had not operated nearly as long as she had calculated. Had the Warriors not been bunched as they were the early discharge of the batteries could have left them defenseless. Yes, they had been lucky.

* Levi *

It had indeed been a wonderful night, but as he woke in the morning he sensed the stress once again in Amy. She had given him a wonderful gift of her love, comfort, and relief from the constant stress of battle and worry and it was appreciated. This was, however, another day and it was time to join the battle again. He had his R&R. He enjoyed donning his new clothes. This was good because he was quite sure Mama had burned his old ones. She probably enjoyed doing it, too.

As they reached the waiting group in the main entrance area he was receiving some odd look. He was confused for a few minutes until he realized they were unaccustomed to seeing him dressed this way. Somehow that made him feel special, and he turned around in jest to show off his new look. Moon found this humorous and started hiccupping in laughter and was soon joined by the others. He noticed that Mama even seemed to take pride in his appearance and the other's reaction. Admittedly, his feeling for Mama had changed, and he couldn't bring himself to taunt her. For once he simply openly smiled warmly at her. Mama's shock was clearly visible and soon turned to a radiant smile of pride. He didn't even know a Simian could smile that big, but it was clearly a smile accented by big black teeth. Amy was radiant in her beauty and appreciation of their finally displayed affection.

Their display lasted only brief seconds, but their relationship had been altered forever.

The addition of Sparks clad in her shiny armor completed the new team. It somehow seemed appropriate in their world of Lancers to see a Knight in shining armor. He slapped Sparks on the back and said, "Welcome Sir Sparks." The humor of this private joke soon faded as Amy quickly had them standing in a new world of danger facing an oncoming army of Simian Warriors.

He had complete faith in Amy, and she said the laser would work so he believed her. He stood as bait and focus for the Warriors and waited. When it came, it was like the devastation outside the facility door. The lasers had unleashed total destruction on the Warriors at that time, and this was no different. The assault of the laser was unmerciful. The Simians fell as flies under a swatter. The devastation happened so quickly that the bisected halves of the Warriors seemed to work independently of each other. He remembered as a child watching his grandfather wring the head off chickens and seeing the headless bodies running around without purpose. This was much the same situation. The two halves were dead, but hadn't realized it. Hundreds fell in waves until none were left to kill. Fortune had smiled on some of the Warrs at the rear. They had seen and registered what was happening in time to run. It was obvious they would have no more problems from them. They were not showing in any way an attempt to regroup. They just ran individually and would probably continue to run in any direction they were headed until they fell over with exhaustion. Those that escaped would never return, and the word would spread through the Simian Colonies, thus ensuring peace for these humans. Well, he hoped anyway, assuming the Supreme One wasn't here to drive them.

The battlefield was sickening to observe. The screeching of the dying Warriors was straining his ears and seemed to continue. There was no blood because the laser slices had burned closed behind the cuts. They would die slowly. Smoke was rising from the bodies, filling the air, and the stench of burnt flesh assaulted his nostrils. This was horrible.

Suddenly, he realized that Amy was in shock. He started chastising her to bring her mind back, but he also realized that whatever they had to do now must be rushed. Amy might not be able to go through the shock of this carnage again with a rational mind. He must take over and force the next battle.

He quickly gave orders to the group, startling them. They too were staring in awe at the carnage. He told Moon and Bambi to get with Mosley and follow the plan that had been laid out. They nodded and left headed toward Mosley and his army. Next, he told his body guards to stay with the Simian army. They were reluctant to leave him until he said, "I know you want to go with me, but you can't help with what I have to do now. You will just be in the way and I will need to come and go quickly. Sparks will be with me, and you saw what she can do." With that fresh in their minds, they agreed and left.

It was now or never. Amy was still mentally numb, but he pressed her by saying, "Amy, take us to the combined Simian army. We must destroy

618

them. Remember, their home is in our area. They have no other place to go, nor any reason to go anywhere else. They have been hot on our trail for many days with blood lust. They will attack our army at the Yuma Bridge and we will lose friends. Take us to them NOW!"

He wasn't sure Amy fully comprehended what he was telling her, but she blindly complied with his wishes. The timing was perfect. Even with a numb mind her calculations were precise. They materialized about five hundred feet in front of where she believed the Simians would be. The Warriors were already compressed as they were coming through a pass on Interstate 10. Their sudden appearance looked to the Simians like it might have been a mistake on their part, and the Simians responded quickly and charged them. As they came within a hundred feet, he nodded to Sparks.

As Sparks began her issuance of death upon the Warriors, he spoke to Amy, partly to keep her mind occupied and partly because he wanted her ready to take them away quickly. He said, "Amy, pick a spot at the rear of the charging army to teleport to. They will all soon be running in that direction, and we can attack from that end." Her eyes were glazed, but she managed to nod. He saw her look inward to the task he had given her, thankful that she was not fully concentrating on the carnage being wielded in front of him.

It was over almost as soon as it started. Hundreds of Warriors lay kicking and screeching within the range of the laser. Again the laser batteries dispensed their charge, but Sparks was still trying to fire. Sparks was in blood-lust and almost out of control. He touched her on her head to get her attention. Sparks turned with fire in her blazing eyes, but he saw comprehension slowly return to her eyes and heard the click of the trigger disengage on the laser.

Amy's image was still not focused. He said loudly out loud, "Amy! How long will it take the laser batteries to recharge?" After a short wait he again said even louder, "Amy?"

Amy refocused and said, "It will take fifteen minutes to charge for another thirty seconds of laser fire."

He resumed their internal communication and asked her to take them away so they could watch the Simian army from a distance while the batteries recharged. Amy was quick to comply and vacate this place of death, whisking them away to the top of a medium size mountain. It was as he hoped. A good third of the combined army had been killed and all the rest were running east in retreat, still in a compact group due to the enclosing mountains forming the long pass through the mountains. This would work to their advantage.

After the fifteen minute wait Amy teleported them again to a spot in the line of charge. It was a repeat of the same savage decimation. Again hundreds fell to the wicked bite of the red sword of death. The only difference was the fact that the Simians kept charging toward them still trying to escape from the attack from the rear. It was like they were not charging them, but fleeing and they were in the way. He had to ask Amy to move them to the vantage point again to escape the onslaught.

They had totally destroyed eighty percent of the army. That was enough. The surviving Warriors would spread the word now, and he wanted that to happen. It was part of Amy's plan for safety for California. She wanted a safe base of operation from which to work from to deliver salvation to the humans and now Techs and Fems around the world.

Amy was not enjoying seeing her plan fall in place. Actually, she had completely withdrawn and was just blindly following his instructions. If the situation wasn't so horrible he would have laughed at Amy. When he looked at her image, she actually had her eyes closed... like that would really work since she saw through his eyes. It was totally symbolic, but he understood.

He gave Amy the fifteen minutes of battery-charging time to calm while Sparks and he relaxed. Sparks seemed to be truly relaxed, almost happy. They signed back and forth as he probed her history. Of course, he knew she was a Grey beyond breeding age, but was shocked to find out that she was one hundred and ninety Earth years old and she had seen the atrocities the Warrior Race had inflicted upon the Technical Simian and how they treated the Female Race with total contempt, subjecting them to breeding only. She had been holding back her hate and rage all of her life, and now she was feeling vindicated with the revenge she was dispensing for all the Female Race. No wonder she felt no remorse.

After a while he said, "Amy?" It was said gently and with love. "Are you okay? I love you." He let his words settle on her for a while. "We have one more thing to do, and I need you for this. It will take both of us to kill the Supreme One."

CHAPTER 15
(THE END OR NEW BEGINNING)

* Amy *

She was still in shock. It had been horrible, and her sense of morality could not take anymore. Her computer mind had logically told her this was right and good, but the living moral mind and person she had learned to be through her emotions said NO! She allowed her computer mind to continue to function, but her emotions simply shut down. It acted like a fuse to disconnect and protect her from tilting and going insane. Her mind registered everything that happened but without allowing herself to accept it. Levi had mercifully taken over, directing her in what he needed and when. How could he stand the sights, sounds and smells of this grotesque slaughter? It assaulted all her senses and violated any sense of morality in her being. She was thankful for Levi and his strength.

Her mind was still reeling as she became aware of Levi trying to reach her. Finally, she comprehended what he was saying. When he expressed his love, she focused on that emotion that was so strong within her. She loved Levi with all her being and grasped hold of that emotion to focus her mind. Yes, she understood. They had to find and kill the Supreme One, or all this mutilation and slavery had no meaning. She said, "I am all right, hon. I understand." Levi gave her a warm smile and waited.

Before the earlier events of the morning, she had given much thought about the Supreme One. She believed the hate and rage of the Supreme One would bring him out. He would not be able to resist a face-to-face opportunity to kill Levi. All they had to do was show up in the general vicinity of the Supreme One, and he would sense her presence. If there was only Levi and Sparks, it would look simple to him. He would come to them, and with a single shot from the laser, it would be over.

She concentrated and let her mind search. The Supreme One was predictable now, and she located him within a few moments. Her search was not masked and hoped to set his rage off as she had in the past. She was right. Again the hate and rage flared forth at her in addition to the verbal explosion of abuse. She smiled at the demonstration of his lack of control, while she blocked out the actual meaning of the words. She said, "I have him located, and I have a general location where we can teleport. Are you ready?"

Levi said, "Hell, yes! Let's do it!"

She smiled but could sense his fear threatening to escape, and she didn't blame him. The Supreme One was the most formidable enemy they had ever faced. Not only was his mental power extremely dangerous, but the physical size would make Levi look like a small child facing a gorilla, even worse. The Supreme One was over twice as tall as Levi and many times the weight. They were fortunate that this confrontation would not be physical. If it were, Levi would not have a chance. She expected a mental attack on her and was prepared. Levi and she would have to be the bait to draw him out. If all went well, Sparks would kill him quickly and the mental attack would not have to last long. She too was afraid of the Supreme One more than she could admit. He had almost destroyed her on several occasions, and this could be equally as dangerous, but she had to admit they had an advantage this time.

It was time, and Sparks and Levi both said they were ready. She began this the longest teleport yet to a position in Texas calculated from the topographical maps to about six hundred feet from where she knew the Supreme One was protected behind a rock outcropping. The area was open by necessity since she had never actually seen the physical location, but this worked toward her plans by presenting an open invitation for an attack.

The Supreme One was still bombarding her physical location with his hate, but she was not expecting the increase in intensity as they materialized close to him. She suddenly realized that she had made a critical mistake and failed to account for the vast distance through which the Supreme One had been projecting his mental energy. How could she have been so careless?

The intensity of evil rage and pure hate bombarded her through Levi's mind link. The Supreme One was walking out from behind his cover staring with those intense white eyes directly at Levi and her. The focused power of this dark evil soul burned into her. She was trying to close off the link to reduce the intensity, but in doing so she would reduce her link with Levi. There was no choice. Her mind was dizzy from the force of mind energy, and she felt her mind losing. Just as she was reaching her limit of endurance, she began to feel a counter energy forming within her, altering and growing. The familiar feel of ASONE begin to take over just before she blacked out.

After what must have been long minutes, her mind began to slowly focus... remembering. She remembered as if an observer, the sight of the Supreme One, huge and overpowering. The huge evil monster was trembling with fury and rage, all directed at her. This power of hatred was contrary to her ability to comprehend and repel, and this power of negative fury began to overcome her. It was then that ASONE rose out of her and Levi to defend them, but it was more than that. ASONE met rage and hate with his own rage and hate. ASONE seemed to be emerging to a challenge as much as defense. She felt Levi's deep hate and yes, hers also, merge with the unexplainable power of her mind. The Supreme One must have felt the resistance, but was rational enough to detect another threat from Sparks. Suddenly, the Supreme One turned his attention to Sparks just as she was turning the laser to him. Two things happened simultaneously. Sparks fired the laser as the Supreme One's body seemed to jerk as a dense, blazing ball of fire erupted from him. The ball of fire collided with the red laser beam half-way between them. In shock, she saw the deadly laser beam disperse and shatter around the ball of flame. In horror, she watched the ball of flame eat its way up the laser beam, following it slowly to its source. Soon the ball of flame engulfed the screeching Sparks, and combined with the stored propane, exploded with great force.

Although part of ASONE, she was helpless. ASONE answered only to himself or herself, she had never figured out which. ASONE was acting in total rage now preparing to do something, but before it could, the explosion knocked ASONE to the ground. As an observer only, she could feel Levi's body ripped and torn from the explosion. He was down on one knee holding his side with one arm while pushing the other arm and hand forward toward the Supreme One. Already another ball of flame shot forth toward Levi, but it was met with a sparkling blue ball of energy projecting from Levi's hand. The blue ball was projected and held at the end of a ray of blue shimmering energy radiating out from his hand feeding it. The forces clashed against each other in a continuous battle of blue and red fireworks. Slowly the red began to push back the blue, coming closer and closer.

As the red ball got near, ASONE made a final hard push of energy and both balls exploded and dispelled.

As the smoke slowly cleared, she suddenly saw the Supreme One standing just behind the explosion. He had obviously walked closer behind the ball of flame, thus providing the additional power behind it. No matter what the reason, it had worked for him. The Supreme One lunged forward through the smoke driving his huge broadsword through Levi's body. Remembering and reliving the moment through a numb mind allowed her to accept the facts without experiencing the emotions, but it was starting to register.

ASONE had been defeated, but in desperation, Levi's arms shot out to grasp around the Supreme

One's legs. It was at that point, even with a numb mind, that she realized what ASONE was going to do. She had felt the energy grow, building then suddenly released in a hard teleport imploded in upon both of them. That is when she blacked out completely.

As she resumed thought, realization slowly fell on her like a building. ASONE had destroyed itself, but took the Supreme One with him. Only now did she comprehend that ASONE had destroyed Levi in the process. There was no input from Levi, no input from Al, Jimmy, or Fred. Levi was dead! Why was she alive? She wept. It felt like her heart had been ripped from her.

She was in mourning for a long time, maybe hours. She wanted to die, but her promise flashed back in her mind. She had promised Levi to live on without him and help their friends. Levi had been prepared to die and would have approved of ASONE's action. She just wished she could have died also. It was not fair.

As Levi had pointed out, she did have communication with Mama through the facility, so she would not be in the total prison of darkness as before, but she would miss Levi. She would miss all his smartass remarks, homespun wisdom and his strength, but she would miss his love the most.

She had all his memories and experiences recorded in her memory and she could revisit them when she wanted, but it was without life. Humm SHE HAD ALL HIS MEMORIES! SHE HAD HIS DNA!

THE END OR NEW BEGINNING?